HEAVE

HEAVE

A NOVEL

CHRISTY ANN CONLIN

DOUBLEDAY CANADA

National Library of Canada Cataloguing in Publication Data

Conlin, Christy Ann
    Heave

ISBN 0-385-65807-9

    I. Title.

PS8555.O5378H42 2001   C813'.6   C2001-902720-6
PR9199.4.C65H42 2001

Jacket images: landscape © Marie Cameron, 1995; woman, Terry Doyle/Stone.
Jacket design: CS Richardson
Printed and bound in the USA

Published in Canada by Doubleday Canada,
a division of Random House of Canada Limited

Visit Random House of Canada Limited's website:
www.randomhouse.ca

Excerpts from a traditional anniversary rhyme appear on page 52.
Lyrics from "A Canadian Boat Song" appear on page 63. This ballad, written in 1805 by Irish writer Thomas Moore, is based on a traditional Canadian air, "Et en revenant du boulanger."
Excerpts from the Irish ballad "Molly Malone" appear on pages 159 and 160.
Lyrics from "Farewell to Nova Scotia" appear on pages 215 and 220.
The poem "Break, Break, Break" by Alfred, Lord Tennyson appears on pages 308, 309, 311 and 318.

BVG 10 9 8 7 6 5 4 3 2 1

To Heather Morse
and to
Valerie Thompson and Marie Cameron

After awhile Haze got up and started walking back to town. It took him three hours to get inside the city again. He stopped at a supply store and bought a tin bucket and a sack of quicklime and then he went on to where he lived, carrying these. When he reached the house, he stopped outside on the sidewalk and opened the sack of lime and poured the bucket half full of it. Then he went to a water spigot by the front steps and filled the rest of the bucket with water and started up the steps. His landlady was sitting on the porch, rocking a cat. "What you going to do with that, Mr. Motes?" she asked.

"Blind myself," he said and went on in the house.

—FLANNERY O'CONNER, *WISE BLOOD*

Wild animals run from the dangers they actually see, and once they have escaped them worry no more. We however are tormented alike by what is past and what is to come.

— SENECA, *LETTERS FROM A STOIC: EPISTULAE MORALES AD LUCILIUM.* FROM "LETTER V.", TRANSLATED BY ROBIN CAMPBELL.

FLOOD TIDE

DEARIE ALWAYS SAID, "GO TITS TO THE WIND."

And I am.

Going so fast it seemed as though I was hovering above myself, watching as I went veil first into those massive oak doors in the foyer because no one makes a getaway in high heels. Just look what happened to Marilyn Monroe — naked, bloated, DOA. That's what happens when you wear high heels. I put my hands out, just like they taught us in high school gym class, you know, when spotting someone on the trampoline: hold up hands, don't push, let the person touch and then bounce back to middle. But only an idiot would wear high heels on a trampoline and there was no bouncing back to the middle as those shoes took me down on that hot June day, my sweaty hands flat on the cool oak door panels only long enough to feel the old wood on my palms and I was crashing straight through the doors that hadn't been properly latched, yards of silk dress floating behind me like a flock of angels as those carved oak slabs were falling silently shut. Magic it was that pieces so large could move with no noise, wrought-iron hinges no doubt well-oiled by the latest sexton. I slipped through the crack and left the musty church behind, all those pews full of stunned guests, and then the sweet outdoors was in front of me but I was crashing backwards as the doors slammed shut, the stupid billowy dress jammed in the doors, and I was smashed back and up, three feet off the top step, hand pounding back into the hard wood, pain dull and distant, and then me, dangling there, garland of flowers down over my eye, battered bouquet of freesias and roses still in my right hand, its scent floating up on the hot summer air, enveloping me in the sweet and squashed miasma of my life.

My life seems to have been about crashing backwards. Ever since I finished high school, which really wasn't very long ago, I've been on the run, so to speak. On the road. I mean, I bolt in the middle of things. Well, I finish some things and bolt. I took off to Europe and then landed in a rehab-sort-of-nuthouse (I wasn't insane, believe me. I was just temporarily unable to communicate.) I started a degree — Classical Studies. I enjoyed the Greeks and Romans. I enjoyed the books, always looking to them as a getaway, a portal in time. Actually, I enjoyed the building the classes were in. The Classical Studies Department was located in a series of grey Victorian houses that ran along a quiet Halifax street with huge sweeping trees. I still don't know the name of the trees.

I was pulling at my dress, the skirt wedged up there with the bodice, and the goddamn jeesly antique lace train that Aunt Galronia had insisted on attaching was pulled tight in the door, most of it still inside. I was pulling, wiggling, tugging, my sweaty skin squeaking against the wood, trying to demolish my vintage 1940s wedding dress, and just thinking about the dress made me so mad that I pulled even harder. "So much for antiques," I hollered. Somewhere in Foster a lawn mower buzzed. A huge jerk and then ripping and buzzing were one roaring sound as the silk and lace tore and I fell to my knees, hands out in front, drooling libations on the indoor/outdoor green carpet covering the steps. And then I was up with the remains of the dress on me, and a bit of the train hanging off my butt with yards of it still inside the doors. I wondered if it was laid out along the aisle like a banquet tablecloth with all the guests on either side waiting for me to be served up and then I heard Grammie say in her clipped dry voice, *You know that old saying, he who hesitates is not only lost but miles from the road out*, so I launched off the steps, kicking one high heel over the railing, and sending the other soaring over the heads of the late-arriving guests, second cousins from Ecum Secum with lips going round, opening and shutting, not saying anything, me thinking how people mostly get that piscine look when they are horrified and then it was me smiling and panting, not knowing whether to say hello or goodbye or to cry or pose for a picture and then Grammie's voice again, *Now or never, Serrie.*

I threw the bouquet up in the air and took three steps at a time because being in bare feet is being eight years old and eight-year-olds don't worry about how many steps to take, not like a twenty-one-year-old woman in high heels and a princess dress who can only do various forms of teetering.

Flaps of dress fluttered as I ran down Main Street, pulling at the ripped bodice, shedding pieces of silk until there was the red bra that I had worn, the only vestige of the rogue I had thought I was. At least up until we were in front of the preacher. Actually it started when I saw Elizabeth's head, the back of her head. I admired her wispy bits of hair and thought what a flattering style it was, wondered why it was done so daintily, with little daisies in it. And the hairdo got blurry and I wondered about that too, realizing the daisies were blurry because Elizabeth was right up there now, at the altar with my groom and the preacher and the best man who had been making bad jokes and smacking everyone on the back. And then it was all blurry.

And so I went. I walked up to the front, wondering if the guests could see my red bra, or at least the suggestion of the bra. It was lacy, really pretty, a push-up. But I didn't think so. I was the only one who knew about it besides Elizabeth who had helped me dress. I focussed on the teeth. There were so many teeth. I assume this is because people were smiling. At weddings, people usually smile, right? Goddamn, it was like being surrounded by Mormons. I always think of Mormons as people with big white teeth. But no one was Mormon here. It was the Foster First United Church, in old-style Nova Scotia, where change is slow like winter and tradition as strong as the forty-five-foot tides of the Bay of Fundy.

Those white teeth became a haze of cotton and the music was squeaking. God, it was terrible, which surprised me — my brother is a concert violinist. I must have put my hands to my ears because Elizabeth, standing beside me at the altar, asked if I was okay. I could see her then, her brown brown eyes, and I could see her lips moving but I only heard the

Okay, Serrie?

The soloist started singing so beautifully, *Ave, Maris Stella*, and hearing that, well, then I knew I was going to bail, shaking my head at Elizabeth, my eyes filling up with tears because even I'm not so selfish I didn't feel a bit of guilt, and I bolted down the aisle.

At the edge of town I leave pieces of my wedding dress in the ditch and head for the North Mountain. I'm on the Lupin Cove Road (what the government calls Route 445), a country road that cuts right across the pastoral Annapolis Valley, passing apple orchards and fields of grazing sheep and cows, honey farms, a stinking chicken farm, then twisting up the Mountain and over to the Bay of Fundy. It's high noon and my feet hit the hot pavement but I'm going so fast the burn is a memory before it's even had time to hurt me. It's as though my life has been at arm's length, long fingers holding the world away, me watching on the sidelines, just trying to stay standing. But now all those past days fly around my head as I run.

The humid June air rushes in and out of my lungs as I begin to find my rhythm, knees up high, arms in close, passing fields of purple clover and Queen Anne's lace, a few cars slowing down and people staring, me waving out of habit, passing corn fields rustling in my wind because this summer day is unseasonably hot and still. Tripping and landing on my elbow, skin scraping off but back up, not even that slowing me down because I don't feel it. This time last year I would have passed out in the ditch, groping for a smoke, but so much can change in a year and I know that all those days we live weave and fold together, we make those days and they in turn make us. Laughing makes it hard to run. I float on my jubilance like a butterfly on the summer air, right by the renovated general store in Loomer, the store with the famous tin roof, the wood and glass display cabinets inside that American and German tourists keep trying to buy from the owners, the whole insides they try to buy, as if everything they see can be purchased just for their asking. As I run through the crossroads a little girl in braids is sitting on the steps eating an ice cream. She giggles and waves. I wave back and then the jubilance retreats. My eyes go watery again, the pavement searing the soles of my feet, the long fingers falling away and time moving in me on the Lupin Cove Road.

You can't run and cry at the same time. Running demands pacing and steady breathing: when you lose control of your breath the race is over. I creep up the final bit of mountain, forest on either side of the road, white and pink lupins in the ditch. It's a long road, I think. My croaks and pants break the stillness of the lush summer air as I take the oxbow bend and then head up to the brow of the mountain. Gravity pulls at me, but I resist, focussing on my shimmery purple toenails, then lifting my eyes and finally, our old place there at the edge of the North Mountain, the dilapidated white Victorian house with the million-dollar view, ready to fall down into the Valley. My old room in the tired turret, the "new" wrap-around verandah, already needing repairs. My father's outhouse collection encircles the house like a garland, each wee house restored and perfect, covered in morning glories.

The heat flows out of my feet into the cool lawn, down into the dry earth, but my soles still burn. Chest heaving, soaked in sweat, I lean against an outhouse wall on the south side of the house, Outhouse Number Nine from Tatamagouche, one of the first in my father's collection. He's restored them all with a new purpose: for reading, some as little work sheds, a gardening shed, only one, way out back behind the house, is still an outhouse proper. I put my hand in the old marble bird feeder beside Number Nine. Sweat beads trickle down my face and I taste salt and hair spray as I pant, unable to find shade. Maybe it's heatstroke. They say it makes you do irrational things. I take a sip from the bird bath by the side of the outhouse, splash water on my face and then tip the bird bath over so the water trickles down on my aching feet, cooling them, relieving the burn. And I lean back against the outhouse wall as the silence of the day falls upon me. I take a deep breath, hold it and then slowly let the air out, shutting my eyes. There is nothing rational about doing what everyone else wants you to. And honestly, there is nothing rational about trying to be a good girl. A pathetic ethos, I think, as a butterfly floats around the corner of the outhouse and lands on my wet forearm. Its proboscis laps at my sweat; I'm a big flower. Oh, a poor ditch flower, you are, Serrie, I think, wilting into Number Nine with the weight of the last year on my back. The holes are gone, now it's just a cushioned bench, and I sit with chin on my knees.

There is a tiny window inside the outhouse. Its warped glass faces south but it doesn't look out on the view — the window casing outlines the green fields, and the South Mountain, and tacks the Valley on the outhouse wall like a faded picture postcard put up years ago. The door faces east, opening onto a little rose garden. My brother Percy says the outhouses are like Buddhist meditation houses but I've never known any Buddhists, not even any of the Shambala ones in Halifax. There is a little Victorian shelf mounted to the right of the door, and on it I can see an old candle, waterproof matches, a package of stale Drum tobacco and rolling papers I put there years ago. To the left of the door an old calendar hangs on a nail, a birthday present from Grammie when I turned thirteen. It's still on October, a big star on Hallowe'en, the day I was born. The picture is of autumn leaves down on Cape Blomidon, where the North Mountain runs into the Minas Basin. An old man leans on a giant pumpkin, holding a live lobster. Maybe he thought he could carve a jack-o'-lantern with the claws. Beside the calendar, written on the wall, is my list of significant events. My father told me to record them here, in the old way. You can read the notes people made over the years, a cross between graffiti and a journal. A pencil stub hangs on a string wound around a rusty nail. My father's idea of a significant event is a big storm or spotting a rare bird. My idea of a significant event is something that almost kills me.

Sitting there, my scraped elbow tingles back to life and I blow on it as I swing my legs up and sit with my feet on either side of the window, my back against the wooden wall, my *Luscious Lisbon Lilac* toenails coated in dirt. I don't know if it's my stinging elbow or the pain in my gut that has me bang the outhouse wall with my foot, rattling the window, shaking the wall, remembering the last time it shook, when Dearie came over after school, when we were first friends, after her mother had died, and then her grandmother, and it was just her and her nasty dad who was never home anyway, which is maybe why she always hated being alone. She lived next to my Grammie in Foster and Grammie had driven her over to my house after the funeral because it was just a bunch of oldies at the reception afterwards. We were nine that November. Dearie had disappeared, and after searching the whole house for her, and out back in the barn, I'd seen the outhouse shaking, just a little bit, and found Dearie sitting inside. The hole was still there then, but she was tiny enough to curl up beside it, leaning against the wall with her chin on her knees. I curled up on the other side of the hole. She was crying but with no noise or tears, it was her body crying, and so I told her about the trip to Cape Breton, my Grammie always said a story or a song was better than a pill.

It was when we lived in Halifax, when my father was in the navy, and when he'd be home we would go for weekend trips, around the Cabot Trail. He liked it up there because everyone's Catholic, just like he is. Percy and I were baptized but we only know that from the white fluffy christening gown in my mother's bottom drawer. We couldn't afford to stay at the Keltic Lodge at Ingonish Beach so we'd rent a seaside cabin at Wong's Ceilidh Cabins, the same people who owned the Chinese restaurant where we would beg to eat and my parents would always say no, we were getting good home cooking. My father would barbecue hamburgers and wieners and salmon steaks, drinking cold beer in the suppertime sun, giving me little sips, salty and sweet, I used to think I was drinking a burp. My mother holding salad dressing: "Cyril, don't go giving her booze," she'd say. He'd take a sip: "It's only beer, Martha." My mother would toss the salad: "There's no such thing as *only*." Who'd have known she'd be right? She'd shake her head and then we'd all eat at a picnic table while seagulls squawked and dove about like rats with wings.

It was during those summertime trips my father started having this thing about heritage buildings as he called them, driving us all over God's Green Earth to look at falling-down houses but he couldn't afford to buy them so he'd go for the outhouses, and bought his first in Ingonish. We drove home with the outhouse tied to the roof of the old station wagon and he put it in the garage until we moved back to the Valley. On one trip we drove into a long tree-lined driveway with a falling-down house at the end, a huge collapsed verandah on the lawn, fancy trim and ornate wooden arches hanging off it, wood all silver from the sea wind. It must have been abandoned for years. There was a sweet faded outhouse with the same fancy trim and ornate corner arches, so we got out of the car and started towards it. The outhouse door flew open and an old woman with white hair like a sheepskin rug came running out, pulling her dress down, waving a cane, running faster than any old lady I've ever seen, screaming, "Get the bloody jesus off my property ye cawksuckin arselickers." My father tried to explain he just liked her arches and wanted to have a closer look. That was enough for her to start swinging the cane at us with these big lunging steps in her old rubber boots. "Jesus, Mary'n'Joseph, I'll wrap me arches right round yer trespassin' necks, arselickers." We jumped back in the car, my father putting it in reverse, laughing so hard he turned too sharp and my mother grabbed the wheel to keep us from the ditch, my father hitting the gas to miss the swinging cane, me saying, "what's a cawk, what's a cawk?" and us laughing all the way back to the cabin.

Dearie didn't laugh or even smile but she wasn't shaking anymore. She pulled at her hair and then whispered to her knees, "Arselicker, nothing will ever be the same again." I let her sign her name on the outhouse wall to make her feel better. *Dearie Margaret Melanson*, it's still here, in her big awkward printing. Writing on a wall or spitting in a ditch, picking a scab — doing something you're not supposed to do always makes you feel better. Maybe that was my problem, I was always doing stuff I wasn't supposed to do, always trying to feel better.

That's not the real problem, now is it, my dear girl? The problem is thinking others can decide your life for you and only a goddamn coward lives like that. You are who you are and that's it, and until you accept that, well, you'll always be sitting in an outhouse wishing things would never change. Change is life, Serrie, and when there is no change ...

But look at what I am, I tell Grammie. I'm a twenty-one-year-old drunk with no job.

Well, now, there's plenty worse things to be.

"Oh, like what, Grammie?" I yell it out the door, wishing I had a smoke.

Like a leper or a goddamn pervert or a hypocrite or a liar.

A breeze bangs the open door on the side of the outhouse and delicate breaths of wind fluff my hair.

"Did I ask to be born, Grammie?" I scream it out the door and wait, but Grammie has no more words for me so I pound the wall of the outhouse with my feet and somewhere I think hear her sighing or maybe laughing, you just never knew with Grammie. My toe throbs, and I pull at the underwire in my red bra and snap back to my first run-away.

ONE

ANGLO-ACADIAN DEARIE IS SHAKING HER HEAD WHEN I COME OUT THE gate at the Halifax airport, saying Elizabeth is at work, waitressing at the Liquor Dome, this big bar that's really lots of bars and you can walk from one to the other. She just got a job through her roommate, Clare, who is a loser, but Dearie won't go into detail, just says I should have called her first and not Elizabeth because Elizabeth isn't dependable.

I see her first by that dark curly corkscrew hair, exactly like her father's. He may have lost his heart but at least not his hair. Dearie says it's Acadian hair, a recessive gene. You could see her hair in the window when you'd drive by the drugstore, when Dearie was working, because when she was a teenager she started wearing it piled up on her head in this beehive sort of style, until she went to university, and then she let it down again, coating it in some kind of special hair laquer to make it stiff, shiny and completely controlled. It looks like she's wearing a ring of long ceramic sausages. Both she and Elizabeth were cashiers at the drugstore in high school. But me, I never worked at the drugstore — I was the caretaker of the Foster First United Church, sexton is what I was officially called. There was even a belfry with a bell on a rope that I had to ring like it was the frigging Middle Ages or something. After work, on Saturdays, Dearie used to drive over to the church, and while I'd be polishing the pews, she'd sit there at the altar, telling me about how stupid her father was, playing with her hair. She's got really dark hair all over and with her white skin you can't miss it. Dearie knows every way possible to remove hair, from tweezers to beeswax to melting sugar with lemon and comfrey.

She and her hair are standing there looking at me and my hatbox suitcase and I look at her and smile but my lips vibrate so I look down at my feet. A stupid tear drops on the toe of my combat boots and then I see Dearie's loafers on my toes and she just stands there on my boots, nose to nose now, and she puts her arms around me. I don't know if she's hugging me or trying to hurt me and then she says, "you have steel toes." That's me, I think, Steel Toe Serrie. Standing on my feet, arms around me, she pinches my waist to see if I've gained any weight, but I never do. Aunt Galronia says it's the genetics. Always the genetics. Dearie says diets make her fat, flipping through fashion magazines that Elizabeth brought home from the drugstore when we were in high school, always looking for a quick fix. She refused to bring the magazines home and somehow Elizabeth doing it made Dearie feel like it was okay to read them. She still thinks we didn't know, but we did, we just didn't say anything.

So standing there on my boots Dearie starts telling me how freaky my head looks, not just my cropped-off hair, or my nose, but my head, like there's something wrong with my head, and I can't really argue. Anyway, I'm too sick to tell her to shut up, but who am I kidding, because when have I ever told anyone to shut up? And then she hugs me again and I'm glad Dearie's here as she chokes up and squeezes tighter, hurting me, so I start walking, with her still on my boots and we both laugh as I break out in sweat and a wave of sick slides over me. My heel is so bad now I'm limping along behind Dearie like Dustin Hoffman's Ratso Rizzo in *Midnight Cowboy*. There are no movies like seventies movies, my mother says. I think of Al Pacino in *Serpico* and I wonder if I should have gone to New York. But I didn't, I went to London.

Dearie lights two cigarettes as we drive on the highway to the city. It's a real highway, with double lanes for each direction, unlike Highway 101 that takes you to the Valley with one lane each way and the occasional shared passing lane more commonly call *death lane*. We speed along in Dearie's big white van. The Christmas of the year we graduated from high school her father gave her three presents, typed up as a memo:

1. Free Christmas trips to Florida condo with her father and the Neddie Family, what she took to calling them when her brother's wife starting popping out babies.

2. All university expenses paid for (except spending money — she has to have a part-time job for this) on the condition she study Commerce.

3. The old delivery van from Melanson's Drugstore, she could have her own wheels.

That day of our graduation ceremony she had called me up to rant about his so-called gifts. It was just one more example of how her own father had no idea who she was, that he could care less about what would really make her happy. She couldn't stand the Neddie Family for more than an hour and she didn't want to study business. But Dearie loved the van, the idea that she could just pack it up and drive down to New Orleans, when the time came. She keeps it clean and tidy but it needs work that she won't get done on it, saying it's a waste of money, she'll sell it soon, but it's three years later and here we are roaring down the highway in the van. She'll never sell it, the symbol of her dreams. All her extra money goes into her Acadian account, for the someday-soon trip to New Orleans to find the people with French names, the Cajuns, standing there chomping on shrimp and playing accordions. I tell her she should do some research on the subject but she always shrugs. Dearie also knows I'll find out whatever she wants to know or my brother, Percy, will keep her going with an endless supply of books. Elizabeth just starts singing away when we go off talking about history and stuff, humming radio songs and thinking about things like lip gloss, boys and dancing — she says too much thinking makes you weird, like me and Dearie, but Elizabeth likes weirdos. I mean, how picky can you be about friends when you grow up in Foster, Nova Scotia? You take what you can get.

The airport is outside the city in the middle of nowhere to avoid fog and it makes for a frig of a long drive to her apartment. Dearie keeps telling me I look ridiculous. I cough and say, "Yeah, I suppose I do." I try to tell her about the music in London, but I don't know anything about music except for Percy and the violin, stuff like Bartok, and what I heard over there, and so I try to sing some, but she says it hurts her head. I'd rather listen to the wind anyway but I don't tell her this. Dearie snorts and says I should just get it together and stop being different. I curl up in the seat and tell her I'm trying to be an Epicurean, that I want practicality as well as style, a haircut that gives me pleasure but service, and I don't finish the sentence as Dearie rolls her eyes puffing on two smokes like some kind of manic mobster chauffeur.

"What the fuck's Epicurean? People who hate fucking hair? What's wrong with hair? Why didn't you call me to come get you? You know, you've got to get your epi-fucking-shit together. And what about the Reverend Rafuse? What did you do *that* for?" Dearie says as she finally hands me a cigarette, half-smoked already.

I don't know what the hell she is talking about so I look out the window at the snow and hope that anytime soon she'll shut up. She must think I went and got religion, as Grammie says, that maybe I'll settle down and do the right thing, whatever that is. I don't say anything, just look at the snow and trees and think if I look long enough we will just keep driving forever, this moment will just be the forever which wouldn't be too bad, cigarettes, heat, motion —

"It would help if you would listen to me. God, Seraphina. What are you going to say to the minister? Galronia is flipping out. She's called me three times."

I take a drag and it makes me feel worse but that doesn't stop me and I don't know why she keeps talking about the frigging Reverend Rafuse because I haven't seen him in three years except at Christmas up there in the pulpit and that doesn't count. My sexton days are done and no one even knows I went to England except Elizabeth and Dearie unless Dearie told them, which I wouldn't put past her as she always thinks she knows what's best for me. I get sweaty and finally ask her what the fuck is going on, but Dearie wants to know what happened in England.

It's Friday afternoon, the last week of November. Bleak. Who needs November? It's only been three weeks that I've been away but it feels like a lifetime. They say a schedule orients you but there hasn't been one in my life since I finished high school and I'm floundering. I feel like I did when I would skip school, walking through the woods with no purpose other than killing the day until 3:00 p.m. when it was okay to be in public again, in accordance with the schedule. Everyone else is in the schedule but you, you're outside of it, aimless, no bells ringing to tell you what to do next, no lunch breaks to separate the day into chunks you'd stumble through, one to the next. Grammie always says we need to find our purpose in life, why we've been put here, and then it makes sense, that you are busy with living, not thinking about living. As my grandmaster hangover chews into my brain, I think that living just sucks.

Dearie hits the brakes as we zoom up behind an old station wagon crammed full of people peering out the windows like fish in a tank. The brakes squeak and my stomach jumps. The station wagon pulls over into the passing lane but there is no one for them to pass.

"What's the deal with Reverend Rafuse?" I say with my eyes

shut, partly so I won't be sick and partly to pretend I'm not here. You know, what you can't see isn't real, it's the first lesson of childhood. Dearie snorts, coughs, leans forward into the wheel, all hunched over, and roars up beside the station wagon as she starts to pass it on the right.

"Don't these damn people know how to drive? Why are they in the fast lane?" she barks.

Dearie hates slow drivers and the only place I know she's insane is on the road. Dearie admits it, but says it's controlled insanity, however to my thinking, as wild as my thinking may be, controlled craze is worse than fancy-free madness — I mean, how can you control anything forever? Die trying is what my Grammie says.

We're up high in the van and down below some lady in the backseat window is holding up a *Watch Tower* magazine. She's pointing at it and smiling. Dearie rolls down her window and glances at me with this dark look on her face, and then back out the van again, at the station wagon. She's looking in and out and the breeze pulls at her words. It's like tuning in a radio trying to hear her.

"God, I can't believe you, Seraphina. It's no secret anymore. Everyone knows where you were — religious bastards." She's keeping speed with the Jehovah's Witnesses and then she leans out the window, her curly hair going crazy in the clammy wind and the van zig-zags on the slippery pavement. I brace myself but my sweaty hands slip down the window and I try to rub it clean so Dearie won't be disgusted. We are coming up behind a truck.

"Look at the road," I yell. "I was safer passed out in a park in London."

"Stop trying to convert us," Dearie hollers at the woman in the station wagon, who cups her ear, smiles as she shrugs and leans forward for Dearie to repeat. Dearie snuggles up to the door, her elbow on the window like a trucker and screams each word separately, like she's reading a bumper sticker:

"KEEP YER RELIGION TO YER GODDAMN SELF."

She hasn't taken her cigarette out of her mouth the entire time until now when she takes a big drag and tosses it out the window where it jumps up like the last flap of a firefly. I slouch in the seat as Dearie floors it, roars past the horrified-looking folks in the wagon and zips ahead, just missing the bumper of the truck in front of us, and then squeals over to the fast lane, right in front of the station wagon. She looks in the rearview mirror and goes faster on the slippery road. "I can't stand goddamn converters. And who the hell was goddamn Gee-ho-vah anyway?" The whole van is vibrating. That's it, I think, the end.

"I'm sorry for everything," I scream at her. "I'm sorry for getting you in trouble. I'm sorry I didn't call you first."

It's a lie but I'll lie about anything to make her slow down. She looks out the window, bouncing on the seat as we hit potholes and bumps and the engine is so loud I think it will explode.

"It's no big deal, Serrie. It's just how it is with you. Wish another election was coming up and they'd pave the road again," Dearie screams back at me. Her voice echoes in the big white van and it hurts my head, my freak head. I keep looking at her but she looks in the side mirrors, floors the gas pedal and pulls back into the regular lane. Just as I take a big drag of my smoke she taps the brakes and I gag as they squeak.

"Earth to Serrie," she barks and I gag again as she stomps the brakes one more time. This time I burp.

"Don't fucking throw up in my van, Serrie. You've made enough of a mess already."

"Well, don't stomp on the brakes," I say. "You're fucking crazy, Dearie."

She hits them again. I take another drag of my cigarette, feel my mouth slowly fill with drool and roll the window down and let the cool air slap me.

"Why don't you tell me what happened then?"

"I went to England, I met this girl named Deborah, and then a girl named Zara. And I hurt my foot in the youth hostel. And Zara, well, she was crazy . . . " I lean my head back on the seat.

"I'm Deborah from Philadelphia."

It's morning. I'm lying in my bunk trying to guess how many feet it is to the ceiling (it must be lots) and then I'm sitting on the edge of my bunk looking down at the curly blonde head, chubby cheeks and blue eyes peeking up from the bottom bunk beside my stack. I notice tubby Deborah from Philadelphia doesn't say she is Deborah from the United States. But she is saying she is from somewhere, so I say, "I'm from somewhere too. I am from everywhere and nowhere."

And she laughs, "Oh that's really funny." I keep looking at her and feel like a jerk.

"I'm Seraphina from Nova Scotia."

Her cheeks bounce as she giggles, "Wanna go see London Bridge, Seraphina from Nova Scotia?"

In hostels, I will discover, someone asks you to go shopping in the showers, someone asks you to suck their cock standing next to the clothes washing machine, someone else in the TV lounge asks you to go to Oxford to see Christ Church College, and washing dishes in the kitchen, a guy asks you to go to a movie. After a minute, an hour, a day. There is no time count here. I wait for Deborah in the lounge. This guy, Nevin, gives me a cookie and goes on and on about his band in New Zealand. I can't look at him when he talks because he looks at his elbow the whole time so I focus on the safety pins in his nose, lined up like the ones in my mother's sewing box. They don't move at all — quality pins, I think.

At London Bridge, Deborah and I stand and look. It's a big bridge. It's got towers. And it's my first experience seeing things that don't mean dick to me. They've been in pictures for years and that's where some of them should stay. I wonder what will ever impress me.

No cameras allowed.

We're at the Tower to see the crown jewels. We walk around this glassed-in container at a breathtaking pace, urged on by the guards who bark if you even slow down and then you're back in the hall. Nice big red yellow green chunks of glass, maybe plastic, for all we dumb tourists know. Fuck, they might as well be fake. Another thing just as good in pictures. They must let someone snap lenses in here. I've seen the photos in Grammie's coffee table books in her house in Foster (she loves the Royals) where she must be sitting now, in her chair, perusing *Reader's Digest*, Aunt Galronia bringing her tea.

We stop at a market Deborah has been constantly pointing to in her guide book. I'm tired now and couldn't care less about sightseeing but she wants to see this and that. I buy a pair of second-hand pointy red shoes with laces and buckles that are so tight I have to hop-skip. Click click click all the way down the sidewalk as Deborah's tummy growls. She wants to get something to eat and we go to McDonald's at Piccadilly Circus. Over fries and milkshakes, Deborah says she's been in London for two days and is going to go to Ireland to hitchhike. Do I want to come — how old am I — do I travel alone — do my parents think travel is a good idea — she's Jewish — isn't it exciting being here — french fries falling from her lips. I'm twenty and what's a blintz, is what I want to know. Deborah giggles and says it's a type of pancake, rolled up with cheese inside, if it's a cheese blintz. She says that I have to watch it at the hostel, there are types like us who are travelling and stuff, but there are other types who sort of live there, hang out, go away after they've been there more than a month and then come back. There's a guy named Alec, from Glasgow, and he's sort of weird. Wears black. Some other people who hang out with him wear black. "You should stay away," Deborah says.

We go back at suppertime and I'm so exhausted I eat a piece of bread and go have a bath. I'm in a room full of tubs, separated by thin wooden walls, even the floors are wooden. I know I'm tired because all of this is starting to remind me of a concentration camp and that's ridiculous — it's more like an ultra-economy Swedish sauna. I dry off and go to my bunk in the empty room, get in bed in my tee-shirt and pink cotton panties with the snapped elastic, gash my heel on the metal frame on the way up and fall asleep on top of my sleeping bag. I wake up freezing, sometime in the dark, with a throbbing foot and I can hear weird, muffled sounds coming from the other side of the room. My feet are wrapped in the mattress sheet. Someone's masturbating. I jerk my foot in the sheet and it peels off the cloth with a sandpaper sound. I roll up like a sausage in my sleeping bag and lie there until the noises and the ache separate as I fall asleep.

And then it's morning again.

"Look at your heel."

Her eyes are enormous, like huge brown chunks of chocolate and her hair is long and black. She looks up at me from the bottom bunk across from me. Gorgeous and tiny.

"Look at your heel."

Her voice is light, bubbles. My heel is covered in dry blood and red-looking skin. I'm looking at it.

"Seraphina, from Canada."

"Zara. From Geneva."

I can't place her accent. She isn't French and she isn't British and she isn't from Philadelphia, but Deborah is, and she wants to know if we want to go to Buckingham Palace today.

Zara rolls her eyes, sighs back on her bed. The bleeding Royalty put her to sleep and I think Zara is the coolest girl I have ever seen. She's wearing a black T-shirt and tiny black lace panties (knickers in England). I roll over to the other side and there's curly hair and big blue eyes and pink cheeks saying Buckingham Palace is something we should really see, tugging on huge shapeless sweats. I roll back to Zara and say that she should come with us just for fun and she smiles and pads off to the shower.

And then there we are at Buckingham Palace, all big and dank-looking, behind walls and gates with some guards in big hats, like in front of Parliament Hill in Ottawa, but at least Parliament Hill is accessible and it isn't someone's home like this is supposed to be, though I can't damn imagine anyone living here and as I think this, Zara, in her straight leg black pants and old-man black coat and her huge clomper combat boots, snorts and coughs, "Fucking rich pigs."

Deborah sighs, "Wow-oh-wow-oh-wow-I-don't-believe-I'm-here."

Later, Zara and I grab a coffee and sit on a bench. She's eighteen and her father's Turkish and her mother's English — he took off after she was born and so all she knows about being Turkish is that they have eyes like THE ONES IN HER HEAD.

"Yeah, my Mum works for the U.N. She's a secretary for some bleeding rotter idiot and she's shagging him, too. I go to the International school with rich fucking spoiled dip kids. My boyfriend, Sylvan, he's Swiss. We love each other because we're the only bloody two who aren't fucking stuck-up assholes there."

I'm sure dip means diplomat but I don't risk asking and sounding like a loser. I want to be just like Zara. Cool. Being cool is everything. I say maybe her mother will marry the man she's shagging. Zara gives a delicate burp: "The diplomat is already married."

And then it's enough talk and she gets down to business. She wants to shop. Says we can find me some other things to wear, some darker things, new shoes maybe. So we go shopping in this huge, bizarre stretching market made of little rooms with cloth walls where you can buy surplus army wear, weird jewellery, biker clothes, incense, records, gigantic shoes and boots like Zara's, and I realize Zara's gone. Music thumps and I feel like I'm lost in a giant music video. My heel is starting to ache again, right up in my leg, and my jet lag is taking over — it's only been

three days, I realize, though I know at the same instant that time means nothing now
nothing nothing.

I limp down this aisle and some guy shouts, "Hey hey, Red Shoes." I look at him and he asks me if I want to buy some comfy boots. "Spacious boots," he says, "the red ones are squeezing the life out of you, girlie." He holds up some black combat boots for £30 and I don't have any idea how much that is in dollars. He gurgles, all slimy and grinning with brown stumps of teeth and though he looks ancient, I know he is my age. Maybe if I give him money, I can go away. I buy the shoes and wait for him to give me some change but he keeps holding my hand, smiling as though it's a competition he's going to win if it kills him, which it might if he doesn't let go. I whack him hard on the head with my red shoe and take off down the row, looking into all these weird, makeshift boutiques. Music throbs. Zara Zara Zara, I think, and there she is, with people wearing gigantic hairdos or with no hair and black clothes, with safety pins in their noses, huddled in a group, and I come ploughing in.

"Zara Zara Zara."

The group disappears and Zara sighs and walks down the row. Bubbles bursting as she tells me I know how to bloody well fuck things up.

"You don't have a clue, Sa — "

She doesn't even know my name.

"Seraphina," I say.

"Okay, Seraphina. The deal is that I want to score some drugs and you don't walk up and yell. You don't walk up and say anything. You wait for me and you talk if I bloody well ask you something and you only answer what I ask. Nice boots."

I'm still puking in the wind when Dearie pulls over on the highway shoulder. She hops out, comes around and opens my door. There is coffee vomit on her white van and on my face, some natural beauty treatment, an acid masque. I fall to my knees by the ditch. Dearie pats my back but I shrug her away. Touch hurts. I think of Grammie and tears drip out my eyes. I'm glad she has never seen me like this. Dearie just stands there smoking until I lean against the van, listening to the traffic go wetly by on the slushy road and she squats beside me. "I bought these combat boots in London." I point at my feet and see vomit. What am I supposed to tell her about my trip? "And then we got haircuts, and then we got pierced." Dearie rolls her eyes and mine shut.

First Zara wants to get a haircut, so we walk to this place she heard about, a shop in a house. I follow her, no idea where in the world we are. I limp through the door and sink into a chair. Zara lights up a smoke and hands me one, saying my foot must hurt and we'll take care of that real soon. I'm leaning my head on the windowsill and then I'm sitting in an old-fashioned barber's chair while an enormous woman named Gladys, with huge blue hair and safety pins and pointy black shoes, comes at me with clippers, old-man-style clippers. Zara is beside me getting a cut from Big Dog as Gladys says "Luvvie, we'll take a bit off here and here and here and then you'll look like something."

So I'm bald.

But being bald is the least of my concerns when Big Dog comes over with a needle and I put my hands to my ears, which are pierced ears like any normal girl. I've even got extra holes up the right one from a high school party. I was loaded and this girl rammed a darning needle through my ear and into a potato. She put dots on my lobe with purple magic marker and then started jabbing away until Dearie and Elizabeth showed up. I was in a black-out by then but that's what they say happened. Who knows? Anyway, I've got the holes to prove I was at the party. Big Dog tells me not to touch my nose and then he's sticking a tongue depressor up my nostril and then he has me count and breathe, count and breathe — and a needle goes through the nostril. It hits the wooden stick and a thread of blood drops down from inside my nose to my lip. I wipe it away with my tongue as Big Dog holds my forehead and slips in a hoop.

I guess it's like a package deal because we go into this room with a table, like in a doctor's office, and Big Dog pierces our belly buttons, or navels, as he calls them: a navel piercing. He cleans my navel, puts a clamp on it above the hole and then — count, breathe — this big frigger of a needle slides in and then I have this hoop with a silver ball on it. It's 22 gauge, like a shotgun. He says to keep the area clean and be easy on the pints, the chemical drugs, sleep and eat well, this will all help avoid infection and promote healing and seasoning, as if I'm a turkey. We should make sure our bed linen is clean too. I mean, ha fucking ha, what bed linen? Zara hasn't listened to a word and I'm thinking the gangrene may just as well set in now.

Next we're sitting on the Tube, whirring along, while Zara pores over a map: *The Drug Addict's Guide To London*. Every time I've been on this in the last few days I've thought of the war and people hiding down here. She laughs, banging her head against the window and smiles at me.

Finally we get out. It's dark and the houses are shabby buildings stacked on the street. Up the hill, she foams, and we go up the hill. A black man comes out of a house and she asks him how we get to this corner we are trying to find. I can hardly understand him.

"What you wanna go up there for?"

"Because."

"How far?"

"You don't wanna go up there, girl."

And she walks on. He looks at me and I look at him and I want to go in and drink tea at his kitchen table. But Zara walks on. I can see a street corner ahead and lights so I run up behind her. And the

second we are under those street lights we are surrounded by pushers, aliens, with pierced noses and lips and faces, shaved heads, stinky
holey clothes, rattling off the names of drugs I've never heard of:

"What you want girls? You want some junk horse smack,
smack you on the bum, you want some speed, you want
some hash, girls you want some meth, you want to be dusted
with love, love you, oh sweet ecstasy? Want needles? You
gonna trip tonight. You want some pills, you gonna dream,
you want to go up or down, a little sniff of snow, fly like
birdies on acid."

Somehow we've ended up in some black slum in London, I
keep thinking Harlem, but then I think Jamaica because of the
accent. And I'm running down the street, pulling my foot with me.
This is the seediest place I've ever known. Oliver Twist can fucking
pop out any minute. Isn't there a goddamn coffee shop, a Tim
Horton's, some roadside fruit stand? Isn't there somewhere I can go
inside? And there is, a seedy place that says restaurant, a neon sign
that says restaurant over this shabby door with a crooked frame that
is colourless in the night and streetlight. I smash it open.

"I need the loo."

Right in front of me is another shrivelled dude in his early twen-
ties or late nineties speaking in English, I know it must be English,
and he points, as I stand there, chest heaving, which is a bad thing
but I am too stupid and drunk to know this. I bolt over to a door with
a pair of tits carved in wood, hanging in the centre.

I rip open the boob door and smash it shut. I'm in a hole. I am
in a fucking shit-covered hole. I stand over the piss-coated toilet,
pull up my skirt. I'm holding it in one hand and I don't want to pull
my underpants down — they are underpants now, not panties or
knickers — so I pull the crotch over, feel a burn as the elastic waist
catches my navel ring and I realize I didn't come here to pee, I

came here to hide. I start to cry but I am heaving too hard to cry so it's only tears and me trying not to swallow my tongue. Fuck — the door isn't locked — it doesn't lock. Knock knock it's the toothless toady guy speaking in tongues.

"Just a minute — just having a pee — "

I slam my foot against the door just as Toad Man pushes it.

Dearie hands me a Kleenex. I tell her I got in with a bad crowd. That I ended up in some places I shouldn't have been in. That I ended up doing some drugs I shouldn't have done, that they made me sick. She wipes some drool from my lip and shakes her head. I was in a sleazy pub and had to keep the door shut with my leg so this guy wouldn't come in. Dearie just stares at me and then snorts.

I'm glad my legs are tight and strong from some distant healthy rural childhood and there is no way he is opening it, and standing there hovering over the dirty hole, with my clothes twisted, hand on my underwear crotch — the word gusset zaps into my mind — one leg up and balanced like a music box ballerina on my burning foot, I pee all over myself.

A stream tinkles in the toilet and on my foot. I think of Zara and wonder if she is dead or high and I think of Ariel in *The Tempest* and want a tempest to blow them all away or some magic, any magic, to get me out of here. Fuck off, I scream at Toad Man, the only universal words I know, in my full-blown Nova Scotia Annapolis Valley twang.

"I'm taking a piss, you Jesus bastard."

The banging stops. I wipe my crotch on the gusset, my hands on my skirt and hair and then jump down and make a plan. Run. That's it. Run out the door. Find the guy who told us not to come here, cry and ask him to call the Bobbies to come and get me and take me home. To take me to the Canadian Embassy. I'll go back to university like a good Canadian girl. I'll apologize to my father and mother. Anything, I'll apologize for anything. I want to call Elizabeth and Dearie.

And I rush out past Toady who's outside the door holding a pint. Did he plan to woo me in the fucking toilet? Jesus lordy. And I hobble across the restaurant. I don't even look, just know there are a few tables and it stinks like sour beer and grease.

On the street it's the lights again and there's Zara and I want to cry because it's Zara, and I want to scream because she's with one of the pushers. He's tall and black and he's wearing a brown leather jacket and I wonder why drug dealers always look like rock stars. And my breathing goes again. In front of Zara and the dealer are two of the shaved head dudes, coming my way. Zara and her man catch up and pass them. Shaved heads veer off down a lane. She grabs my arm, her soft hand on my elbow.

"What the bloody hell? How's your foot, girl?"

"I had to find a loo."

Liar liar, but she doesn't know.

"Those guys, man, they were coming for you, Seraphina."

Seraphina. He likes my name. Jack. Jack likes my name. Likes my boots. He likes everything about Zara. And he tells us not to worry about those blokes. And so the deal is she's scored already, we smoke some with him now and then he'll tell us how to get home. Yeah, fuck, sure. Sounds like a great deal. And then we die. Great goddamn deal she wrangled. I can tell she's been around the U.N. Jesus. Then we're raped and bludgeoned to death. Hacked into pieces by Jack the-fucking-dope-pushing Ripper.

It's only been fifteen minutes since getting off the Tube. Fifteen minutes and Zara is walking down a lane and I limp down the lane behind her and I don't care anymore. I don't care and I suck back the smoke into my lungs and smell that tarry hash smell and shut my eyes. I stand there and my foot disappears and so does my belly, my nose, all gone. As I open my eyes, Zara's voice floats by my head, each word in a bubble and I know Ariel must be around somewhere. Back on the street and the dingy light is white now. Somewhere, back there in my mind, I know it wasn't just hash we smoked as Zara bubbles go slowly by

                         Taxi
          Fucking pigs
                         Bleeding Coppers
Taxi
                                   Wehavetotakeataxi

The taxi drives slow and I'm wedged by the door. Orchid Zara sits in the middle, Jack's hand on her knee. Big cat purrs, "You are fine for a white girl." Where is my foot? Jack and the driver watch the rear view mirror for the bleedin' coppers. Zara puts her head on my shoulder. I am the best friend she's ever had. Her voice is full of echoes. Elizabeth and Dearie float by, Christmas ornaments looking for the tree.

And we're by an old graveyard near the hostel. My eyes are wrapped in the dark and I see Foster, Nova Scotia, fall off the map. I'm leaning on a wrought-iron fence, so thirsty I want to suck the cold out of the metal and feel it slide down my throat. Zara's leaning in the taxi door talking.

Slam.

She's leaning on the fence, sweating.

"It's fucking junk. He's fucking smoked us up with heroin."

She vomits. And my world slides into velvet blue on fire as Anne Of Green Gables Does The Big Time.

I'm shivering and Dearie takes her coat off and puts it around me. "Serrie, maybe you should stick to coffee. I don't understand why you have to do things like this," she says with this worried little laugh. I pull on her arm, looking up at her squinting in the winter sun as it lowers its self downward to the earth.

"Jehovah's God, Dearie," I tell her, watching the stinking sinking sun. "It's Hebrew, in the Old Testament, Jehovah, God, same thing. Like Jahweh, you know, what Rastafarians say for God. They think our world is Babylon, you know, the white world."

Dearie smiles, at least it looks like smiling, and she laughs out her teeth in a hiss. "God, Serrie, why can't you get something useful out of a book, like how to live a normal life? What's Babylon? Isn't it a river?"

I sit there by the ditch looking at the blinding sun thinking about Gee-hov-ah and other non-practical things while Dearie helps me stand up and get in the van, as I tell her the rest. She's disgusted and fascinated at the very same time.

The Big Time is me waking up glued to the pillow with puke, my head feeling so big and wobbly it's like having a globe full of rocks and sand on my neck. I want to just die 'cause my body hurts so much and I can't remember how I got wherever I am, which is the hostel, I realize, when I open my crusty eyes. I remember sobbing and drooling into a telephone, vague bits of Dearie and Elizabeth on the phone, me screaming about the ocean, high tide, pieces of voice stitched together with static and clicks and gull squawks, big stretches of blackness, then choking on snot, the receiver sliding from my slimy palm like a flipping fish.

It's total body cancer, I've got total body cancer, I think, from my bulgy head to my sore belly to my throbbing heel. Sweat drips, the bed spins and my eyes fill up with tears. I can't feel my lips and I know this isn't a good way to start the morning. Someone has pasted me with puke to the bed, keeping me in my place, because it doesn't seem to matter what I do since I'm always forced to be in a place I don't want to be in. Some little part of me screams that I'm the goddamn jesus glue master, but I don't want to hear that so I take a deep, blubbering breath and pull at my neck. It makes a big crack, my head rips off the pillow with a dry, coarse noise, the smell of piss in the air — I've wet the bed. So much for being cool.

I lick my lips. Huge — must have smashed them on something but I can't remember what and my throat goes tight. I can taste blood and then I hear "Zazazazzaaaa." In my head I'm thinking Zara and I say Zara again but it sounds like I'm retarded and maybe I really am. I sit up slowly, my foot screaming back to life and the room whirling about. It stops. There is no Zara, only Deborah, chewing her lip, looking at me from her neat and tidy bunk.

"How are you?" Her curls bounce and she bites her lip. Automatically I bite my own and wince with pain.

"Oh well, you know." I say. "I'm okay."

And she looks away. It's been two weeks? I don't know . . . Europe by blackout, I think. Every night starting in a pub with Zara ordering gin-and-tonics and me saying I feel like some old lady, Zara's eyes rolling, me drinking up and blacking out. And then drugs in dark parks and clubs with music music music pounding down on me in splinters, fragments, slices, pulses, like being inside the tune. Coming to on my feet, smoking something, taking something. On my feet in a conversation that I can't follow, coming to in a crazy apartment in bed with some guy, thinking for a second I am in Halifax, but there is Zara on the living room floor. Getting booted out of the hostel in the morning and dozing in a park in the early afternoon sun, feeling so old and lost, crying about it, Zara always rolling her eyes because Zara never cries, and giving me more smoke, more pills. It's easier to be drunk and high in the dark than it is to be sober in the horrible truth of your own life is the only brilliant conclusion I come to in England.

Deborah keeps looking at me and I stretch my big lip to smile like she's going to take a snapshot (because everything's always great in holiday pictures, right?) but my lip cracks and I taste blood sharp as iron and my stomach heaves. I swing my legs over the edge of the bunk and stare at her, break out in a sweat again and then my stomach rolls and the bunk feels like a dory in big seas. Rocking back and forth, I wish was home, but a long-time-ago home, so I could have a new start, do it differently. I get sick on my T-shirt and Deborah takes me into the bathroom. She sticks me in a tub and pours water over my head and there is a bang at the door. Deborah says we'll be out in a minute. I try to wash my face but I'm shaking too much to hold the soap so Deborah makes it all foamy and washes me like I'm some discarded old lady in a home, in the Norton Hill Manor where my Grammie would rather die than be stuck away like so much old linen.

"Look, Serrie, I think you're a nice girl but you've got to get out of here. Right?"

I'm shaking in the cold and Deborah pours more hot water down my back. I soap up my navel and rinse.

"The police were here last night and you can't stay here anymore."

And I tell Deborah I don't know what happened at all and she tells me that everyone in the hostel was asleep until they heard a horrible screeching out in the park in the darkness. The hostel night manager went out and found me rolling around in the grass with a bottle of whisky, screaming. When he asked me what I was doing I said I was a bagpipe. If the manager wasn't such a nice guy he would have turned me over to the cops who came looking for Zara who's run away from a reform school somewhere in northern England.

Dearie looks like she wants to shake me, shake some sense into me, like the babysitter who ruptures the blood vessels in the baby's eyes. The stupid baby that cries and cries even when it has food and clothes, a clean diaper, a tidy crib, when it has everything it could ever need but it is never enough for the baby troubled by horrible existential pain that it wouldn't share even if it could talk because it would be despairingly pointless. It is only a floppy creature whose agony darts out and cuts the night up into little pieces that stick in eyes and ears and brains.

Shut up, Dearie, I think, covering my ears, watching her mouth make perfect shapes, reading her lips. "You called the Reverend Rafuse up in the middle of the night, screaming about London and God and your parents and how bad it all was and who would help Trevor, that you hated Nova Scotia and goddamn bagpipes, where was the queen anyway, and what was so special about paperweights and teapots?" She took a breath. "What's the deal with teapots and paperweights?" Dearie worked in, before telling me that the Reverend Rafuse phoned my parents who phoned Dearie who then heard from Elizabeth that I was coming home after my three weeks in the old country without so much as even sending anyone a flippin' freakin' friggin' postcard.

I keep the window rolled down the rest of the way into the city. The lights are twinkling as twilight falls, twinkling in that welcoming way twilit cities have, *the cozy time* my mother called it when we lived in the PMQ. Dearie keeps saying she is hungry, that it is suppertime. It's good she's there to tell me because my internal clock is temporarily shut down. The days are short this time of year, short and cold, especially in the city where the harbour fills it up with dampness. They say the Valley has the best weather in the province, and Halifax the worst, cars spattering slush and snow until April. Nova Scotia is so small there is only one real city and so people don't even call it Halifax, just *the city*. We come in to it through Dartmouth, the smaller city across the harbour from Halifax. There are two suspension bridges, the Angus L. MacDonald and the A. Murray MacKay, or the old bridge and the new, though I can't even remember the new one being built. If you aren't from the city, you never think of Dartmouth as a separate place, just an extension of Halifax, a bedroom community. Dearie calls it *Darkness*.

After we pay the toll on the new bridge and start off again, the sick feeling comes back, but mostly from thinking about Dearie and her controlled craze, my parents, my mother all mad and quiet, my father helpless, the poor Reverend Rafuse and the outraged Galronia. And Grammie, my Grammie wondering why we can't just get on with it, the whole damn lot of us. I start doing the burping thing again but Dearie says we can't stop which I already know because big signs everywhere say:

No Stopping
No Turning
No Reversing

It's just too much like my frigging life. I go hanging out the window with dry heaves: vomit as you go — my goddamn ethos. The salty, soggy wind whacks my face as we zoom over the steel-blue Halifax Harbour, the city so small after London, and all I can think is I'm back where I started and it's worse. The sun is setting in the West, same old sun in the same old West over the same old city. Dearie reaches over to pat me on the shoulder but it's hunched up so close to my ear there is nothing to pat and I feel her hand on my head. My shakes go into her arm and she presses on my head to steady me.

"Serrie, things will never be the same if you keep doing stuff like this." She says it looking straight ahead, like she's reading a sign.

Looking down from the bridge I see the house where we lived, all those years ago when we lived in the city on the navy base by the bridge, and I wonder if I walked into that house, whether I could travel back in time, have one more chance.

We moved to Halifax from the Valley when I was three and Percy was five, because my father was in the navy then, a mechanic on big ships, making their engines go. He had an older brother, Roan Sullivan, who was tall and looked like a cigar, so says Grammie, but I never knew him because he got the tuberculosis on a big warship in World War II from the cramped cabins, my father says. He says he remembers Ro playing the piano, some piano in the orphanage I guess, because instead of foster homes they had orphanages in those days, along with the TB, and they must have had sing-a-longs or whatever people did back then for fun. I don't even know what tuberculosis is, except my mother says it's alive and well on the Indian reserves and no one gives a good goddamn what happens to them, oh no, just stick them away out of sight and let them rot like so much compost, frigging government. There's not much career satisfaction happening for her these days.

When Ro Sullivan came off the navy ship he had to go to the sanatorium in Bigelow Bay, where he sat around playing the piano and drinking rum until he was dead in the bone. My father never talks about him except sometimes when he hears piano on the CBC radio and his eyes empty out and I don't know where he is — my father's whole life before us is a mystery, except what Grammie tells me. But he joined the navy, following in the footsteps of dead old Ro, which you might have thought would set some kind of gong off in my father's head, some, you know, portentous bell tolling out, but he joined anyway and when I was three we moved to the city, into a little PMQ, Private Married Quarters, like being in the middle of the alphabet, and I loved it. Back then, my mother was at home all day. She was a nurse, following in the footsteps of Grammie. She stopped working when she had Percy — it was what my mother always wanted, Aunt Galronia told me once when I was six, out in the Valley visiting her and Grammie, and we were picking cherries. Gallie, as we mostly called her, told me that my mother had always wanted to stay home and be a housewife, a mother, she was born for it, that's the main reason she got married, because the clock was ticking and she was no spring chicken, almost forty years old. Having kids at that age takes a toll on the body and going back to work was most likely going to give her a heart attack, which she could have avoided if she'd just left Nova Scotia, but, oh no, she had to have a family. "We make the bed, we goddamn lie in it. We bake the bread and we goddamn eat it," Gallie informed me. I managed to climb high enough in the tree so Galronia's voice became a hum just like the ones bees and bugs make, those summer sounds that always soothed me.

When she wasn't being a housewife, my mother would do watercolour paintings and make the most delicious pies and jams, me helping out with everything until I started school, my mother taking us that morning, leaving me screaming and crying in the classroom doorway, her saying, "Pumpkin, you'll get used to it," and looking very sad as she left me there. Percy stood beside me at recess and gave me all his cookies, telling me I would soon get used to it. But by October, when I turned five, I still hated sitting in my little desk and colouring pictures, the sweet dumb teacher standing behind me saying, "Good girl, Serrie, nice work, but skies are blue, not pink and purple. Make your sky blue, the sky has to be blue, any shade but always blue." I knew then that Percy didn't know everything, even though I wanted him to.

My father was nearly always at sea and when he wasn't, he was in the basement in his workshop inventing things, "top secret things," he would say. My mother would take us to museums and parks and sometimes out of the city for day trips to little villages on the coast, for fish and chips in New-Medford-on-the-Beach as opposed to New Medford-in-the-Woods, where we would collect sand dollar shells and sea urchins caught up with the seaweed and driftwood, washed there on the smooth sand by the waves. The fingers of the sea, my mother would call them. Sometimes when the waves were small we'd lie down on the sand, just at the waterline, and let the waves touch our heads, "a scalp massage," my mother would say, the waves coming and going, cold cold and then the warmth of the sun and air. Who could stay the longest, who could brave a wave crashing on their face? Percy hated the water and as soon as it would start touching his hair, he'd sit up and watch us. Sometimes he'd splash around playing war games, Big Navy Cruiser or Mighty Freighter, Nuclear Submarine Destroys the World. My mother and I would sit on the blanket, her smoking, us both reading, the smell of cigarettes and suntan lotion, lemonade and ocean, a heady summer fragrance twirling in my nose, her holding the pages of the book open with her toes, pink rose polish on the nails, reaching out and stroking my hair, then turning the page. She kept my hair long and wouldn't cut it, not even when I'd get food and crap in it and she'd patiently work most of it out, clipping a few strands if she had to. At the beach I'd chew on the end of a braid while I read and my mother would reach out with one of her pink-tipped feet, taking a slow drag of her smoke, ashes on the sand, and gently tug a braid: "How do you do, pumpkin pie?" And she would giggle back into her book.

But those times ended so fast, my father coming home from sea, sitting in their bedroom drinking rum, reading science books and spy novels. My mother crawling in bed with me at night and holding my hand. We'd hear him calling her name and I'd squeeze her fingers and she'd squeeze back, whispering not to cry but to go to sleep so it would all go away, her hand stroking my hair until his shadow would fall on my quilt, him saying, "Martha, come on Martha, you have to get up, I'm sorry, you know, I don't mean it." And she'd get up saying, "Cyril, you're scaring Serrie." He'd say "that Serrie's not scared of nothing," and I'd cry into my pillow so they wouldn't know how weak I was, that I couldn't even do a little thing like not cry, that Serrie was scared of everything, even her own ugly toes. He'd yell about how it wasn't fair, how it was all passing him by, and I'd hum the doxology over and over:

The Lord bless thee and keep thee,
the Lord make His face shine upon thee
and be gracious unto thee:
the Lord lift up his countenance upon thee and give thee peace,
Amen.

But he wouldn't stop, he'd keep whining like a big baby, and then my mother would play him yoga tapes from the library. The next day he'd still be in bed or gone and my mother would be quiet with a tight mouth, slamming breakfast down, yelling at Percy for reading at the table, telling me to eat faster. My father started being in and out of the military hospital and taking what he called nerve pills. And then he had problems with his pancreas and his liver and his kidney and then he became an anatomy system, like the pictures in the books Percy would bring home from the library when he was babysitting me. Our mother would be at the hospital, visiting, and Percy'd flip open the big books with the coloured body systems, "Christmas tree people," I would say, and he would laugh, his ten-year-old fingers carefully turning the pages to show me all the human systems, the respiratory, the circulatory, the skeletal system, the digestive and the nervous system, showing me exactly what systems our father was hurting in.

My school days stretched out in a long row of dominos, one falling into the next and the next, this endless line of time we were caught in. Our father would be home for a few weeks, a few months, it was impossible to tell how long it was, as the days pushed down on each other. We didn't know how long he would be home or when he would be gone again, to the hospital or to some big building where we would see him in WAITING ROOMS and VISITING ROOMS, sitting under the NO SMOKING signs, standing by the PUBLIC TELEPHONE, by the hall that led to the X-RAY DEPARTMENT, in a hospital bed in a JOHNNY SHIRT sitting by a painting of BANFF donated by THE LADIES HOSPITAL AUXILIARY.

I was seven when they took out one of Cyril Sullivan's kidneys and my mother had to go back to work for the Department of Health, and she'd be there at the sink in her work clothes, slamming dishes in the drying rack, muttering that having a family had ruined it for her, had ruined it all, that it could have been different, me crying into the Froot Loops. Percy would take me to the bathroom to brush my teeth and would get my book bag, pulling me out the door with him, our mother in a chair in the living room smoking, her head in her hands, fingernails never painted anymore, skin stripped down the sides to the first knuckle, all sad and remorseful when she'd come home at night, making little glass bowls of chocolate pudding, and then falling asleep in her chair. Percy creeping upstairs with me in front of him, putting me to bed, telling me Micmac stories of the Valley, stories of the great Micmac God, Glooscap, who paddled his canoe over the Bay of Fundy to where it narrows and roars around Cape Split, *Plekteok*, into the Basin. Glooscap set up a lodge there, near Cape Blomidon, surrounded by the huge red cliffs and sparkling amethyst beaches. Percy would tell me to go to sleep and go canoeing with Glooscap, that he'd look after me. I could hear Gallie saying Percy was trying to make me a pagan but I didn't care, I wanted to be in that canoe gliding over the water, with a god steering in the back.

A year slipped away, us scurrying about, until the day I came home with gum in my hair at the beginning of June. I didn't even remember it getting stuck, there was just so much hair, and I slept on it. The next morning, I couldn't even get the pillow off my head and Percy just laughed in the kitchen, bits of cereal hanging on his lip, falling back into his cereal bowl. Laughing until my mother's hand jabbed out her morning smoke and ripped at the pillow and then at my hair with a brush. The white cotton pillowcase with hand-embroidered daffodils flopped in my eyes as my mother pulled harder and harder until I was crying. Percy dropped his cereal bowl when she started whacking my back with the bristle part. I could hear china shattering as Percy grabbed her hand that held the brush. He had turned eleven on May Day, a skinny, girly-voiced eleven, but he was as fast as wind, pulling me up the stairs into the bathroom, locking the door, shushing me as he cut the gum out with toenail scissors. Martha was outside the door, saying she was sorry, so sorry: "Come on, kids, let me in. Perse, I'm so sorry, Serrie, I'm sorry." Percy, he was turning the taps on full blast and flushing the toilet so we wouldn't have to hear, then holding my hand all the way to school. That night my mother crawled in bed with me, holding my eight-year-old hand all the way through the night, so tight it hurt the bones and I knew then that even bones, the bones that held you together and upright, even they would eventually break and crumble, fall into dust. You couldn't even trust your bones. So much for the skeletal system.

T W O

DEARIE'S APARTMENT IS IN AN OLD FOUR-STOREY HERITAGE BUILDING.
She moved there in September, the year we all started third-year
university, just before I took off for England, after the Thanksgiving
Debacle. It's a giant bachelor apartment, what would be called a
studio if it was renovated. The whole place is furnished in antiques
she inherited and I don't know anyone else our age who lives like
this, but then I don't know very many people my own age. She has
some big bookshelves but not too many books, and the books she
has are usually introduction books, you know, *An Introduction to
World History*, *Introduction to High Fibre*, *Befriending Hegel*, weird
stuff like that. They all look brand new and the pages crack when
you turn them. We don't know if she reads them, but at least it's
an effort, right? There are also her log books, books where she
writes down all the music she wants to buy, places she wants to
go, perfume, foods she wants to eat. Dearie's great at making
lists but not so great at putting on her dancing shoes, if you know
what I mean.

 I start running a bath in the old claw-foot tub and Dearie brings
in clean yellow towels. Watching the water pour in, I ask her how
Elizabeth is, shouting over the water noises. Dearie shrugs and
leaves. She comes back with a cup of tea for me, and puts it on the
toilet tank. She leans in the doorway with a smoke.

"So how is Elizabeth?" I ask again, sitting down on the cold black and white tile, waiting for the tube to fill. The steam is warming up the room and I feel my body begin to relax. My butt is so scrawny I have to get a towel to sit on.

"Oh, she's always working. I never see her. Or she's with her roommate, Clare. I don't like her." Dearie doesn't mince words.

"Why not?"

"Because Clare's not very nice, that's the fuck why. It's like she doesn't have time for anyone who doesn't work at the bar with her. She got Elizabeth her job there. Elizabeth hardly goes to classes anymore. Clare, she was going to university in Vancouver but she dropped out and moved back here. She's from out near Blockhouse. I think something bad happened but Elizabeth won't tell me."

"Well, maybe she asked Elizabeth to keep it a secret."

"Well, it's not like I'm a stranger or anything."

Dearie doesn't understand the idea of a confidante. "So is Elizabeth coming over?"

"Yes, but just because you're here. She got the night off, if you can believe it. I just called her because I said I would when we got back from the airport. I told her about your trip."

The tub is almost ready. "You told her about my trip? Dearie, why don't you let me do that? Don't tell anyone else, okay?" I twist the taps off but I'm too weak to make them stop dripping.

"Fine, fine, you don't have to get mad about it, Serrie. I thought you'd want her to know. I mean, are the three of us best friends or not?"

Dearie pushes me out of the way to gets the drips stopped and I say, "Sure, we're best friends but let me tell, okay?" My head starts to throb, in this quiet way, as though something inside is trying to come to life.

Dearie shrugs and takes a drag. "Whatever," she snaps.

"Maybe you should tell Elizabeth you would like to see her more."

"What would be the point of that?" She takes another drag.

What's the point of this conversation, I wonder. I put my toe in the water and it's boiling so I struggle with the cold tap. "Is Elizabeth okay?"

"Yeah, she has a new boyfriend. Some guy named Reggie. He's old, thirty."

Dearie leaves to find an ashtray and I slide into the tub. She comes back, sits on the toiletseat and lights another smoke.

"What's Elizabeth's place like?"

"Don't know. I've only been in the front porch. She's never there when I drop by."

The warm water soothes me and I lean my head on the sloped enamel back of the tub. A tiny blue and green stained-glass window above the sink glows with some end-of-day sun that has battled its way through the winter sky. When I open my eyes Dearie is gone and the door is shut and then so are my eyes again. The chlorine smell of city water hangs under the cherry bubble-bath steam and dulls my mind. London, my sick body, it all melts away until I gong my head on the side of the tub and knock off the wire soap and shampoo holders that are hanging off the edge. My head rings like an old phone as I hear Dearie walking over the squeaky hardwood floor.

"What the fuck are you doing to my bathroom?"

The doorknob turns. Can't I even *bathe* in private? She comes in and stares at my feet that are propped on the edge of the tub. My heel is ketchup red. "Jesus, I dropped the goddamn bar of soap, that's all." I rub my head. "I'm not doing *anything* to your bathroom."

She leans against the sink. "Well, you don't have to make so much noise."

"It's my nature to make noise," I whisper. What a pot of crap I talk. Shampoo on my head, stuff that smells like sweet bananas. I'm not hungry or I'd probably eat it. We look at each other and she shakes her head. "Don't you want to know where your stuff is?"

I don't know what stuff she's talking about.

"My suitcase?"

"No, not your fucking suitcase. All your fucking stuff you left at the guys' house."

I rub my head. "Isn't it still at the house? There wasn't really anything anyway."

"No, it's all packed up in my storage locker, not that you had much of anything but goddamn books. They had to rent out the dining room. Another swimmer. They kept your furniture because you didn't give notice."

It's my parent's furniture, or was. More old stuff from the attic. Just junk, not any of the Spinster Sullivan's valuables, not this stuff. I rest my feet on the faucet.

Dearie stares at my heel as she tells me not to get water on the floor. "You have to go to a doctor about that foot. What the hell did you do?"

"Bashed it in England. I told you already."

"Well, what did you go and do that for?" And then she sees my navel. "Jesus fuck. What's that?"

"It's supposed to be sexy." I pat it gently, like a kitten.

Dearie can't stop staring. "That's sexy, is it? Looks like you pulled it out of the bathtub plug. Hardware in your nose, your belly and a shaved head. Right out of a death camp."

There is no point in saying anything so I sink down under the water until my ears fill and I'm almost sucking bubbles up my nostrils. She shakes her head and leaves. I shut my eyes and just feel the warm water and think about the Reverend Rafuse, the messes I keep making. I go lower in the tub and the water covers my eyes but it isn't enough to close out the world. I hear Dearie come back in again but I stay still as she sits on the toilet. I can hear the tinkle even with water in my ears so I open them and it's not Dearie — it's Elizabeth sitting there, staring at me with her big brown eyes, smiling. I smile back, not even moving, and she giggles and starts ripping off toilet paper, first 5 squares, then 4, 3, 2, 1 squares of toilet paper. Then odds,

5, 3, 1, then 4, 2, then the whole thing one more time. Elizabeth has always done this. She points, with the sequence of 3 in her hand, to my nose. She smiles and wipes. And they think I'm weird.

"Welcome home," she proclaims, and then begins the sequence of 2. She crumples it up in a ball and sits there, giggling. "Well, it's quite the state of affairs." And then she wipes with the piece of 1 and reaches behind to flush the toilet as she apologizes for not being able to come to the airport. Elizabeth hopes Dearie didn't give me a hard time.

"I didn't give her a goddamn hard time, Elizabeth. Jesus, you think everything is so goddamn frigging funny." Dearie comes in with a cigarette and a bottle of wine and three glasses. She sits on the bath mat and hands the bottle and corkscrew to Elizabeth, who is waving the smoke out. She hates smoking, everything about it, unless she's absolutely loaded and then she smokes like a mime, every drag a big production.

Elizabeth starts tugging on the cork, giggling with each pull. "She called up the Reverend Rafuse in the middle of the night, for god's sake." Then she just bends over the bottle with laughter.

Dearie lights a cigarette and frowns as she drags on it. "It's not god-damn funny, Elizabeth. It's sacrilegious. That's what Galronia said."

"Oh Dearie, do you really think she should start listening to Galronia?" Elizabeth keeps tugging at the corkscrew while Dearie stares at her and Elizabeth stares back, still hee-heeing, saying, "look at her hair, look at her hair."

The cork hits me in the head. Silence, and they crack up, swigging out of the bottle like we were back in high school at some shore party, looking at me like I'm the night's entertainment.

Elizabeth reaches over the tub and hands me a glass of wine, the stem catching in the bubbles. It's sweet and cheap and the smell mixes with the bubble-bath. I drool.

"Serrie, there's lot's more, so just take it easy and don't go crazy or anything."

Elizabeth doesn't get it. I push the glass away so not to puke in the tub. "It's just the jet lag," I say and sink even lower in the water. How can I explain that I'm scared of a glass of wine?

"The *jet lag*," Elizabeth echos, and Dearie snorts, "She's got the jet lag, she's *so* sophisticated." Dearie reaches through the bubbles and tugs my navel ring. It burns and I bat her hand away.

"Now Serrie thinks that right there is a sexy man magnet. How about that?" Dearie says, sipping her wine.

Elizabeth makes a face and then turns to Dearie. "Hey, did you go out with that guy who asked me for your number? You know, the one in the bar who asked if I knew you."

Dearie on a date. I can't see it. Dearie takes a drag and then a big drink. "Jesus, he thinks everybody knows everybody in the Valley. No, I didn't go out with him," she blows.

"Because everybody *does* know everybody in the Valley." Elizabeth takes the bottle. "Everybody knows everybody from one end of the province to the other, except in Yarmouth. I mean, who goes to Yarmouth, except for the people who live there?"

Yarmouth is at the far end of the province and you can catch a ferry to Maine from Yarmouth, a big fancy ferry with gambling and a Vegas-style show, right here in the Maritimes. It's even got an international airport, or a make-work-port, as my cousin Gordie calls it. Not many flights really land there. Grammie always said Yarmouth was Nova Scotia's best kept secret but Elizabeth has always hated it. To my knowledge, she's never even been, just heard her cousin complain about having to drive three hours there and three hours back and that was it for poor historic Yarmouth, damned for life.

Dearie and Elizabeth start arguing who knows who and I submerge.

Under water, I hold my breath and remember being fifteen at Dearie's house on one of those cold snowy days in between the years, you know, after Christmas and before New Year's, when there is absolutely nothing to do in a small town and certainly not on the Lupin Cove Road. We were in her family room watching TV and I'd come over with a plate of squares and fruitcake. Dearie was polishing them off like a five-year-old with a bottle of orange-flavoured painkillers. They hadn't gone to the Florida condo that year, some business thing Mr. Melanson had to do over the holiday. Her house was so clean, so much cleaner than mine, as she'd point out with a grin. No dust-balls, no piles, no crumbs on the floor, no drafts blowing in the windows. It smelled like plastic, new things — the smell of prosperity, I guess. Her father came into the family room and ignored me. Nothing personal though — he ignores everybody under twenty-five except Dearie and she says it's just because they are directly related that he talks to her; he's obliged to.

"Now, don't let her smoke up the place. Make her blow it up the chimney."

The doorbell rang and I watched Mr. Melanson strike through imaginary clouds of smoke as he answered the door, holding it wide open to let in the December wind, just to flush the place out. Dearie winked at me as the Clarks walked in, saying "hi, girls" to us. As they headed to the living room to play cribbage, Mr. Melanson pointed to a new wooden wall unit by the sliding glass doors. "Got that for Christmas. How much do you think that cost, Turner?" Mr. Clark guessed a hundred dollars and Mr. Melanson laughed like a food processor chopping a shoe. "Guess again," he crowed as they disappeared down the hall.

"You told him I smoke?"

Dearie rolled her eyes.

"Well, sure I did. You *do* smoke."

I couldn't believe it. "But you smoke, too."

"Yeah, but I'm not allowed to."

"But I'm not either. They're going to think I'm a bad influence on you."

"Well, they already think that. And your mother doesn't care about smoking."

"Well, maybe my mother does care."

"Oh, come on Serrie. Give me a cigarette."

"But I don't smoke at home," I say. "You know I don't."

"So you understand why I tell my father you smoke and not me. I don't smoke at home either. So give me one."

I didn't understand anything, but, like a moron, I took one out and threw it to her as she stuck this foot-long fancy match with a fuchsia head into the fire. It flared up like a torch.

"Drag?"

She held it out like a peace offering, and I took a deep puff as Mr. Melanson walked in.

"Make sure she blows it up the chimney, Dearie."

And she winked again.

Elizabeth and Dearie leave for the Star Fish while I'm still in the bathroom, peeking in one more time before they head out to the bar for a pre-weekend, Thursday-night-good-time drinking session even though they both have exams tomorrow. Elizabeth lights me a candle and Dearie brings in a cup of hot milk, to relax me, they say, but I know they just want to have one more peek at the freak show. I take a sip and swallow but my stomach lurches so I put the glass on the floor and turn on more hot water.

Elizabeth is right, everyone does know everyone in the Valley. When people refer generally to the Valley, they could mean a whole bunch of different places besides the actual physical valley floor itself (unless you are *from* the Mountain and then you'd never say you were from the Valley, and vice versa). For instance, they might mean somewhere on the North Mountain, somewhere like the Mountain Edge Road, or on the top of the

Mountain itself, or over in Lupin Cove on the Bay of Fundy shore, the Bay with its rugged beaches and the highest tides in the world, curving in from the Atlantic down near Digby, where my mother and Gallie were born, though it's more famous for scallops than their births, right to Cape Split, then sweeping around by Cape Blomidon, where the mountain ends or begins, "depending on your attitude," Grammie says, the Mountain there dropping into, or rising from, the Minas Basin. But referring to the Valley could also mean the South Mountain. And it's always *the* Mountain, always with a definite article. The only people who say North Mountain or South Mountain are people who come from away or those journalists who wrote about the incest scandal over in Long Road. They kept saying "on South Mountain." Everybody knew it was just another book by people who weren't from around here, who just liked a scandal and had to go hanging out all the Valley crap like flags at the United Nations, just to make a buck. We here in the Valley would like to pretend that it never happened at all.

Incest and articles aside, it was a picture-book-pretty summer in Foster when we moved back home to the Valley that June when I was eight. After the bubble gum incident, my mother told us we'd be moving to Foster as soon as school was out, that our father might be sick for a long time and if he started getting better, we'd be the first to know. And that was all she said, and started packing the house up after work, Percy getting us to bed, her coming up to tuck us in, knowing how sorry she was from her hand on my forehead, crawling in bed with me late at night when I was asleep, getting up before I was awake.

One night I awoke to rain sound, the spatter kind when it falls straight down to the earth and smacks dead on. There was no Martha beside me. But there was a heavy perfume smell on the air and I crept down the stairs. My mother was still packing, folding the crocheted afghan that was always on the couch, a cigarette going in the big glass ashtray on the coffee table. She was folding the afghan into a neat rectangle and I could see the beige wool squares by the light of the single candle she was burning, the scented silver candle. She folded the afghan over and over and the green afghan squares just disappeared into the night, as she started to sing through the smack smack smack of the rain:

> The first is paper, on which you can write
> The second is cotton, all crisp and white,
> The fifth is wood, a box full of dreams,

She started crying into the afghan, and then mumbling. Me on the bottom step pulling on my hair.

> The eighth is bronze, metal in an elegant form
> The ninth is copper, and tenth is tin,
> If you have got this far you are bound to win.

And then she just burped up each word: *The fifteenth is crystal, cut glass at its best.*

I looked at the candle as it burned up all her words — *the twentieth china, cups, plates and the rest* — a beautiful tall silver pillar in a silver candle holder, handmade by an artisan in Bear River, a wedding gift from her best friend Yvonne Illsley, who lives out in Vancouver now. It had always sat up there on the mantel, waiting. I could see the cigarette smoke slithering over in the air, a cloud snake waiting to drop down around her neck and choke her dead. I was crying into my elbow then, as she took a big drag on her smoke and coughed — *the twenty-fifth is silver, really swell.* And then it was just quiet, the rain softer now, and I rubbed my eyes as she wiped hers with green squares of the afghan, blew her nose in her apron and began to pack the Hummel figurines on the mantel, another wedding gift. I only woke up as I felt her lips on my cheek and smelled the smoke on her breath as she tucked me into bed.

And the next two weeks flew. It was the only time I had ever seen her move that fast, giving her notice at work, getting all the boxes ready, putting an ad in the *Buy and Sell* for our furniture on a Wednesday and us sitting on the floor by the weekend. Our father was still in the hospital and we heard her tell Grammie that he could sober up and come to Foster or he could keep drinking and stay in the city, she was sick of it, and Grammie didn't seem to be saying anything as our mother did all the talking. And when Grammie came up to the city with Gallie to help us move down, it was like Cyril had never existed. We drove back to the Valley with Grammie in her red mini Austin, Percy in the front wearing giant sunglasses reading a book, and me in the back squinting. The three of us stopped at the Chicken Burger in Bedford for chocolate milkshakes and I looked at the brown spots on Grammie's legs while she told Percy we all were going to stay with our Grammie for a spell, that we'd have a darn good time in Foster, it was better living for children than in the city. As I sucked the last of the milkshake up the straw, Grammie said I would be able to play with Dearie Melanson, who lived next door and was four months older than me. Gallie and Martha tooted as they drove by in our old loaded-up green Chevy. Grammie gave us dandy wipes for our hands and told us to drink up. I liked to rub the dandy wipe all over my hands and face and legs, drying and making me cool, the alcohol smell sharp in my nose. It was morning, but the air was hot already. It would be a scorcher summer, you could tell. The kind where everyone and everything becomes a Sunday drive.

On the highway, Grammie shifted into high gear and caught up to Gallie and Martha, Gallie at the wheel on that beautiful June day with blue sky and delicate dabs of lacy cloud. As we buzzed past the Chevy, Gallie shook her head at Grammie's driving. I could see her lips saying, "Mum, slow down, you are seventy-nine years old," but Grammie had on these old cat-eye sunglasses and she just gave Gallie a smart little nod as we went by. I waved at my mother from the back window of the mini and she waved back, but I could tell she was crying, her face all crumpled up. The sun was pouring in the window, and I was sweating on the bouncy vinyl that vibrated with every bump as my mother's sad face was left behind. And right then, with school over for the year, and summer upon us, and the Valley before us, I felt a lightness come through me, starting deep inside, doing tiny reels in my belly as we rolled over the highway, up a big hill and under the West Brooklyn Road Overpass to see the Annapolis Valley spread out there before us, a pastoral postcard, the North Mountain against the blue sky, the Minas Basin at high tide, tidal channels cutting through the green fields and meadows, Cape Blomidon with its red cliffs high and magical. The world I had known slipped away as anticipation of summer filled my body. I was flying up there with the seagulls as we drove down into the Valley.

In Foster, Percy and I were put in the bunk beds in the upstairs spare room, Grammie in the room beside us, Gordie across the hall, and Gallie in the room beside him. Martha was sleeping on a cot downstairs in the glassed-in verandah at the front of the house, which was fine with her, seeing as she had the insomnia. Gordie was always working at the peat bog and I'd only see him in the early morning when he'd be holed up in the bathroom, me waiting to pee, nightie caught in my crossed legs. He'd slam open the door, hitching up his jeans, with the smell coming out behind him like a barn animal. I slid by with my fingers squeezing my nose, but not slipping fast enough, whacked on the butt with his girlie magazine. Then he'd stand out there listening to me pee. One time, to escape this routine, I slipped out the window, over the porch roof, onto the

cherry tree and down, walking in the dewy grass for a squat behind
the old garage by Grammie's roses, looking at the spider webs strung
from the green blades, webs Gordie would mow down every
Saturday morning. I walked back to the porch after and sat in the
shade, listening to the town start up. Gallie came out to water the
fuchsias in the hanging basket before it got too hot, going around it
to water every bit. And then she finally saw me and jumped.

"Lord god almighty, don't sit there like that."

"Like what?" I whispered.

"Don't be smart. You know like what. Like some creepy little
ghost. We need to put a bell on you."

"Gallie, you'd think little men come in and put you in a rack at
night, just to get you strung good and tight in time for dawn. Lord,
the air is close and it's not yet eight o'clock." There was Grammie
sitting down in the porch swing with her coffee, her little rice paper
fan going, the mother-of-pearl handle in her long fingers.

"Well, she sneaks about..."

"Gallie, she does not sneak about. She goes out the window
and down the tree. If you took a few quiet moments to start the
morning instead of crashing and banging about sweeping the floor,
you'd know."

"Good Lord, Mum, you think it's okay for an eight-year-old to
crawl out the window? What will people think? Serrie, did you spill
lemonade out here yesterday?"

"Yes, yes, I do think it's okay, and I don't give a good goddamn
what people think. Gallie, you're getting old before your time. You
and Martha certainly made good use of that window."

I giggled, picturing Gallie in her flowered apron and green
pumps coming down the cherry tree, fly swatter between her teeth,
mop strapped to her back, cleaning up the great outdoors. Except
for the little mole by her lip, there was no evidence that Gallie had
ever been that imp girl in the frame going up the stairs on the photo
wall, white hair bows, smiling and glorious beside the young

Martha, our mother, who still had the same smile, even when it was a tired one that strolled across her mouth. She had stood in the porch doorway with her eyes on Gallie, watching her pick at the hanging basket as she sipped coffee from her golden orange Fire King coffee cup.

"Well, that was all my doing, the climbing. Must be hereditary." My mother sipped through her smile.

"Oh, Martha, you know Gallie would have climbed a telephone pole if she could have. I may be old but I certainly remember the time she climbed to the top of Mr. Weaver's tombstone and couldn't get down and the police had to come."

"Mum."

"Yes, that's enough about the old days, now we all have our memories refreshed. Listen to the robins."

And off to the kitchen Gallie went, chucking me a glare.

Sometimes we'd hear Gordie come in late at night. We'd switch our flashlights off and hide our books when he'd come creeping up to the doorway, whispering that if we were bad kids he was going to send us down to the dump in North Bigelow Bay, the bad part of town, and that he'd tie us up and leave us there for the Davids to eat, that the Davids gathered at night and went out looking for a snack, preferably rotten, just like us. Percy and I wouldn't say anything, just shaking in our beds, me petrified of the boys named David. Grammie and Gallie and our mother would be downstairs talking outside on the front porch, having a drink in the summer night. Gordie would stand in the door whispering in the hot thick air that caught and held each of his words: he knew we were wide awake, that we'd just better stay out of his way or we'd find out what bad really was because he was a bad master (sometimes Gordie didn't make much sense). And if we so much as mentioned his name to Grammie or Martha or Gallie, he'd take care of us, if we knew what he meant. We knew. And then he'd bang down the stairs and turn on the television, up loud so we'd hear Gallie yelling at him to turn it down, our mother yelling they would wake Serrie and Percy up, Grammie saying they were all ruining her peace and quiet. Gordie went away on fishing trips pretty near every weekend and you could hear the house creak as it relaxed. After being scared of the Davids for a good month, I finally asked my mother if she knew of the boys with the same name going about in a gang. I could feel her smiling in the dark as she told me that David was the surname of many of the Micmacs down on the reserve near Fundy Central High School, and they had better things to do than go about in a gang, like working and raising their kids, just like anyone else. I should ignore Gordie, she told me, because he was as racist as his father, Bennie.

Grammie's house was a century home. It was clean and airy, never dusty, the parlour always in perfect order. But it was comfy, with chairs made for sitting in, Grammie would say, not just for looking at, or breaking your back. It was never off limits, and on rainy days we were welcome to curl up there with books, to colour and play games on the floor by the old Duncan Fife coffee table. It had been a farmhouse, way back when, and the garage was one of the small old barns that my Grampie had put a garage door on. There was an upstairs in the garage, but it was starting to fall in, so we were banned from going up the ladder. But sometimes we'd sneak in, past two of Gordie's old cars in the back, and then up the ladder, where we found Gordie's girlie magazines and a two-four of Ten Penny beer. And a creased snapshot nailed to the wall, finger smudges on Grampie's face, Grampie and little Gordie smiling up in Margaree, holding salmon and fishing rods, like nothing had ever gone wrong.

Grampie was already dead from a stroke when we moved back, but Gordie was old enough to remember him, in that salty way that had him leave the room whenever Grampie's name came up. My mother says he was the only father Gordie ever had, his own not wanting a thing to do with him. All I remember of Grampie is him cooking all the time in an old sleeveless white undershirt, making big pots of sauerkraut, the kitchen so vinegary my eyes watered. He'd lift me up on the counter where I'd sit beside him. Once he put me up on the top of the fridge, where I sat like a cookie jar, watching Gallie come in and fuss over him, not even seeing me, and when she did, saying nothing. He would hand me up treats, me saying "thank you, Grampie," in my whispery little voice that drove Gallie crazy.

My grandfather's family were originally German settlers down on the South Shore, in Lunenburg, and then some great-great-grandfather or something got a land grant near Digby at the western end of the Valley. On a tip of land down near Digby Gut there is Meissner Point, with an old lighthouse on it. My Aunt Gallie says some rich German (a real German as opposed to a *descended German*, which isn't really a German at all, according to Gallie, but not according to my mother, who says you are the sum total of everything, like a blender drink) will probably buy it up and turn it into a schnitzel gasthaus sort of place, whatever that's supposed to be. Grampie didn't make schnitzel but he did make pickles and rye bread and sauerkraut. And baked beans and brown bread on Saturday nights like everybody in the Valley, and even over in New Brunswick. Places I've never been to are what keep me going, just knowing there is some-place else, someplace bigger, better. Like Heaven, where my Grampie went straight, direct, no stops, no side roads, breakdowns, or stopping for the view, just right straight to Paradise, Gallie always tells us. No purgatory for us Meissners, Gallie says, not like for you Catholics, able to be as bad as you want, what with a built-in safety net provided by the Pope. Percy and I would look at each other with raised eyebrows because the only thing Catholic about us, aside from the baptism gown, was our father and, of course, our in-grown guilt.

Gallie loved Grampie best, so she always would say as she mopped the floor that summer we came home, or passed me dishes to put away. "Oh, I loved Dad the most, you know, your grandfather. He was a good, solid, stable man." Me lugging the cast-iron frying pan over to its hook of honour by the stove, good and solid, the ever stable and ever steady cast iron frying pan.

Stable or not, Grampie died while we were in the city when I was four, but I don't remember him going on, just my mother back from the funeral, standing on the stair landing of our PMQ house, crying, our father holding her and whispering her name, the same landing I stood on and watched her from when she packed and cried the anniversary song. I don't remember Grampie in the coffin, which is just as well, Grammie says. In my mind, Grampie cooks and puts me on the counter, the counter where I sat by the invincible frying pan, when Gallie made the sauerkraut after we moved back to Foster that summer.

Percy and I were born in Foster when Grammie was still the head nurse of the hospital, when Grampie, Garnet Meissner or Garnie, as they called him, was alive, selling insurance and putting back whisky with the local politicians. My father and mother were old, almost forty, when I was born. Only Gallie started younger because she's not a freak like the rest of us, she'll have us know, she was twenty-five. But old or not, my mother managed to have me at dawn on Hallowe'en, right at pumpkin time, and I became her pumpkin pie. I guess I was a fat baby, or what my mother calls plump and rosy, like a frigging piece of fruit or something, no pumpkin. I walked when I was ten months old, but I didn't talk until I was almost four.

They thought I was retarded, Aunt Gallie told me, everybody but Grampie, who said I appeared to be more interested in thinking my words. My mother said Gallie was being foolish, they didn't think Serrie was retarded, maybe there was just a learning disability. I could say words, all kinds of words, but I didn't put them together. Just went around like I was reciting the dictionary and was hauled off to the city for tests, the smarts tests, as Grammie called them. The specialists said I had better than average hearing. They were right about that, everything sounded loud, mostly all the talking. Maybe I was autistic, they thought. I was just sorting through the words, Grammie said, and Grampie too. And the doctors agreed, saying to just give me time.

The talking. I remember it started when we were in an apple orchard, a family outing. We had come out to the Valley for the afternoon. There is a framed picture in Grammie's house, hanging on the wall where you go upstairs, taken by the Gallie of yore. We are all wearing shades of brown and green, bright we were under the blue sky marbled with clouds; the sky dreams in clouds, my mother had said one long-ago summer day.

Red apples in the trees, and Percy up there on one of those old-fashioned wooden apple ladders ending in a point, metal bucket hanging from the branch by his right hand. The photo was taken just before the apple fell on my head.

"Ow," I had whispered. "Ow, Percy. It hurts my head."

And then they had looked at me.

"I want up the ladder too," said I, "where it's safe."

"We should have hit Serrie on the head sooner if that was all it took," Gallie remarked.

Grammie stared at her until Gallie looked at the big sky dreams. "Well, I'm just kidding, Mum."

What I learned from the apple-on-the-noggin outing was if you weren't able to speak up for yourself, no one else would, but talking is no guarantee of being heard.

Gallie was the town librarian after she came home from Toronto. That was after Gordie's father, Bennie Arsenault, had an affair and beat Gallie to pieces (which I never understood, because *he* had the affair, but one of the select things my mother told me was that love isn't something you will ever understand). Gallie never pressed charges because back in those days, Grammie says, you didn't do that because people would have thought you were off your proverbial rocker. Galronia did pack Gordie in her car, though, and drove from Toronto to Nova Scotia in one day, right through the night with both black eyes and nothing else, not one bit of furniture, just left it all behind and moved in with Grammie. Gordie stayed there until he finished high school and became *just like his father* and went Out West to make it big.

At first, that summer when we went back to the Valley, Percy and I were reluctantly happy — we were holding our breath for fear if we exhaled it would be into a vacuum, no air to come back in, suffocating on our own relaxation. But the pain flew out of us in a kite, spinning and pirouetting above until the string snapped and there were only memories left, bits of colour against the boundless blue sky, and then even those were gone as each day grew longer and longer. We played outside, in soft rains, in downpours, coming in to dry off, reading in the sun porch as we watched steam come off the road. Those days shaped our hearts, whole and strong and full of summer, a summer covering us with blossoms and breezes and stupid innocence. There would never be an autumn at all.

There were no sharp grown-up voices cutting and slicing through the night anymore, but I started getting up in my sleep, walking down the stairs in my smocked cotton nightie. The next day Percy would report at breakfast, reading from his notebook as I sat eating cereal and strawberries in my eye-watering bright green shorts. His little sister, Seraphina, the somnambulist, had yet again crept down the stairs while Grammie was playing bridge, drinking gin and tonics with her cronies. Grammie had observed the spectre

gliding over the floor, heading out the screen door, down the verandah, and onto the warm sidewalk. Grammie had gone out after her,
and had taken her back to bed, where Percy was busy making his
final notation-by-flashlight, the flashlight then taken away by
Grammie, which was really his sister's fault but could be rectified
by her forking over her strawberries.

Early in the morning, after my pee, before breakfast and Percy's
night report, I'd sit outside on the steps and my mother would bring
me a glass of orange juice to drink in the sun. She'd go back inside
to get breakfast and I'd stare over at the Melanson house, this big,
fancy, two-storey place with white pillars that Mr. Melanson had
built after he tore down the old house on the property. It looked like
the funeral home up on Main Street and more than once people
pulled up, looking for the memorial service of someone they had
read about in the obits. It mad him really mad, that did. Mr.
Melanson would be out there early, putting chemical stuff on the
lawn to make his Kentucky bluegrass grow perfect, and if my mother or Grammie or Gallie were out, he'd come over and talk about
the weather. He said Dearie and her mother were in Portland,
Maine, for the whole summer, visiting cousins, and she wouldn't be
back until September for school. Dearie's mother was American
and missed her country. She had that New England accent, all
those consonants bumping the As that would stretch out and brush
the Rs for *baar* and *caar* and *staar*.

Our mother got a job right away, working part-time as a health
nurse out of the office at the Foster Hospital. As soon as she had
work, she put Percy in violin lessons and she'd drive him into
Bigelow Bay every Monday night. That was Gallie's bridge night, so
it would be just me and Grammie, having a cold supper — chick-
en and potato salad, frosty lemonade — and then out to the garden,
Grammie telling me stories about growing up with no plumbing,
about making pear wine, how they'd hold the arm of the clock so it
wouldn't gong midnight when they were late coming in, getting off

the horses a mile before home, walking them so they wouldn't be panting when they came into the yard. I guess waking up Great-Grandpa McKay was a dangerous thing to do. And then when it was twilight, as we'd walk in to get me ready for bed, we'd sing the bed-time song, this Irish air that Grammie learned in Belfast when she was an army nurse during the war.

Faintly as tolls the evening chime
Our voices keep tune and our oars keep time
Soon as the woods on shore look dim
We'll sing at St. Ann's our parting hymn
Row, brothers, row, the stream runs fast
The rapids are near and the daylight's past.

Me still chanting *row, brothers, row* through a mouthful of tooth-paste. In bed, questions about Belfast and the war, and Grammie would say she didn't want to talk about it. Martha and Gallie said she never discussed it and there was no exception, even for the one and only granddaughter. "Some things are never to be spoken of," she would whisper as she tucked me in. I'd be asleep when my mother and Percy would came back late because they would always stop for a milkshake on the way home. It took me a long time to understand that the song was about more than just bedtime.

I'm dried off and in a big flannel nightie of Dearie's tucked into the bed she made up for me before she and Elizabeth went out. There is a candle and the shadows flicker on the wall as I stretch out, my body relaxing, my head sinking into the down pillow. It's two decades I've been alive now, so much time, so much water under the bridge, as they say. So many waves having broken on the shore, Grammie says. That summer back in Foster, who would have thought things would unfold as they did. The best thing about being a child is the lack of worry. Sometimes I think the end of childhood is signalled by the arrival of worry, so even if you are still a kid, when you walk around with that strained look, it's already too late, you've skipped over the last of those carefree days without even knowing it.

My mother was grateful to have work that summer, to be able to be kind to people. There was a bounce in her voice when she told us her good news, what the job would be. She had an area to cover, doing home visits, stuff with pregnant ladies and fresh babies, old people, and in the autumn she'd have to go into the schools. When she wasn't working, she'd go over to see our relation, the Spinster Sullivan, to tend to her. The Spinster was big and fat, and sudden noises made her lurch, so we had to be quiet, "you have to be mindful," our mother would tell us, as we hopped out of the car after supper on those warm summer Thursday evenings. I never quite understood it, as so many sudden noises came out of the various holes in the Spinster herself. Sometimes we'd get there late, if we had to go over the Mountain first to visit at Kenny and Wanda Mosher's so our mother could check on how Wanda was doing with her pregnancy. Wanda was agoraphobic and wouldn't come down to the Valley for the prenatal classes at the Foster Hospital, so the community health nurse, our mother, would go to her. We'd pass the Spinster Sullivan's on the way to the Moshers, white clapboard peeling, faded black trim.

All the Moshers were from over the Mountain, some living in Lupin Cove, a whole bunch of them living in little houses and shacks along the Mosher Road, this bumpy dirt road that the county sometimes forgot to plough in the winter until a Mosher would call up with swearing threats. We'd park in the driveway and our mother would leave us in the car with books and lemon drops and we'd sit there looking at the house with its Dr. Seuss chimney, all the pieces from various yard sales and scrap metal yards welded together. The house was tiny, a shack surrounded by birch trees with a brook running through the backyard. There were old cars piled all around and a stack of rusting mattress springs. Old John, the dog, sitting by the shack door, deaf and blind. Kenny would carry Old John in at night and put him on his blanket by the stove. It was strange to see so much junk about in the middle of the woods, sweet-blossom breezes, wild roses growing in the ditches — *rugosa, originally from Asia* — and all along the side of the house, tangled better than barbed wire.

Kenny would always come out so our Mother could have her "woman talk" with Wanda and he'd lean on the car door like he'd known us all our lives, calling us by name, rolling a rollie, smoking a rollie, offering us a rollie, Percy glaring at me when I'd reach for it, as Kenny laughed. Bits of tobacco would stick on Kenny's puffy bottom lip, his long and heavy red moustache drooping on either side like a dead squirrel, making the sides of his face look as though they were sliding off his head. He had long brown fuzzy hair and we only knew that he was thirty-five because our mother told us. His youngest sister, Fancy Mosher, was only eleven, but she had a different father and lived over near Lupin Cove. Kenny had a gut that would jiggle as he told us about his home renovations.

"Put in that stove for the winter."

Percy would nod. "Good to have a stove." Man talk.

Rollie still in his mouth, Kenny nodding back. "Goes to Canadian Tire and buys some chimney parts. On special. Some good specials, those." Smoke blew in the car and I sucked it in. Percy and I looked at the chimney, wondering if it would stay upright in a wind, if the roof would just go smack straight down with the weight of the metal and the satellite dish.

"Yup, takes a shotgun and points it up and shoots through the roof. Puts the chimney right there, yessir." The rollie was just about to burn his lip but he cartwheeled it off with his tongue, workboots squishing in the dirt.

"It's good to have a wood stove for the winter," Percy would say through a mouthful of lemon drops, offering Kenny one. He would decline, holding his hand up from the wrist and shaking it, the queen mother waving, and then he'd point to his woodpile. Kenny was a chainsaw man for hire, cutting down trees for various logging contractors. He was missing bits of finger but you only saw that when he'd do the rollies.

"Serrie, look at that wood. Piles it up ready for the snow."

I'd nod, sucking on a drop.

"Don't talks much, Serrie?" And I'd shrug and whisper that sometimes I did. Kenny would laugh, and then look towards the house as our mother opened the door.

"Good little woman talk?" he'd call to our mother.

She'd smile and nod, carrying her nursing bag. "You should join us, Kenny. It's talk for fathers, too."

Kenny would light up another rollie from his pocket. "S'pose so," he'd say as he handed one to my mother, and she'd take it, letting him light it with this fancy silver lighter he won at the Foster Summer Fair, at the roulette booth on the midway. They'd stand there and she'd tell him to make sure that Wanda had lots of fresh milk and vegetables, that she shouldn't be on her feet. Martha said Wanda was obese and that her legs looked like Kenny's chimney. We didn't know what her legs looked like because Wanda didn't so much as peek out the window. Martha said it was because it was exhausting for her to get up off the couch where she had been watching the satellite television for the last three months. She told Kenny if it got any worse, Wanda would have to go down to the Valley to the hospital. Kenny would nod, *uh-huh, uh-huh, uh-huh,* standing there by his home. The little shack would look soft and fairytale-cozy in that golden summer evening light, the end-of-day light smudging everything soft and gentle, the evening light that is so forgiving.

After the first home visit at the beginning of July, when we had backed out of the driveway, waving to Kenny, Percy told Martha not to smoke a rollie with him, that it wasn't appropriate. That was so

Percy, *it wasn't appropriate*, like we were living by some manual. It would have helped if someone had given me a copy. She turned the car onto the Lupin Cove Road. In between the trees it was dusky, and the cool smell of night forest came in the window. I had no sweater and pulled my knees up under my dress right to my chest, thinking about little elf people who might be dancing about in the woods.

"That's Kenny's way of being friendly, and you and Serrie may as well get one thing straight now that we're living back in the Valley: you're no better than the Moshers or anyone else, just because we were living in town, because your mother happens to be a nurse." She spit out the word nurse as the Valley twinkled before us, the Spinster's house just a shadow. She glanced at me in the rear-view mirror to make sure I was listening. "Serrie, you listen when I talk or you'll be sitting in the front seat."

She continued as we turned in the Spinster Sullivan's driveway. "At least the Moshers all have something to live in. They may get by without much but they've got no debt and they are good people, so you can stop your snobbery right now. We've got nothing, not a pot to piss in, nor a window to throw it out of. If it wasn't for the charity of your grandmother, we'd be on the streets."

Percy never mentioned the rollies again.

The Spinster Sullivan's real name was Auntie Ruth. She wasn't really even our aunt or even our father's aunt, but a distant cousin, I don't know how many times removed. We were all that was left of this branch of the Nova Scotia Sullivans. There had been a sister once, the one that died from licking the moss-green wallpaper. It had a gold Ionic column pattern on it, turn-of-the-century Victorian wallpaper that had arsenic in the dye. Grammie said Sally was nine when she died, and a nine-year-old should know better than to lick the walls. Arsenic was in all kinds of things then, along with lead and mercury. "It's a miracle the race didn't die off or completely mutate," Grammie says.

There were two little girls in the old black-and-white photo on the dusty mantel in the Spinster Sullivan's parlour, and one of those sweet little girls in a white lace dress with sausage curls in her hair was none other than Herself, the Spinster Sullivan. Her arm was around her identical twin, Sally. Grammie said the Spinster Sullivan was so traumatized by Sally's death she was never normal afterward. She trained to be a teacher, but never worked after she inherited money from some relative in New England, and then she travelled the world, finally settling into the old family house when she was in her fifties, after her father died. She cared for her mother until she went and then the Spinster took in a long hard breath that sucked her deep into the house, the years falling down heavy on her until senility brought a bit of relief. From the looks of old Spinster Sullivan, she had completely mutated from the little picture girl to the lumpy old lady with long old toenails yellow and curled, garden snails perched on the end of each toe, nails that our mother would clip as she did the Spinster's foot care, us sitting eating dusty cookies in the corner of the old-fashioned kitchen that would become our kitchen when the Spinster broke her hip and died.

I couldn't believe we were related, except for those green eyes sunk way back in her bread-dough face, eyes just like my father's, like mine and Percy's. Sometimes we'd go right after supper, when the summer day would be stretching on into those safe pales, the fuzzy end-of- day rays, long shadows creeping from the trees around the Spinster's house. We'd be outside by that time, running along the overgrown hedge surrounding the property, a shabby black ribbon that tied together this place full of dust, and toenail clippings, faded sofas and quilts, black-and-white pictures of stiff, poisoned people in weird clothes, pictures that captivated Percy and me as we'd sneak into the off-limits parlour through the front door that the Spinster never locked. I'd lounge on the fainting bed, and Percy would sit in the slipper chair, pretending to take off his shoes. It was like a museum, all her old furniture, china and glass things, paintings, even her eye glasses were old. She despised the antique-dealers who would come by and try to buy pieces off her, my Grammie said, like that Mr. Burgess on the Lesterdale Road on the other side of Foster, driving around in his 1942 Bentley. The Spinster had sold some salt and pepper shakers to Earle Baltzer, who has Baltzer's Collectibles over in Lupin Cove, and she had sold off the farmland years ago, first half of it to Mr. VanderKloets, this Dutch farmer who immigrated just after World War II, and then the other half of it to the Hiltz Family. They had a big fruit and vegetable farm and a country market. They were good neighbours, buying most of the Spinster's pumpkins, bringing her fresh vegetables. But that was it for the selling.

From the outside, the old Sullivan house was the kind that made you believe in witches and magic. Inside, it was the kind of house that made kids desperate to explore and adults desperate to have an auction, a giant yard sale, a shop vac. The Spinster wouldn't part with a thing in the house, not the grandfather clock that still gonged the goddamn hour on the hour (and the quarters, and the halves), not the barrister bookshelves with the glass fronts that pulled out and then rolled back inside when you opened them to get at one of the old leather-bound books, not her china, her glass, her crystal, the old Indian stuff, not her quilts, not a piece of her furniture, not the old apple crates out in the barn, and never her antique glass paperweight collection. The dust just quietly came, settling everywhere, getting in the cracks and the walls, resisting all forms of cleaning. Even the faded lace curtains wouldn't give up the dust, no matter how much shaking and wiping you'd do. The deadly green wallpaper had been stripped off years ago. We had peeled up the faded flower print, and then the layer under that, and the next layer and the next and the next, but no green, just the old horsehair plaster at the bottom, plaster that would fall off as our fingers pulled away, our mother clearing her throat in the parlour doorway, scratching her face. She had red scaly patches under her eyes, eczema, said Doctor O'Leary, the town doctor in Foster who had delivered me and Percy, Elizabeth, Dearie, everybody I knew. He said the eczema was from stress. Our mother said it was from the change in water, from going from the foggy Halifax climate to the dry Valley. And she'd still be scraping at her face as we were told to be good.

We'd head immediately for the turret room on the third floor, up an old dry wooden spiral of stairs that only I could get up without Martha hearing the creaks all the way down into the kitchen where she was tending to the Spinster. Percy would do his flat-foot tiptoe and be furious at the creaks, the floor should know he was tiptoeing, it should be quiet, according to Percy's Logic. If only the world operated by his logic. Le Mont, the Spinster Sullivan's great big marmalade cat, would be sitting up there on the turret windowsill like some ageless wizard. He'd lick his paw, thud to the floor, and then pad down the stairs, me behind him, scooping him up, ever the gentle beast, staying still until I took him to the kitchen to say goodnight to everybody before he went out for his tom-catting. Auntie Ruth loved Le Mont like a son and she wouldn't have him fixed, even though our mother kept telling her that if he was neutered he wouldn't always be staying out all night and getting banged up in fights. But Auntie Ruth would say she'd no sooner let the vet chop off his basket of goodies than she would let herself go to a nursing home. Martha would let it go, shaking her head. There was no one to care for Ruth. Grammie had been doing it, but she was getting too old to go over, almost eighty herself, if you could have believed it. So our mother took over, trimming the toenails of the Spinster, her sitting in her big chair smiling at us, asking about Cyril, thinking he was still at sea riding on destroyers, our mother letting her go on thinking it, because it was true, just in a different way.

Those summer nights at the Spinster's would have us finally end up, tired and dirty, on the verandah waiting to go back to Foster, listening to the frogs and crickets, counting fireflies. Even in the dark night with the Valley lights twinkling back up at the flirty sky, it was the kind of view that made you know what birds saw when they flew; it gave meaning to a world without end.

By July, when Martha got on work full-time, we'd spend the mornings with Grammie in the garden, going uptown to do errands, and then having lunch, usually cucumber and tomato sandwiches. Grammie would make us brush our teeth and then send us up to Gallie at the library to read books and assist her with *the folios*, to Gallie's rigid delight. Foster wasn't anything more than a main street called Main Street with residential ones that flowed off of it. Driving into town you'd pass big old houses on an elm-lined street, the big wooden Baptist, United, Anglican and Pentecostal churches, all so close you could hold your breath and walk easily from door to door, sampling various manifestations of the Lord. Before World War II, before the bottom fell out of the apple market, when there were still trains running before the goddamn government pulled them out of the land like so many varicose veins, Grammie says, Foster had a thriving agriculture distribution industry. The warehouses still stand empty, down by where the tracks were, by the small houses, Foster's attempt at a bad side of town, right by the little Catholic church. There were still a few apple orchards in the town but the local developers, Mr. Melanson and some other guys, were after the old farmers to sell. Grammie said it would be the end of an era.

The library was in the old town hall on Main Street, a building with tall glass windows and creaky floors, a building that the town would just rip right down one day, without even a thought for heritage, issuing a memorial china plate in less time than the demolition took. Main Street was the only street with stores and there wasn't even a stoplight, no pay parking. The mayor, the town council, the clerk, the treasurer, the tourist bureau, public works, the police, every tiny office behind a tall wooden door down the long hall to the door that opened into the library.

The best thing about the afternoons at the library was reading the books and the second best thing was the huge

NO TALKING

signs Gallie had put up, so even she had to obey them — most of the time. When Gallie found me leaning on a table reading *Alice in Wonderland*, she whispered that it was drug-induced filth written by a Victorian pornographer, I should read C.S. Lewis and writers like him, I should be reading books with good morality, tours of the forest.

Percy was in the back with the reference books, sitting by the window that looked out onto the Foster town park, and when he came up to get me to walk home, I told him Gallie was making me read nature books when she wouldn't even go camping because of the germs and bacteria. Percy scratched under his arm, his favourite T-shirt sleeve ratty, smirking: "*Tour de force*, not tour of the forest, stupid. A great feat. You know, like building a big building." That summer was when he started being short with me, first with the rollies and then with my vocabulary, maybe worried I would end up on the back of the destroyer myself. It was the first time he wouldn't tell me the meaning of a word so I found "pornographer" in the big dictionary and I didn't understand it so I looked up "erotic" which was about sexual love and then Gallie slammed the dictionary shut.

Galllie wasn't one to waste time, especially not with signs of our imminent corruption right in front of her. The next day we were enrolled in Foster Youth Ecumenical Bible Day Camp where we had the pleasure of singing Jesus songs, colouring Jesus pictures and writing stories on why Jesus was our very best friend. The Bible camp was run by the United Church minister, the Reverend Rafuse, a kind, tall, thin man who trembled like a wire in the wind, always flicking at his right jaw with his index finger as though there were some invisible bug he was trying to tap off. His wife's body resembled an apple, and Grammie liked to call them the Reverend and Mrs. Jack Sprat, eat no lean, eat no fat. Grammie said it was hard to resist with the Reverend's first name being John. He wasn't that old, Gallie would say, mid-thirties, but he shuffled about like an old man, maybe from being so skinny he was scared of snapping into pieces. The Reverend oversaw the ecumenical camp that mostly Protestants attended, but there were a few Catholics, and a little Chinese girl whose father was a doctor in Bigelow Bay. She was a Christian but that fact never took hold, seeing she ate her rice lunch with chopsticks, because why would a Christian be eating with sticks?

The groups were sloppily run by high school students, our camp counsellors, who led us through all kinds of boring activities. When we got too rowdy, the Reverend would come by, flicking his jaw, giving us the Jesus eye, as we at my table called it. He'd deal with all the discipline problems and the only time he wasn't around to handle a crisis was when he was at a morning conference in the city. Mrs. MacDonald, who lived just outside of Foster, brought her little boy, Simpson, to camp one morning, demanding to know why her son was bringing home pictures of a brown Jesus, making him look all *ethnic*. It was early, and we were all just arriving, putting our lunch boxes in the corner. I was still sleepy, and hadn't even had time to explore my latest bug bites, which I usually would survey so I could pick them during the morning prayer. But Grammie wasn't sleepy, not one bit, as she told Mrs. MacDonald that Jesus of Nazareth was dark because he was born in the Middle East, not Iceland, so she should go home and stick that in her head in place of whatever nonsense she had in there now, and she might also find it helpful to read through the Bible with a map handy, so as to avoid having to harass a poor high school student who was just trying to do a good and accurate job.

The day camp program was held at the Greater United Christian Camp Meeting Grounds, a huge property on the northeast side of town, built way back in the 1860s, in the midst of a huge stand of beautiful old pine trees right on the edge of a small lake, the Lake of Redemption, or Lake R, as it was usually called. They only took down enough trees to build sweet little cottages. The church had some of the cottages but many were still privately owned, with the arrangement that they could only be sold to the church itself. There was a camp kitchen and eating area, and some buildings for offices, meetings and, of course, day camps. None of the cottages had electricity or stoves for fear of fire. Almost since the beginning you took your hot meals in the common eating area. This was because of Zane Pineo, who in 1930 skipped the Sunday morning church service so he could boil an egg. But he had the sleeping disease, narcolepsy, and his cottage caught fire, and after that there was no more cottage hot cooking. All the buildings circled around the big outdoor worship space, the space where my mother remembered the travelling Evangelists delivering their sermons in voices that soared out through the pines.

It would have been a beautiful place to be that summer, if we hadn't had our hearts set on roaming around unsupervised, playing in the yard at Grammie's. Percy refused to be a good sport about it. He would glare at me at juice break, saying if I have to look up *those* words I should do it in private. I'd roll my eyes at him and pick at my mosquito bites until they bled. We were put into groups of three to do a Christ mosaic. It was me, Elizabeth Baxter, and bad-ass Fancy Mosher, Kenny Mosher's littlest sister, set to do a nice Jesus mosaic with the multi-coloured pebbles we'd collected off the beach over in Lupin Cove on a day trip to see scallop-shucking.

Elizabeth was tiny, with wispy bits of short blonde hair standing up in the humidity, long flappy puppy-ear eyelashes. She told me and Fancy that when she was a little baby the summer heat had made her head sweat and lots of her hair had been *affected*. That's what her mother had said, and she was a hairdresser so she knew. Fancy and I had nodded, impressed by the science, sitting at the picnic table, bare feet on the cool pine needles.

"I was born on Mother's Day," Elizabeth lisped as we glued on a nostril for Jesus. She'd put her head to the side and shut her eyes, giggling, like she was remembering how much fun she'd had coming down the birth canal. "I'm a DES daughter. It's a drug, so I wouldn't be born early, you know, like an egg yolk. It could make my organs weird but we watch them carefully, the organs." Fancy and I had nodded. We were best friends, me whispering, Elizabeth lisping, and Fancy Mosher, eleven years old, with boobs, a bra, and a mouth like a septic field. Fancy talked constantly if she liked you. And if she didn't like you, she'd just sit and stare, twisting her hair, making you want to turn around, pee your pants, and run through the pines. She got a drive into camp every day from over the Mountain in the big blue United Church van that Michelle McIver called the Charity Van. Michelle's father was a lawyer and her mother worked at Melanson's Drugstore, and when we'd be on juice break, Michelle would say the quality of the camp was coming right down, that was what her mother was saying, when shack people started coming off the North Mountain, and if *those people* weren't in the classes at school the teacher would have more time for the town kids, the kids from good homes. The school didn't need the illegitimate ones. "That's the right word for bastard," Michelle would say. And she'd look right at Fancy. Fancy would just look back at her with those dark eyes until Michelle's throat went dry.

On juice break Fancy would tell us stories about living in Lupin Cove, how she'd get up every morning and go down to the beach, except in the winter when the wind blowing in off the water could freeze your eyeballs hard as glass. She said her cousin had his eyeballs frozen when he was out on the water fishing with the Ryans, and now he had marbles for eyes. And Fancy would tell us about the pirate who had buried his treasure over on the Isle Haute, and had asked for a volunteer to stay and guard the booty.

"Oh, he was a right wicked captain, he was, and this one sailor wanted to escape, so he put up his hand," Fancy said. "And so the Captain smiled, and then took his sword and went *whish*, just like that, and chopped off his head. My brother Tucker, he saw the headless skeleton when he was over on the island. They say to get the treasure you have to slit the throat of a little girl and let her red blood drip down through the rocks. And you have to do it at midnight on the second Saturday night in August, only by firelight, without speakin' one word, or the hole closes up, and the sea water rushes in."

Elizabeth would sit close to me and we'd hold shaking hands. When Elizabeth would be ready to cry, Fancy would say she shouldn't worry because she lived in the Valley, only Fancy should be worried about being carted off over the water. But that didn't help, because Elizabeth liked Fancy, so I would get them to sing the bedtime song. Fancy's voice was low but it sounded so nice layered with our girly voices, and we sang until the camp counsellor told us it was pretty but we could only sing about Jesus. We changed it to *row, Jesus, row*, except for Fancy who sang *jesus christ, Jesus, row*. None of it made any sense, but we were asked to sing it at the end-of-camp variety show anyway and everyone clapped and smiled, Grammie, my mother, and Gallie in the front row, Grammie rolling her eyes at the Jesus stuff.

When we first came to Camp, Fancy had heard Percy lecturing me about sex words and what was appropriate for me to be asking about. I had told her about the pornography and she had laughed. While Elizabeth and I were busy glueing rocks onto plywood to do the Jesus Mosaic, Fancy was on the other side of the picnic table, writing down appropriate words on pieces of paper and holding them up, one after another:

COCK   CUNT   FUCK   TIT   LARDASS

We just sat there with our mouths open. Fancy would draw illustrations and hold them up, flipping her messy ponytail, tapping her too-small sandals on her dirty feet, toenails black and chipped underneath the red polish. She was a tomboy going through puberty too fast, not able to halt the onset of hormones, as Gallie called it, wanting to play fort and hide-and-seek, but ending up with her shirt up when older boys would get her against the wall. Fancy would lower the paper as soon as a counsellor would glance over at our table, and she'd pull her red lips into a beautiful smile, like Jesus himself was looking at her, and would glue on a strand of seaweed for hair. When the leader would start telling us more about how Jesus was Lord and all that stuff, Fancy would flash the cards again, and this time Elizabeth started mouthing the words like we were in school. I was wishing for a dictionary to look up LARDASS when Elizabeth started lisping the words. I elbowed her as the counsellor looked our way, and she elbowed me back and put her finger in her mouth and giggled, and then I started too, as Fancy flashed us again, me and Elizabeth whispering each one, until Fancy got bored and drew a picture of Elvis.

We wouldn't have been caught if Michelle McIver had been doing her own mosaic instead of watching us through the new binoculars she got as a present for barely managing to pass grade five. She waited until the end of the day and then the three of us were pulled into Reverend Rafuse's office. The Reverend wanted to know who had been writing such filth when we were supposed to be making a mosaic of the Lord. Elizabeth started her lispy crying, saying we had too made a mosaic of the Lord and she was right, bad words and all, we'd completed our activity. The Reverend said, "Why, yes, you have and a fine depiction it is, very artistic, girls, very artistic, but these words have nothing to do with art." I was thinking the Reverend was being just as bad as us, because he was lying — at best our work looked like Jesus as a fossil, you know, Petrified Saviour. Fancy was standing there with her arms over her chest and the Reverend Rafuse started saying that she was lucky to come down off the Mountain to participate in a summer camp and she could just as easily stay up there and write bad words and make Elvis pictures. Elizabeth's face fell again and he quickly said there was nothing wrong with Elvis, but we weren't here to be learning about *that* King. While he was talking and scratching away at his jaw, I could see Michelle McIver outside the window, looking in, smiling away, her permed hair around her face like clown hair. It was me who had been caught by Aunt Gallie looking up *erotic*, so it was just as easy for him to think Serrie Sullivan was still obsessed with *those* words. And so I got in trouble — I whispered it was me. But not because I was brave or anything; it was too easy to blame Fancy and that didn't seem *appropriate*. And mostly it wasn't appropriate for Michelle to be watching our *in camera* trial, nor for her to start yelling that I was lying, that it was really Fancy Mosher who wrote all those bad words.

Michelle had her binoculars taken away as punishment for spying and swearing and I spent the last two weeks of August going to bed at six o'clock right after supper. I wasn't allowed to read or even draw but was supposed to meditate on how I could mend my bad-girl ways. When it would finally be getting dark, my mother would come in and tell me I had to be good, that I couldn't go getting into trouble, that she was trying to figure out what we were going to do. I had to help her by being a good girl, and I should come to her or Gallie or Grammie about new vocabulary words.

They separated me and Elizabeth and Fancy. It was funny because Fancy was put in Percy's group and he had to like her because, in addition to swearing and staring, she liked to read books even more than we did. He found this out when they had to make a modern-day martyr story and they based it on *Moby Dick*, which they had both read in the abridged form. They had to do it story-telling style and when they were telling it, Fancy would look right at Michelle McIver when she said, "Moby *Dick*." Percy had a crush on Fancy, though she could have knocked him down with a swing of her tits. When we made wallets, she embroidered little pink roses with green vines and gave it to Percy to give to me.

After lunch we'd have a quiet time where we'd have to lie down on blankets among the trees. It was cool and quiet there. The little kids would have nap time but we'd get to listen to a story that the Reverend Rafuse would read to us, and then he'd tell us the adage for the day: *Fear knocked on the door. Faith answered and no one was there.*

"So what does that mean to you, kids?" He picked his jaw and folded his arms. It was weird seeing the Reverend without his religious gown, the one he wore in church. We'd all be quiet, wishing it was time for the afternoon outing, and then someone would say, "Faith was slow getting to the door." He'd smile and nod, "Well, yes, that can happen," and then he'd ask someone else would say, "Faith didn't like Fear," and he'd nod and say, "Well, sort of, children," and then Fancy Mosher, without putting her hand up, said in a loud voice, "If you believe in the Lord, then you'll stop being scared." And the Reverend Rafuse smiled with his whole skinny body, bobbing up and down with his arms flung up and out.

"Exactly right, Fancy Mosher," he said, "and none of us will be scared if we believe in the Lord Jesus — He will take our fear away — and we should now silently pray for Jesus to relieve us of our fear." And then he looked right at me, as Halifax and sad nights, my father and my mother, came into my mind like he'd put them there with his look, so I turned my head, but Fancy Mosher was staring right at me and I knew she knew my secret, that underneath the weightless summer, Serrie Sullivan was scared of every single thing. And Fancy Mosher, she knew I knew her secret, that her eyes had started to freeze over long ago.

The candle fizzles out and I lie there cold and clammy in Dearie's flannel sheets, biting my lips as that chill memory of Fancy Mosher's eyes drapes over me. The Halifax streets are quiet, and in the darkness I could be anywhere, any time in my life, in bed, shaking and wishing for sleep. Dearie's hard guest bed reminds me of the chaise longue, the fainting bed, at the Spinster's house, where I had curled up with books and a blanket after we finally moved out of Grammie's and up on to the North Mountain.

That autumn our father was discharged from the navy and the hospital or detox or wherever the hell it was (no one's ever told me or Percy what really happened that whole time, and when we did ask, they said, *now why do we have to go and talk about that?*). At the same time, Old Spinster Sullivan broke her hip and then died during the replacement surgery. She was just too old and fat but, as my father said, she'd lived a good life. Our father had stopped drinking and had come out from the city so we could start over. And so we went to live in that big rambly house on the Lupin Cove Road that was about to just give up and fall down, just in time for Christmas. We spent the holiday trying to sort out the old Auntie's piles and stacks but it was too much work so we just shoved what was in the way up into the attic. Our father had inherited the house, but some distant cousin living in New England had to be consulted — the Spinster had said he was to have some of the china and glass, several pieces of furniture. But the will was so old that the lawyer, who was the son of the lawyer who had drawn it up, said he'd have to locate the distant cousin, though the cousin was probably dead, too, which meant finding his descendants, and it could take years, but he'd do his best. His efforts had been prepaid by the Spinster Sullivan, in some all-inclusive will package, but the prepayment had gone to his father and so my mother said she didn't expect him to be moving on it any time soon.

There was no furnace in the place, just a bunch of old, drafty fireplaces and a rusty oil stove in the kitchen, where my parents hauled mattresses for us to sleep at night until my Grammie found out and paid for a proper oil furnace down in the cellar and a mason to come and fix the fireplaces, up and down. My mother kept working and my father went on a temporary disability allowance, spending his time putting in the outhouses and fixing up the house. At first it was okay, all that country living and beauty. We even had a pumpkin patch, inherited from the Spinster Sullivan. My mother got us cross country skis at a yard sale and we'd go out in the fields, the three of us. Cyril couldn't come, he said because of his condition, having one kidney. We were all scared he was going to start drinking again, because he wouldn't go to the AA meetings, didn't want to go anywhere except to the hardware store and the library, or in search of outbuildings. Percy would just stand quietly listening to his excuses, not saying a word, just looking out the window, while our mother would say it would do him good to get some exercise. But he'd say we didn't know what it was like to have health problems and my mother would sigh, Percy would be in a trance, and I'd be crossing my fingers in my mittens that they wouldn't have a fight. But there were no more big fights, just tight lips, white knuckles, a house full of ornament people in danger of falling over and shattering. Cyril would stay home keeping the fire going for us, hot chocolate ready when we got back, and things would be better after being out in the trees, skiing through the apple orchards, our mother lagging behind with her smoker's lungs, as she called them. We didn't talk about Cyril, we just let him retreat from us, and us from him, a sad man left in the doorway who grew smaller and smaller as we skied off over the fresh, white world.

By the time I was thirteen and we'd been in the Spinster's house four years, the disability money was cut. My father was sent out on a work placement at Stronach Meat Packers, at first burning the hair off of animal carcasses, then working as a mechanic on the hot dog line, the pork chop line, line after line, trying to invent things on the weekends. We had an old car and a truck by then, previously owned vehicles, as the car dealership guy told my parents, and our father would tinker with them every weekend to keep them on the road. He'd go into the university library in Bigelow Bay every Sunday afternoon, sometimes taking Percy and me with him or just one of us, where we'd be fanning through giant atlases and looking at all the books until we headed back for Sunday dinner at Grammie's.

Grammie pulled us through those first autumn months, coming over on weekends to help sort out the Spinster's things, just to be there like she always was, sipping a cup of tea, holding my arm as she looked around at the garden, telling me there was always an adjustment period, where you just had to go about your business, even if you felt bad, and let things settle, allow life to find a pace and a routine. I wanted to be back at her house in Foster, not up on the top of the North Mountain in a pile of dust. The first weekend we were there, I cried in the Spinster's rose garden, and Grammie stood up, rubbing her dirty fingers on her gardening smock. She told me the Spinster's roses had outlived the Spinster, and I had to be like the roses. No, Grammie, I snapped, I'm no plant. And then she gave me the *just go through the days* speech and I told her I was only eight years old, that she wasn't making any sense. And she said all she meant was for me to just keep on keeping on, which makes more sense, because who wants to be a rose.

That second Sunday, when Percy and our father were at the university library in Bigelow Bay, Grammie and I went out to the garden to put in bulbs so there would be flowers the next spring. So much of the Spinster's garden had died and gone to weed, which bothered Grammie more than the dilapidated house. We finished and put the gardening tools back in the barn, and then walked slowly to the house with Grammie on my arm, looking at the leaves changing colour, the September days soaking into each tree, up the trunk and then sautéing each leaf into spicy shades of chili and saffron. The vintage Bentley was in the driveway as we came around the corner of the barn and up to the house. Grammie's hand went tight on my arm all the way into the back storm porch.

"Now, Martha, I know Miss Sullivan didn't want to part with one little thing but that was, as you and I both know, sen-ti-men-tality, and it's natural, of course, for that to take hold when you get to be her age. But prac-ti-cality is what we should think of. And I'm telling you that it would be practical, not to mention wise, to think about what you need and what you don't need in this house." Mr. Burgess's voice was booming out from the front foyer, down the hall, past the kitchen, and right into the back, to us. Grammie wasn't saying anything, just moving into the kitchen, straightening her sweater and then sitting in the armchair in the corner of the kitchen while Mr. Burgess's voice slithered in to us.

"Now, Martha, she had some Cheyenne saddlebags, ones that were made before the Indians went on reservations, oh, circa 1870 or so. She used to keep them right here on the bannister, last time I was in. That was a few years back, mind you."

"Yes, those are up in the attic now. Nice fringe on them. Pretty beads. Lord, the things she picked up in her lifetime, I tell you . . . " And then my mother sighed, from all the carrying up to the attic we'd had to do to make enough space to move around without crashing over something.

"Well, Martha, *I tell you*, that kind of item is sought after by collectors. Now in good shape, they'd be worth, oh, five thousand dollars. Course they haven't been properly stored here so I'd only be able to give you, oh, about half that, seeing the restoration work that would have to be done to even interest a collector. Now most wouldn't even give you that, but I know Cyril's had a hard time of it, and this old house, why she's certainly seen better days. Martha, may I trouble you for a glass of water." And then he started coughing. "All that hymn singing this morning. I should hold back, but the Good Lord gave me this voice and it's only right to praise Him with it."

Grammie crossed her legs. "Praise him indeed."

His voice was louder as they came down the hall to the kitchen. "The thing is, Martha, old people just store so many things, always thinking about a yard sale, a flea market, but never doing it, just hanging onto every single thing. It's what I was saying, the sen-ti-mental factor, and then what happens, just like what happened here, is they pass on. But do all those dirty things pass on? No, they just take up space and then the relatives, like yourself, have to sort through everything, and most of it's just plain junk. And I could certainly take some of that off your hands, give you a bit of space and a bit of cash. Old folks mean well, but —"

There was nothing sentimental about the look Grammie gave him when he came into the kitchen. "Why, Mrs. Meissner." A smile jerked on his face, invisible hooks on either side of his lips.

"Why, Clarence Burgess. I do believe it's a sin to work on the Sabbath, but it could be that I'm so old the Commandments have changed without me noticing. You know us old folk, can't tell day from night, what with all the junk in the way of the light."

The smile got bigger. "Oh, you know me, always the joker. Just out doing some Sunday visiting. Thought I'd bring a housewarming present over from me and the wife. She's out for a drive with the girls and her mother."

My mother was holding a bottle of wine with a bow on the neck.

"I see." Grammie leaned back in her chair and crossed her arms.

"Well, if it isn't Seraphina. Look at you, all grown up. How old are you now? Must be almost a teenager."

I leaned against Grammie's arm. "I'm almost nine," I whispered as Grammie put her arm around me.

"Isn't she some cute. Going to be a good looker, that one, like her Aunt Gallie. Can't believe she never married again."

My mother handed Mr. Burgess a glass of water, his eyes bulging with each gulp as he looked around, gaze finally settling on the carnival glass marigold compote on the shelf where it had been for the last twenty years.

Grammie's eyes fixed on him. "Our Gallie's not one for settling."

Mr. Burgess started laughing and slapped the counter. "Mrs. Meissner, you're quite the lady."

"Yes, and it's been quite the visit. I'm sure Ruth would be happy to know you were just stopping by on your Sunday visitation round to make sure Cyril's family is taking proper care of her antiques, just as happy as her lawyer and New England relatives would be, and the Good Lord Himself, no doubt. When they are located and come to cart off their inheritance, or junk as you call it, I'm sure they'll express proper gratitude. Goodness, listen to me. Must be the sentimental factor. And look at that old grandfather clock there. My land, it's almost time for supper, Martha. We'd best be calling Gallie to see if she needs anything. When will Cyril be back?"

"Cyril and Percy are going to drive straight into Foster from the library."

Mr. Burgess coughed into his hand. "Well, give Cyril my best. I should be heading home for my own supper." And he nodded at Grammie and winked at me as my mother took him down the hall to the front porch.

Grammie turned to me as soon as he was gone and took my face between her hands. "Now that's what you call a picker, Serrie. Going round the countryside, barging into old folks' homes, trying to buy off their antiques for next to nothing. Thinks he can get whatever he wants for a song. If he ever comes by when you and Percy are alone here, you don't go to the door, you don't open the curtains. You just let him knock until he goes away. And you keep the door locked, because a picker like him will just walk right in like he owns the place, because in that mind of his, why, he already does."

My mother came back into the room pulling her sweater tight. It was cold when the sun went down. "Lord, Mum, you don't have to be so bloody rude. It's not like I was going to sell him anything."

"Martha, I can't believe you even let him in the house." Grammie shook her head. We could hear the Bentley purr, and then the high-pitched back-up noise as Mr. Burgess drove out the driveway.

"Mother, he was just standing in the front hall when I came down the stairs. It wasn't like I was inviting him in."

"Well, you lock the door then. And just watch out for him, Martha, because he'll hover over you like an eagle over a trout pond. Ruth will rise from the dead if you sell her things to Clarence Burgess."

"Lord, I'm not a fool."

"No, Martha, you are not a fool but you're hard up, and the hard up can do foolish things. Burgess knows it and don't you ever underestimate the patience and the rapacity of his kind. Now let's get over home and have a nice dinner. Gallie's making apple pie with the new Gravensteins."

"Me and Percy picked them with Aunt Gallie yesterday," I said, my voice breaking, digging my toe into a pink patch on the old hooked rug under Grammie's chair. I didn't want any fighting, my stomach was hurting already.

"I know you did, my darling." Grammie said, patting my arm.

My mother put Mr. Burgess's water glass in the sink and began to scrub it. "Serrie, you go get ready. I told you to wear your boots in the garden — look at your feet. And you've got a leaf in your hair. Be sure to wash your face with soap and hot water." I ran off down the hall and Grammie's voice floated up the staircase.

"There's nothing wrong with her hearing this, Martha. Lord, you act like she's made of china."

"She's my daughter, Mother, and you don't need to go scaring her to death about Clarence Burgess."

"Yes, yes, she is your daughter." Grammie said with a tight voice and then she was quiet, like me, all the way over to Foster, and through supper. That night in bed I had to think about Cape Breton beaches to get to sleep.

We only went back to Cape Breton once, me, Percy and our mother, when I was fourteen and Percy was sixteen, old enough to do some of the driving, me still stuck in the back seat. We stayed at Ron's Eat'n'Sleep Waterfront Motel Cottages, where Ron had a big buffet barbecue every night for all the guests. The cottages were ancient, once-bright blue and white paint peeling off the clapboard, but each cottage still charming, with a big verandah and a porch swing. I wanted to stay forever but Percy said that would be impossible, because it wasn't insulated and I'd freeze to death by Christmas.

All day my mother sat on the beach, still smoking, holding a book but mostly staring at the sea, me calling to her over and over from the water to watch my wave dives. She'd take us out to see the sunset and we'd pick out as many colours as we could, her telling the names: fuchsia, aqua, magenta, azure, amaranth, ochre, turquoise. And then dark time, still and mysterious with crickets and other gentle night creatures. When Martha and Percy would fall asleep (they both snored, they say it's genetic), I'd go get her cigarette butts from the ashtray on the kitchen table and sneak out far in the grass to light the first one so she wouldn't hear me flick the lighter, though with all that snoring I could have puffed away at the foot of her bed. I'd light the next off the dying end in my lips, sitting on the verandah, watching fireflies glitter by, wave sounds coming in on the sea breeze, and I'd wish we could stay forever in Cape Breton summertime. The next day we'd head out to the beach again, turning brown and playing, Percy building sand castles and forts, and then trying like crazy to keep the tide from destroying them, building dykes and walls, all of us trying to keep the water back and finally standing there by the lump of the kingdom that was. There were no more holidays after that. Day trips to beaches, to lakes, church teas and dinners, stuff like that, but never with my father coming along. And no more painting. And that lightness of spirit, it just went away, for my mother it was so-much-for-being-a-landscape-painting-housewife-and-living-the-dream. It just stopped.

Bang.

As is my habit these days, I wake up in the dark and have no idea where I am. At least it's not a blackout I'm coming out of, but thick, sticky sleep.

Another bang.

"Motherfucker," Dearie hisses. Keys clink on the hardwood. I hear her hand smacking on the floor trying to find them. Thud. Dearie falls over. "Sweet motherfucking basket of misery."

I'm in the bed, Dearie's couch, the antique sofa trunk she got when her grandmother died. It's very narrow, so I had crossed my arms like a good corpse to keep them from hanging over the sides, you know, like I was waiting for someone to come through the door and drive a stake through my heart, and then I just lay there in Dearie's apartment under a quilt and five wool blankets, listening to the cars outside on the slushy street as I fell asleep. There is another thud as Dearie gets up and then drops her keys on the table by the door. I hear her shuffle off and the fridge door open, the sticking seal making a smacking noise, Dearie gulping whipping cream, her hangover cure. She tiptoes into the living room and then sits on her brass bed and lights a smoke.

She's talking really slow, with this drunk drawl, and for a minute she almost sounds French. "God, it's cold out there. And damp. Wish I was down in Louisiana, walking in New Orleans with my long lost family."

I'm Acadian, Dearie Melanson always says. Arcadian, I say back. Dearie always screwed up her face when she didn't get it and when we were older she'd light up a smoke. If Elizabeth and I hadn't pulled her through French in high school, Dearie would have failed. We even had to help her learn the Acadian national anthem, which we learned in Latin because our French teacher was an Acadian priest, Father LeBlanc, and he said it was in Latin because the Acadians were good Catholics when they chose it, way back in 1884. "Ave, Maris Stella," Elizabeth and I would sing to her, "Felix caeli porta." But Dearie said she liked it better in a language she understood, "Hail, Star of the Sea," she'd mouth, "blessed gate of Heaven." Any trace of Acadian in Dearie's family was anglicized out by the time Dearie's grandfather was born and so just the surname tumbled down the years to Dearie. She can't even put on an accent, sounding more like some Eastern European factory worker, whatever they sound like. Dearie wanted to speak French so much, but she just mangled the words, even her own last name. The way we Anglos say it, Melanson sounds more like molasses than anything French. That's assimilation for you, my brother Percy once said, and went through all the names of the absorbed Valley Acadians near Foster, in our part of the Valley and the Mountain: LeBlanc, Landry, Comeau, Martin, Robichaud, Sauliner, Boucher, Dupuis, Bernard, Surette, Lambert. A found poem, he said.

Dearie kept saying she was going to find her roots, that all her relations went down to New Orleans and became Cajuns, and that she was going, too — any day. We'd tease her, but you didn't tease Dearie for very long. Dearie thought that everything would make sense when she finally got to Louisiana and ate cornbread and shrimp and stuff, with her *real* family, even if they were only descendants. She'd clung to that as long as I knew her, though her father says it's just history and he has better things to think about than a bunch of dead French people. Dearie said Elizabeth and I didn't know what it was like to be assimilated. Elizabeth always said Dearie should change her name to *ma chère*, and then Elizabeth would sing *ma chère, ma chère* to some tune she just pulled from the sky. Elizabeth hears music in everything. I told Dearie if she didn't want to be an Anglo-Acadian then she should to go to New Brunswick where there are real live Acadians, or up to Cape Breton, or even right here on the French shore, as we call it, farther down the Valley in Clare, in Digby County. But she'd just scowl. Immersion at the Université Sainte-Anne in Church Point, or Pointe de l'Église, depending on your tongue. If she wanted to find out who she was, then what was stopping her, Elizabeth giggled. Every year Dearie would pile us in her van for a tour of the local deportation sites and assorted Acadian points of interest, her favourite over on the Mountain in Morden, down past the lady artist's studio in the renovated church, at the French Cross right on the Bay of Fundy. And she'd take us down to Grand Pré, to the museum near the deportation site, back in 1755, when Colonel John Winslow put them on boats, burned their villages to ashes, and sent them all over the world. In our first year of university, when we were home at Christmas, we did go down to Church Point. Destination: St. Mary's Church, the tallest wooden church in North America, with rocks packed in the belfry as ballast to anchor it against the wind. Imagine, anchored in the sky. The year before, our last year in high school, we went to Meteghan to La Vielle Maison, this Acadian museum. Meteghan was founded in 1785 and you can feel the spirits. It's the least I could do, it seemed, accompany Dearie while she tried to figure out how the *grand dérangement* affected her — it was the only thing I could do for her.

"Serrie, you awake?" Dearie whispers as she lights a cigarette.

I can see a bit of moon out the blinds, blinds Dearie would close if she wasn't looped because she says that's what people do, close blinds at night, I suppose just like the sky is always a shade of blue. But I like the moon, flower white, lily-of-the-valley white. Dearie says she's sorry for being such a bitch, she's just worried about me and I've still got my family to deal with and the Reverend. I'm not easy to be friends with sometimes.

"I know this because you keep telling me," I say. "I know how hard I am to be friends with, I'll probably never forget. I'll start changing immediately."

She doesn't hear me because she's got bed spins and starts moaning. I feel for her, I really do. She says it's funny for her to be loaded and me stone sober. I'm always the drunkest, and so I say, like someone else is inside of me for a flash, "Maybe that's my big problem, *my specific problem*." Dearie doesn't say anything at first and then she asks me what I mean, and in the dark there, with the foot pain far away and dull, lying on the coffin couch bed, I tell her there's something bad about me and drinking, about me and drugs, I'm just like my father maybe. She's slurring her words now, says I'm just exaggerating, being melodramatic. I should just cut down a bit, it's just about being resolved, it's about being responsible, we are too young for those kind of problems, we are in our prime, we can do anything we want, the whole world is out there for us. She keeps talking away, saying that in New Orleans they have aboveground graves.

"Mausoleums, sepulchres," I tell her. I don't know where these words come from, they just float to me as I fall away from the moon to a quiet place where my mother is hanging out laundry on the line, cows mooing, she is hanging *my* bras out, one by one, "seven years of brassieres," she whispers as she turns and looks at me, then back to the line, hanging out bra after bra, so many bras I know they can't all be mine. She is sad because she can't go anywhere until each bra is on the line but the pile is too big and the line is too short and she keeps asking me what to do but I just don't know.

I wake up crying, with Dearie shining a flashlight in my face and I put my arm over my eyes. She asks me if I'm okay and I shrug, hot tears sliding through my hair to the nape of my neck. My heel really hurts and I'm scared she's going to get mad again, but she doesn't. It's what I find hardest about her, about Dearie, that I never know when she's going to be nice and when she's not. Whenever she gets near crying, she gets mad, whether it's her or someone else with the tears. A match flares and her eyes glow like the tip of the cigarette as I tell her about the bra dream. Her dry lips scuff the filter and she sucks in and says she's getting as weird as me, she's been dreaming of digging up her mother in the Foster graveyard, but when she opens the coffin, it's full of accents, the little symbols on French letters.

"Like cedilla? The squiggly one?"

"Yes, Serrie, exactly like that. What does it do?" Dearie whispers.

I can see her nod, her chin brushing the quilt. "It makes the C sibilant," I whisper back. She won't know what that means so I say it gives it a *hiss* sound, the snake sound.

"Great, snakes and bras. There's no hope for us, is there?"

THREE

I LOOK AROUND AND SEE ELIZABETH HANGS UP ALL THE FRAMED photos her mother sends her. There are family photos taken every year, and a huge one of Elizabeth in her high school graduation gown, as big as the picture of the Queen in the lobby of the high school. Elizabeth's mother has the piano top lined with big blow-up school pictures of Elizabeth and her sister, in these ugly gold frames, but frames nonetheless. The coffee table in the Baxter living-room is piled with family albums, the dates on the front of each one, little stacks of history. Here, in Elizabeth's city room, there is a bookshelf with some clothes on top and junk on lots of the shelves but I can see her photo albums. We have none of these at my house. There are a few family pictures, baby ones and stuff, on my mother's dresser, but there are no albums, no big framed deals on the wall or on the old pump organ. All our photos are in boxes my father keeps hidden in case there is a fire someday. I try to tell him that if he died, none of us would be able to find these family pictures and that it would be nice to put them in albums now, for us to look back on all the good times, but he's stuck on outsmarting the fire and who am I kidding about the good times?

Elizabeth's roommate, Clare, let me in. She's really tall and has red hair, dyed red hair, or maybe it's her eyebrows that are dyed, because they're black and people do that, don't they, dye eyebrows? She stood there in these old-man pyjamas.

"Is Elizabeth here?"

"You must be Serrie." She said it like she meant, *you must be the person who drowned my kittens.* "You'll have to take those clodhoppers off. We've got carpet here."

And they do have carpet, this old orange, two-tone shag with cigarette burns. I propped myself against the door and started unlacing my boots, with arthritic slow fingers. Clare leaned against the wall and watched like a prison guard. I looked at her big bare feet as I eased off boot number one.

"Elizabeth's still in bed. You can go wake her."

I wobbled off down the hall.

"Keep going," Clare barked. "Go through the kitchen."

Why didn't she give me the instructions all at once, I wondered, rather than this game of Clue: Mr. Plum in the Billiards Room, Miss Elizabeth in the Boudoir. The sun porch, it was her bedroom.

"Just go in. She sleeps like the dead."

Elizabeth was nowhere in sight. The blinds pulled, junk piled everywhere. Products — beauty products, travel size, some dating back to age fourteen. Elizabeth just keeps collecting them, little shampoos and little creams, powders, the leftover cosmetic samples from Melanson's Drugstore, little soaps still in the wrappers. She never uses them and they smell more like the packaging they're in than whatever it was they were simulating in the first place. Purple light, the only light, comes from *my* purple lava lamp. She had to have taken it out of the house-of- swimmers after I went to England. The lava was going up and down so fast it must have been on all night or, knowing Elizabeth, since I took off for London, a month ago today. I limped over to switch it off, because even a lava lamp needs a break, right?

The whole room is decorated in lawn stuff, yard furniture stuff, plastic, like from a K-Mart sale. I pull up a deck chair and elevate both my legs on the end of her bed. I'd like to have a smoke but she'd kill me so I don't. There's a walkman on the floor so I put on the headset and snap the play button. God, ancient Olivia Newton-John, *have you never been mellow*, and I think, Olivia, actually, I've never been mellow. Her voice is like a marshmallow and I sit there in the weird little sun porch room on the lawn chair, surrounded by the patio-frigging-furniture. Dearie is still home in bed. The cream cure must not have worked. She only groaned when I got up, and put her pillow over her head. Dearie won't let anyone drive her van so I've limped over on my own. Waking up early must be the jet lag — you know, still on the Greenwich mean.

Elizabeth's father, Smokey, is a strawberry and dairy farmer and her mother has a hair salon in the basement of their home. They don't have much money and there's certainly no extra furniture for her to take to the city. The Baxters don't have one old thing in their house in Foster — everything looks like it was mail-ordered from a catalogue or from one of those bargain furniture stores. The original Baxter family farm sits on the south edge of town. All her neighbours are her uncles, aunts and cousins. Her grandfather lived in the main farmhouse (which has a heritage plaque on it) and divided up enough of his land so that his nine sons and one daughter could all build homes near him. Only one went away to Toronto, to be a lawyer. He used to come home (before the cancer got him) with all of his kids, who hated the smell of cow shit. No one else even finished high school in Smokey's generation. Education is a big thing for parents like ours.

Elizabeth's mother, Ardyth, runs the household — she even does all the budgeting, counting every damn penny. She always did everything for Elizabeth, and when she went to university, her mother filled in the application, did her student forms. Elizabeth said she was a lazy kid then so it was fine with her. Ardyth is calm and composed, held together by a series of tight smiles and frowns. I've only seen her hug Elizabeth one time. Elizabeth always had short haircuts and had to have trims all the time. Me, I'd just need an occasional snip on the end of my long mop. I'd sit in a hair dryer chair reading celebrity gossip magazines and watch Ardyth comb out her daughter's hair and snippity snip with only the shiny chrome blades touching the young neck and forehead and then we'd be shooed away for a paying customer, some old lady for a wash and set or cut and perm. Ardyth gave the kids one piece of meat each on a meat night, or two fish sticks if it was a fish stick night, one glass of juice and on and on — never any seconds or extras. Ardyth's parents died when she was five and she worked as a secretary until she married Smokey Baxter, who was still living with his parents when he was almost forty. Then she studied hairdressing in the city so she could work at home while Smokey ran the farm with his brothers.

The summer we were thirteen, an arsonist set their cow barn on fire and though most of the herd was out to pasture that night, the damage was so extensive and the insurance they had so minimal that the Baxter Family Farm went hundreds of thousands of dollars into debt. It was Elizabeth's birthday that night and we were sleeping in a tent on her lawn, me, Elizabeth and Dearie. Somewhere in the middle of the night when Elizabeth got up for one of her famous pees, she saw the orange glow across the strawberry field. We watched the fire from the tent door and then walked barefoot through the dewy strawberry rows in our pyjamas, sleeping bags around our shoulders, knots of tightly held hands not breaking as Elizabeth pulled us, jumping the rows, the sleeping bags flying behind us like capes as the Strawberry Princess ran with her ladies-in-waiting on either side until we could hear the jaws of the fire crunching away on the Baxter family heart. Elizabeth stood in the middle of us and I watched shiny fire-red tears fall from her eyes and dot her cheeks in a straight line, tiny crystal balls, never taking her eyes off the fire. We stood there in the berry field right across from the barn and listened to the cows trapped inside wailing as they roasted. The Foster Volunteer Fire Department was spraying water, big red trucks and flashing lights, aliens in helmets and giant boots, Mr. Baxter running around but there was nothing he could do, and we watched him cry as the barn fell in, the men holding him back.

The next morning we went down and listened to the bloated cow bodies bursting from inside the rubble, at least that's what Elizabeth's cousin Laird said the noise was. It turned out the arsonist was the next-door neighbour and off he went to the nuthouse. Mr. Baxter changed after that, always worrying, talking about what could go wrong, how you could never be safe from anything. It was like he thought worrying might be able to help him, but he just seemed to get older with every month.

Mr. Baxter drives a tractor and does farm stuff, driving around in fields, ploughing, planting, harvesting, you know, right out of Ecclesiastes. He doesn't talk much and when he does, he repeats most of what he says like some kind of echo. Elizabeth and I are bonded by our fathers. We don't have to explain their "marching to the beat of their own damn drums" syndrome, as Grammie calls it. Mr. Baxter is the only man in town my father seems able to have a conversation with, which involves looking at machinery or my father's inventions or talking about history. Then there's more pointing and then sometimes laughing, but I never can figure out what in the name of God they are talking about. My father, being a progressive type, says "coloured folk," while Mr. Baxter is still saying "Nee-gro." It's enough to make me want to die. They both say I-talian and A-rab, which is better than wop and rag-head. It's beyond me why no one ever understood my need to expand my horizons. Both our fathers read and have some interest in the world, though no desire to actually go and see it. Mr. Baxter still comes over from time to time to check out my father's invention shed and you can hear more of the same: *uh-uh, how 'bout that; isn't that something;*

well, I never, never never never. He's always got a smile for you, Mr. Baxter, and even my Aunt Galronia likes him. Everyone does, even after the barn burning and him then getting dark and worrisome forever after. Except Elizabeth. And it isn't that she doesn't like him, he just seems to set something off in her, you know, this inner gnawing, and he never means to.

For instance: Mr. Baxter was teaching us both to drive one hot July Sunday when the Valley was in drought. Elizabeth was five months older than me, and she was sixteen. Sixteen was the age for getting your beginner's license and we were keen to be able to drive, because when you live rural, it's not like there are very many places you can walk to. We were in his metallic pine-green Plymouth Fury III, in the peaceful Foster Cemetery beside their farm. We kept going down shady lanes, passing the dead people and the dead grass, Mr. Baxter telling us about everyone, every single damn dead person like he was the keeper of the memories. *Old Mrs. Kenneally, poor little headless Junior Doucette, Hepzibah Foster, Rupert Atkins, Clarkie Bishop, Grace McKinly, Simon Best, Thankful Palmer*, and on and on. Elizabeth turned the radio up and started singing along to some golden oldie hit, but Mr. Baxter just kept naming off the dead. I started counting tombstones to the tune of "Ninety-nine Bottles of Beer on the Wall," mouthing it, as not to disturb the soliloquizing in the front, tapping my sweaty thigh to keep rhythm. At seventy-two grave markers of stone on the ground, seventy-two grave markers of stone, Mr. Baxter gave a loud mutter, "Take 'er left now by Garnet Meissner's stone, right here by Serrie's grampie's stone, just take 'er left, take 'er left."

Elizabeth started screaming in this voice, like a kitten set on fire, "I hear you, I hear you, I'm taking 'er left, I'm taking 'er left."

And he took off his hat, rubbed his head, and said, "Just calm down there, Lizzie, calm down," while I waved to Grampie's stone, wishing I was anywhere but in the metallic pine-green Plymouth Fury III.

"I'm friggin' calm, I'm calm, for the love of God," Elizabeth screeched.

Mr. Baxter and I jerked back in our seats as she hit the gas and spun left on the dirt road, yelling, "No more about the dead, no more about the dead," clouds of brown dust rolling in. She squealed onto the road, going the wrong way, taking us out of town. Mr. Baxter just sat there and let her drive, Elizabeth crying now, eyes never leaving the road, sweaty hair plastered to her head, gasping she was sorry, but she just didn't want to hear about the goddamn dead, screaming again. There was a car coming and it was the Reverend Rafuse, smiling and waving in that dumb, hopeful way of his, index finger going up to flick his jaw as Elizabeth ignored him, roared past and turned down the Lesterdale Road, roaring by the sign at the end of the road: Burgess Antiques, Five Miles.

In the ditch we could hear frogs over in the pond by the willow trees. There wasn't any wind at all and we just sat there as the stillness came back, Mr. Baxter patting Elizabeth's head, asking me if I was okay. She was crying with her mouth open and her eyes squinted shut, making little noises that sounded just like the frogs. Mr. Baxter jumped out, surveyed the car, and walked off to the farm to get the tractor to haul out the car. We were only half a mile down the road; it doesn't take very long to lose control going at that speed. There was a smashed headlight and some scratches on the green paint, but the ditches were tangled with Brown-eyed Susies and Queen Anne's lace — wildflowers and wild grasses had padded our crash. When Elizabeth had taken the turn onto the dirt road, she had floored the gas and the wheels had caught in loose gravel until we careened into the ditch. Mr. Baxter didn't even grab for the wheel, as we all knew the car was out of control. At least Elizabeth had good enough sense not to pound on the brakes; I guess it was that instinctive farm part of her. I piggy-backed her over to the pond and we sat there, waiting. Elizabeth kept up that burp crying thing, and then she jumped in the pond and swam to the other side, where she sat wet and alone, staring at a waterlily, until her father came back.

Elizabeth never would talk about the accident again, not at all; maybe the whole episode reminded her of all the miscarriages her mother'd had before she had Elizabeth, and then Elizabeth was only born because her mother took DES, *diethylstilbestrol*, the word Elizabeth taught me when I first met her in Bible camp. Elizabeth was still scared there were things weird and deformed about her organs, her *reproductive* organs, that she would get some kind of cancer. She'd been having a pelvic exam every six months since her first period and she'd say the doctor would poke and prode at her, scrape her insides, her legs up in stirrups, shoving freezing cold metal up her. The only other girl in Foster who everyone knew was a DES baby was Jennifer Parker, but she was out in Vancouver, so who knew what was happening to her.

It's hard to believe there could be anything wrong with Elizabeth's organs as she jerks up in her lawn-chair bed and swings her feet to the floor. She kicks a pile of clothes to the side and stands up wearing pink bunny pyjamas that zipper up the front. She stretches up high on her toes and then walks over to me like some fuzzy toy and hugs me.

We have coffee in the living-room, sitting in the worn out La-Z-Boy chairs. Clare joins us, lighting up a cigarette, Elizabeth coughing and opening the window, where a few snowflakes sink by. Clare starts telling us about some guy she met at the bar last night, some guy named Harold who wants to take her bowling.

"Reggie's almost thirty," Elizabeth tells me. "He's taking me to Palm Springs in February — he won best salesman of the year. Sold more BMWs than anyone else in the dealership."

Elizabeth has lost her mind, this is the only explanation. A car salesman. She says he went to university and studied all kinds of neat stuff, geography, business, management, history, just a whole bunch of stuff, but he dropped out. I think that will at least give us something in common.

"Reggie is quite the salesman, indeed." Clare sips her coffee.

Elizabeth throws a cushion at her. "What's that supposed to mean? Anyway, Serrie, he's going to teach me to golf." She giggles with bliss. Golf and bliss, it could be the name of a club.

"Isn't Florida really touristy?" I sip the coffee — it's weak so I just gulp it down and start having fantasies about moving to Florida and opening up The Golf & Bliss, with the help of Salesman Reggie. A real job. Galronia would be thrilled.

"No, that's Palm Beach. This is Palm Springs, in the desert, where Bing Crosby went. You're the big traveller now, aren't you? You should know where Palm Springs is at least." She takes a sip of coffee and then shouts, "Hey, guess what day it is?" Elizabeth hops up and puts on a Bing Crosby Christmas carol CD. It's another one of her rules — no Christmas carols until the first day of December and then every day, all day, nonstop until December 27, and then it's on to New Year's Eve, singing "Auld Lang Syne," and then into the new year itself. The three of us dance around to "Deck the Halls" with coffee, Clare adding Bailey's Irish Cream, saying the heat will burn the alcohol off. She keeps staring at me and her eyes are as red as holly berries.

I get back to Dearie's and while I am waiting for her to come home I call my parents collect. My father answers and starts talking to me like I'm Smokey Baxter so I just say "Uh-huh, I see, oh yes." He tells me they've been hit with a snowstorm — who'd believe it when it's just turned December? — but it'll most likely melt. It's weird to me, just a couple hours away and the weather can be so different. My interest ends there but not Cyril's; he goes on and on about the weather like any good Canadian and I almost fall asleep. My lips squish against the receiver and my spit tastes like sour plastic so I light up a smoke to keep me energized. There is a pause when the match flares and I wonder why we pretend I'm smoke-free, but before I can start saying anything he starts telling me about the latest outhouse he picked up for his collection. "This one, she's right some old," he says, "from the Georgie Hall place in Scott's Bay, right near Cape Split. Writin' on the walls goes back to 1900. Old Mr. Hall said he was happy to see it go to me and not some dealer from the city."

The yard at our place on the Lupin Cove Road has outhouses everywhere now. I can never figure out how my mother feels about the outhouses, one day complaining how ridiculous they look and the next day going out and weeding the gardens around them. Percy calls them artifacts, "my father collects artifacts — he's sort of an amateur anthropologist-archaeologist," I hear him say on the phone to some guy the second Christmas he is home from university. And he does collect them; our father hunts the outhouses down all over the province, towing them home on a trailer, then setting them on the lawn, fixing them up. And in the spring he plants morning glories, using the outhouses as trellises. Gallie always says that morning glories are just weeds, relentless bloody weeds, but Cyril keeps them pruned and perfect, knows the names of all the varieties. He keeps lists, lists for everything, posted on the bulletin board in the kitchen, and makes up special outhouse lists to keep track:

PLACE OF ORIGIN	CONSTRUCTION DATE	MORNING GLORY
1. Middle Barney's River	1894	Blue Waves
2. Margaree Forks	1940	Pearly Gates
3. Malagash	1917	Scarlett O'Hara
4. Malignant Cove	1899	China Blue
5. Walton — Noel Shore	1925	Pearly Gates
6. Isaac's Harbour North	1939	Flying Saucers and Summer Skies
7. East Pubnico	1904	Roman Candy
8. Shubenacadie	1902	Heavenly Blue
9. Tatamagouche	1927	Moonflower

He replaces the clapboard and shingles, restoring them to what they must have looked like when they were first built as outhouses proper. Only Number One is a working outhouse, Middle Barney's River, and that's where you go if the one bathroom the Spinster Sullivan had put in is busy. *Taking a memorial shit for Barney*, Dearie says. My father's got Numbers Five, Six, and Seven done up as woodsheds and digs little paths to them in the winter. Outhouse Number Three, Malagash, still has all these old black-and-white snapshots of someone's long-gone family put up with old tacks. My father took them down when he cleaned the outhouse and fixed it up and then put them right back, not in a box hidden away, but then it was someone else's family. Ladies in funny bathing suits, old black cars, a farmer with a plough hooked up to work horses. Number Nine, my favourite, has writing on the walls going back to when it was built in 1927:

> *Clear skies, hot today, June 24, 1934, Harold Barbour.*
> *Had a good dinner, August 18, 1940, Toby McKenzie*
>   (in a little kid's printing).
> *Nothing but rain, November 2, 1935, Harold Barbour.*
> *Praise the Good Lord, June 6, 1944, Manly Withers.*

The August before I left for my first year of university, Cyril wanted me to type up a new list with all the family information he had gathered, seeing as I was such a good typer from the typing class the guidance counsellor told me to take, which was offered in place of art, seeing as it was a rural high school and we had to take what we could get, what with the funding cuts and all, whatever the hell that was supposed to mean. I yelled that it was *typist*, not *typer*, that he shouldn't sound like some hick and that I wasn't typing up some crazy list of his outhouses anyway. He got all hurt, saying I would have before and I screamed that before is gone, before was when nothing mattered, but I'm no kid anymore and I'm no *typer* either,

I'm going to be more than that. And he put on his hat and went out-side to sit in an outhouse and there was no one left for me to scream at but my mother, who came into the kitchen and told me that's just his way of trying to be involved with my life. So I took another breath so as not to lose my momentum and screamed at her that it's involv-ing me in *his* life and none of them have any interest in *mine*, that she just wanted to make me into a freak like them. She yelled back that if people really knew what I was like when I was out in public I wouldn't have any life, no one would have any time for me. I ran outside and cried in Outhouse Number Nine. It was getting dark by then and I sat there looking up at the moonflowers, the night bloomers, white petals like tissue paper covering the old warped win-dow, knees to my chin, and wished I didn't have to go away, that I could just stay in Number Nine forever. I went and stood outside of Number Two, Margaree Forks, where I could hear Cyril breathing. "Sorry," I said, just like Mr. Baxter, "sorry sorry sorry."

"It's okay, Serrie," my father said, and then he was silent, and I went back to Number Nine.

One spring day at Grammie's, just after my father retired, when I was fourteen, she told me to be patient with my father, with both my parents, but especially Cyril, because he'd had a hard life, orphan-ages, the drink and all of that. Aside from being Irish and Catholic, he was a good man. She poured the water in the teapot and put the cozy on, saying she didn't understand my mother anymore, going all morbid about the past, not talking about anything, walking around like a ghost these last years.

"Cyril, your daddy Cyril," she said, "was put in a home as his father was beating him the colour of pansies, and his mother, the long-dead Grannie Sullivan, would only say, 'Make sure you don't hit him in the head,' but then she died having an appendectomy (everybody knew the doctor was dead drunk when he cut her open), and there was no one to say, 'Don't hit him in the goddamn head.' So *he did*, he hit him in the goddamn head. And then, of course, off he'd go to the confession, to get all cleaned out before he did it again. One day, the older brother, Roan, beat the living shit out of the father because he was finally big enough to do it, but Cyril's head swelled up anyway, from all those years of beatings. The size went back to normal, but then he was all different, doing his own thing. And the boys went into the orphanage, and their father kept going to the confession. Now it seems to me there's a lot of similarity between the confessional and an enema, I tell you. So there you are." And Grammie sipped her tea and patted my cheeks, shaking her head, telling me that the most important thing was having a good head on your shoulders, that Serrie Sullivan would do all right with the one she had. It was the only thing Grammie was ever wrong about.

"So what kind of flowers do you think I should put in there when spring comes?"

Right, he's talking about the new outhouse. I say I don't know and then I start to get pissed off 'cause here I am calling, but I may as well still be in London and so I yell, "I don't know what kind of flowers you should put in your frigging outhouse, Dad."

I can hear the silence between us, and then he clears his throat. "So you got into some trouble, I hear."

"Yup," I say and take a drag. "That's what I hear, too."

And then my mother gets on the upstairs line and she's tired, her voice thin as wire. She doesn't say much, just that I'm going to have to come home so we can sort some things out. She hasn't told my brother Percy anything yet — he's busy at the University of Toronto — she says it like he's a professor or something. Percy's only doing his master's, but he may as well be the Dean of Arts. Silence and the three of us breathing. I know what's she's thinking about, and she knows what I'm thinking about: Burgess Antiques, Thanksgiving. But we'll never do more than play that think game. And then she tells me I'm going to have to apologize to the Reverend Rafuse and I tell her I know, I know, and then she gets mad and says I don't know a goddamn thing and she's sick of me and what am I going to do about university. I hear my father in the background saying, "Let's just stay calm, folks." My mother starts to cry. Click. She hangs up. I let some time pass and call back and tell her I'm sorry, that Dearie will be driving me out on the weekend.

I have a fever that night and Dearie tells me to take it easy, looking at me from the kitchen table where she's studying. She's going to Florida for Christmas, to spend the holidays in the condo with her father and the Neddie family. Neddie's now with a venture capitalist business in California, doesn't ever want to leave Silicon Valley, and holds forth at the dinner table about topics like high technology and due diligence and market analysis and business plans and turbo growth. And so Dearie's grouchy, just smoking and drinking tea, flipping the pages of her textbook and staring out the window. She has more exams and Elizabeth is working all the time so she can have Christmas off. I spend the next four days propped up on the coffin bed, smoking, hobbling out to the coffee shop, and reading magazines and books out of my box that Dearie pulls out of storage.

By Thursday I'm going fucking stir crazy and I just want to hop on a plane again, but my student loan money is almost gone. I'm supposed to meet Dearie and Elizabeth for supper at the Old Spaghetti Factory, so I have a whole afternoon flopped before me. I go wandering about the slushy downtown streets listening to the foghorn. My combat boots are soaked from the slush and my foot is sore. I end up near the docks in front of this seedy bar, the Lobster Trap, the bar everybody laughed about at university, where guys go for their stags. The room is long and curves around at the back, where there is a round wedding-cake stage with tables encircling it. I can just imagine the bands that play in here. The air is stale, familiar and reassuring in that dull, hopeless kind of way. The bartender looks at me, this old guy who looks like he should be at the helm of some briny, barnacle-crusted ship, Old Ahab himself. The first thing he says is "You better have ID or you turn around right now and go shopping at the mall."

I freeze.

"Got ID?" he says again.

"Yeah, yeah, I got ID." I can tell he thinks it's going to be fake because I'm acting like it's fake. So much for being sophisticated. I haul out my passport and slap it on the counter and say when he's finished looking at it he can give me a gin and tonic. He looks at my picture and smirks, "I see you had a makeover."

So I sit at a table like some loser from a Hemingway novel and my feet are soaking wet. The heel feels better already — amazing what a few days of mould can do. I'd managed to make it to the student health clinic, still had my university ID card. I remember to take some more of the pills, washing them down with my gin. It's just me and a few old guys slouched over the bar having a good god-damn time at The Trap. A warm glow comes over me and I relax for the first time since I got here. But then as soon as I let my guard down, the panic slips in and my stomach goes watery. I'm in Halifax with no money, I've dropped out of university, I'm dreading seeing my family and the Reverend Rafuse, though *I don't even know why* I'm hiding out from him. There is no memory of that conversation. That's why I'm hiding out, I realize.

"Hey hey."

I look up. Some oily-looking dude is standing there in a suit like he's going to church, but a seventies-style suit, like he's got decade confusion, just like my mother.

"How you doin'?" he says.

But I'm smart now from all my worldly experience and so I get right down to business. "Fuck off," I say.

"Hey hey, I'm just makin' conversation."

Old Ahab yells at him to leave me alone and he does, first spitting on the floor by my combat boots. Maybe I can hitchhike to Toronto. Maybe not. I go back to figuring out my life. Maybe I'll figure it out. Maybe not. Blackouts. There's no doubt I'm an alcoholic but I'm only twenty years old, I think. You can't be an alcoholic at this age — you're still a kid. I've been having blackouts since I started drinking, when I was fourteen, so that would mean I was an alcoholic at fourteen and that's an impossibility, isn't it? Maybe I'm just, you know, a blackout drinker. Maybe not. And the Good Reverend Jack Rafuse: I don't remember and it would seem those brain cells are gone forever. I have another drink. My main experience with the Reverend and religion was being the sexton, though most of the time I was alone cleaning or just hanging out. It wasn't that I didn't go every Sunday, but I'd have to go ring the bells at the beginning and end of each service, so I started sitting up there, reading or sleeping, depending on the state of my hangover, creeping down for the sermon, standing in the back with the latecomers. Mr. Burgess would be there most of the time, leaning against the wall, no doubt checking out the stained-glass windows and what have you. Gallie and Grammie were always in the same pew up front. My mother gave up attendance shortly after our return to Foster, and Percy along with her, saying the only time he could practise the violin without interruption was when I was out of the house. After puberty, it was all downhill between me and Percy. Hormones can make you so mean. That wasn't true though, about his music, because sometimes I would creep outside his room before I went to bed and he'd play my favourite songs for me, the same ones he'd play before puberty, only I was allowed in the room then.

And my father's some kind of Catholic, you know, lapsed Catholic — he doesn't go to Mass — and he can't figure how everyone but the Catholics go to Hell, seeing as the Protestants are good people, the Jews, the A-rabs. He wants no part of it. In spite of all of the minuses he wants a Catholic funeral, so he told me once. And he wanted me to make a gentleman's promise to do a religious exploration, as he said, religious research, until I found something that suited me. We even shook on it. All I can figure is I must have been in a good humour at that particular moment.

Anyway, I may not be religious, aside from all my own quirky ideas about God, but I love that church, the building, I mean. I can still smell it, still see the sunlight streaming in the windows, not just the fancy freaking stained-glass ones but the clear old windows, panes rippled and bubbly, the ones they wanted to replace, "the fix-it-all-to-hell committee," my mother called them, one of Galronia's committees. We could have used a bit of the fix-it committee's inspiration on the Lupin Cove Road, what with everything held together by dust, nostalgia and cobwebs.

I take a sip and look at the glass and I'm back in front of those truly awesome windows. And, sure, you can't see outside perfectly — everything is warped — but you can bet that seems more real than anything to someone like me. There was so much wood, good solid oak, and the whole place smelled like it. When I was little I thought it was the smell of the Lord, you know, God smelled like a good slab of oak, and I thought this until Galronia set me straight, saying the Good Lord God smelled as clean as a hospital. As sexton, I'd scrub the salt stains from under the pews in the winter and spring. Summer was great for sitting barefoot in the cool basement in a Sunday school room, smoking cigarettes, a joint if Elizabeth managed to show up. It was good to just sit there reading a book with no one knowing where I was, in the same room where I learned the nine choirs of angelic creatures from Miss Taylor, the Sunday school teacher we had who was into angelology, as she called it. First Choir: seraphim, cherubim, thrones; Second Choir: dominations, principalities, powers; and Third Choir: virtues, archangels, and angels. I would shout them out as I padded up the stairs and through the front foyer, running down the aisle to the altar, the sanctuary bright with sun, feeling the light inside of me, the warm smell of lemon oil and hymnals, mixed with the west wind, what Grammie calls a zephyr, blowing in the windows.

I feel dull heat on my finger and I light another smoke and take a drink without even breaking my zombie stare at the panelled wall of the Lobster Trap, music muffled and far away, hardly enough brain cells left to be here and there at the same frigging time.

It all changed when we entered the University Bound period. That's what they call it, being *university bound*. And what of those not so bound? There was never any name for them really, just general or non-academic. Dearie and Elizabeth's marks were just high enough to get in, but *just* — too many hockey games, parties, too many good times, those teenage good times that I'm sure I had too. I just don't remember them. It's some predestined thing that we have to do, *you kids will have an education*, my parents said, like there was something to prove.

And there I was, seventeen, University Bound, with a partial scholarship, filling out student loan forms in triplicate, all these applications and documents like I was some lawyer preparing a brief, whatever that is, and we had a big screaming fight when I asked my mother to help — she gets weird about money, about anything official. Just follow the instructions, she yelled. I said I didn't understand the instructions, and I didn't — I've never understood instructions, not even on a cake mix box. I can't even make Jell-O. Elizabeth's mother still fills out everything for her and Dearie's father is still footing the total bill, and why was no one helping me, is what I started to rage about. My father came in then from the unending work on the solar panels, as my mother was snapping she couldn't stand it anymore, and then I yelled at my father that I couldn't stand it, and he said to count him in, that he couldn't stand it either. He helped me fill out the student loan forms, saying to my mother, "Now Martha, she's awful nervous about goin' away to the city and all, we gotta be patient with her." Her hissing back: "There's no money to be sending her, it's all gone to Percy and that was nothing anyway. The government's going to tell us we have to pay for her because they don't give a good goddamn about our debt."

And you know, I just started rustling papers because that type of noise is a lot easier to deal with. And then my father telling me, "Mother's awful nervous about you goin' away and we gotta be patient with her, she just can't stand talk about financial matters. We're gonna get you to university, don't you go being afraid, now." His hands shaking from all the pills to *take the edge off*, to relax his back, the pills he keeps hidden in his shaving kit in the bathroom, on the top shelf, way in the back. I watched every tremor and felt each one shake through me, as he filled in each box and line on the application, wearing his glasses, me sitting there snorting and wiping at my eyes like a sick barn cat that crawled up from the cellar, waiting to be hauled out back and shot. It killed me watching him, my father going from line to line, everything still working in his head, just in his own way, saying slow and soft, *his girl's going to university no matter what, not to worry about a thing*, turning the application over, looking at the instructions from the government, figuring it out bit by bit. Without even looking at me, his big shaky, calloused hand reached out and patted mine and then went back to scribbling on the forms. There's nothing I hate more than being sad.

"Well, Seraphina Sullivan at the Lobster Trap on a slushy Halifax day. What is the world comin' to, my land? Now look at you there. My oh my."

Panic surges through my body, I jump in my seat, and my hands go wet and sticky as I squint under the dim light. My eyes are drippy so I dab away at them like a Southern Belle and peer up at Wynnette Doucette, her hair dyed blonde but with black roots, like she's rotting on the inside or something. A long way from Melanson's Drugstore but then, look at me, right? Long way from the belfry. I thought she was down the road in Toronto. The last place I want to see someone I know is at the Lobster Trap. She asks me if she can sit down and I look around to see if anyone else I know has taken to frequenting dives and turn back to her, with one hand over my nose hoop, trying to hide my haircut.

"What's wrong with you, Serrie? Got some kind of palsy?"

"No, just, you know, stretching."

"Are you okay?" she says.

I've still got my hand on my nose.

"Don't want to be seen with me?"

She's supposed to be a prostitute in Toronto now, or at least that's what they say in Foster. That's what they say about everyone who is trashy and leaves, that she's a hooker in Toronto. And I'm ashamed of not wanting to talk to her, of just wanting to be alone, like I think I'm better than her. I want to shout, "It's a two-fold problem, Wynnette, a two-folder. I'm ashamed of my nose and I'm ashamed to be here." I settle for muttering, Mr. Baxter-style, "No no, oh no, just meeting someone . . . someone." She rolls her eyes, because who would I be meeting at the Lobster Trap, a drug dealer, some longshoreman, whatever a longshoreman is? Mobster maybe? Who knows?

"Sure, sure, you can sit down," I say, my hand still on my nose. She keeps smiling at me. "It's okay there, Serrie. I don't care what fashions you're into. Suits you actually."

That's the thing that's different about her: she's always polite, she's got manners, no matter what, unlike the rest of us. Wynnette's parents, the Cruickshanks, owned the Hotel Majestic in Lupin Cove. It was well over a hundred years old when it burned down to the earth. I was only about six, so I don't remember, though I've heard the story from Grammie so many times you'd think I was manning one of the bloody water hoses, watching Wynnette's parents burn up, all that history going up in a torch that would have broke Percy's heart to pieces. Wynnette was fourteen and had to move down from the Mountain to Foster, to the trailer court behind the hospital with her aunt and uncle and a zillion little cousins with blue eyes. And that was it — her whole life was wiped out and she was a trailer court girl. Dropped out of school and married in three years to Tommy Doucette who worked at Stronach Packers with my father. They had a little baby boy named Tommy Doucette, Jr., who promptly became Just Junior because they were always telling people his name was *just* Junior, and if you ask me, it would have been easier to call him Bert or name him after someone dead.

"My Aunt Lola says you were seeing a bit of the world," she says with a smile, and takes another drag. She's wearing a low-cut top and there are these crinkles around her eyes, and straight lines by her lips, bags under her eyes, like some hard case off a soap opera. It hits me then, that Wynnette's not really that old, I mean twenty-eight is pretty old but it's not thirty, right? She's got that hard look to her, as though she got all scorched up in the fire even though she was off at the Bible camp paddling around in a canoe when the hotel went up. I haven't seen her for a long time because she left town just after my period started. It's a great time tracker, that.

"Yeah, well, you know," I say and take big gulp of my drink. She orders a beer and tells me it's a bit early to be having cocktails. I'm getting a good buzz on now and don't even know what time it is, but any time is a good time for a cocktail, I tell her, and then giggle like Elizabeth. This little voice inside of me says I should just go home but I shut it up by lighting up another smoke. I ask Wynnette if she comes here often and she starts laughing, bending over and slapping her knee. I just smile like I'm all savvy.

She stops laughing and shakes her head. "I work here, Serrie. That's why I'm here."

Does she make good tips is what I want to know, because maybe I can get a job waitressing. She doesn't answer so I ask again and Wynnette laughs and then starts hacking away, like she's terminal.

"Oh, great tips, Serrie, I make great tips,"she says, and takes a chug of beer.

When Just Junior was three, Wynnette started going around with these friends, going shopping all day and having lunch at the Burger Barn, at the Pizza Hut, the great lunch spots of the Valley, Just Junior always along. Tommy was at work making the money and her spending it up, according to Galronia. Until the day she was roaring along home in a car with her friend, Wendy the hairdresser, when they had an accident. Wendy died two weeks later from massive internal injuries. Just Junior flew through the windshield and his head was chopped right off and he was buried in the Foster Graveyard with his name on the tombstone:

Thomas Starr Doucette, Junior
"Just Junior"

The official report said the car had got caught in loose gravel on the side of the road and the driver, Wynnette, had lost control of the car. No charges were laid, but everyone in Foster was convinced she was hammered and had bribed the RCMP, though as Grammie says, what would she have to bribe anybody with, that poor thing? Tommy Senior wouldn't even look at her and she moved back to the trailer court and started working at Melanson's. Tommy didn't talk to anyone anymore, not even at the meat plant, like he was a shadow, my father said. And then she just left, Galronia said, just packed up and headed off to Toronto. Dearie said Wynnette gave two weeks' notice at Melanson's Drugstore, but no one knew she was going away. Who could blame her, is what my mother said, living in a town full of gossips.

And then it starts to be one more blurry night. We keep drinking and talking and smoking. Whenever that little panic thing starts poking at me, I just take another big swallow. I know it could be black-out time, anytime soon, but I don't give a fuck any more. Planning, apologizing, it just drips away, bit by bit.

Wynnette starts telling me, "Serrie, you've got to take control of your life, you're some smart, you are, and you can go places."

I'm really loaded and it strikes me as hilarious that Wynnette Doucette is giving me advice on how to go places, so I just laugh. She keeps telling me I should go back to university and make something of myself. I ask her what exactly it is that I'm supposed to make of myself and she says I can be whatever I want to be but I tell her I don't know what I want to be. It's too expensive, I tell her, and she says that the money will appear if I really know what I want, like she's some New Age counsellor or something. And I think about my mother and my father and start that stupid drunk boo-hooing into the glass, hearing slow-motion Abba songs playing all over me. She puts her hand on my wrist but there is no feeling, I can only see it there.

And then I black out. When I come back, the place is packed and the music is booming. Coloured lights splash about and a magical mist hangs in the room. Two identical gnomes wearing silver tank tops sit at the table with me. I'm finally dead and I'm glad to know that heaven or hell or purgatory or Hades or Tartarus or whatever you want to call the Great Beyond is just a sleazy Nova Scotian bar full of pervert elves and the like. There is a pile of half-eaten chicken wings on a plate in front of me. My throat feels raw and my mouth has a bitter powdery taste. I start smacking my lips and look about for a drink. The smoke is so thick my eyes hurt and I rub them with one hand as I grab a chicken wing with the other. As I take a big bite, I look at the gnomes, and speculate that these are my companions for eternity. Why can't I be with angels or highly evolved light-beings like on "Star Trek"? Because I'm not highly evolved, I hear myself say. One of the trolls sneezes — they are just short muscle guys, twins with moustaches, facial hair, snot, shit — you know, humans. Wynnette's crying to my right and this one twin says to her,

"You gotta get it together before you go on." Where is she going? She's talking about Just Junior and then one of the twins says something to me. It's so loud I can only see his lips move so I say sure, great, whatever. He smiles and gets up. I watch him walk away until my eyes cross. The other guy says, "It's just what you need, Wynnette," and she gives him a trembly smile. I am so drunk and so stoned the room tilts when I stand and then swings back. Who needs an amusement park? In some little reptilian part of my dying brain I remember thinking this would never ever happen again. So much for never ever.

Wynnette and I go down a hall so narrow you'd barely be able to sling a cat through it and then we are in a little, dirty, dank room in the back, a dressing room, with big mirrors and a few dull round bulbs in some of the sockets. I stand there against the wall, lighting a cigarette as I watch Wynnette splash her face with water and put make-up on. I take a big drag and nothing happens so I suck harder. Wynnette laughs at me in the mirror and it's the fucking filter on fire. I stomp on it and torch up another. While I'm doing some deep inhalation Wynnette says it's hard but what I've told her really helps and I say, yeah, yeah, no idea what it is I've told her. She tilts my head back and puts some eyeliner on my inner eyelid. If I wasn't so drunk, I'd be squinting, but it's too much work so I just stand there, the wall holding me. She covers my mouth in lipstick and asks me when my friends are coming. What's she talking about? I tell her I don't have any friends and she laughs and the lipstick goes across my cheek and then she starts kissing my neck and then her tongue is in my mouth, on my jaw. I just stand there, watching in the mirror, my face hollow under the fluorescent lights, all scribbled up. I can't even feel her lips on my skin but I can see the lipstick marks she's leaving, each lip print a photograph. Way down below there is a faint throb in my heel and I snap out of my drunken-druggie stare and take a step back, each blink now a strip of negatives, shaking my head, looking for my eyeballs. Wynette looks at me and I shake my head again, find the eyes and turn my nose hoop. I'm too out of it to throw a fit and it doesn't matter anyway because that awful sad feeling thrashes through my intoxicated state into my stomach, a fish on a dock with the hook in its eye. The lipstick marks look like so many mouths sprouting on my neck. Wynnette is saying she's so sorry, she doesn't know what came over her, I shouldn't tell anyone. Wynnette cries.

The moustache guys float through my brain and I say, "What about the moustache guys?"

Wynnette says we'll meet them in the back room but I shouldn't get my hopes up because they're *fun boys*. It's easier to just lean against the wall and look at the ceiling. Somewhere a fan roars and my ears fill up with it, and I'm scared we're in some industrial park, and then I realize how stoned I must be. My head swivels back to Wynnette and she's putting this red satin bathrobe over a gold sequin bikini, pointing to a door on the side that leads into another little dirty change room. The moustache guys are sitting at a lop-sided card table snorting lines of white stuff. I just stand beside one of them, I don't know which one, the one that looks like the other. They are both wearing identical purple sparkly bikini bathing suits now, looking just like Christmas crackers waiting to go off. The roaring starts in my ears again as one of them points to the white stuff and so I snort up a line as my eyes bulge and I'm doing the highland fling on the dirty goddamn linoleum floor in front of me.

Then we are sitting at this little table in the back, near the stage. My nose burns so bad I take an ice cube out of a drink, a drink being held by some guy in a suit who just happens to have his hand on my thigh. I hold the ice cube to the nose ring and look at him. He must be in his forties and there are lipstick marks on his face. I look away and see Wynnette dancing on the round stage, the moustache twins clapping and cheering at our table. She takes off her top and her tits jiggle. Her stomach is flat but there is this loose skin and white marks. There are cat calls from all around; I can't see anything in the audience because it's so dark, but under the stage lights you can see Wynnette is crying to the beat. Her lips are moving, she is saying, "Just Junior, Just Junior," as Abba blares. Wynnette keeps thumping and shaking her tits as all this white fog rolls around her feet. Sweat trickles down my face and into my panting mouth. The twins are clapping to the music — their hands, together and apart, over and over, mesmerizing me, and my heart pounds with every slap of their hands. Then one hand comes up and points and I follow it, past all the Liberace-style rings right to the tip of the finger, and there at the end I see a tiny Dearie, Elizabeth, and Clare standing on his fingernail. I look back to the clapping hands and fall into them, the palms as soft as all the wings of the nine choirs of angels.

FOUR

I'M SPENDING THE CHRISTMAS SHOPPING SEASON IN THE INSANE ASYLUM after my evening of festivities at the Lobster Trap. We had grown up saying, "Better not do that or you'll get locked up in the NS like Chester Chisolm," all the s sounds in his name hissed. That's what it was always called, the NS, for the Nova Scotia hospital. You don't even know the proper name of the place you are in. It's another one of those famous blackout moments, but the first time you have come to in a hospital bed, some doctor saying you overdosed on booze, coke, heroin, speed, and codeine. But you still have no memory of it, Chester the only familiar thing about the ward. You don't hiss his name here. Chester in the city to have his medication adjusted — the doctors saying it's not working quite the way it should. Chester thinking it was working fine, his trans-mu-ta-tion commencing *right the frig on schedule*, but he was all for making the doctors feel important. He thinks he's becoming a lobster.

"Gettin' a little trip out of 'er without havin' to pay for a hotel. Can't lose. Get some Christmas shoppin' done and be on the island in time for the reunion. This year I'll make'er, girl. You just wait and see," he tells you as you give him a cigarette and watch Hawaii Five-O reruns together, Chester whispering, Danno, Danno, Danno.

He was put in the local hospital one New Year's when I was ten and stupid enough to think it was funny. Davie Baxter, one of

Elizabeth's many cousins, lived over the Mountain and fished scallops and lobsters in the Bay of Fundy. He saw Chester going down the Loveless Road, this little dirt road that runs right along the cliff by the water, the last to be ploughed in the winter. Chester stark naked except for a big cape, carrying a big, antique sword that he'd taken from Earle Baltzer's Collectibles. Davie went out and yelled at Chester, but he kept going, a slow jog with his little feller hanging free, bare feet covered in dirt and snow. He showed Davie his truck stop paper placemat map of Nova Scotia — the Isle Haute, out there in the Bay of Fundy, circled in red pen. No one has lived on the island since the lighthouse burned down thirty years ago and was replaced with an automated one. But Chester was going to a family reunion, he said, out on the Isle Haute, and he needed someone to take him out in their boat, because if he didn't make it, why, he'd be disinherited. Davie told him he'd do it if he would come inside while he got into his fishing clothes, so Chester went in and paced naked by the fire, telling Davie's wife about the importance of family. Then the ambulance came and he was committed.

It was now the first week of December and I'd been back from England for one day less than a week and in the hospital for forty-eight hours. The hospital had called my family and then Elizabeth and Dearie had called them. Elizabeth and Dearie, who had shown up at the Lobster Trap just in the nick of time, the doctor had said. Your family couldn't make it down to see you though — it was full-on winter already and another blizzard had the Valley closed off from the rest of the province. But Dearie and Elizabeth came to visit, driving over the harbour to Dartmouth, Dearie listing off the details like it was an oral exam. All of us in the beige patient lounge at the end of the hall, the only place to have visitors because I wasn't allowed off the ward. There was some sort of intensive watch, with orderlies peeking in, looking right in your face, and your head would fall and stay there, your hand to your mouth, so ashamed. The elevator was locked, the staircases were locked, the windows were sealed shut and everyone around you was crazy. Maybe you were too, you didn't know about that, but you knew you were a drunk and a doper, you knew that for sure after hearing Dearie fill in the details.

You had called Elizabeth, hammered and hysterical and slurry, then Elizabeth had called Dearie. Dearie then drove to Elizabeth's house, where Elizabeth and Clare were waiting. They all piled in the van and drove to the Lobster Trap. You were making out with some business guy, sitting with two homosexual twin strippers, snorting coke and drinking Singapore slings and whisky sours while watching Wynnette Doucette do a striptease. You started to shake, sweat, and turn grey, then passed out into the arms of the midget strippers. You were taken by ambulance to the emergency. Your heart stopped. They resuscitated you. You were admitted. You regained consciousness. You were transferred to the provincial psychiatric facility in Dartmouth for observation and addictions evaluation.

And it feels likes sleepwalking, but part of you is awake, seeing, but everything distant and numb, part of you outside, watching, not able to get back in. Dearie and Elizabeth sat on either side of you on the couch, close, protecting, but you realized *they* were scared, and sitting close as though you, Serrie, could protect them from the crazy people coming in and out. A tall man wringing his hands and smiling, straight from the Bates Motel, a middle-aged lady talking about being an Interpol agent, a big fat guy sitting in a chair and staring at the television, Chester Chisolm waving to them from the doorway. They each took one of your hands and it was then you realized how cold you were, how cold and dry. You couldn't squeeze back, especially when they both started to sniffle. Then you asked them to go because you couldn't stand it, their pain, your pain, any pain. You walked them to the elevator wearing the pink fuzzy slippers and carrying the green grapes that Elizabeth had brought because that's what you bring people who are sick, *sick like*

Serrie. And the nurse had unlocked the elevator for them, a big orderly standing by, exactly the same as a bouncer in a bar but here to keep people in, not out. Dearie and Elizabeth facing you, more people getting in, standing in front of them, only Dearie's hair sticking up, Elizabeth poking her head around, holding her hand up, palm out, fingers spreading like flower petals as the doors slid together and there was nothing but the dull green paint of the closed doors, doors that quietly closed off every tiny bit of hope.

You were asleep when the whole family arrived for their only visit.

Your father stayed home, your mother told you, he said to say hello, the car ride in would have made his back stiff. Aunt Galronia cut her off, saying it was just as well he stayed home. Percy, home for Christmas, was standing there all sour and you tried to will yourself back to sleep but no luck. They were all dressed up for something important, a wedding or a funeral, Christmas shopping in the big city — dressed up for the hospital, for you.

Your mother leans over. "Serrie," she says carefully, as though it wasn't you, like maybe you were some crazy wearing a Serrie suit.

You haven't seen her since Thanksgiving.

"We brought your clothes and books," she whispers.

"Look, missy, I know you're not having a nap," says Aunt Galronia.

A few drops of her spit land on your face and you know she was staring at your nose.

"Sit up and say something to your mother."

You open your eyes and Aunt Gallie is hovering like a gargoyle.

"I'm having a nap."

"Oh, I see. Your family comes all the way from the Valley to see the likes of you and you decide to have a nap —"

"I'm not having a nap now —"

"Oh, it's perfectly clear what you're doing," she says.

"I *was* having a nap. Look, I'm sorry . . . " and your voice stops.

"Serrie, pumpkin pie, stop being silly," your mother says.

Percy comes over and waves in your face, fanning you like it was a case of sunstroke you had, not alcoholism. "So I hear you're having a nervous breakdown," he says, all casual, as though you were merely meeting by chance in the post office.

You let out a big sigh and bite your lip until you taste blood.

Your Grammie waves her cane around. "Everybody get the hell out. I'm going to have a private time with my one and only granddaughter."

You lie there while the grandmother keeps twirling her cane. She's so slight and little you don't know how she ever had babies. The grandmother spins the cane like she's the head majorette in the Apple Blossom Parade. She bellows for everybody to shut up and go to the cafeteria so you can have a few minutes to compose yourself for company. Galronia protests that they are family, not company, but Grammie isn't having any of it.

They leave for the cafeteria without a word, Gallie looking back over her shoulder. You get dressed and go down to the visitor's lounge with the grandmother who sits down and takes out a cigarette. Chester wobbles in and lights Grammie up.

"Thank you, Chester dear. Now you go off and find your marbles," she says.

And Chester trots out one more time as you lean against the window and Grammie leans back in her chair.

"Well, my dear, why don't you join me. You know you can't get anything past this old girl. They're just upset, Serrie, that's why they are so rude. Lord, though, you'd think one would have some good sense, at least enough perspicuity to know to keep their mouths shut."

She passes you a cigarette and with her old wobbly hand and good manners, lights yours. She uses wooden matches, and you notice that Grammie's hands shake now, as she hits the match on the little box and it pops alive. You lean in to make it easier for her and see how faded her eyes are now, behind the glasses. It's the first time you see it, that Grammie is old. She pats your knee.

So you sit there smoking with your Grammie while she pulls her new coffee table book out of a giant handbag, flipping through the glossy pictures of the Scottish Highlands. She tells you all about her bridge club and how boring the Reverend Rafuse's sermons are getting, that she wants some exciting preaching in the church to keep her from nodding off and snoring as this seems to be disturbing other members of the congregation. Then she says you aren't the only hoyden in the family, she stole a Model T Ford from her brother, Irvine, back when she was doing her nurse's training in Boston. "By the time I came back, he'd moved to California, working on some man's farm. Don't think he ever knew I took it. Poor old Irvine. Serrie, you must get your ways from me." You sit and nod and smile and say yeah, yeah, and she pats your cheek and you weep in her boney arms because you know she is the only person alive who loves you no matter how stupid and feeling sorry for yourself you are, she loves all of you, especially the parts that you would like to take a jack hammer to. She says you just need a rest but you know that no matter how old and wise she is, you need more than a rest and there is no happily ever after, not even your Grammie can give you that.

The rest of the family return with tea. The visit is almost over and no one has mentioned why you are here. And no one has mentioned Thanksgiving. No one will. You talk about the weather, Christmas craft sales, holiday specials at the Micmac Mall that you read about in flyers left in the lounge. You think you need some better reading material. Your aunt loves them however; nothing like a sale. Percy tells you about his latest project, building a model of some trestle bridge he's been researching. This one is a commission for a museum.

Gallie beams. "Imagine, Percy's already getting paying work in his field and he hasn't even graduated yet," she says.

Percy rolls his eyes. He gives you a Nova Scotian tartan ball cap with a picture of the trestle sewn on the front and just sits beside you, with his hand on your shoulder while your mother sits on the other side with the aunt's hand on her shoulder. Other patients shuffle by with their visitors but you and your company just sit quietly on the sofa, posed for a family Christmas card shot. Then your Grammie pounds her cane and announces it's almost time to hit the road because she doesn't like driving after dark in the winter.

Midway through the first week, after I've had time to settle, I meet with the psychiatrist. He does rounds in the morning, and appointments in the afternoon. We'll meet three times a week. He tells you that you are primarily in here for observation. He asks questions and questions and questions and always ends with *that's all for today*. We meet in a room with a table and chair, it's not even his office, just a room on the ward for appointments. There are no pictures, no calenders, no signs of personality, just institutional blandness and efficiency, just like the doctor.

The doctor is what they'd call a fruitcake back in the Valley and you bet he never goes there. He always seems really nervous, talking fast, eyes darting about the room. He pulls up a chair so you're sitting face to face. You stare out the window. No big desk between you and him, and you hate that. He keeps asking a zillion questions about your drinking and drug use and you answer but you're getting tired of answering. You ask the doctor for a pass for the courtyard. He asks you why you stare out the window. You apologize. He asks you another question. You shrug at the psychiatrist; that should be a good answer to whatever it was he asks — you don't have the slightest idea.

A few days later you are walking down the hall, past the patient pay phone, to the lounge to watch TV before bed. Chester is making bird chirps and you look up. He hands you the phone, smiling.

"Nice girl, that Florida Dear is." Chester garbles as you take the receiver and lean face first into the corner. You don't say much, you're fine, you say to her, and she complains about her father and good old Neddie, how much she hates it, that all they talk about is money and business. You look at the scuff marks on the floor. Dearie sounds angry, but under it she is tired and sad; this makes you tired and sad and you want to hang up. She says she doesn't want to study business anymore, she doesn't want to be an accountant, and on and on. You are walking through an orange orchard, flowers that smell Florida-citrus-sweet, picking juicy fruit off the branches. Dearie's voice comes to the orchard and brings you back — she wants to have a craft store maybe, anything but study Commerce. She asks what you think she should do and you say you don't know, whatever she thinks is best. She doesn't like that answer and says you are the last one to give advice.

Later, watching television, you wish Dearie would just leave you alone.

The doctor wants to know about home, where you are from. You tell him your friends Dearie and Elizabeth call it Dog Fuck Nowhere. He nods and asks about your childhood. You don't know what to tell him. "What do you want to know?" you ask.

"Whatever you think is important," he says.

Dearie's boobs had grown years before mine and when mine finally started to poke out when I was fifteen, I asked my mother about a bra. You don't need one, she said, an undershirt will be fine, they aren't really growing. What do you say to that? Dearie decided I had to wear a training bra so I wouldn't have guys pointing out my high beams in the hallway at school.

"What am I training my tits for?"

"For real bras."

"Then why don't they make small real bras?"

"Because real bras aren't small, that would be an undershirt."

"Why I am supposed to be having big tits?"

"Because a woman has tits. You still don't have your period so you have to at least have tits."

She would give me these beige padded things that cut into my flesh and made it look like I was wearing little pillows on my chest, pillows made of stiff chunks of foam. Dearie said bras weren't about looking natural, they were about keeping *them* in. They cut into me, little scabs drying on my ribs. I threw the bras in Cyril's weekly barrel fire but didn't tell Dearie. I started wearing big sweaters and let *them* out.

Who invented those kind of bras anyway, you ask the psychiatrist. He looks at you and then makes a note. Then he looks at you again and shrugs. He doesn't know about bras.

After the bra stuff, the blood came, the monthlies, as Galronia calls them, like some old bag out of another time. It came in August, I was fifteen, and it was just after the graveyard driving fiasco. It had been looking like I'd have my driver's license before my period. Dearie was always saying maybe I had an ovarian cyst that was blocking everything up, Elizabeth telling her not to say things like that. Dearie got her periods when she was twelve. Elizabeth was fourteen, and me, stuck in perpetual adolescence, listening to them talk about it, with only honourary membership in the *blood club*, as Elizabeth called it. Dearie blowing smoke on her every time she called it that. It was disgusting. Elizabeth hated it being called "period." She started calling it *the red friend*, which made Dearie roll her eyes and say period was better. They'd argue and I'd be explaining to Dearie what a euphemism was, Dearie puffing on a smoke, saying that it was words like that were no doubt jamming me up.

The doctor listens, holding his notepad. Maybe it was drinking that loosened you up, you tell him. Drinking was all you seemed to do once you were fourteen. Your sporty days fell behind as the days of smokes and rum took over, as you became a woman.

That day of bleeding: my mother in the backyard stretched in her chaise lounge listening to Gordon Lightfoot drone away about the "Wreck of the Edmund Fitzgerald" from the stereo inside. I whispered *it* had come.

She looked up from her magazine. "What has come?" she asked.

"It," I told her, "*it*."

She looked back to her magazine, it was most likely a bit of diarrhea, she said. I was so mad I burned the stained panties in the trash barrel fire. I stuffed toilet paper in my underpants and went to see Grammie in her flower garden deadheading the roses.

"Oh, yes, I see," she remarked, "Got cramps then, Serrie?"

"Cramps?"

"Yes, indeed, cramps." Aunt Galronia walked over from the mock orange bush in rubber boots with her own giant clippers wearing this weird-looking orange terry cloth dress with a zipper up the front, a beach throw, as she called it.

You cross your legs in the chair and tell the doctor that Galronia hates buying new clothes, every piece of summer stuff she has is left over from the sixties, even this big flowery bathing cap that she wore those times the family would picnic over at the shore in Lupin Cove and she'd go in the water. It was amazing she could float, all skinny like that, and you'd see her out in that Bay of Fundy water that was freezing even in the summer, white rubber cap with pink and blue flowers, spindly arms going around like a windmill, waving at the Ryans in their fishing boat. The doctor writes something down and you go back to menstruation.

If Gallie could take the cold of the Bay, she could take the pain of womanhood. She had no sympathy for me. "Of course it comes with cramps. It's not like you just got a suntan. You'll get used to it . . . well, it's the anniversary of the King's death. What a tragedy, I tell you."

"Lord God, Galronia, you're pruning, not destroying. Easy, easy. Now who's gone and died?"

"Elvis, Mum — it's the anniversary."

I stood there squirming with the underwear going up my crack while Grammie stood up, rubbed her neck, and brushed a long strand of grey hair off her forehead.

"Lord God, Galronia, you'd think he'd been your man. Don't you have better things to do? Now you clip those roses and make sure the stems are long enough for my cut-crystal vase, the tall one in the right corner of the china cabinet."

Grammie gave me money and sent me up to the drugstore to buy pads. Wynnette Doucette was working, not Elizabeth or Dearie, and she waved as I came in. Wynnette Doucette, before her life went totally crazy like her long black hair with the frantic spiral perm. She asked about Cyril's outhouses, waiting for an answer so I knew she wasn't being rude, and I whispered, "Fine, just fine, it's all fine." The other cashier, Mrs. McIver, whom Galronia calls the town hypocrite, came up and said she heard he'd brought a new one from the South Shore. I was in 4-H with Mrs. McIver's kids, in the gardening project, "the wildflower girl" our project leader called me. And Mrs. McIver smiled in this your-father's-a-freak way and then held forth on her own superior lawn ornaments, these jeesly dwarf things. There wasn't one thing on our property that was a joke. If Cyril heard the word *hobby* he'd sit outside for hours looking at the sky with emptied-out eyes — he had only passions.

If you drove by the house on the Lupin Cove Road it looked like some kind of gallery, Martha's gardens of tall, swoopy flowers, prototype solar panels strapped on the house, the outhouses all about. Once some tourists stopped and called to me from their car window — I could tell they were tourists by their fancy mirrored sunglasses like in the magazines at Melanson's Drugstore. I walked down the driveway and the driver smiled.

"How much?"

"How much what?" I frowned.

"How much to come and see?"

"See what?"

"To see your museum."

Staring from the ditch, my own eyes looking back from the designer aviator glasses.

"Mister, that's no museum, that's my home."

And he turned all red and drove away, leaving a cloud of dust behind, as my father walked up and asked what they wanted. "Way to the city, to Halifax," I said. "Musta took a wrong turn."

But Mrs. McIver wanted to talk about Elvis more than Cyril Sullivan on the Lupin Cove Road living in his dead auntie's house with his retarded family and so I headed for the feminine protection aisle, whatever that's supposed to mean. A box of super plus tampons so no one would know it was my first time because first timers use pads — that's what Dearie said. Victoria Gibson, another clerk, from the only black family in Foster, came down the aisle with a pricing machine in her arms. I picked strawberries with her mother, Mabel, at Baxter's Farm every June. She could pick faster than any one of you and always picked the rows clean, smoking a cigarette between her teeth as she went up and down the rows. Victoria was the youngest of fourteen kids.

"These scented ones here are on sale, Seraphina," Victoria said and handed me a pink box that smelled like aerosol rose air freshener and kept going to whatever aisle she was going to price merchandise in.

Before I could make it back to the cash, the cosmetician, Geraldine McMahon with the long bottle-blonde hair, grabbed me and said she would give me a free make-over. I could hear my mother saying make-up was ridiculous and Galronia saying only tarts and Indians needed to have their faces lacquered, but Geraldine just put me in the make-over stool and did me up like a paint-by-number. She took a Polaroid and it didn't even look like Seraphina Islay Sullivan, but a movie star. I felt this happy feeling, maybe bleeding was worth it if I could look this hot, but then I felt itchy between my legs and didn't want to drip on the make-over stool, so I went to pay. I was almost at the cash when the Reverend Rafuse came by with some shaving cream.

"Going to a party, Seraphina, out on the town?"

I looked at my feet and hid the photo. "No, sir."

He smiled, leaned on the shelf with all the aftershave, and flicked his jaw. "Well, dear, it looks like you are prepared to go somewhere." And then all the bottles of Old Spice and Hai Karate and Brut fell down with a big bang and Geraldine came running, while I zipped up to the counter where Wynnette Doucette rang the tampons through, saying "It's hard being a woman, hey Serrie," me nodding, because whatever that meant, I was sure she would know.

Back at my Grammie's, I hid behind the old barn garage, next to the humus pile, hoping Gordie wasn't going to arrive home for a surprise visit and come out to the garage looking for his abandoned girlie magazines that Gallie had no doubt already found and burned. The blood was dripping out my shorts and down my legs. I wiped with some fresh-cut grass, all soft. No one could see me, so I pulled down my pants and tried to shove a tampon in and up. A blinding pain went through me as it slid in and I fell over into the leaves and compost, there to die in all my stunted glory. The shiny white cardboard applicator stuck out from my pussy like a stake and my whole insides felt bruised. Trying to pull it out was even worse — it was impossible — so I just lay there weeping into the rotting apple and potato scraps. I would never even be able to have sex, let alone a baby, all clogged up with a piece of cotton, broken in by a tampon. I wobbled into Grammie's house, hoping they were having a Sunday nap in the August heat but there they were at the kitchen table, sipping iced tea, still in gardening clothes. They just stared and then I remembered the make-up and put my hands to my face. Leaves and compost stuck to all the powder and foundation. I crept by their shock and went upstairs, right to the bathroom, Gallie hollering after me that there was some explaining needed. For the first time I hollered back, "I shouldn't have to buy my own protection anyway, it's just the underpants being protected, not me," and then silence before Gallie started yelling that Martha should be taking care of this, Gallie had a boy and this wasn't her problem, and Grammie bellowing: "Everyone shut the hell up."

I ran a bath and was getting in when Grammie knocked at the door. She was old then, too, but just with grey hair and wrinkles, and she came in. I stood there with my stupid fifteen-year-old body, water around my calves, blood smudge wing prints right down my thighs. Grammie helped me sit down and I started blubbering away again. She washed my back, patting me on the head and twirling my long hair up into a bun. The photo was on the toilet seat and she said I looked some pretty, I was growing up just fine. That made me cry even more, Grammie being so nice. I told her how the tampon hurt and she shook her head, saying I was too young to use them, and she helped me pull it out. I thought that Wynnette Doucette wasn't kidding when she said it was hard being a woman. Grammie drove me home and while she went in and yelled at my mother, I went out and burned the Polaroid, Percy watching from his bedroom window. The picture curled up, lost in purple and orange fire, me and my war paint all burned up.

The psychiatrist is just staring at you and you know he's glad he's a man. He nods, slow this time, chin going up and down, forehead wrinkling: "That's all for today."

Just before supper you check at the nurses' station — he has changed your chart. You go walking around outside in the late afternoon, alone in the courtyard, smoking. Cold aching fingers waving up at Chester in the window, the woman-in-black who is your roommate staring down at you but not even blinking when you wave up to her. You feel stupid and take a drag, looking at the sky. A sweat breaks out all over your body, you can feel it soaking into the crotch of your panties, down your back and soaking into the wool turtleneck, your feet clammy in your boots. Your cigarette shakes in between your stained knuckles. You are freezing and sweating at the same time, and you know finally how scared you are, fear is contained in you, just as you are held behind these brick walls, the walls the pale sun slips behind.

The doctor wants to know about high school days. You tell him it's more accurate to call them drinking days. He nods and writes that down.

High school was about being cold, poor, drunk, and bussed to Fundy Central Regional High School. I just drank those times away, you know, if you can't drop out, then black out. Aside from square dancing, and flowers, it was my only hobby, not that it was much fun after the blackouts started. In Nova Scotia, the legal age to buy booze was nineteen and we were only sixteen: legal to drive but not legal to drink and certainly not legal to go into the Nova Scotia Liquor Commission and buy our own bottle. Sometimes Elizabeth's cousin Laird would get us a bottle of Captain Morgan's dark rum, that was before he got married and moved over to the bay shore. We'd all go down to the cemetery and sit there, me and Dearie smoking, Elizabeth singing with the radio. Sometimes we would use Dearie's van but usually it was Elizabeth's car, her father's car, because Dearie would inevitably pick Elizabeth up, come over to the Lupin Cove Road to pick me up, and then say the tank was empty. We'd go to get gas and then she'd say her purse was empty. And her pack of smokes was always down to the last one. She got her cheap ways from her father and Grammie says he got his cheap ways from his pain after Dearie's mother died, that winter after my family moved home to Foster. His pain turned him sour, rotting him, until he was as jolly as a piece of green meat with worms.

When they got back from Maine, Dearie's mother was feeling really sick, and was losing weight. At first she wouldn't go to the doctor because she said she liked losing weight, even if she felt bad, it was better than a diet. But she finally had to see the doctor and he put her in the hospital the same day. The pancreatic cancer had spread everywhere. Mrs. Melanson knew she was sick, Dearie said, she knew inside, and that was why they had gone to Maine for the whole summer, so she could say goodbye. She just hadn't bothered to tell anyone that was what she was doing, Dearie would say, jaw rigid.

Mrs. Melanson was dead before Christmas. Grammie said it was then that Mr. Melanson got mean and cheap. Elizabeth said he would come down to Baxter's Farm and argue about strawberries, stacking berries in his boxes so high it was like two boxes, arguing for a half-hour that if he could get that many in one, he was only paying for one. He started buying up property everywhere, put his mother in a home when she didn't want to go. He said a housekeeper was too expensive and so off she went to the Manor, where she shared a room with three other ladies, all of them senile and howling. Fancy Mosher's mother was a cleaning lady at the Manor and she told Gallie in the library that the only family who came to visit Mrs. Melanson was nine-year-old Dearie, walking over after school every day with a knapsack full of tea biscuits that she had made just for her grandmother, walking up that big hill, cheeks red, huffing and puffing. I remember Dearie hurrying away after school when the rest of us were staying for track and field practice. I thought it was because she was chubby and already had boobs at the age of ten, she didn't want them jiggling up and down, all the boys laughing.

Dearie's father sold Grandma Melanson's house, and all her furniture and dishes; all the old stuff, except for what Dearie inherited, was bought up by Mr. Burgess, but Mr. Melanson made him pay pretty for it. And when she found out all her stuff was sold off, Grandmother Melanson quietly died. Dearie would go down there, on the anniversary of the death, to put flowers on the grave, and Elizabeth and I would go with her, standing there while she put them down.

We had our share of pain but weren't cheap — we just didn't have a sweet cent. When Cyril lost his job and it was one-income living again, the lights in the Spinster Sullivan's house went out, so to speak. The house had to have a new roof and it needed new shingles. The verandah was propped up with bricks. The house needed new windows on the north side, where the wind was coming straight through and blowing the curtains out like they were on the clothesline, but they weren't, they were inside the frigging house. Almost the entire house had to be closed off except for the kitchen in the back, the family room and the bedrooms. It was impossible to take a shower because there wasn't a shower and it was impossible to take a bath in the old claw-foot tub because it was so cold in there. I'd have these huge fights with Martha about having to wear so many layers inside that there was absolutely no point in ever taking your coat off when you came through the door. And to protest, I wore a big old fur cape of Aunt Ruth's, and a moth-eaten buffalo hat, at the supper table, her screaming that I had to stop being so immature, then screaming at my father that they should sell the house but they wouldn't get a thing for it because it was falling the hell apart, and Percy would be glaring at me over his pork chop, with his three sweaters on. I would escape to the parlour, where I'd build a fire in the fireplace until Cyril told me there wasn't enough firewood to keep that many fires going, one cord was gone already and the winter wasn't halfway through. So I would have to sit there with them in the family room, trying (and giving up) to tune in the television, reading and doing homework on the floor by the fire, saying "yeah, yeah" to all of Cyril's ideas for new inventions, listening to Percy's obscure facts, and Martha hollering, "You all have to start pulling your weight around this pigsty," that she couldn't keep doing everything by herself. But no matter how much I helped, it was never enough. It would take a long time to figure out it could never be enough.

I had to come down out of the turret while they put in new windows which weren't new, storm windows from an old house like ours that had been demolished halfway between Paradise and West Randolph; Cyril had heard about it when he was off scouting outhouses. I'd spend every weekend at Elizabeth's house, to get warm, and also because Elizabeth's bedroom was on the ground floor so we could sneak in drunk and high without waking anyone up. I'd drink in cars, at parties, Elizabeth at the wheel of her car, or Dearie's van, so drunk it was surprising we weren't all drunk-driving-dead before graduation.

The nerdy doctor nods. "Yes," he says, "drinking and driving is very dangerous." He makes another note, caps his pen, and opens his mouth.

"That's all for today," you say.

He shuts his mouth, pushes back his hair, and looks at you. "Is there anything else you'd like to tell me, Seraphina?" It's the first time he's used your name. You realize you don't know his but you don't ask, just shake your head.

In the next session, the nervous doctor tells you there are no signs of depression and he doesn't want to prescribe medication. "You are," he says, "very sad, and angry, but you are not depressed."

There's a feeling of mild disappointment that it can't be fixed with a pill, and you want him to shut up about the sad business. How would he know?

"You are very young for your age," he says.

You feel insulted, but part of you, *that part* of you, agrees. So you sit there and he asks if you think you have a problem with drugs and alcohol and you say, yes, you do think you have a problem. And you mean it.

He nods.

He gives you a pass to go to AA meetings in the hospital every night. People come in and put them on, he tells you, they put on the meetings. When asked what a meeting is like, he says you are going to find out soon and you can tell him. You say no. He looks at you and says he will take away your courtyard privileges and your off-grounds privileges, which he is just about to give you, and that's all for today.

You go. You sit there and listen. It doesn't make much sense, but then you can't listen to people talk for more than a few minutes without the words layering over each other until it's a jumble of sound and syllables, morphemes, you think, your college brain clicking on now and then, a thoroughly unreliable lighthouse. You are the youngest person at the meeting and you keep going back so you can get off the locked ward just for a bit. And because you like it there in the meeting. You don't know why, you won't know why for a long time, but there, you know you can relax, your body knows it before the lighthouse clicks on and you sag into the old armchair. And you also know you don't want to drink anymore, which has nothing to do with AA or your family or your friends or the hospital. You are scared you will die next time. The last thing you want is a drink. A next time could mean not waking up in a hospital but waking up in a coffin or an urn.

It's a closed-discussion meeting, for alcoholics only, or people with a desire to stop drinking. That's the only requirement for membership, *a desire to stop drinking*. That's it. No forms to sign, money to pay, references to give, just desire, big desire, and you've got that. They read it in the preamble that starts every meeting, this preamble from a big blue book with the eponymous title, *Alcoholics Anonymous*, or the *Big Book*, as most people seem to affectionately call it. They read the Twelve Steps, too, the foundation of the program, the nice lady beside you says. There is a big poster of the Steps on the wall and you follow along as they are passed around the table on a laminated poster. Everyone takes a turn reading one — unless you don't want to, and then you just say, "pass," which you always say, but first, like everyone else, you say your name is Seraphina and you are an alcoholic. You don't remember the Steps, even though they are everywhere. You can barely remember your own name and none of theirs stick except for Big Bob, the man chairing the meeting, this guy with a giant swirly moustache. He's tall, and kind of old, but you can't figure out how old because he's really fit and healthy, but has grey hair and is covered in tattoos and you don't associate tattoos with fit and healthy and grey hair. Big Bob laughs this big booming laugh. He is all dressed in black and it makes you think he's going to be just like your roommate and you have to be ready because he'll try to catch you off guard. You're right. After the first meeting he comes up to you and reaches out to your hand, saying he is very glad to see you here. You didn't expect his shake to be warm and firm and you pull your hand away and light a cigarette.

"The black outfit is a giveaway," you blow out at him. If there's anything good about being locked up it's learning to stand up for yourself. He laughs, boom-boom-boom, and claps his hands. Applause. You just keep smoking.

He tells you, "Yes, I do dress the part. You know us ar-tistes."

You don't know them ar-tistes. Where does he think you grew up, in Paris or Rome or something? You tell him the only thing you know of art is pictures of Greek urns and the oil paintings Dearie's mother did, copies of paintings by Monet, Cezanne, Van Gogh, and even El Greco's *Toledo in a Storm*, all from her deluxe-colour calendar, "Monthly Works of Art by Twelve Old Masters." She framed them and sold them for two hundred and fifty dollars at the mall in Bigelow Bay and in the hair salon in Foster. When you asked Dearie what the difference between a copy and a forgery was, she told you her mother had signed her own name to them, not the Old Masters', that was the difference between a copy and a forgery. Big Bob is grinning away at you and you think if you don't get out soon, he'll blow you down with his laugh. Maybe there's no difference between an artist and a nut. He tells you he is an instructor at the Nova Scotia College of Art and Design, that he is a recovering alcoholic . . . just like you. He may as well have pounded you with a piece of wrought-iron fence. It's okay for you to say it, but not for a stranger — but it's a whole room of people just like you that makes you feel good and bad at the same time. Your stomach cramps and you shove your cigarette at him. He takes it, like it's normal to hand him a half-finished smoke, and he says it will all make sense eventually, *one day at a time*. As you leave, he watches, holding the smoke like it's a paintbrush. A big boom-boom laugh. So much for being en-fucking-garde, you think as you creep down the empty hall, hearing the odd scream and wail, which disturbs you far less than Big Bob's laughing. The night orderlies let you in the locked ward.

Back to your room to find a bouquet of flowers from the Reverend Rafuse wishing you a speedy recovery. You sniff the flowers and smell summer. There are purple irises in the bouquet and you wonder where irises grow in the winter. There is a bouquet from Burgess Antiques and you take it to the nursing station, saying you don't need two in your room. You curl up in bed, the middle room-mate crying softly, the other one muttering about Lucifer, you not knowing how anything is going to work out anymore. You fall asleep with an iris in your hand. When you wake up, the dressed-in-black roommate is standing over you and when you offer her the wilted iris, she crinkles her nose and leaves. It's better than garlic or a crucifix.

The doctor wants to know about boyfriends. There was only one boyfriend in high school. You don't count the one-night things, the ones you can't really remember. The doctor just sits there.

I'd met Trevor in the library, where I was reading and he was doing his detention. Only once did I bring him back to the house. Late March, the last year of high school, the year that took as long to pass as the Roman Empire did to fall. Trevor kept asking to come over and I finally said yes. He rode home on the bus with me, Percy already in Toronto at university. Trevor didn't say a word about the outhouses when we walked in the driveway, just nodding at them, waving at my father when he appeared over the roof a new out-house, Issac's Harbour North, hammer in one hand, saw in the other, like some psycho out of a horror movie.

Trevor and I sat there in the kitchen shivering in the cold. The fire had burned down low with Cyril outside working all day, me trying to stoke it up, Cyril coming in to get it going. "Good try, Serrie," he had said, not a word about the room full of wood smoke. Trevor talked about shingles and stuff and then my father went back out and drove off in the truck to Foster to the hardware store.

Trevor held my hand by the stove. "I thought he was going to smell like shit or something."

I pulled my hand away.

"You never talk about him or anything. You don't talk about home at all."

"Like you do all the time, Trev."

He hadn't seen his father since he was three, even though his dad was a bartender in Bigelow Bay and played guitar in some old-guy band that performed all over the Valley. Trevor was musical too, a natural guitarist, just like his dad.

"Running with that boy," was what Gallie and my mother called it. That Trevor was a loser was one of the few things they agreed on. The only thing keeping me from full loser status was my high marks. Good grades made me untouchable, the honour roll some sort of evidence that whatever was wrong was irrelevant, unimportant, a phase. Not that there were too many signs then, aside from watering down my mother's gin. She'd just buy more, only confronting me once, me lying, saying maybe it was Cyril falling off the wagon. Hearing her go at him in the kitchen, his shock enough to have me get booze from Elizabeth's cousin after that and keep it at the church.

Trevor was a great hockey player until there was just one too many falls on his knees at after-game parties. He was always positive about everything, even as his world blew away, turning to sand when he made the odd clutch at it. And loser or not, he was big and hard and strong and good looking (in that James Dean way, Dearie said, because she was into old movies in high school). It was the only nice thing she said about him, even though Trevor was always friendly to everyone, failing because he didn't go to class very much, sleeping in the woods in the back of the school. He lived with his mother in a tiny apartment in Bigelow Bay, sharing a bedroom with his old bunk beds in it, her on the bottom, Trev on the top. Sometimes she'd bring home some man and they'd go at it in the bottom bunk, shaking both tiers of the bed. Trev would jump down and take off in the middle of the night. He'd show up at school with bags the colour of dead leaves under his eighteen-year-old bloodshot eyes. Once, just after we started seeing each other, I was sitting on the beach at a shore party, away from the fire and the rest of the party, and Trevor said she had sold her bed, and most of the other furniture, but not his bunk beds because she was sentimental about his youth. And then he laughed and took a drink of beer, and laughed some more and then he was crying, as I went into my first long blackout.

The doctor asks how often you black out when you drink. Most of the time, you tell him, and then continue.

When he'd been at my house, he had looked all around. "You've got a real house here."

"What's a real house? And anyway, for how long . . . it's falling apart. Just look around."

"At least it's not an apartment. And your mother's got a real job, working for the government. Pension, right?"

"She hates it."

"How do you know she hates it?"

"Because every morning with coffee she says, 'I hate my goddamn job.' That's how I know she hates her goddamn job."

"Maybe she should get another goddamn job." He gave me his slow lazy smile.

I took the lid off the stove and shoved in another stick and opened the draft all the way and then started shoving the wood with the poker to perk the fire up. "She can't get another goddamn job. That's it for her. And you know . . . with my father . . . she has to work. And with us. And then all the money goes into paying for the car and the truck and the house and us and for savings. She says we're just another version of the working poor."

We went out back to Number Nine and smoked a joint. We had fumbly sex there against the wall, bits of wood splintering in my back and butt, bits of blood there on the wall, me too high to even know it hurt. After, when we both stopped laughing, Trevor banged on all the outhouses. Cyril drove in then and Trevor showed him how they made great drums. My father was smiling and I knew he liked the company. Trevor fit right in, that is, until my mother drove in, hands on her hips, staring at Trevor, grunting hello, not asking him for supper. I walked him outside to the road and he hitchhiked somewhere, not home. My mother said I was not going to be dating losers like Trevor Smith, I was too young to be dating — period. I had whispered that I was seventeen and needed a regular life, like any other seventeen-year-old girl, that I couldn't be a kid forever, and then stomped outside wondering where Trev would go for supper.

Dearie came over after to have an end-of-day-smoke out back by Number Four, Malignant Cove. She would call it the tumour shed and we both thought it was really damn funny.

"My father says young people are idiots," Dearie said as she took a drag.

What alarmed me was how she seemed to accept this without considering the implications. And then she held forth on Trevor as a loser and how she wanted to lose her virginity.

"What does it feel like?" she asked.

"What does what feel like?" I said, knowing what she was after.

"You know . . . sex?"

"Like falling to pieces and being melded back together," I told her.

She rolled her eyes and went on about the party on the weekend. I was leaning against the outhouse and still felt sticky between my legs as I looked up at the sky and thought about Trevor out there in the night.

You tell the psychiatrist the best thing about Dearie was that she could talk forever and all you had to do was nod, and make little throat noises. You didn't even have to listen past a certain point. She didn't seem to care about that.

Trevor was really stoned after that and even Elizabeth told me not to waste my time. Elizabeth had a different boyfriend every month and she'd toss them aside like cherry pits. I would talk on the phone late at night, until Martha screamed to get off, and then I would scream and carry on the conversation. One night Trev called after he hadn't been in school for a week. He'd missed exams and I hadn't heard from him the whole time. Some old guy who wore suits had moved in with his mom, and then he was going on and on about playing in a band. He started singing some song he said he just wrote, especially for me, for Seraphina Sullivan, and then he started to cry. I knew, sitting there at seventeen, that he was never going to play in a band that played anywhere but local Valley bars, if he could even manage that. He was going to be just like his drunken father, just like Dearie predicted. He started telling me that I was really smart and would do something great. The wind banged away at the glass in my room as I sat there holding the receiver out, thinking all I could do was read and smoke, as he babbled on. His mother had taken off, the landlord had evicted him, and he was going down the road to Toronto to make it big in music. When I hung up, he was still rambling on about Jimi Hendrix and being up in the Watch Tower. And as I turned out the light, the problem was clear: no one was ever in Trev's watchtower to start with.

You go to the lounge to have a smoke after and Chester wobbles up, all excited from talking to Dearie. He starts flapping around the room and you ask him if he likes birds. He likes to eat turkeys at

Christmas, he tells you, as you peer at him from under your tartan ball cap, the thing that keeps your shaved head warm. He starts chirping. You wonder if his medication will ever kick in. He keeps tweeting away and you want to wring his neck.

"Look, Chester, I thought you were some kind of lobster. What is it, lobster or bird?" you snap. "You have to know what you are, for God's sake." Shouting, "you have to know what you are," knowing the shouts are really at you, but you can't help it. So loud it can't be your voice. A nurse peeks in the room and immediately stop.

Chester stops flying. Wings collapsing all around. "Well, yes, why yes, I am a crustacean, I'm no bird." He sits down in an armchair and crosses his arms, staring at his shoes.

"I'm just pretendin' to be a bird. Just tryin' to have a good goddamn time in this here place. It's just fine and dandy to do them charades and the role-play and what have you in the group therapy but do it yourself and look what happens — people think you're insane."

He starts slowly rocking back and forth in the chair. You feel weepy, it is too easy to crush Chester, like stepping on a daisy. You light Chester a cigarette but he refuses.

"I'm some mad at you, Serrie," Chester says.

You apologize and offer the cigarette again. He shakes his head and you shove it at him. He takes it with his thumb and yellow index finger and curls the rest around, smoking privately through his fist, not looking at you. You tell him all about your father's bird feeder out back by Number Nine. He likes hearing about the bird feeder and starts humming, so soft you could only hear if you were right beside him, like you are.

"Someday maybe I can show you, Chester, maybe someday." But you know that day will never come.

You are so skinny now that the bathtub is torturous, shivering chicken skin, butt bones grinding into porcelain. You switch to showers and check out the stall. The door doesn't lock, but the hinges squeak, so you'll hear it if the creepy roommate decides to drop by. You take off your flannel shirt and sweatpants. Naked except for slippers and your hospital bracelet, you turn the shower on and lean in to adjust the taps. The water stops. You pull back and the water starts again, so you lean back in. The water stops. You jump back and the water sprays down as you see yourself in the bathroom mirror, naked and scrawny, water dripping down from the brim of your ball cap, steel in your belly, dark circles under your eyes. You look like the kind of person that would make children reach for their mother's hands, and old ladies cross to the other side of the street.

The nervous doctor asks how you are finding being in the hospital. You tell him you are enjoying it. It's like the world has slipped away, no problems, nothing to worry about.

"I see," he says. And then he asks if that's what life is, having no problems, no worries, the world just slipping by. You laugh and he just sits there, face like a tombstone, and then asks you to explain why you find that funny. He's not mad or anything, just very scientific, which brings more laughter. You are no more important than a crossword in the weekend paper. You tell him life is defined by problems and worries, that's all you know. He asks how that makes you feel and you want to push him out the window.

"Does that make you angry," he asks. You shake your head. He nods. You wait for "that's all for today," but he just keeps looking.

You stare back.

He shakes his foot.

You just sit there.

He clears his throat.

You snap your neck and say, "All I know about psychiatry is from *One Flew Over the Cuckoo's Nest*. My mother says there are no movies like seventies movies."

He leans forward. "You can imagine how far that particular film set back the field of psychiatry," he says with a tight little smile.

And you automatically grin back at the doctor, who uncrosses his legs, runs his hand through his short hair, and shakes the smile off his face. He has bags under his eyes, the doctor is tired. But he's still listening.

In mid-spring of grade twelve year, sometime while I was out drinking and smoking dope with Dearie and Elizabeth, when Cyril was in his invention shed inventing, and Percy was off in Toronto finishing his second year of university, my mother decided to sell off the Spinster Sullivan's Limoges china tea set, circa 1900. It was white porcelain china with a pink rose design. There was a whole dinner set, too, twelve place settings, including three vegetable terrines, two serving platters, and a gravy boat, and it was worth good money, enough to pay for a new roof — depending on the price Mr. Burgess would give for it.

And that was just the beginning. "There's a veritable fortune in that house," Mr. Burgess had told Martha on the phone that Sunday afternoon when my father was out. Mr. Burgess would be happy to help her out. I was listening in on the upstairs phone at the end of the hall by the window that looked out onto the Lupin Cove Road. The North Mountain was greening, little leaves creeping out, robins at the bird feeders my mother filled, buying giant bags of sunflower seeds, storing them in the back storm porch by the winter boots. Cyril was off at the university library, researching wind power, and my mother had been cleaning up the kitchen all morning while I sat up in my room reading. I would be going over to Dearie's later in the afternoon to sit around and smoke. The phone had clanged and I'd slipped down the spiral stairs in woollen socks to answer but Martha and I picked it up at the same time.

Mr. Burgess spoke before either of us did. "Well, good afternoon, Martha Meissner. This is Clarence Burgess."

It was strange how people acted like Martha had never married. She'd always be a Meissner.

"Clarence. So how would this afternoon be, say around 2:30? I'm sending Serrie over. Too much to do here."

They didn't know I was listening in.

"Why, that's fine, Martha. I'm just back from church. The wife and girls are off to the city for the afternoon, having supper with their grandparents."

Mr. Burgess was a bit older than my mother, mid-sixties or so, and his three daughters were all younger than me, still at the Foster School. Sometimes I would see them at Melanson's Drugstore buying lipstick and hair spray. There was an older brother from Mr. Burgess's first marriage, about Gordie's age, though no one's ever seen him. Grammie said he didn't get along with his father, never forgave him for leaving his mother for a younger woman. Mr. Burgess had brown hair with manly bits of grey, and he looked too much like a celebrity for it to be accidental. He was big and in great shape, Gallie said, from working out in a gym in Bigelow Bay. Grammie said Mr. Burgess was afraid of getting old, that most people were afraid of getting old because there would come a point where time itself would force you to look back and be accountable and it was so much easier to be young and carefree. Nothing more pathetic than those resisting the passage of time, Grammie would say. And he dressed like he was always doing business, pressed shirt and pants, expensive leather shoes, camel-hair coat, driving around in his antique Bentley.

"I know it's hard parting with family heirlooms," he said on the phone, "but in the end, it's a win-win situation for everybody because if you're not using them, well, why store them? It's cash in the bank. You sell them and you get the money they're worth, and money is always something you can use. Believe me, Martha,

Christian to Christian, we live in a world where money matters and there's nothing wrong with parting with a material object when someone else will enjoy it. And I know that times are a bit hard for you now and I'm willing to do what I can to help you out. We all have hard times and I'm just glad I'm in a position to help."

He went on and on like one of the dusty self-help books that were in my mother's bookshelf in our PMQ in the city, before they had been put away in boxes and shoved up in the attic. Mr. Burgess was originally from Prince Edward Island and then moved to Halifax with his first family. It was there he met the next Mrs. Burgess, who was supposedly from money, money made selling land when the city started expanding. He was selling real estate in the city, until he pulled some sneaky deal that had lawsuits everywhere, which he settled out of court. After that, Mr. Burgess took his departure from property sales and moved his second family out to the Valley for what he calls the "good Christian life." He came out here and started up his antique business. Grammie said, when you stack up that many lies, you gotta run before they fall over and knock you down.

After they had said goodbye, I had stood up there in the hall, holding the receiver, waiting to hear her click as I watched a robin out the window.

"Serrie?" she said into the phone.

I kept watching the bird, red breast so bright against the dull tree trunk.

"Serrie, I know you're there."

"No, no, I'm not here," I told her. Soon I wouldn't be, I'd be in Halifax at university, not that I wanted to go there either. I didn't know where I wanted to be.

Her deep breath came back out into the phone and hissed in my ear. "Serrie, stop being foolish. You know not to listen in."

"Well, then you shouldn't listen in on my conversations. What kind of example is that?"

"I don't listen in on the phone."

I put my sweaty palm on the warped glass window, fingers spread out, cool glass as sharp on my hand as my voice in the receiver. "Well, eavesdropping by the door is just as bad."

"Now you listen here, young lady —"

I could hear her way down in the kitchen, her far-off voice like a recording that paused for me to insert my reply. "You listen to my calls with Dearie and Elizabeth and Trevor and you won't even admit it." She'd walked right into it and she knew it but she'd never acknowledge it. It was never about acknowledging, or apologizing, or listening, or being responsible, or admitting — it was always about defence or capitulation.

"That's just like you to go bringing up the past. I work my fingers to the bone around here and you just criticize, criticize. I can't even ask you to do one little thing —"

My hand was shaking against the glass. "I didn't know you were asking me to do anything. I thought you were telling me not to do something," I yelled.

There was a click and I could hear her walking from the kitchen, down the hall, to the front of the house. Her voice rose up from the staircase. "I need to be here in case your father comes home from the library." Then quietly, Martha saying, "Serrie, you need to help your mother with this. I need you to do this for me."

"But the china isn't ours to sell," I whispered up to the attic. She called up that she couldn't hear and said to come down to the kitchen so we could have a cup of tea. My mother, so sharp and so soft. I was a sucker for the softness, desperate for it. "In a minute, I have to call Dearie and tell her to come get me later," I said, leaning over the railing, looking into her face, her tired smile as she nodded. Dearie pissed off at me for changing plans, Dearie not wanting to be alone in the house, telling her to call Elizabeth, hanging up. Elizabeth calling almost immediately to say she'd be at Dearie's that night, too, I could help Dearie with her homework, make popcorn

and use some of the fancy seasoning Dearie had brought home
from Florida.

Down in the kitchen there were tea cups. Silver spoons, butter,
tea biscuits. The skin on Martha's fingers gnawed as red as the strawberry jam in the little glass pot. There was Ceylon tea, her favourite,
steeping in the pot. Her, at the table, apron still on, eczema flared
up again in the Sunday spring sun, asking me to pour, handing me
a cigarette like we'd always been smoking together. It was to pay for
the roof, the house simply could not get through another winter,
she said, looking in her cup, at the pot, anywhere but at me. There
was so much work to do in the summer. It made sense, she said, to
start selling stuff, just the small valuable things that weren't in use.
There were so many payments to make and no savings. Percy in university, me going in September. She'd tell Cyril she'd tucked the
money away over the winter. Not to tell Percy, not to tell Gallie or
my father, especially not to tell Grammie. No, no, it was out of the
question to borrow money from Grammie, borrowed enough, never
pay it back. Cyril would never miss the china, certainly not a tea set.
And he didn't need to know, he was barely coping as it was. No one
was ever in the dining room, it was just me and her going about the
house, battling the dust, admiring the old things. The New England
cousin would never show up. She stopped talking and looked out
the window as though she wanted to be far away but was trapped,
saddled here with this family, trying to take care of them and not
being able to. And even with her wrinkles and bags and grey-
streaked hair, I could see the girl she had been, so hopeful, wanting
to travel out beyond the Valley and now stuck here on and between
the Mountains. I reached for a biscuit and told her how good they
were. She smiled out the window and I thought she'd cry then. She
would have if she'd looked at me, but she continued to gaze outside
at the birds on the feeder until she got her breath back.

Chews of biscuit, slurps of tea, my green eyes gazing out the
window, then colliding with hers, mine dry and hard — teenage

eyes — seeing the long-lost relatives' names still and dead, waiting to be spoken, their ghosts hovering about as I wrapped the Limoges teapot and cups, every delicate saucer, in newspaper, and placed them all carefully in a big box.

There's a ghost in the car with me, driving on the back roads to Mr. Burgess's, me saying "Oh, Auntie Ruth," out loud — too late then, not biting my tongue soon enough, breathing her to life, seeing her in the rearview mirror, the Spinster Sullivan all fat and jiggly, jiggly and accusing, hurt and angry in the back seat, rolling like a barrel with every bump, all rotting like she'd come out of the grave, bulging eyes, accusing eyes, as though it was me masterminding the plan to sell off her treasures. Shutting my eyes, still seeing her there, talking to her, explaining it was just to keep her house standing up, that times were really hard, everyone was trying, really, but nothing was getting better. Wanting to drive to Elizabeth's and sit in her room reading fashion magazines, instead driving down the Lesterdale Road, Spinster Sullivan fading away as Mr. Burgess stood in the door of Burgess Antiques, a renovated old warehouse, a long building stretching back into an endless display of elegant antiques, those things from another time. His hands on his hips, jeans with a perfect crease in the leg, shirt pressed, fine gold chain glinting against his wiry black chest hair, gleaming smile, and holding his hand out to me on that late April day. I wanted to toss the china and run as it shattered, run away from the Valley, fly away to somewhere crammed with people, loud, noisy, where I could disappear into a sidewalk crowd and no one would even know I was alive. Behind the antique shop I could see the tiny green buds on the apple trees and the North Mountain rising up in the distance, the heavy beauty of the Valley unfolding in spring, unfolding on me and around me, pulling me down, twisting into me, piercing skin and pulling it off, the happily-ever-after myth flaking away, leaving soft scales there on the wooden steps as I walked inside the shop and hurried to the counter, tripping and losing my balance, hearing a crack as the fragile treasures slipped from my thin arms.

The doctor hands you a box of tissue and you just look at it until you feel wet on your top lip. You blow your nose and tell him that Dearie saw you when you were driving home, you were coming out of the Lesterdale Road and she was in the white van, driving into Foster. You pretended not to see her and drove into Grammie's, but she came in after you, right into the kitchen with her big mouth. Grammie was having a cup of afternoon tea and then she wanted to know what the hell you were doing on the Lesterdale Road. She turned that hard look on you, those faded eyes bright again. Can't anyone take the scenic route, you asked as you went to the bathroom, Grammie's cup clinking behind you, Dearie saying to come over to her house. Elizabeth wasn't over yet and she didn't want to be there alone.

Dearie never wanted to be alone, but once we all left Foster and were at university, she didn't want to stay in university housing, not after two years with a roommate in the Taylor Residence for Women. She hated her roommate, some girl named Megan who never said more than "hi" to me and, from how Dearie tells it, never said any more to her either, and that doesn't work with Dearie. I was in Cypress Cottage on account of my excellent grade point average. It was a big stone building, so I don't know what the deal with calling it "cottage" was and I'd never seen a cypress tree outside of a book. And it was weird, because I was so lonely like I never had been before, and I had been alone most of the time. Now I was always with people, and getting more lonely by the millisecond. I was always with Dearie and Elizabeth, going to idiotic parties and bars with them, smiling at all the people. I'd go to the same place every Friday night, the Star Fish tavern. It was the place to be, packed with students and artists, actors, athletes, musicians, South enders, North enders — the North End is where the poor people live, where some of the original Sullivans settled. Gallie says the North end is full of black people, like she's scared of them or something. Percy says Halifax is the last city in Canada to have a ghetto like this, though most people would like to pretend there's no ghetto, no racial problems at all. But everyone from every end of Halifax came to the Star Fish. There was a big tank with star fish and seahorses in it. The smoke and thud of the music killed them off on a regular basis but most people were too drunk to notice. I'd just sit there at a table, buying two glasses of draught at a time, reading a book, Elizabeth's and Dearie's purses and coats beside me. They'd be off drunk and giggling, coming back to give man updates. Oh, they loved that first year, party party party, so many people to meet, Foster far behind, young and hip in Halifax, the world before them. It wasn't until second year, when they realized they had to actually pass their classes, that the urban glamour dulled. I'd get through half a book on a good night at the Star Fish, smoking, ignoring the drunk guys who'd sit beside me, which was easier than telling them to get lost because no one could ever hear me above the music and the laughing crowd. I didn't stay home though, by then I didn't do well alone in the city, I was disappearing around the edges.

I would go sit on Citadel Hill with a book, looking out at the damn harbour. Sometimes I'd go to the public gardens and look at the ducks and the roses. And there were the splendid old graveyards with trees and tombstones. Sometimes I'd bike out to the one where the Titanic people were buried — it made me feel close to Percy, what with his love of the past, the times gone by.

If it was shit weather I would be in the bathtub drinking red wine, smoking cigarettes and joints, reading books and forgetting to go to class. The exams were easy if I read the books. At the beginning of third year, to save money, I moved out into a house full of guys that Dearie knew from the university pool. I didn't decide until the last moment and Dearie was pissed off — she had wanted me to be her roommate but I didn't want that, nothing familiar did I want then, I wanted a hotel-room life. But Dearie got over it, as much as she got over anything, and set me up with the pool guys, one of whom was her swimming instructor. As soon as she left Foster, and hit the city she signed up for lessons, but then that's Dearie, wanting to save face in Foster where everyone knew she couldn't swim but as long as she didn't swim she could pretend she knew how — it's a weird thing about her. My bedroom was the dining room and I hung blankets on the doors to keep the guys out but they'd come in anyway, late at night, and would sit on the edge of my bed telling me about how much they drank and then going on about their love lives like I was Dear-Freaking-Abbey. They had big hard bodies, bloodshot eyes, and mouths full of silly jokes, except sometimes when they were drunk and maudlin, and I felt sad about how hard it was to be a guy, you know, having to be big and strong about everything, even when you wanted to just sit and cry, but you couldn't, because men don't cry, right?

The doctor raises his eyebrows and then they slip down again. You wonder if he cries and if he does, if he cries alone. He says you will be discharged in two weeks, you will need a treatment program to deal with these issues, he will check back with you when he has details. You ask if that's it for the sessions, and he asks why you want to know. You shrug. The sessions will continue, he says.

After your appointment, you smoke in the courtyard, holding your cigarette up to the sky as filigree snowflakes come floating down. You try to burn holes in every snowflake you can reach but they just disappear.

Clare says Elizabeth is at work. It's the third time you've called. You ask if she got your messages and Clare coughs as she says yes, that Elizabeth is busy at the bar. When you ask for her work number, Clare says the kettle is boiling and she is expecting a phone call and then you are listening to the dial tone.

Back to your room, and the roommate sits weeping. All you can think is *woebegone the maiden* . . . but you can't remember the rest of the poem and then you think about your mother and Thanksgiving as you pull a blanket over the roommate, patting her head and saying, *shhhhhh, shhhhh,* like she is a baby and you will make it better.

That night, back in the corner by the pay phone you punch in the numbers for your house in Foster and you realize you aren't dialling your house anymore. When your mother answers, she is quiet and says she's too busy to come all the way into the city when you ask her to come visit. You tell her you are being discharged soon and she says it will be nice to have you home for Christmas. You know she's lying, so you don't say anything and she says she packed away the Christmas decorations so well she can't find them for the life of her. You ask her to come get you when you're discharged. "Can't you get a ride out with Elizabeth?" she asks. She says you can take the bus and they'll pick you up in Foster. Leaning against the concrete wall, you bang your slipper on it. Your heel is still sensitive. You bang harder and the pain floods up your leg. She's tired, she says, and you say goodnight and go back to your room to sit on your bed with the curtains drawn. You think about Thanksgiving, but you don't want to, so you stop, but the thoughts come anyway, no matter how hard you bang your heel.

The next day, the psychiatrist asks why you took an impromptu trip to London.

That autumn I was so homesick, always trying to find somewhere in the city that felt comfortable and familiar for even just a moment, but it was impossible. I went home a few days early, before Thanksgiving break, with Dearie and Elizabeth in the van. The moment I walked in the door I knew Martha was blue, face all drawn. Moving around the house as though she was a dust ball. I would jump whenever I looked up, not knowing how long she'd been standing there watching. My father was trying to rejoin society and had joined a heritage group that autumn, to make a case for the preservation of outhouses. He was there the first night back when my mother came home from work, not taking her coat off, just her boots and then going into the living-room and sitting in a chair in the twilight. Cyril went in, saying, "Hard day, Martha?" as I peeked around him, noticing how much weight he had gained. She nodded and I went back into the kitchen. He made her a cup of instant coffee and put in a dab of cream and sugar, just the way she liked it, and handed it to me to take in. My heart cracked looking at her, face so long and thin, lines so deep on either side of her mouth they looked like slits, grey streaks in her black hair, bags under her eyes. I wondered how she could change so in just a few months. Now I see that I just hadn't noticed, that it happened long ago, and another little piece of my heart snapped off as she took the coffee and drank it with a piece of her hair in her mouth.

My father made fishsticks and french fries for supper and the next night, pancakes, bacon and hash browns. He opened real maple syrup and said to have as much as I wanted so I drowned the meal in it. Aunt Galronia called about planning Thanksgiving dinner for Sunday while Cyril was out getting wood. I told her my mother had a cold and was in bed early. She sat there looking at the pancakes. When Dearie and Elizabeth called I told them I was studying. Later that night Le Mont puked on the carpet upstairs and Cyril threw a shovel of dirt on it. I never knew why he did that. My mother was already in bed. The next morning the cat shat on the floor by the puke. The cat box was stuffed with dried turds sticking up like cigars. I went to empty it, but the smell was so bad I gagged and left the whole mess.

I waited outside for Dearie and Elizabeth, who were coming to take me for an autumn drive. When they drove up in the van I hopped in as fast as I could. At the shore, the tide was high and the waves were crashing in. I ran on the rocky beach, straight into the goddamn wind so they couldn't see me cry, long hair streaming behind like seaweed, seeing nothing but the huge crashing green Bay of Fundy waves, my cries gobbled up in the roar.

That night Cyril went to a heritage society meeting and I made frozen pizza. I ate a can of fruit cocktail in heavy syrup. I didn't even know she was home until I went in to the living room to turn on the TV. She had her boots on and was lying face down on the sofa. All I could say was, "You aren't supposed to wear your boots on the sofa with the good upholstery." She didn't answer. I went really close and could hear her whispering, "Who put my dreams in the closet?" I put my ear to her mouth and heard her say how she had dreams once and they went away like waves. I wanted her to cry, because I knew about crying, but she didn't, she just kept talking.

"Responsibilities come and your dreams slip a bit farther away and you can't see them as clearly but you think of them like the seasons, you always remember the seasons, the senses always remember, the smells, the colours, the wind sounds — you remember your dreams this way. And that's when you die, when all your senses slow down and quit, one by one, like your Grammie. Soon she'll die. Your Grammie will die."

She was squinting and I couldn't bear the pain of it all, so I put the lights out. But she kept talking, I couldn't flick her off.

I kept saying, "Remember your dreams then, Mum, keep remembering them."

"Serrie is too young to understand because she has her knapsack of dreams on her back each day when she goes out into the world," she whispered.

It felt as though I was dying inside, becoming old and not even twenty-one yet. I could feel the weight transferring from her to me, standing there in the dusk-gone night while said she had forgotten the sound of the seasons.

I left her there. From my room I thought I could hear her muttering but it was just the branches at the glass, like *Wuthering Heights*. I saw the shape of the trees, black against the moonbright sky, and I wished I was far away on the briny ocean, tossed with my toes in water so blue I could use the word *azure*. I thought about my dining-room bedroom in the city — I hadn't even bothered to unpack there yet — and those five big swimmer guys I didn't really know, just that they left their pubic hair in the bathroom sink. I thought about the fact that I belonged nowhere now, not there, not here — nowhere. Far off the phone rang. The cat began to dig in the dirt pile outside my door. I hissed, "Stop, Le Mont, stop," and wished his name was Mr. Fluffers or Furry Face, something normal. He wouldn't stop digging, so I grabbed him and went outside, shaking him until he meowed and gouged my cheek. I dropped him, whispering, "Sorry kitty, sorry kitty," but the kitty was gone. I bent over, sucking in deep frosty air, thinking if I breathed in enough I would freeze up and feel nothing but a sense of crispness. But it only hurt my lungs and I went over hacking.

I was still coughing from all the cold air when I called Percy at his residence in Toronto. Some guy said he would give him a message. I waited at the kitchen table by the phone for an hour, hyperventilating, willing it to ring. My mother was singing dead-and-gone songs in the living room and I wished her voice would crack but it stayed clear and high.

> *In Dublin's fair city where girls are so pretty*
> *'Twas there that I first met sweet Molly Malone*
> *As she wheeled her wheelbarrow*
> *Through streets broad and narrow*
> *Crying, "Cockles and mussels, alive, alive-oh."*

I called Percy again. The same person answered the phone and said he forgot to give Percy the message — he'd gone to a party.

Alive, alive-oh, alive, alive-oh, crying,
"Cockles and mussels, alive, alive-oh."

I tried to catch my aching breath, wanting my older brother to pour me a bowl of Froot Loops and brush my hair.

Now she was a fishmonger and sure 'twas no wonder
For so were her mother and father before

The guy on the phone was apologizing as I hung up.

She died of a fever and no one could save her
And that was the end of sweet Molly Malone

I called Aunt Gallie.

Now her ghost wheels her barrow
Through streets broad and narrow
Crying, "Cockles and mussels, alive, alive-oh."

Outside in the driveway I had this sense that my whole life was a big joke and that any minute someone would leap out from behind a tree and say, ha ha, and then I could laugh and get on with it. I realized how much easier it was to get on with it when there was a bit of distance between me and reality. I wondered how to make it permanently that way. When Galronia drove in, I went blind in her car lights and stood there, a jacked deer. I wanted to scream when she got out of the car but my voice cracked, I couldn't say anything. She put her arm around me, and I thought that Galronia was a goddess. I leaned against her,

Galronia saying, "There there, there there, Serrie. Auntie will take care, Auntie will take care."

She turned up the heat in the freezing house and told me to put the kettle on for tea, rubbing my shoulders as she went back into the living room. My mother was crying on Galronia's shoulder. Gallie said, "There there, there there, Martha." I made a fire in the kitchen stove and cleaned up the dishes from the fishsticks, pancakes and pizza. The phone rang and I answered it, hoping it was Percy. I told Dearie I had to do some reading and she asked what was wrong, but again I said I had to read and hung up.

Galronia took my mother to the house in Foster and when my father came home I screamed at him about the cat shit pile, listing off all the reasons she was breaking down, that everything was falling apart, why couldn't it be normal? I could see his devastated face as I ran out the door, and all the way down the Lupin Cove Road in the dark, my head a slide projector flicking through the twenty years of our lives together and before, the old-fashioned pictures I had seen, the ones from Grammie's albums, in her room, on her staircase wall, all flashing by in my mind. I was running the Lupin Cove Road from memory, feet guiding me in the coal black night, but there was a patch of black ice and I landed hard on my face. Stunned, I lay there until I was so cold I knew I had to get up or my own ghost would be wheeling a wheelbarrow through the streets broad and narrow. So I hobbled all the way to Foster, thinking somehow I had to go as far away as possible as soon as I could.

And then, somehow, I was outside of Elizabeth's ground floor bedroom window, standing face-to-face with a stern-looking, paper cut-out turkey wearing a pilgrim's hat. I just looked at it until it seemed to be smiling and then I banged on the glass until Elizabeth pulled open her curtains, standing there in polar bear pyjamas. She let me in the basement door and stared at my forehead and then I could feel the huge bump from the black ice, the stinging claw marks. "Serrie?" she whispered, scared, and me, with my head pounding, tried to tell her, but I couldn't talk, just opening and shutting my mouth like a fish on the dock waiting to have its head chopped off. She took me by my cold hand to her room and I sat on her plaid bedspread holding her teddy bear while she unlaced my boots and wiped frozen blood from my face. "There there, there there," she said, just like Aunt Galronia.

Her mother came in, but Elizabeth waved her away. Elizabeth went to run a bath for me and I could hear them talking, then her mother on the phone with my aunt. And Elizabeth sat on the toilet peeing, doing her toilet paper sequencing while I slid down into the bubble alps. She sat there singing old Fleetwood Mac songs and then washed my long hair, making soapy hair sculptures, me with the round hand mirror she gave me, looking at my ugly face. Eyes like piss holes in the snow, all that fancy soap hair as I listened to her beautiful voice singing, "Sara," as the steam misted up the mirror and I was finally gone.

After putting on Elizabeth's nightie I sat on her mother's lap and she rocked me and I finally was able to cry hard into her shoulder while she told me grown-ups sometimes had problems too, but that just made me cry more. Ardyth Baxter stroked my hair. I had never seen her do that to Elizabeth or her sister and she kept stroking until I stopped crying and Elizabeth brought in hot chocolate. I sipped it and burned my lips as Ardyth called my father to say I was staying all night.

You can hear the psychiatrist breathing — he has a cold. You tell him your biggest regret is having to be an adult because it certainly seems that life is worse the older you get.

Dr. O'Leary came to Grammie's house and filled up my mother with anti-depressants but I only know that because Gallie told me when she picked me up after church before I went back to the city with Dearie and Elizabeth. She told me it was time I grew up and stopped being such a strain on my mother, both of us kids, me and Percy, and our father too. And I didn't argue with her. I just sat there and let her go on: you weren't any lady of leisure, you were a grown-up and it was time to realize that life is not about having fun, no sir. And on and on while I looked at the red and orange leaves of huge trees lining the Lupin Cove Road, the cold blue sky all around. And that was it, no one never mentioned it again, like it never happened.

I went back to the house and apologized to my father, who nodded and went out to his workshed. Back in Halifax I started going to the university library to read and drink sherry out of a cycling water bottle until the library closed. I would walk alone across the deserted campus in the dark, not ever thinking about being raped by a maniac or anything. I would do anything to avoid going back to the house full of swimmers, where life was one big party, one big swimming pool, one big salad day, whatever that meant.

When I went off to university, the only place I could ever temporarily relax in Halifax was standing up there on that stupid Citadel Hill with the fort and its moat on top of the world, the harbour down at the bottom past the downtown, city streets pinwheeling off, tidy blocks of wooden houses with sweet storm porches, houses painted in bright colours, houses lining streets that led only to each other. Houses snug and warm through the windows, houses full of people you would never know, people passing on the city street sidewalks, people who would look ahead. I managed to get through the first year. The second year, sinking low, Dearie and Elizabeth saying the city was making me weird but no one really noticing *how* weird, just me and books and a bottle of sherry. That third year, unable to keep anything down — figuratively and literally. Skipping classes for a month, the kind Classical Studies professor calling.

"I am so very busy," I kept saying.

I hadn't gone to class after our last meeting, and it was the only class I went to on a regular basis, just fifteen students. I would smile when the professor would teeter on the edge of the elevated lecture area, the professor full of rapture talking about any of the gods and I was all for at least seeing rapture.

In his office, after Thanksgiving, he had told me I had to come to class, hand in my papers, he was concerned. We had discussed the possibility of graduate work, me staring at the antique glass Clichy paperweight on his old oak desk, stomach feeling full of sea urchin shells, thinking of the teapot. It was very cold for October, bone-rot damp, and I should have worn more than a sweater. Hearing his voice: "Seraphina, your paper is overdue, you absolutely must hand it in. You'll lose your scholarship. Everyone in the department believes you should be thinking of graduate work."

And then his phone call in early November, asking why I hadn't come to class. His voice echoing through the receiver: "Oh, Seraphina, my dear girl," his satin-soft English accent, but I had hung up already and was out into that day's end, where the sun was dripping down like marmalade from behind a strip of grey cloud, then a jar of black night spreading smooth and thick across the sky. And I came to on the top of Citadel Hill.

It was a place with a view. Even in the dark, to see the lights go on and on. Looking at the city all around, sipping sherry out of my bicycle water bottle, knowing that I was of no consequence at all, that into the world you are born alone and out of the world you also go alone, with eyes on that unbearable expanse ahead. I am the celestial sky, every luminous celestial body.

Venus, Hesper, the evening star rising in the winter sky; Antares, the Rival of Mars. I am every constellation: Orion, Auriga, Taurus, all of them. The Star Showers — the Perseids, the Leonids, the Geminids. I am the moon, moonrise and moonset, the moon at perigee, the harvest moon, the blue moon, the new moon that licks the meadow clean. All the twilight definitions: civil, nautical, astronomical.

I am a twenty-year-old drunk on historic Citadel Hill on a cold autumn night.

This world I am in must be bigger, hoping but not even knowing how to be in a small part of it, to be at once in and of it, but there is no move you can make next, no move of consequence. I am outside the game in the dark November night, with professors calling and parents folding themselves away like sheets.

I blew hot air into that Halifax night, the dragon melting her tail, and I was then just a cheap sherry drunk, pitching down the white hill to the snow crunchy sidewalk and step, step, step, back to the house full of roommates where I grabbed a few things, packed my idiotic little black suitcase, cleaned out my meagre bank account, and called Dearie and Elizabeth, who were so taken back they drove me out to the airport in the van, thinking it must be some big Serrie joke, even as they watched me get on a charter flight to England, even as they stood there waving, Elizabeth giggling and chewing her fingernails and Dearie frowning, with her hands tugging at her curls.

The psychiatrist nods.

You wish you'd been blacked out for the last few months, the last year, so there would be no memory. You wait for *that's all for today*, but he just keeps looking at you. You stare back. He shakes his foot. You just sit there in all your quiet sadness until he speaks. His voice is quiet. You will be discharged at the end of the week, for Christmas, but on the condition you go to a treatment program, the Weeping Willows Treatment Centre. Your primary addiction is to alcohol and it seems to lead you into other substances. And you are maladapted, he tells you. Missing key life skills, the kind that enable people to make the transition to adulthood, a transition you are resisting and he isn't sure why, something to address at the Weeping Willows. The Weeping Willows is on the hospital grounds of the Fundy Regional Hospital in the Annapolis Valley, he tells you, but you know all this, of course. You know that if you had overdosed in the Valley they would have sent you there, not to the NS. They will have a place for you two days after Christmas. You will be close to home, he tells you. And you nod. There is silence. He asks how you feel about being close to home. You don't want to cry so you don't answer. You are trying to be a Stoic and everybody knows that Stoics don't cry. He tells you most people take years to get a handle on alcoholism. You are young, intelligent, your chances of having a normal, productive life are very high, he says, with his legs crossed, his hands folded like handkerchiefs. He nods and keeps looking at you. You fight to control your breathing. It occurs to you what a flop you'd be as a Stoic. He watches all of this, you struggling to stay in control, just watches without a word, until your breath is calm.

"Good luck, Seraphina," he says, nodding.

The night before you leave, all those things you told the doctor stay in your head, all this stuff he knows, facts to him, pain to you. Elizabeth calls to arrange a visit on her way to the Valley the next day and you tell her you need a ride home. She's thrilled and you just scuff the floor while she babbles and then, later, sniffle away on your hospital bed. You keep seeing faces in your mind, your poor pathetic family. The roommate hears your sniffles and pulls the curtain aside and holds your hand, not saying anything because there is nothing to say. You compare slippers and go to sleep. In the morning she is gone when you get up. As you are packing, you put the bouquet that smells like summer on her bedside table. You wait for her to come back but she doesn't, so you head to the lounge to say goodbye to Chester. She is there watching TV, a big smile as you thank her for last night. She keeps smiling. She doesn't remember; she has just had electro-convulsive therapy and her short-term memory is gone. You don't know whether to laugh or cry so you do neither, say nothing, just leave, thinking of the flowers by her bed.

FIVE

CHESTER WAS WALKING DOWN THE HALL WHEN REGGIE AND ELIZABETH got off the elevator. He gave her a formal nod and wobbled away. Elizabeth shrieked "hi" and hugged me close and tight, smelling of sweet shampoo and conditioner. From over her shoulder I saw Reggie stare at Chester. I watched him while I looked at his hair; it resembled painted hair on a plastic man doll. And Reggie was dressed like a plastic man doll: pleated pants with loafers and a big sheepskin coat. He stared at my head — I had just shaved it for the holiday season. And then his salesman senses found him and he gave me that *hey hey, take her for a test-drive* smile as he grabbed my hand and pumped away. I stood there all stiff until he slapped me on the back and dropped my arm.

"So Elizabeth says you've been having a few problems," he said, slapping me on the back again. "Reggie, short for Reginald," he told me. "Reginald John David McLeod."

Chester wobbled by again, did a complete turn, and continued back down the hall. He started this low humming, what he calls *shell harmonics*. I nodded at Reggie. He pointed at Chester.

"What's with him?" Reggie's arm was suspended in the air.

Elizabeth answered. "Oh, that's just Chester. He's never been right in the head."

"Ah," said Reggie.

All was clear to him then, ye olde problem in the head, which he must think I have, too. It's not far from the truth, really. Chester came by again.

Reggie nodded in that business way. "How ya doin', buddy?" He whacked him on the back and Chester flipped out, hands in the claw position, going for Reggie's eyes.

"Jee-sus jee-sus jee-sus christ," is all Reggie can say as we drive over the new bridge and off to the highway. "Mother of god, the guy's a fucking nut." I look at the afternoon sky, that faded blue colour only winter brings. What was he expecting to find in a mental hospital? The city falls behind and we are homeward bound to the Annapolis Valley. We stop for hot chocolate in Windsor, halfway there. Elizabeth heads for the bathroom and Reggie and I stand in line. He says to order anything so I start reading the wall menu and he whispers, "Tick-tick-tick, Serrie, the early bird gets the worm," and orders us all the Christmas hot chocolate mint special and a box of assorted doughnuts that I carry to the table. Reggie admires his chocolate dip doughnut from every angle and nods his approval.

"So, Serrie, you really worried Elizabeth, with your little trip to England and all. She wasn't much fun to be with, so worried about you. You're hard on your friends, buddy."

He keeps checking out the doughnut, flashes a big smile, and I realize it's his food, he's smiling at his doughnut. I sip the hot chocolate. It tastes like toothpaste. On the wall there is a big poster of a chocolate block and chocolate curls, sprinkled with green mint leaves, *Have Yourself a Minty Little Christmas*. Elizabeth never went out with anyone like this before, old and all polished. They were always the regular sort of guys, predictable, solid, funny. And heartbroken when she dumped them. Reggie bites into his doughnut and leans forward, chewing as he speaks.

"You know, buddy, you should be nicer to your friends, especially Elizabeth. You and that Clare chick."

My hands go sweaty. Who the fuck does he think he is, *buddy*? I take another sip and feel the steam on my face. For the first time I feel a kindredness with Clare. I peer up at Reggie. We're so close I can see a few hairs his Braun shaver must have missed. "I hope you're nice to her yourself," I say, looking at the hairs on Reggie's chin. He's hairier than most guys our age. I guess facial hair is a sign of old age.

"Well, that's none of your business, is it now, Serrie? *Serrie.* And what kind of name is that? Serrie? What's with you people in the Valley? Inbreeding? *Dearie. Dearie?* Isn't she in Florida? Vacationing at Disney Land, like the little Bambi she is?"

He thinks he is funny and I watch him laugh and chew. He laugh-chews, laugh-chews, as though he can't do both at the same time. Maybe it's some rhythm thing, maybe he's into experimental music. I can only hope. He keeps staring at me and I think he's going to start that buddy-whacking thing on the arm. Elizabeth comes out of the washroom with strawberry lip gloss shining in the fluorescent lights, the Christmas spirit onto her, as my Grammie would say. She skips out to the car, us following behind.

I'm curled up in a ball in the back, pretending to be asleep. It's easy, because the hum of the car is putting me in a trance. The bumps are almost imperceptible because there's nothing like fancy shocks. In my haze, I hear Reggie say, "It's just alcohol, right? And pills? And coke?" I can hear a rolling paper, one sound that can never get by me.

Elizabeth turns around, giggling, and pokes me. I remain motionless. "You still can smoke pot, right, Serrie?"

Very slowly I let my mouth hang open and keep my eyes shut. I grunt softly.

"Serrie's asleep," she tells him. "It was heroin, too, I think. She just doesn't know when to stop when she's drinking. She'll do anything, just goes crazy. She hasn't had a very good life."

It's good my face is pushed into the leather, hearing Elizabeth talk about me. What's a good life? I wonder. Her life? Maybe. Life is what you make it, Grammie would say.

Reggie takes a big toke and lets it out. It smells like cat piss. "Well, she's gotta get her shit together. Her poor family, having to put up with that. I hope she doesn't drool on the goddamn leather. That's genuine calf leather, Elizabeth. Do you know how much that costs? I could get you a deal on . . . "

I listen to his spiel, like Elizabeth can afford to buy a BMW. "Maybe you should get some new friends," Reggie tells her. Elizabeth giggles. She always laughs and the more she doesn't want to talk about something, the more she laughs. Maybe if I could do that, everything bad would go away, and then nothing bad would ever happen in the first place. "She'll always be my friend, no matter what," she says, taking another haul on the joint.

I drift into sleep and then wake up not knowing where I am. I sit up and see we are barrelling down the Highway 101 into the Valley and, as cold and wintery as it is, there is nothing more beautiful than that view. The Minas Basin spread out at low tide, the lowering sun varnishing the red mud that ends at the snowy white banks of the tidal channels. The North Mountain high and dark. But I'm so tired even the beauty can't keep me up. Reggie and Elizabeth don't seem to notice I'm awake, they are just looking straight ahead, so I just drop back down and wake up when I feel the bumps of the Lupin Cove Road as we head up the Mountain, potholes so deep not even a highly engineered German luxury sedan can soften them. Reggie's mumbling about pencils. I sit up and stretch, rub my face, all hot and itchy from the drool-soaked leather upholstery, and take a look at home sweet home. The outhouses are decked with flashing lights, the latest one, Number Ten, Scott's Bay, stands alone, a guard outpost by the road. The verandah is decked with a wobbly strand while the mailbox blinks like something on a runway. My bedroom window in the tower is covered in purple lights. I sit there in the back, looking at the place, some Victorian spaceship waiting for its twilight launch.

Reggie is a genius. "Looks like a bunch of outhouses." He turns into the driveway.

"Yes," I say. "It is a bunch of outhouses. That's why it looks like a bunch of outhouses."

"Aren't we sassy," says Reggie. "You didn't tell me she was so sassy."

Elizabeth looks at me. "You never know with her. Serrie's family do their own thing. Her brother makes these model trains out of stuff. He's into history."

Sometimes I really wonder what her brains are made of. She has them but maybe it's just different brain matter, like strawberries and fucking sunshine. She does that little girl giggle, head to the side. I know her eyes are closed.

"Yeah," he says. "Oh yeah? How old is he? Ten? I do the log throw in the Highland Games."

Log throw? He has to be kidding. I ask him what the real name is for log throw and he gets snotty, wants to know what's wrong with log throw. Reggie's from Antigonish, where they all act like they just got off the boat and if you say that to them they're liable to beat you with a bagpipe or smother you with a kilt. I smile and wonder what the hell Elizabeth is doing with Reggie. Clare was right. And he's old, too, thirty, but he looks even older with all these lines that must be from concentrating on selling so many fancy cars.

Elizabeth has the munchies now and she's rolling around in the front seat. Reggie's so mellow I wonder how he's managed to drive. It's "Good King Wenceslas" he's trying to sing, but he can't pronounce it so he says "Good King *Pencil*." I start laughing and Reggie glares at me in the rear-view mirror. His eyes are slits. "What's so goddamn christly funny, Serrie?" but I don't tell him because it's the Christmas season, right? I just whisper, "'Tis the season, Reggie, to be jolly."

"Fa-la-la-la-la," warbles Elizabeth.

"Shut up, shut up," he barks as he points out the window. "Who put the outhouses there?"

"Santa's little helpers," I tell him, hopping out of the car. He laughs. What does he think? Someone just delivered them one day? My stuff is all in the back seat so I just grab it and throw it on the snow. I can see my mother peeking through the curtains, wondering what the hell we're doing out here. Elizabeth giggles with red bunny eyes as I slam the door.

"Easy, easy," Reggie barks as he rolls down his window. "Easy with the door. It's imported." Just then he sees the Valley out there, how far you can see from my parent's house. He takes it in, and then looks at me and nods, his lower lip sticking out. I nod back and Reggie backs up as I turn towards the house. *Beep-beep* and I spin around.

"So how about going skiing with us on Boxing Day?" Reggie has a big stoned smile on his face. I just look at him. "How about it?"

I nod and smile back.

He's waving, and calls, "Merry Christmas, Sassy Sullivan."

"I'll call you." Elizabeth shouts, waving with her hand in Reggie's face, him shoving it away. He guns the car and they disappear down that bumpy road. And then I feel heavy and alone, standing there, the cold freezing my tears before they can even fall off. I close my eyes and then open them. The Christmas lights are blurry and neon, like my life. Who needs to go to Vegas? Gallie says Elvis went to a Vegas in the sky. I imagine him up there singing "Blue Christmas," backed up by nine choirs of sequined angels, white mist floating around, playing poker, maybe with Grampie, sitting at some white marble table with flashing lights. Maybe Heaven is just whatever we think it is.

I stand there and look at the house. Le Mont is sitting on the verandah, all puffed up like an orange porcupine. He regards me with familiar indifference. He neither holds grudges nor forgives. He is a true Stoic, I realize. Apatheia. I look at my bedroom window and then the whole house again. The new paint is starting to peel and there is a bit of moss growing on the roof — the roof that was just shingled. We fix it and the winter eats it. It doesn't matter what they do, it always gets back to looking run down. It's a cycle. Cyril wants to get siding for it next time, no more painted clapboard, but my mother tells him she's not having any of that damn aluminum stuff on the house, it would just cost too much. Cyril will keep putting the ladder up, moving slowly to the top and painting away. It occurs to me that maybe she doesn't want siding on it because, aside from the money, then what would my father do? What would happen to him if it was just the outhouses? What if there were no chores around the house for him? If he had no work shed? If he had no ideas for inventions? What if he had stayed at Stronach Meat Packers? Why did his back go out on him all of a sudden? What if he was into man things like hunting and tractor driving? What if burning the hair off pigs with a blowtorch didn't bother him? What if no one had ever hit him in the head? What if he owned a real business like Dearie's father or a farm like Elizabeth's? Why do I have to be just like my family? I don't need to know these things, I tell myself; these questions are best not asked.

They're just putting the tree up when I come in. I stand in the living room doorway. We've never been ready for Christmas until it's right there. Will it ever be any different? Nothing changes really, the big lesson I keep learning, even if it looks like it's changed. My father and mother steady the tree while Percy screws it into the stand. It's straggly but it smells wonderful, like a forest. My father waves and my mother looks over through the branches. I can't see her mouth but it must be right on a branch because the branch wags up and down with her words. The tree is talking, I think. Chester the lobster, the outhouses, a talking tree. What would the psychiatrist think? I bet he'd just nod.

My mother waves a hand from the tree. "Well, we weren't expecting you until late tonight. The roads must be clear if you got here so quick."

"Go out and get the saw, Serrie, I gotta cut off another foot." Percy doesn't look up.

The tree is wobbling and he starts barking for them to hold it still. I can't see anyone, they're all tree people now.

"What's the name for the log thing at the Highland Games? Log throw?"

Percy pops up and looks at me now, pine bits in his hair, prince of trees. "No, it isn't called log throw. It's caber toss. It's a spruce log, twenty-two feet long —"

My father's voice comes muffled from the tree. "Grab that side, Percy. There's a sheaf toss too, Serrie. Did that in my day. Tossin' a bag of straw with a pitchfork."

Ah, the glories of the Highlands. The tree flops to the right and my mother sighs from the branches, the sighing tree. It wobbles back to the centre and I wait for it to walk over to me and just tell me how it is. Percy comes out to the middle of the room and demonstrates the caber toss, leaving my parents bracing the shaky tree while he performs.

"You have to toss the caber end-over-end with your feet in the six o'clock position and flip the caber so it looks like the hands of a clock at twelve o'clock. Now could we continue the highland history lesson later and get on with the tree? We need that saw, Serrie."

The tree sways to the side and he jumps back in and grabs it as I head out through the kitchen, past the half-dozen kinds of Christmas baking my mother has started and not finished. There is a big extension cord running through the porch with a piece of masking tape on it and my father's crooked printing: Outdoor Porch Strand Activation Switch. He's got a list on the wall where he's keeping track of what time the lights are switched on and off, some kind of Christmas record, I suppose. I snap the switch and wait for them to shout at me, but all I hear is Percy:

" . . . to the left . . . to the right . . . no no, I said to the right."

My father rumbling: "Take it easy, let's all just work together."

I snap it on again. The click echoes in the cold. I put on some big rubber boots that remind me of being a kid and I walk down the driveway, wondering what Elizabeth's family think of old Reggie. Through the bay windows I see the tree fall over.

I take a long time finding the saw in the workshed. Tools hang on the wall and there are all kinds of half-started inventions, one big thing that looks like a giant metal buoy with electronic stuff. Maybe my father is making a robot, a buoybot, a friend for poor old Chester. I think of this old movie, *Rocket Man*, where his super-duper rocket switch gave him all the options: up, down, fast, slow. What else do you need with choices like that? I light a smoke.

My father comes out to see what the big delay is. I'm sitting on the workbench, saw on my lap, smoking and looking at the robot, now just a dark blob.

"Well, that's makin' you like a dragon kinda, just hibernatin' out here," he laughs.

I shrug. He's glad I'm home, he tells the ceiling beams, that we're all together. I look the saw in the teeth. "It's good to be here with each and every one of you." The evening sky is cool pink through the warped old glass panes and the mountain looms dark in the north.

"Enough light to still see the new birdfeeder, Serrie. Like those purple lights I put on your window?"

I smile and follow him out to Number Eight, Shubenacadie, walking like a soldier. The white and green feeder has three levels with compartments. Feed is scattered about the bottom, dark on the snow, like a stain.

"Early Christmas present from your mother," he smiles.

"Different birds come, the ground eaters, ones that perch up high. Blue jays chase everyone else down below. They sure look pretty but they're mean buggers, they are. Whole flock of pheasants back again this year. Counted fifteen three days ago. Man from the Research Station says they're like a flock of chickens now that we feed 'em grain."

There are a few stars twinkling out of the magenta sky and I don't know if I am twelve or twenty. My father puts his hand on my shoulder and I put my stinking cold smoke hand on his. We just stand there, and I think about being really little, all bundled up, looking at the night sky, Cyril showing all of us the winter constellations. And the summer sky, us out on the lawn, staring up, dizzy from the twinkles, tumbling up into the night. You know, staring up but it feels like falling, rising and falling at the exact same moment. Before we go in the porch door, I look up, wishing I could be there, a patch of fading colour and then dark and quiet, a little piece of the night.

Christmas Eve Day my mother calls me down to have a coffee with her while my father and Percy shovel the driveway. I light up and sip. She doesn't say a word about my smoking but I'd like to say a word about coffee. It's dark and bitter and I hate how it tastes but that's what coffee's all about or why would people drink it? It's learning how to handle it that makes you a bona fide adult. So my mother starts with how she knows I've had a bad time, she's done the best she could; my father, mental health problems and all, has done the best he could. Percy just doesn't understand, and actually, none of them do, but the doctors say my chances are good, though Lord knows if they really know anything. We'll see how things go at the Weeping Willows. And then she just sits there for awhile and she looks really young, staring out at the bird feeder. I can hear birds chirping and the crunches of metal shovels biting through the crisp snow and frozen driveway dirt. My mother wonders why there are so few chickadees and I tell her maybe more will come, you never know. I think she's going to cry, so I eat some of the fruit cake on the table and say how good it is.

"Really, Serrie? Is it good, pumpkin? I thought it wasn't going to turn out this year. Is it good?"

I keep telling her I wouldn't be eating it if it wasn't tasty but she just stares out the window again and then *snap*: she's back, sixty years old and haggard.

"Aunt Galronia, Grammie, and Percy are taking you Christmas shopping in Bigelow Bay this afternoon. Seeing as you don't have a cent left and the bank will soon be after you, I'll give you some money."

Our silent pact, where the money came from. My stomach is tight in the silence that breaks when I chew a piece of fruitcake and tell her again how great her recipe is. She nods and smiles at the plate. I take a deep breath. My mother sighs and I start bracing myself for shopping with Galronia.

The one and only time before was in search of a bathing suit when I was fourteen, just when my tits were starting to grow. A birthday treat, all the way into the city. My mother forced me to go, Aunt Galronia would be hurt if I refused. I stormed around but ended up in the car with her anyway, Dearie and Elizabeth along for the ride, Dearie in the front seat talking to Galronia about Mr. Melanson's plans to expand the pharmacy. Galronia asked Dearie about the latest sales and then looked at me in the rear-view mirror, oh, what a sale we're going to, oh, the greatest sale ever, at the Halifax Shopping Centre. They were selling off these old-style-no-stretch-nylon suits. No lycra for me. That would come when it was obsolete and everyone was getting some new space-age stuff, walking around like Star Trek people.

All the suits had these pocket things for *bosoms*, as Galronia said, and I'd grow into them. What did she think I was, a goddamn plant or something? Galronia came barging into the dressing room and squinted. I was covered in maple leafs, one where each boob should have been. A freezing draft was coming in but she kept the curtain open, hollering for the saleslady, this old woman with white hair and pink lipstick who came running. They looked at me like I was a mannequin, some dummy. Dearie and Elizabeth appeared behind them, Elizabeth making faces and Dearie elbowing her, putting her hand over Elizabeth's mouth.

"Oh, she'll grow into that in no time," the saleslady said to Gallie, "in no time at all. And the durability. Lord, the durability. This material will just hold its shape, not like those new ones. They get all stretched out, they do, but not the old, reliable ones. And the chlorine will take years to eat away at this fabric."

Even toilet bowl cleaner couldn't eat at this, I wanted to scream. My face was hot and red like the maple leafs. Why can't I be from a country with more taste, more elegance, I thought. Why can't I just be a citizen of the U.N. and have a simple blue suit with a circle of stars? Why don't they just cover this one in Mounties and igloos? The nylon made my skin crawly and I wanted to wrap up in the dressing-room curtain. But they kept standing there, "Oh, what a great deal it is. Isn't it lovely, just like they wear in the Olympics." I wasn't much of a sportster but even I knew Olympic swimmers didn't go splashing around in material most people would make a tent with. I crossed my arms.

"Put your arms down so we can see the fit," Aunt Gallie barked.

I moved them down but they wouldn't go, my arms defying Galronia, parts of me trying to take control. She glared, I glared. How long did they need to *see the fit*? I was on the verge of throwing one and then they would have something to see. She took a step towards me and my arms and neck sagged at the same time. *We all give up so easily*, I screamed at my body.

"Now straighten up. What is with you, Seraphina Sullivan?" Gallie demanded.

She poked and prodded at my waist, like it was going to smooth the fabric wrinkles. Elizabeth started snorting and Dearie dragged her away as Galronia looked over her shoulder and then up at me with a smile. Aunt Gallie thought it was fun and that she was one of the girls. I shut my eyes then and imagined I was swimming naked in the Bay of Fundy, but then I remembered how cold the water was, even in the summer, so I just stood there shivering until she patted me on the head and left me to dress.

So the great-bargain-maple-leaf suit was purchased and Galronia bought us chocolate milkshakes and fries at the Chicken Burger in Bedford that we ate in the car on the way back to the Valley. The three of us sat in the back together.

"Must be nice to have a personal chauffeur," Galronia said all the way home. "Some people don't know how good they've got it, oh my."

Elizabeth kept making faces, Dearie kept elbowing her, and I just sat there by the door, wondering if it would hurt if I opened it and dropped out on the highway. Dearie started elbowing me, whispering for me to get over it. I contemplated elbowing her back but my arms betrayed me again and I just went closer to the door. At home, Elizabeth tried to tell me it wasn't that bad, giggling the whole time. Dearie told me it looked god-awful while Elizabeth stuffed socks in the boob spaces. They fell on my bed laughing. The next day the suit went in Cyril's fire barrel.

So much for sports.

But that was then. Now my mother slams down the rolling pin. "Serrie? Seraphina Sullivan? Are you listening to me?"

"No," I say.

Her eyes narrow. I smile and shrug and say I'm just kidding.

"Percy will have the money and that's not up for discussion. I hope things work out, Serrie. We've done the best we could. Now I've got to get back to work. I put Percy's Christmas present somewhere last summer and haven't seen it since." She climbs down to the cellar and I finish my smoke, staring out the kitchen window at the feasting pheasants.

When Gallie and Grammie drive in, my father stops me at the porch door and gives me a magazine he says I might want to read on the way. It's *Popular Mechanics*. I say no and Percy rolls his eyes and pokes me in the back. My father insists and I start to get angry, saying I will be car sick if I read, it's only a twenty-minute ride to Bigelow Bay anyway, and I get this feeling that I want to rip my hair out. When he's really upset, my father just goes quiet and looks at his boots. Gallie lays on the horn just then and Percy tells me to just take the damn magazine but I cross my arms. He takes it and shoves it under my arm where it rests of its own accord. As we walk down the steps he tells me I'm a stupid idiot, I know what Cyril is like, and why can't I just humour him, just a little, just for once, like I did when I was little?

In the back seat I flip open the magazine and there is a piece of paper with a fifty-dollar bill inside, and in his jagged handwriting: "Serrie, you get yourself a little treat. Between you and me. Love your father, Cyril."

Grammie starts telling us about Christmas in her day and jingle bells on the sleigh. Elvis sings "Blue Christmas" on the radio and I stare out the window at the North Mountain, trying not to picture my father standing there alone, waving as we backed up, Cyril standing there with his shovel, smiling, just wanting so bad for us all to get along. He was still smiling as we drove away, and he was still smiling in my mind, Cyril's soft face that just wanted a bit of kindness.

We drive down the highway, my face pressed to the steamy glass so no one can see me cry. I have on my big lambskin mitts but even through them I can feel Percy squeeze my hand, and even though I want to this time, I can't squeeze back, but he holds my hand all the way to the jammed mall parking lot, where Gallie starts doing this race-car thing trying to find a parking spot. She hits the brakes so much I shut my eyes and do deep breathing so I won't get sick, and then Percy elbows me — I don't even know the car has stopped.

I help Grammie out of the car and give her my arm to help her to the mall door. Bits of snow fall from the grey sky, the wind so damp and cold. Grammie's wrapped up in so many layers I don't know if it's the bulk or rheumatism that make her hobble. It's like some parts of her work these days and some parts don't. She's getting older and there is nothing I can do to stop it.

The County Fair Mall. It's warm inside, warm and tacky. Canned Christmas music blares fuzzy carols, big balls of white stuff hang from the ceiling, maybe snowflakes, who knows. Blinking, multi-coloured lights are draped all about.

"My good lord god on high. Enough flickering to have you take a fit, eh, Serrie?" Grammie screams over the music. "Where are my sunglasses, Gallie? The blindness will set in if we don't get away from all of this."

Gallie screams back that we'll all do our shopping really fast and glares at us. Percy and I nod at her but she keeps glaring. Galronia arranges a meeting time at the food court, arranges it with Percy. I don't know what they think I'm going to do, get a bottle of rum and go sit in the parking lot?

We go to India Imports and I power shop. I buy everybody something made of brass because I can't stand being here and the last thing I want to do is bump into anyone I know. I walk right in and pick up candle holders for all, a big gong for my father, and head to the cash. Percy looks at my stuff, starts to say something, and then stops. He takes out his wallet, this thing he made in Boy Scouts with a frigging maple leaf and a beaver pressed on the leather, and pays for the whole damn lot.

We walk through the mall, passing all these tables where people are selling ugly homemade crafts. A few people wave at Percy and I just look at my feet until we get to Earle Baltzer's Stack of Books. It's a new shop, he closes Collectibles over in Lupin Cove in the winter and works here, he says. And that's exactly what it is, a store filled with stacks of books, with ladders, stools and a few comfy chairs. He's even got a cat named Marvellous that just sits in the doorway looking out at the mall, yawning and turning back into the store.

Mr. Baltzer nods at us. He never says much and he never takes his pipe out of his mouth, so I never know what he is saying anyway. He rocks back and forth on his feet with one hand in his pocket and one holding the pipe. Right away I find a book about the history of the Dominion Atlantic Railway, the DAR, lovely and old with faded colour pictures, pieces of tissue paper over them. I hide it on a shelf and tell Percy he has to leave so I can buy his present. He says he'll wait on the bench outside, handing me a twenty-dollar bill. The book costs almost forty dollars, so I use the money Cyril gave me. When I'm paying for it, Mr. Baltzer tells me to pick a paperback from the box on the floor — one free with every purchase over five dollars. I hold up two and he recommends the tattered copy of Brave New World. When I leave, he's talking to Hans Zimmer, who owns the pie factory out near Foster. He's a rich German who's buying up the waterfront property, my grandmother says, like they actually won the war. He does own half of Lupin Cove. They say he waits until people get old and then offers them more money for their property than a local ever could. He is old, mid thirties, Gallie thinks. He's a widower; his first wife died in a car accident, she's heard. Hans is dressed like a model for some outdoor clothing company, with these boots right out of Heidi. He's movie-star handsome. Everything is ironed, and his hair is trimmed to perfection. He nods at me when I leave. Maybe I can get a free pie from him. Heading out the door, I smile back and trip over Marvellous, as Percy shakes his head on the bench by the fake plants.

"So give me the change," Percy says. I'm sitting beside him and hand him a dime. He asks to see the receipt. I can feel myself getting mad. He sees me holding *Brave New World* and I tell him Mr. Baltzer gave it to me but Percy's eyes narrow before I finish the sentence. I'm condemned for life.

"Fuck you."

"Isn't this typical."

Then my voice breaks. "How could you think I took it? I'm not a criminal. You never used to go that far." And I blubber away about one free book with every purchase over five dollars.

"You sit there on that bench."

So I sit there like a big baby, thinking of Grammie saying *damned if you do, damned if you don't.* Where exactly do you go from there, is what I would like some grown-up person to tell me. Staring at the end of my lit cigarette, I think how much easier it would be if I was dead and buried and they could all come and visit me, feeling so bad they didn't treat me right when I was alive. There's nothing like feeling sorry for yourself.

Percy sits down beside me. "Serrie . . . sorry about that. I just don't know what to . . . how to help you."

He feels bad but I don't care. Policing me isn't going to help. It's not like I'm busy trying to sneak a drink or anything, score some drugs. Mr. Baltzer must have not told him the price of the book; he'd have known it was a gift for Percy. Protected by strangers. "Yeah, whatever." I take a drag.

"Look, Serrie — why are your eyes crossed?"

I'm still staring at the end of the cigarette and it's making me dizzy. A big ash falls off the end, lands on my toe, and I bounce it up and watch it fall like toxic snow.

"I didn't ask if you stole it, if that's what —"

I turn my head slowly and glare at him and he shuts up, finally. We sit there and hands cover my eyes, fingers that smell like nicotine and cheap perfume, making me gag.

"Guess who?" says a voice.

I sneeze and the hands go away fast. It's Wynnette Doucette, looking hard and tired, bulges under her eyes, wiping her fingers on her skin-tight jeans. Percy's just staring at her.

I wonder when I'm going to get a break, it's like I'm caught in some loop. I wait to have a stroke from embarrassment but I don't feel anything but hopeless. I'd just like to curl up and go to sleep in the fake palm tree pot. I elbow Percy and he says "Hey there, Wynnette," and smiles this big fake smile.

"Hear you're making us all right proud of you, Percy, the big schol-ar."

It's all over his face that he is shocked she even knows the word *scholar*; she can tell and I can tell and he knows we both know so he says, "How's business?" as though she's some entrepreneur and not a stripper. I roll my eyes. She asks me for a cigarette. I've got one left and so I say we'll share it. Percy rolls his eyes. Wynnette whips out her own lighter, shocker pink nails clicking as she snaps out a flame, talking through the side of her mouth like Mr. Baltzer as she lights up.

"Excited about Christmas?"

"No," I say. "How about you? Home for Christmas?"

"Just for two days."

She'll be going down to Just Junior's grave, no doubt. Wynette takes a big drag, hands me the cigarette, and asks Percy what he thinks about travelling on trains. She took the train from Halifax to Montreal last year, slept in a berth and it was a fine sight better than the bus. Percy starts talking about the spirit of Canadian history embodied in the trains. I hand the cigarette back to Wynnette and point out that the bar car's fun. She takes the cigarette, and points the glowing end at me. "You, missy, shouldn't go anywhere near the bar car. How you feeling?"

I raise my eyebrows, bite my lip, and shrug. "Oh, just fine," I reply. About as fine as she must be doing, I think.

She nods and blows out a tube of smoke while she stares into the mall crowd. Hans Zimmer walks by in this stream of people wearing

Christmas scarfs and ball caps. Hans sees us and does that formal Prussian nod thing and the three of us wave in synch, like we are at a goddamn parade. The people behind him think we're waving at them so they wave and we wave and then the people behind wave so we wave to them and it seems no end is in sight until Galronia and Grammie appear. By then I'm thinking about the brass gong I bought for my father. What would we do without India Imports? He can put it out near the outhouses. I don't know why really, some kind of spiritual thing, I'm thinking, gonging in the morning, echoing through the trees. Grammie is still complaining about the Christmas carols and has a hand over her ears, the other arm linked through Galronia's, who's got a grin on like she has a dislocated jaw.

"So how are you doin', Mrs. Arsenault, Mrs. Meissner?" Wynnette smiles at them.

"Oh, fine, fine, just fine. Now, you kids, I've been sitting in the food court for the last thirty minutes. Isn't this just typical? Percy, you should know better."

Thank god for trains and being the irresponsible one, I think, as Aunt Galronia stares at Percy. I'm saved and start humming along with the Christmas music, "Silent Night" turned up to distortion.

"What?" Grammie screams at Wynnette. She smacks the rubber tip of her cane on the floor.

Wynette screams, "I said, how are you doing, Mrs. Meissner? All ready for Christmas?"

Grammie points at her head. "If we don't get out of the goddamn mall, I won't make it for Christmas, though with the way I've been feeling I think it'll be my last anyway," Grammie screams good-naturedly. She sits down in the middle of me and Wynnette. "How about a smoke for Grammie, Serrie?" Grammie barks.

I rub my bristly head. Galronia looks like she's progressed to lockjaw now, just at the thought of her mother and niece sitting in the middle of the mall having a smoke with Wynnette Doucette. I give Grammie a drag and she puts her arm around me.

Gallie rolls her eyes. "All right, it's time to go. The snow's falling out there and I'm not having any car accident. No hamburgers for you."

"Oh, shut up, Gallie." Grammie takes another drag and passes the cigarette to Wynnette. "We'll just finish up this smoke." Grammie holds it out to Gallie who rolls her eyes and looks away as Grammie giggles and Wynette and I join in.

Gallie seethes and repacks her shopping bag until Grammie is ready to hit the road. Just before we head out to the parking lot, I turn around. The music is clear here by the mall doors and underneath all the bad instrumentation there is a pretty soprano singing about snowflakes and snowmen. My eyes find Wynnette Doucette still sitting there on the bench, smoking, looking into the crowd, but you can tell she doesn't see anybody at all.

None of us go out for Christmas Eve church service. I'm still not sure what to do about the Reverend Rafuse and it's clear I've got to make some big changes in how I live. I can't trust myself. I stay at home wrapping my father's presents for my mother and listening to him tell me about the his plans for a rock garden for Number Seven, East Pubnico. He tells me he has special news for us on Christmas morning and not to say a word to anyone. Probably a new outhouse, I think. My mother sits in her room wrapping Christmas presents. Percy's building a new model train, and when I finish the big pile for my father, I go to his room.

"Coming in to sniff the glue?"

"Ha, ha," I say, and then sit on his bed. His room is a sty, exactly how it was when he left home, like some weird museum. But I'm one to talk, with my bedroom completely empty.

"You know, you're going to have to get it together, Serrie. You're not a kid anymore."

I stare at my hands. There is a yellow stain on my smoking fingers, dull yellow, the colour of old book pages. I sniff it — it smells like nicotine, no matter how much I scrub. Maybe I should use bleach. It's better to be clean and raw than dirty and comfortable. I look up and Percy is staring at me. I sit on my hands and look at his model. "So what train line is that from?"

"Don't change the subject. There are people who want to know when you are going to start growing up."

I shrug and say that I'm sure the treatment will help out.

Percy blows on a piece of plastic and then glues it to the side of the freight car; it's a door. "The Dominion Atlantic Railway. It was a special design for them. You know that old railway track you ski on, or used to ski on when you still did things like that, but I imagine you can't remember, seeing how long ago that was. Well, that railway was the DAR and it was discontinued in the 1940s. They ripped up the tracks and sold them but the line still stretches across the Valley like a corridor."

It's still what I like about him best — all the things he knows about, history, all the facts, the details. When he talks about history his hands wave around, pure Percy, making things from hundreds of years ago come alive, telling me bedtime stories that were true, my hero then.

"Maybe we can go out for a ski," I say, "before I go to . . . away, before you go back to Toronto to university." I don't say the name of where I'm going out loud; he'll cringe. The Weeping Willows Treatment Facility. Everybody cringes. Even the people who run the place. They like to call it *The Willows* but everyone else always adds the weeping. It was built on property donated by Evangeline Comeau, an Acadian whose family came back from Louisiana in 1920s during the Acadian renaissance and bought up heaps of land. Evangeline Comeau lives here in the summer on a great big estate in Pereau. She's down in New Orleans in the winter, on another big estate, I imagine. There's heaps of weeping willows all over the property, most of them surrounding a nice pond that the residents skate on in the winter. There is an indoor pool that looks out on the pond. Galronia calls it the Alkie Resort. Madame Comeau said they could have the land for free and call it the Weeping Willows Treatment Facility or they could buy it for thousands and call it whatever the hell they wanted.

"Nothing like a deportation," I say, and Percy looks up from his model and raises an eyebrow. I look at his walls, painted olive drab. Percy keeps gluing little railings and wheels and stuff on the train car. I ask him if he'll play the violin for me sometime while he's home, like he used to when I was little. He shrugs again and doesn't look up, so I head down the hall and up the stairs to my tower room. The clean flannel nightie my mother has laid out on the bed smells of fresh air — it's another one I haven't worn in years, clothesline-dried so stiff it could walk around the room, go down and have a chat with the tree probably. I roll around on the bed until it's soft and cozy.

Elizabeth calls and asks why I didn't come over. I tell her I'm tired and she says to call tomorrow. Dearie calls, grouchy and bored. I wish her a Merry Christmas and then read in bed until really late, my father calling up the stairs, "'Night, Ser," my mother, "Seraphina, don't forget to brush your teeth." But I do, I do forget to brush my teeth, and as I turn out the lamp, I'm too tired to care. I hang on to my navel ring as I start to get drowsy. The dark makes me feel safe and I pull the quilt to my chin. Le Mont jumps up on the bed and curls up at my back. His purr runs up my spine and then violin music spirals up the staircase: "My Home," one of the first pieces Percy learned, some delicate Scottish ballad, my favourite when I was a kid. I want to go tell Percy I'm going to grow up and be well-adjusted, but sleep sucks me away from the music of my brother.

Percy is shaking my shoulder and I'm so stiff the whole bed is squeaking. My breath blows out white in the frigid Christmas morning air of my bedroom. Out the east window I can see the pink morning sky as the sun starts to rise. The early light twinkles on the branches outside the window, the temperature low enough for the wet snow to have frozen. Percy shakes me again. I open my eyes. He's wearing these too-small pyjamas from years ago; we are both in our old nightclothes.

"Serrie! Serrie! It's morning. Let's check the stockings."

We run down to the living room, where Santy has made a stop. Cyril has been up early to make a fire and turn the furnace up so it is cozy warm by the tree. And he's made coffee for us.

"Strong, just the way you like it, Ser."

It's water-weak but I manage to bite my tongue, as he hums, mixing the pancake batter. Our mother is still in bed, sleeping in like a lady of leisure, Gallie says when she calls to see if we are up, to say Merry Christmas.

Percy and I open our stockings and I leave Percy with his book to go out and feed the birds. Cyril's got feeders at every outhouse, little ones. The wind chimes are caked in snow and make no noise even though there is a breeze. It's Christmas Day and the air smells of evergreens. There is a feeder outside the kitchen window at the back of the house, away from the road. Yesterday's seed is buried under snow and it has to be brushed off so it doesn't rot and mould, making the birds sick or high, you never know what chemicals are going to come off rotting grain. The snow is deep and the birdies are hungry, just flying a few feet away when I come to the big feeder. They sit there watching me, the chickadees, the purple finches, the pileated woodpeckers, even two crows up at the top of the maple tree. After the seed is poured, I stand still with my mitt full of seed, arm out. The birds don't come at first, but in less than five minutes they are at the feeders. I keep standing there and after fifteen minutes my arm is aching. But then, just as I'm going to go in, a chickadee lands on my finger-tips, fluffed up to keep warm. The claws grip my mitt as it grabs a peanut and flies way. I wait and it comes back again for another nut. While I can feel the pressure of the claws on the mitt, I can't notice the weight of the bird, the feed in my hand is heavier. And it keeps coming back until my palm is empty. Turning around, I see my mother watching in the window. She waves and smiles, still in her housecoat, a cup of coffee in her hand.

Inside, after I brush myself off in the porch, she's amazed that the birds ate from my hand, even more that I was able to stand there for so long. "I can't believe a person like you would be able to stand out there that long. It's remarkable," she says as she hands me a coffee.

I don't take the cup. "You don't have to be so critical. God." I whisper.

"It's just an observation, Seraphina. You can't take any kind of feedback at all."

"Well, telling me I'm impatient isn't really giving me a compliment or *feedback*."

"It's impossible to talk to you," she says.

I don't know what I did. Maybe it's just me being here that makes her angry. My coffee cup smacks on the kitchen table as my father comes in. "So everybody's having a nice Christmas." It's a plea, not a statement or a question. I pick up the coffee and head in by the fire and my mother follows with a plate of ginger cookies, made with fresh ginger, my favourite. She puts them in front of me and rubs my bristly head but I ignore her and she leaves the room.

Late morning I have a nap and when I get up there is Christmas music playing and Cyril has hot cider on the stove with cinnamon sticks. The fire roars. My mother goes out to the porch to pour a shot of whisky in her cup and then takes her cider in by the tree. We begin the present opening, my father starting us off with his big news. He's got a grant to do solar power research. We just sit there and stare. Who'd've thought, I think, and then feel ashamed — I'm turning into Galronia. He explains he's going to make some solar panels to heat hot water with, that he got a government grant for the alternative energy. And he shows us the letter and the check. I ask if the buoy thing in the workshed is for this and he tells me that's for a future project, tidal power in the Bay of Fundy. I don't know what the hell he's talking about really, sun-heated water, big panels nailed on the south side of the house. I can just see it now. But he's beaming. My father puts on "Jingle Bell Rock" and my mother starts dancing around like a kid, pulling me up and swinging me around while my father claps in time. My mother belts it out and I howl along with her. Wrapping paper and bows fly up in the air as we twirl around the room and when my mother dips me, a red ribbon sticks to my head and then she sticks more on and I am a giant dancing Christmas bow. We forget that any of the hospital stuff ever happened, that I am about to go into rehab. For a moment we are back in time.

All but Percy. He just organizes the presents, and the ornaments, and the pillows on the sofa, and he organizes the goddamn tree branches, like they were rearranging themselves when he wasn't looking. He barely talks to me when we open the presents. He loves the train book, though, and almost forgets that he's mad until he opens this big huge red-and-white sweater, like a candy cane. His face wrinkles and my mother tells him everyone's wearing them. From South America, she tells him. He glares at me like I picked it out and then rubs his hands on it.

"It's nice wool," he says.

"Quality wool," my father says.

They give me a pair of heavy-duty hiking boots for Christmas, leather and big laces.

"You can climb Mount Everest in those, Serrie," my father says.

My mother sits beside me in a pile of wrapping paper, her apron on. "Well, you seem to be into the big boots these days. These are waterproof. The fancy Gortex and treated leather."

I kiss her on the head. My father holds the train book and tells me it's a real find, a real find indeed. He doesn't know what to make of the gong, but he is touched I didn't get him something run-of-the-mill like socks or chocolates, like I usually do. We set it up and whack at it until my mother yells from the kitchen that she feels like she's in a goddamn temple.

For the rest of Christmas day I just hang about, doing odd chores for my mother, staring out the window counting all the tree branches and twigs until my mother says I'm acting like a lunatic. Her eyes go wide and she puts her hand on her mouth.

"I didn't mean it like that, Serrie."

Percy walks into the kitchen, gets a glass of milk. "It's the truth, though."

My father limps in and says everybody should just try to get along. I stare out the window. I hear "White Christmas" playing in the living room.

"Who's not getting along?" my mother says.

"Well, what's the commotion about? Why can't we just try to get back on track and have a nice day?" Cyril sighs as he looks at the bird feeder.

Percy gulps all the milk and slams the glass down on the counter. "I can't act like nothing is going on. She's just out of the asylum and we're acting like it's a normal Christmas."

My mother glares at him. "Hospital, Percy, hospital. And do we have to talk about that? It's bloody Christmas Day."

Nuthouse, hospital, shit-house, outhouse, asylum, what's the difference, I think so loud it hurts my temples. I can feel myself losing it. My father starts with the *now Percy's* but all I can think is that I don't stand a chance in this family.

"Christ, it's not all my fault. That's what they told me in the hospital. It's a family issue. And what about Thanksgiving?"

That stops them dead, me, too, even. But there's no talking about that stuff, *no sir*. Percy gets another glass of milk and my mother puts her hands on her hips and then tells me not to cry. My father leans against the wall and looks out at the bird feeder again. "Now why do you have to go saying things like that when everyone's getting on just fine?"

"Because we never talked about Thanksgiving. Can't we ever talk about anything here? Things aren't always fine, you know."

Percy drains his glass of milk and shoves me when he walks by. I throw a wooden fruit bowl at him. Red apples fly through the air. He ducks and starts screaming, "See, she's a lunatic, she's a lunatic. She can't control her temper."

So much for everyone getting along just fine. My mother takes off her apron, throws it down, picks it up and then ties it on. We watch as she ties and unties, reties it so tight I wonder how she can breathe. Maybe she doesn't want to breathe. The phone rings and we all just stare at it, ringing and ringing until my father answers, shaking his head at all of us. It's Dearie from Florida.

I pull the phone cord around the corner and sit on the floor in the dining room. My mother is listening.

"Merry Christmas. I was talking to Elizabeth. She says you haven't even called her yet."

"Merry Christmas, Dearie. Got a tan?"

Dearie sighs and says she's bored crazy. They're staying in the condo and there's nothing to do and she wishes she was back in Foster and she can't wait to get back. My mother picks up the extension, saying I've got help put stuff in the car to go to Grammie's. I still can't get Dearie off the phone, she's so homesick. She asks me if I was over in Morden, did I go see the French Cross

for her, her Acadian Christmas pilgrimage. I tell her I can't go anywhere alone, so getting over on the mountain to the Bay of Fundy
is a big goddamn challenge. She says that's fine but she's a terrible
liar and I wish she'd just fucking say she's pissed off, but I don't say
that either, just goodbye and hang up. The phone rings while my
hand is still on the receiver. Elizabeth wants to know why I haven't
called her so I ask her why she hasn't called me. She says she's been
busy. I say I have to go. She says they'll come visit after dinner. I say
who's *they*? Elizabeth says that Reggie's out for Christmas dinner. I
tell her Galronia just wants family this Christmas. I'm trying to cut
down on the crowds, I tell her. Elizabeth is quiet, and says she'll
call me later.

Christmas-food smells smack us in the face as we come into
Grammie's. Gallie taking the turkey out of the oven, the kitchen
just as it was when my grandparents bought the house, wainscoting,
old sink and cupboards, linoleum, an ironing board that pops out of
the wall, hardwood floors perfectly maintained. Joan and Buster
Hayes are sitting at the kitchen table, friends of Gallie and
Grammie's. Kelly, their only daughter, and her family are in Florida
for Christmas, so they are dining with the Meissners. We are an
hour late, as usual. Gallie stands there in her apron, giving us orders
as we take off our boots and coats in the porch.

"Martha, Mum's upstairs getting ready, so you go check on
her and make sure she hasn't had a stroke on the toilet. Isn't
that something about Cyril's grant for what . . . what is it he got
a grant for? Martha, please go check on Mum. My, oh, my.
Now, Serrie, you put the wine glasses on the table . . . oh dear, that's
not a good idea, is it?" She points to my nose. "Now do you
think we're just going to get used to that? Always gotta be different,
eh, Serrie?"

I twirl the nose ring at her and she shakes her head. "I see.

That's lovely. That what they do over in London these days? Or maybe that's what they do on the ward in the NS." Before I can say anything, she shoves her head in the fridge. I just stand there shaking, so Buster salutes me, Joan takes a swig of her drink as she asks how Dearie is.

"Fine," I say. "Fine. In Florida."

"Must be nice," Galronia shouts from the fridge. "Everybody's in Florida 'cept us. Guess we're not good enough for that."

Percy sighs and Gallie pulls her head out of the fridge and takes a swipe at him with her eyes and then goes back in. I start wishing it was a gas oven.

"Florida's full of the Kay-bek-cois," Joan says. "That's what they like to be called. I know because I was there last year this same time."

Percy unzips his coat. I can see his new red-and-white sweater. "Well, that's what they are, *Québécois*," he sighs.

Joan takes a gulp. "Well, whatever, *Qué-bé-cois*, franker-phoners, whatever turns your crank. Florida's full of 'em in the winter."

"Yeah, and it's full of oranges. Hemingway lived there, too," I say.

Percy hangs up his coat and smiles at me. Truce.

Galronia pulls her head out of the fridge and stares at Percy's sweater. Then she looks at me. "That Hemingway blew his brains right out." Galronia stares at Percy's sweater again. "Percy, you look as gay as eighteen balloons."

My mother grabs an apron. "Gallie, that sweater's from South America and you know it. You were with me when I bought it, for lord's sake. You picked it out."

"Well, now, it certainly looked better in the store."

My mother ties on an apron and glares at Galronia. We go to the den; they'll call us when it's suppertime. It's the first time I don't have to help out.

Galronia's voice comes behind us like a mosquito. "Now don't tie up the phone, Serrie. I'm expecting a call from Gordie."

My father comes in from parking the car. We can hear him in the kitchen. "Now let's everybody have a good time, Christmas dinner and all."

Percy looks at me and rolls his eyes. "When's he going to get a new line?"

He flops on the couch and I take out *Brave New World*. Our father comes in and joins us and we can hear Martha and Galronia in the kitchen.

"Now where's the gin, Gallie?"

"Under the sink."

"What?"

"The gin is under the sink, I said. Are you deaf?"

"Under the sink?"

"That's what I said, sister, less than two seconds ago."

"With the Comet and Mr. Clean?"

"Yes, with the Comet and the Mr. Clean and anything else that's down there."

"She'll kill us yet, Marthie." Grammie has arrived from the bathroom.

"Very funny, Mum. I thought it would be better out of sight now that there's two of . . . them."

"Two of what?"

"Well . . . you know . . . Cyril . . . and now Seraphina. You know."

Grammie coughs. "No, no, I don't know."

"Lord, you'd think *I* was the nurse."

"No, I'd think you were something else and I'd rather not say what. God almighty, they're not rummies. Now give me the gin." Grammie's cane thumps.

"I'm just trying to help out." Gallie opens the cupboard. "There's Fresca in the fridge for mix. And I got Sussex ginger ale *for them*, the really gingery stuff that Cyril likes."

My mother comes in with a tray, eggnog and rum for Percy, and ginger ale for Cyril. For me she's gone and made a Shirley Temple with maraschino cherry juice, cherries and oranges.

"Now just sip that, pumpkin pie." She pats me on the head and I pat her on the bum. I look over at Cyril and he raises his glass to me. I wonder how he's managed to stand it all these years. I raise my glass back and Percy holds his up. "Chin-chin." We read until we are called to dinner.

The table is sparkling in the candlelight. Cut-crystal dishes full of pickles and relishes: nine-day wonders, chow-chow, bread-and-butters. Gallie's good china plates, Blossom Time pattern with all these pink flowering apple trees, crystal butter dish and salt and peppers. Grammie's sterling silver gleams. Gallie sets the table with every piece of frigging cutlery in the silver chest. No one knows how to use most of it, though she barks *eat inwards, eat inwards* at every family dinner we've ever had. Percy ignores her, my father just scoops the whole meal up with the big fork, and I use whatever I want and plead confusion. Most of it goes back in the cutlery box unwashed. It never changes.

But I'm not at the table. I'm in the corner at a TV table to make room for all the adults. The TV table is wobbly but it's easier not to trade it for another one, to just take my seat and wait for my mother to bring me my plate. She stands beside me.

"Gallie, you have her over here like she's got some kind of contagion." My mother puts a cut-crystal glass full of tomato juice by my plate. She always pretends to forget I hate tomato juice and I always remind her, our little ritual. This year I don't say a word. I even take a sip and put my hand on her arm. "It's okay, Ma." I haven't called her this in years.

Gallie comes in from the kitchen. "Time for Grace."

My mother glares at her and I reach up for her hand, squeezing it. "Really, let's just eat."

And my mother sits down at the table while Grammie launches into the Grace. "Praise God, Holy Christ, thank you for the food and family, grant us peace, amen, Gallie, get the gravy."

I focus in on all the little piles of food: mountains of mashed potatoes, squash, turkey, stuffing, all covered in gravy. It's easier to eat one mountain at a time. For awhile I think we might have what my father is always asking for, everybody just having a nice time, me the contented outcast in the corner. There isn't much talk because everyone is eating, congratulating my father on his grant, though no one seems to know what he's up to. He's proud though, smiling away. Grammie's muttering that she can't see her food so Galronia and my mother keep putting more candles on the table until it looks we're having a seance.

Gallie takes a sip of wine and says, "Seraphina, I hear your old boyfriend Trevor got religion and goes about with the Pentecostals. He had trouble with the law but he's a clean liver now. See him sitting in that blue church van they have to pick up everyone and drive them in for service. Sits in the back seat, though, so some of his old ways must still be hanging on."

I make gravy lakes and giggle; I can't see Trevor as a Pentecostal. My nose ring catches the candlelight.

"You look just like a lady pirate, Serrie, my dear." Joan smiles at me and I give her a little wave from the corner.

"Yes, and lives just like one, too," Galronia adds as she stuffs in a forkful. My father sighs and my mother puts her napkin down.

Joan says, "Speaking of pirates, did you hear the money the government's planning to pump into the *Bluenose*?"

Percy frowns. "The *Bluenose* wasn't a pirate ship, Joan."

"No, no, it wasn't, was it? Privateers then?" She dishes out more pickles.

"No, she was a banks fishing schooner, for racing, too."

"Quite a ship she was, though. Lord god, you can't beat a schooner," Buster says.

Grammie squints at Buster over a forkful of mashed potatoes and I wouldn't be surprised if Grammie sailed on the *Bluenose*, if she was the ship's nurse — you never know with her.

"No, no, you can't beat a schooner. There's nothing like a wooden boat. Except a good light, I might add. Now I wish I could see what the hell is on my blessed fork."

Another candle lands before her and my mother sits back down. "Lord, Mum, sometimes I think you do this just to keep us on our toes."

Grammie winks at Percy.

"I saw a book, *Shipbuilding in Lunenburg*, at Earle Baltzer's yesterday," I tell Joan.

Gallie lets out a food-coated laugh and talks to her plate. "Well, I imagine some people won't be having much time for reading. Some people will be getting a job, as that's what folks do who drop out of university, unless they just happen to be independently wealthy and forget to make that known to their own family."

"I don't want a stupid job that's boring." I shovel food in my mouth.

"And what kind of job does a drop-out get? Some people might think they can get a job reading books and I'd like to welcome those types to the real world. People take what they can get in this economy and that's just how it is, plain and simple."

The turkey turns to sawdust in my mouth. I don't know what kind of job I can get; it's not like I have a plan. The plan was always I'd go to university but there was no back-up plan, there was no planning the plan, there was just always the plan.

"She's got the Weeping Willows to go through before any job, Gallie. That's enough. Can't we just eat?" My mother crosses her arms.

"Imagine, a Meissner at the Weeping Willows. Good goddamn thing Dad isn't alive to see this. He must be having fits in the grave as it is." Gallie presses her lips together and her eyes narrow. Grammie looks at Gallie and waves her fork.

"Eat your supper before it gets cold. Your father, Garnet, God rest his soul, would just want his granddaughter doing what she needs to."

My father clears his throat and rubs his back as Percy talks with his mouth full. "She's a Sullivan, Aunt Gallie. We're Sullivans, not Meissners." Percy glares at Galronia and I bet he's wishing he was in Toronto.

Grammie takes a sip of wine. "That's Meissners with two s's. Your grandfather didn't go and change it, no sir, not like that second cousin of his who was Lieutenant Governor. Taking the s out to hide the German. Now who did he think he was fooling? Everyone knew they were from down in Lunenburg."

"I think Aldous Huxley was onto something with his idea of genetic engineering," I say, wishing Gallie had been conditioned never to leave the kitchen. Grammie puts her fork down.

"Now, Serrie, I don't want to hear *that name* at the Christmas dinner table again. Your grandfather had Jewish blood, you know, and so do you. German Jews from the Black Forest. Where the hell are you anyway? Where's my one and only granddaughter?"

"Huxley," I scream. "Hux-ley, not Hitler. I'm over here at the TV table."

She turns her head around, my Grammie the Owl. "Oh, I see," Grammie says. "Now who in the name of God put you over there?"

Percy scoops up some food and then waves his fork around while he talks, the potato falling off, lump by lump. "Grammie, according to you we're Jewish, Micmac, and Gypsy, in addition to being German, Scottish, and Irish, and that's what accounts for us being so dark."

"I'm not any of that," I call from the TV table. Percy looks at me as he sticks the empty fork in his mouth and his teeth clang on silver.

"And what are you then, Serrie?" Joan asks.

And so I say I'm trying to be of the Stoic persuasion. Percy chokes on his fork, Gallie rolls her eyes, and Grammie takes a sip of wine.

"Well, now, that's a new one, Roman. And I like it, I do. A little bit of Imperial blood spices up the old family tree, now doesn't it, Percy, my boy?"

Percy giggles like he hasn't since we were kids at the beach. He smiles at Grammie and then at me. My stomach relaxes.

"Maybe we should just say we're Nova Scotian and leave it at that." Grammie winks at us, shakes her head, and then commences eating her turkey. "Oh, what a nice dry bird. Nothing like a dry bird. I love a dry bird." Some food sticks to the side of her cheek. Her face is still with just the slow denture mashing motion of her jaw.

"Well, maybe we should plant a weeping willow tree out back to mark this momentous year." Gallie takes a sip of wine and pats her mouth with her napkin. "Now that's one of my better ideas if I do say so myself."

My mother slams her fork down. "Can't you let well enough alone? Can't you let it drop? Can't you let us just get on with it? We have company but you'd never frigging know it, now, would you?" my mother says, each word slow and separate.

My father looks around at everybody but not making eye contact, smiling nervously. "Now, everybody, let's just enjoy this spread of food."

Gallie keeps eating. "I'm not saying anything, now, am I, Cyril? Do you see me talking? *I'm* the one who made the spread of food. A lot of thanks I get. Martha, you still have your apron on at the Christmas dinner table."

Grammie looks at Gallie. "You're certainly on your high horse tonight, Galronia."

In my safe seat over in the corner, I think that Aunt Gallie would do well to stop acting as though every single thing is an issue of morality and noble living.

"Well, aren't some people all high and mighty? Issue of morality and noble living, indeed." Gallie says.

They're all looking at me; Percy's got that raised eyebrow. I'm talking out loud, jesus god. Grammie bangs her fist on the table.

"Now who said that about morality and noble living? I'm all for a little recitation, like the old days when we had to put verse to memory. 'This is the forest primeval —"

"Some people would do well to learn morality," Gallie says.

Buster's eating like it's the Last Supper. Joan pushes her chair back and my mother slams her fork down.

"Now, just because that Gordie never bothered to call doesn't mean you have to go and pick on my goddamn kids, does it, just because your son can't be bothered to come home even at Christmastime, not once in the last five years."

The table shakes as my mother stands and strides to the kitchen. Everyone goes quiet but Grammie. "Any more red pepper jelly?"

"Oh, Mum, not now," Gallie barks.

Grammie puts down her fork and wipes her mouth with her napkin. "Pardon me, Galronia? This is *my* house, young lady. I worked for years at the Foster hospital to pay for this and it is mine, free and clear." Gallie opens her mouth and Grammie holds up her long index finger and Gallie's mouth shuts. "If you ever talk that way to me again, I'll ship you back to Toronto with your philandering SOB husband Bennie Arsenault. I may be old but don't you ever forget whose house this is, girl, or I'll put you out like fish guts for the gulls. Have I made myself clear?"

It is so quiet I can hear Grammie's dentures shift. Gallie just sits looking at her plate.

"And wipe that lugubrious look off your face before I do it for you."

Thank god for company is all I know, because Joan jumps up and takes over. "Now let's everybody just digest and then we'll have the plum pudding. Who's for hard sauce?" She starts piling plates and my father heaves himself up to help her. Gallie rushes into the kitchen crying. I can feel my eyes fill up. The plate disappears from in front of me and it's just me and the TV table. My father comes back to the table and Buster asks him about the solar power and, grateful, Cyril launches into a technical explanation of the panels. Grammie looks at me as Percy knocks over his glass of milk.

"Might as well laugh as cry, eh, Serrie?" Grammie says.

After the plum pudding, Elizabeth and Reggie stop by Grammie's for a visit. Reggie is wearing his Clan McLeod tartan tie and the gold Volvo cuff links he got from his dealership for Christmas. My mother and Joan hand out hot rum toddies and hard eggnogs as we all sit in the parlour eating fruitcake, squares and shortbreads. Elizabeth tells everyone about the trip to Palm Springs at the end of January and Reggie talks cars with Buster and my father, telling them they haven't lived until they drive a BMW. Percy loses interest in about ten seconds and starts reading the coffee table books. I sit there rubbing my scalp and Reggie winks and shakes his head, downing his drink. My mother goes to fetch him a refill as I escape to the upstairs bathroom. I peek in the TV room on the way up and Gallie is in there by the phone, with a migraine coming on. As I go up the stairs I look at all the photos hanging, ones of us as little kids, black-and-whites of the ancestors, Gordie as a little boy with his giant space-head, so big that Aunt Gallie had to have a caesarean section. There are pictures of him leaning on his red Trans Am, him holding up a lobster. That autumn after we moved there, when I was nine, he went out on the oil rigs on the Grand Banks off Newfoundland. Another rig went down with lots of his friends on it and not one person survived. After that, he headed out west to Alberta, to work on the oil fields.

The summer when we were living at Grammie's, we'd bug Gordie to take us for a drive in his car, but the only thing I recall him saying was that I was a stupid brat and Percy was a damn fag and we should stay out of his way or he'd kill us. We stayed out of his way, especially when he was babysitting us, except that Saturday afternoon at the end of August when his friend Brian came over to help *mind the kids.* As soon as our mother left, they told us to get into his Trans Am for a ride, which confused us, so we just stood there, the brat and the fag, until he started yelling and pushing us into the back seat while he and Brian jumped into the front laughing. I saw Dearie out the Trans Am window, in her yard, just back from Maine, her mother just going into the hospital. We backed up and squealed down the road, me a bug against the window, looking at her, mouthing for help and her running into her house. Gordie roared us up the North Mountain and down all these dirt roads, into Lupin Cove, straight for the harbour, swerving at the last minute, the Bay of Fundy a big blue blur and me throwing up in my mouth and swallowing it back down. Gordie and Brian kept looking back and laughing. He put on Pink Floyd really loud and I couldn't even hear myself over the roar of the engine and the music. Gordie started swerving on the gravel, looking in the rear-view mirror and crossing his eyes at me.

My mother was home early, standing on the steps with her hands on her hips when we burned in the driveway. Dearie beside her with her arms crossed, Dearie to the rescue. And Grammie, she was standing behind them both. Grammie and Mum took a strip off Gordie and he tried to say we made him take us for a ride, but Dearie had already told Mum and Grammie and they got even madder at his lying. Gordie felt bad because he had a soft spot for Aunt Martha, though you'd never know it from the way he treated her freaking offspring. Gallie came home from the library and went at him again. And then Gallie and Martha went at it. Grammie told them to both shut up. Gordie left a few months later for the oil rig.

At the top of the stairs there is a picture of him on the deck, all covered in black goo with a hard hat on, with all these guys that died out in the Atlantic. He is kneeling in the front, smiling.

I'm sitting in the empty tub with my back on the air cushion and my feet on the tap. There is no shower. Grammie's bathroom is really old and hasn't been renovated yet, despite Gallie's attempts. That will come when Grammie is in the grave. I'm reading *National Geographic*, an article about Madagascar. Who wouldn't want to go to a place with a name like that? There is a dance beat tap on the door and Elizabeth comes in with her eggnog. She laughs to herself and sits down on the toilet to do her pee thing. She is wearing a straight black skirt with a pink angora sweater and I can tell by the way she hauls the skirt up around her hips that she's got a big buzz on from all the Christmas visiting. I watch each toilet paper square come off.

"So can you even drink spritzers or Singapore Slings? You know, girlie drinks? Eggnog, holiday drinks?" Elizabeth asks as she tries to wipe and slips to the side of the toilet seat. She looks up at me and holds out her glass. I can smell the rum from across the room.

"Nope," I say. "A drink is a drink is a drink." And the smell is making me feel sick. I don't know why and maybe I never will know why, but I have no desire, no urge, no nothing to drink. The passion is gone, that special feeling, and I could almost cry from the emptiness. What comes after this?

"Not even punch?"

"Nope."

"God, that's terrible." She's finished wiping but just sits there, sipping her eggnog, pantyhose around her ankles, skirt about her waist like a cummerbund. "I thought you'd grow out of it, you know, all your weird high school drinking. Not grow into drugs." Her big bottom lip trembles.

I wonder how I am going to manage now, because I don't know anyone who doesn't drink. It's the Maritime culture, for the love of God. It's what young people do. We drink in parks, we drink in cars, we drink at parties and then we go off to university and drink in bars and drink at parties and drink at beaches and in the privacy of our own residence rooms and apartments. We see who can hold the most liquor. It's a prestige thing. Rehab is not. And here I am sitting in a fucking bathroom with everyone else downstairs getting smashed but gentle Cyril, who sits there looking like he'd be happy to go sit in the truck all night reading with a flashlight.

Elizabeth kneels down by the tub. I'm a priest in a lavatory confessional, which reminds me of the Reverend Rafuse — I still haven't apologized or thanked him for the flowers. I smile and tell Elizabeth not to worry about a thing.

"Why, Serrie, why do you do what you do?"

I look at my yellow fingers. "I don't know, Elizabeth, I don't know. I'm not doing it anymore now. There's hope yet." But she doesn't seem to think so, like she wishes I was still boozing it up, not knowing any other way to be with me. And she goes into what Grammie calls tippler tears and dabs at her big brown eyes with a wad of toilet paper.

"You know, I bet after awhile you can drink again. But you should probably stay away from the drugs. Things will get back to normal, Serrie. Maybe you can get a job in the city. And you can live with me and Clare. And you should go back to school. You do great in school. You just need a break. We all need breaks. I don't think Dearie will stay in university full time. She hates it so much, but Mr. Melanson won't let her study anything but business." Elizabeth is really inspired now and climbs back on the toilet to pee again. "I can't wait to go to Palm Springs. My parents gave me a real bed for Christmas. With springs. You can jump on it." From the tub I look at Elizabeth and smile.

And then we go downstairs and hug goodbye. Elizabeth and Reggie are off to do more Christmas visiting, like an old married couple. Reggie pulls on his toque and slaps my shoulder.

"So we'll come over tomorrow to get you at four o'clock."

I raise my eyebrow.

"Skiing. Remember, we're going skiing."

I had forgotten. It wasn't like I'd been budgeting for a ski trip. And I hadn't skied since I was fifteen. "Oh, I have to help out my mother," I say. "Lots of cleaning up to do."

"How long does it take to clean up?" Elizabeth asks.

"That'll be the day, when Serrie cleans up." Gallie's come into the kitchen for more wine.

My mother is behind her, holding out her glass. "Gallie, now how the hell would you know?"

Reggie ties his scarf. "Skiing is good for what ails you. That's what they say."

Now who says that, I wonder?

Reggie takes out his smooth leather gloves and continues. "It's especially good after all the festivities. Don't want to get a roll." He pats his stomach.

Elizabeth giggles. "We'll watch her, Mrs. Sullivan. Don't you worry."

"Lord, let her have a bit of fun. It's not like she killed anyone. I'll pay for it." Grammie's in the kitchen now, looking for the wine. Grammie shakes her head as she takes the bottle from Gallie and heads back to the parlour.

"You look after yourself, Mrs. Meissner," Reggie calls after her. He thinks Grammie's a character.

Her voice floats back: "Yes, indeed, Reginald, I take care of everything but my mind — it does what it wants these days."

Reggie starts laughing and then looks at my mother. "It's on me, my Christmas treat. How about it, Mrs. Sullivan?"

It's like I'm being signed out for the day.

"Now, we can give you money, Reggie."

Reggie takes my mother's hand and shakes it. "No, no, it's on me, a day on the slopes with two Valley girls. "

My mother giggles and Gallie stares at her with horror, and then turns to Reggie. "Serrie's a Mountain girl, Reginald. Isn't that right, Elizabeth?"

"Oh, well, whatever," Elizabeth laughs, and she and Reggie head out the door. I shut it behind them.

My mother just rolls her eyes at Gallie and starts putting more shortbread and fruitcake on plates, getting ready for visitors. In a few minutes there is a knock at the door, and then people from town start arriving, trickling in over the next half hour: the Churches, the Taylors, the MacNeils, the Littles, the Camerons, the Browns, the Wagstaffs, the Armstrongs. They all crowd into the parlour and I sit on the sofa, jammed between Galronia and Joan. The conversation centres on Percy, his graduate program, fancy old Toronto, and the goddamn government. I stare at the rug, at the old brass clock on the mantel, a clear bell jar sort of thing, Grammie's retirement present from the hospital. I think about skiing tomorrow, wondering if it's just like riding a bike, and the conversation spins on the parlour air. I quietly slip from the room and put on my winter things. Just then the phone rings and I hurry with my boots but Gallie hollers that it's for me.

"Merry fuckin' Christmas. I am so bored. Getting some fat on those bones?"

"Merry Christmas, Dearie. How's Florida?"

"Same. You know, sun, beaches, blue skies, it's okay, nothing great. So what are you doing?"

"Just going out for a walk."

"That's weird," she says.

"That's me," I whisper and look at my boots.

"So did you see Elizabeth?" she asks.

"Yup, we're going skiing tomorrow, me and her and Reggie."

"No fair. How come you always wait until I'm not around to do stuff?"

I say, "Dearie, you don't even ski. And it was Reggie's idea. Jeez —"

"Well, it's not like you ski. Where are you getting the money for that?"

Just then Gallie comes in. "Now don't go tying up that phone. Gordie and Bobby are going to be trying to call and I don't want them getting a busy signal on Christmas Day. You know Gordie, he only tries one time."

Dearie's heard every word so she doesn't protest, just asks who Bobby is. "My first cousin once removed, you know that," I tell her.

"Oh, right, I forgot."

A light snow is falling as I walk on the sidewalk smoking a cigarette. The street lights are dull and muted, but the Christmas lights on all the houses blaze away, and I wonder if this is what Vegas looks like, but just more, you know, bigger, brighter, tackier. I wonder about Christmas in Florida, beach-ball Christmas. No one is on the streets, but then no one walks in small-town Nova Scotia unless they are on doctor's orders because of high blood pressure or a heart condition or if they are a bit touched, or a rebel maybe, some horrible agitator trying to stir up trouble. Walking is no longer a means of transportation; that's why we have cars. It's so quiet I can hear my boots go squeak on the snow sending shivers up my spine, so I try to walk like a sprite. My foot has healed up now and I can skip and run and jump if I want to.

I walk past the church and only the front light is on. All dark in the sanctuary. It is the only Christmas I've not gone to the service. The manse is lit up with green lights that go with the green house paint. It's very pretty, I think, from the sidewalk. There is a crèche. I stand on their front step for a long minute, my finger on the doorbell, and then I sigh and push it. Mrs. Rafuse answers and her lips go from a smile to a big circle of surprise. I scuff the toe of my boot and whisper, "Merry Christmas."

"Well, well, Merry Christmas to you, Serrie." She just stands there with the cold air blowing in and I can hear the Reverend coming. I just stand there smiling like a jack-o'-lantern.

The Reverend comes into the hall. "Oh, my goodness, Seraphina, dear girl." He flicks his jaw.

They stand there looking at me and I look at their slippered feet. I can hear people laughing in the living room. Their little boy,

Andy, runs out in elf pyjamas and stops and grabs his father's leg. He points at my face and giggles and then hugs my leg. I kneel down and he asks me why I have an earring in my nose. I tell him I don't know, because that's the truth — I don't have the slightest idea. "It's very pretty," the little boy says.

"Come in, come in, and let's shut that door. Now, Andy, you let your mother put you back to bed. Give me your coat, Serrie."

"I like wearing it," I say. "I mean, I won't stay . . . I just wanted to stop by and —"

"Let's go in here." I take my boots off and then follow him down the shiny hardwood hall with hooked area rugs to his study door at the end. The Reverend's study is a big room with French windows. The green light from outside spills in on his huge oak desk. It's covered in papers and he starts apologizing for the mess and clears a big brown armchair for me. I sit down and he sits opposite me, crossing his legs. The Reverend flicks his little fringe of hair over his bald spot and smiles. There is no way I'm taking my hat off.

"Well, Merry Christmas," the Reverend says.

"Merry Christmas," I say automatically. I take a deep breath. "I'm sorry for calling you up from England. I've been having all these problems, you know." I can feel my eyes water and I'd like nothing better than a big smoke, but that would be ungodly. "Anyway, I wanted you to know I was very sorry and I didn't mean to be rude and I hope you will forgive me and it was very thoughtful of you to send me flowers in the hospital and I shared them with this woman who had shock treatments but I didn't have shock treatments and I should have sent you a thank-you card but I'm having trouble seeing people these days and I'll be going to the Weeping Willows and I hope you will forgive me for being such a selfish fucked person." I put my hand to my mouth and bite my lip but the Reverend Rafuse leans over and puts his hand on my knee.

"It feels good to say 'fuck' sometimes, doesn't it?"

I smile and chew back my crying. He says of course he forgives me, that I am already forgiven, I have to forgive myself. *What did I expect he would say?* I think. He is a preacher and it is his job to forgive. He asks why I called him and I tell him I don't remember, I was in a blackout. It's the first time I've ever said this out loud and he nods, not in that clinical way like the nervous psychiatrist, but with compassion, you know, looking at me with this softness. I keep waiting for him to yell, not that he ever did yell at me when I was the sexton, but I just keep waiting.

"Serrie, you kept saying that Mr. Burgess had taken your china."

Oh god, is that what I rave about when I'm in a blackout? Let the dead bury the dead, Grammie says, but it's like the past is crawling out of the grave. I tell him I just don't remember, maybe being in England must have made me think of teacups and stuff.

He nods. "Serrie, do you know what the whole point to Jesus' life was?"

I just stare at him. It's like I'm back in Bible camp.

"Serrie, Jesus came here to tell us not to be afraid."

I smile and nod. How can I tell the Reverend that Jesus just obviously couldn't have known what-was-what. We talk a bit more about the Weeping Willows and he says it is a miracle I am dealing with this now at my age, some people live their entire lives in misery, that my family are good people who mean well but he knows there are problems at home. And he says I should turn to God for help now, for the strength to deal with these problems, that the Lord is right beside me.

The Reverend stands in the doorway as I go down the steps. "Serrie?"

I turn and raise my eyebrows.

"Serrie, the answer is yes." He clasps his hands together.

I just look at him.

"You kept asking me, would all the angels carry you to God?"

What an idiot I am. Doesn't he know that the last thing I want to hear is what I actually said to him? I just keep looking at him, snowflakes falling on our heads.

He goes into his sermon voice: "The Almighty will let you know when it's your time. Okay? He'll just take you himself, okay? Don't go calling on the angels. He'll send them. You just have to keep living, keeping the faith. Carrying the torch, okay, Serrie?"

I nod at the Reverend Rafuse. I was a Classical Studies scholar in another life. I know about carrying the torch, a good pagan thing to do. The Reverend holds up his hand like he's at the Olympics. I hold my hand up, too, and leave. When I turn back, the Reverend is still on the step with his still hand up, glowing in the green light by the nativity scene. Maybe I could take his picture, make holy cards and go up and sell them to all the Catholics in Cape Breton and make enough to retire on. I turn and march home with my arm up.

It's almost midnight when I get back. Joan and Buster are on their way out the door and my father too, to warm the truck up. Gallie gives me a big liquored-up hug. God love the hard eggnog. Grammie is in bed and I zip up the stairs to kiss her goodbye and then back down to the kitchen, so clean and shiny you'd think there wasn't even a big dinner. As we are finally heading out the door, the phone rings. It's Gordie and the first thing Aunt Gallie does is lay into him about calling so late. In the car, my mother says she doesn't know why Gallie bothers with Gordie and she doesn't know why Gordie bothers calling.

After we get home, I sit upstairs in my tower room, but I'm so twitchy I can't stand it and I go down to Percy's room and ask him if he wants to drive over to Morden to see the French Cross.

"Ah, Dearie's journey," he says, looking at his violin, and I realize he has hardly played at all this Christmas. He regards my nose ring as he would an old map or an artifact.

"Do you want to drive over to the shore or not?" I ask again. He stretches. I can't go anywhere if he doesn't agree and he knows it.

"Where did you go tonight?"

"To the Reverend Rafuse's."

"And what did he say?" Percy crosses his arms over his chest. He starts singing in his flat, tone-deaf baritone, so funny coming from someone who plays a gorgeous violin:

> *I have three brothers and they are at rest*
> *Their arms are folded on their breast*
> *But a poor simple sailor just like me*
> *Must be tossed and driven on the dark blue sea.*

He stops and licks his lips. He is truly one of god's great wonders, I think.

He asks again, "And what did the Reverend say?"

"That I should keep the faith, carry the torch."

Percy nods like this makes perfect sense to him. "You're so impatient, Serrie. You'd be a horrible farmer, digging up the crops every day to see if they were taking root."

"Look, Percy, I'm being really patient right now. Just call me Job. Now do you or do you not want to go for a drive?"

He scratches again, still in his big gay sweater. "Sure, the tide will be high. I'd like a drive."

We bundle into coats and scarfs. Our parents are still up; it's taking us all a long time to wind down tonight. Percy yells from the kitchen door, "We're going for a drive over to the shore, so don't wait up."

"Fine, kids. Mind the road and have some fun," Cyril calls from the living room, where he is reading Christmas-present books.

Our mother comes in with Le Mont in her arms. "Percy better be doing the driving."

"Of course I am," he sighs and we take a step into the porch.

"Well, be careful of the roads and going across the Mountain at this time of night."

Percy bites his lip and then snaps, "We're not planning to do power turns or anything."

He jerks the outside door open and it looks like they are going to have words so I start thinking about driving. It's really funny because we all know I am a better driver than Percy; Cyril says I'm a natural-born driver.

"Well, I'm just saying to be careful. Why you kids want to go over there in the middle of the night is beyond me."

"I'm always careful and what's the difference with the time of day? We aren't driving with the headlights out or anything. God."

Percy pushes out ahead of me and I shrug at our mother and follow him out, thinking there was a time she would have been the one packing us all in the car. We don't talk while we sit in the truck, letting the engine warm up, and as we start backing up, Martha comes running out with Cyril's coat and boots on over her nightgown.

"Jesus, what is it now?" Percy hisses under his breath as he rolls the window down.

She hands us a thermos of hot chocolate.

It's snowing when we head over the North Mountain. We are in low four-wheel drive and creep along through the snowdrifts, clunking down into first gear so we don't go in the ditch. I keep expecting Percy to turn the truck around, but he doesn't, just cranks up the heat and the defrost. The fan makes too much noise for us to talk, which is fine with me. All the way over, the snowflakes hit the windshield and we can see only white, but Percy keeps going and the engine roars as he shifts into second. There is nothing but white until we near Lupin Cove and then the snow fades and the night is dark and clear. Percy puts the truck back into first gear as we pass the old farm and then the Lupin Cove Church at the top of Moon Rise Hill. The little graveyard sits at the crest, the dead looking out over the Bay. We start down the steep drop into the village. In June the hill is lined with purple, pink, and white lupins, but now it's just a big mother of a snowbank. And then the harbour is there, right-smack-in-frigging-front of us, shiny black wavelets in the truck lights, the water quivering, alive. You have to turn hard to the left, the road then going over a little white bridge and circling the harbour, and then up another hill and down along the shore. Right where you make the sharp turn is the one-of-a-kind cottage, this amazing little arts and crafts style house, the windows dark at this time of night.

Going around the Harbour, just before you head up the hill, where the Lupin Cove Road becomes the Bay Road, there is a Victorian home with fancy dormers, towers, and gingerbread, just like the Spinster's house, but well-maintained, late nineteenth-century. This is Earle Baltzer's Antiques & Collectibles, where in season you can dig through his piles of stuff to find a treasure. It is across from the little general store and in the summer you can have fish and chips and sit at picnic tables painted in salt water candy colours, soft blue, pink, yellow and green. Halfway up the hill, on the way to Morden, is the old hotel, the Cliffside, a prime example of classical revival architecture. It hasn't been a hotel since the late forties, and no one has even summered in it for years. It really will go cliffside soon, our father says. The other hotel, the one owned by Wynette Doucette's relations before it burned up, was at the top. All that is left is the old Victorian house the Cruickshank family lived in, a house much like Earle Baltzer's but with a widow's walk at the top of the house, restored three years ago to turn-of-the-century splendour, the residence of Hans Zimmer. His house is dark, except for little electric candles in the windows.

When we were kids, Galronia and our mother would bring us over to Lupin Cove for picnics and at low tide Percy and I would walk on the sticky mud bottom of the harbour, in the little stream trickling under the bridge. When the tide is out the lobster and scallop boats sit on the harbour floor, and when it is in, they float in over twenty feet of cold water. The boats are all hauled out now until the next lobster season in early spring. We drive by the green-and-white Cape Islander boat, the *Ruby R.*, owned by the oldest fishing family in Lupin Cove, the Ryans. Ruby was the grandmother, but she died a long time ago, though the old grandfather still putters about. Highest tides in the world along these shores, forty-five feet in, forty-five feet out. Lupin Cove was a port-of-entry, had a shipbuilding industry, lumber mill on the stream, and a thriving agricultural community until the trains came and the Valley developed. At first the train tracks were laid right over the mountain and out onto the wharf but they stopped coming eventually. That was back in the glory days of Wynnette's family, the Cruikshanks with the big hotel. The village is in a state of decay, Percy says, what with the lighthouse being torn down last year and replaced with an ugly metal pole. It's like being in a ghost town.

The sky is clear by the French Cross, with the stars glittering enough to give you a seizure if you happened to be an epileptic but neither of us are, so Percy and I just stare until we almost go in the ditch. I don't say a word while he gets us back on the road, just look out at the Bay at the glow of Saint John on the other side in New Brunswick. Percy curses the development. I know nothing would make him happier than to see a schooner in full rigging go sailing by now and find we'd been transported back to the 1800s.

The parking spot by the French cross hasn't been ploughed so we just park in the middle of the road and sip the hot chocolate. Morden is a fishing village turned summer cottage spot and there will be no traffic tonight except for lunatics like us. The truck lights shine on the plaque and I don't need to see it to know what it says, I've read it a thousand times before. "Tradition has it," it reads, and then tells about the Acadians, the ones from Belle Isle, who got advance warning of the expulsion and fled over the North Mountain to hide out on the shore at Morden. They camped out on the beach all winter, eating mussels and shellfish, perishing in the brutal cold. In the spring some survivors crossed the Bay of Fundy and settled in northern New Brunswick, led by this man named Melanson, with the help of the Micmac. The story is he went over the Bay with a few natives who got together a rescue flotilla. They crossed back to Morden to rescue the survivors, but the return trip took Melanson to meet his Maker. The British had moved the Loyalist settlers in by that time and they took the huge piles of purple and mauve mussel shells over to the valley and made plaster to build their church down in the Valley. I wonder what happened to the huge piles of bones that were left there on the beach. Did bones make good plaster? When Dearie, Elizabeth and I would come here, we would sit and have a memorial smoke. Way back, she is related to that Melanson who died, but she still won't research the family tree, let alone go to New Brunswick. I'd have a smoke for her tonight, right in the truck, but Percy hates cigarettes more than Elizabeth and it's so wild outside I wouldn't even be able to get one commemorative drag in.

We get out and the frenzied thick wind off the water grabs at the doors. I have to use my body to shut it. Percy leaves the truck running but the blow is so loud you can't hear the engine outside. Out in the Bay we can see the Isle Haute lighthouse light burst out into the sky, another place where Acadians were rumoured to have fled and died, where Chester wanted to go for his his inheritance, sword in hand, where pirate ghosts chopped off heads. Huge waves smash the rocks, surf saintly white in the truck lights, mounds of snow on the rocky beach and big chunks of ice. We hold out our arms and lean into the blasting wind and it holds us there, stealing our breath, making our eyes tear but not letting us fall. Percy sings:

When I am far away on the briny ocean tossed
Will you ever heave a sigh and a wish for me?

And then there is nothing but wind and waves as we float there in the night, Atlantic shore angels come to mourn the long gone dead.

SIX

THE FAT GUY DOESN'T LIKE THE RULES, ESPECIALLY THE "STAIRS ONLY" rule. During orientation, Robert, the fat man, complains. He is told if he needs extra time to haul himself up and down, then he'll just have to plan for extra time to do that. The elevator is off limits, except for the elderly or anyone with a disability, which includes morbid obesity, but not a beer and nacho gut, exactly what he is suffering from. So Robert takes the stairs with the rest of us at the Weeping Willows Treatment Centre. The place resembles a university residence, at least to me, freshly failed out of academe. It's in a red-brick building and though a relatively new structure, it is built in a traditional style, three storeys high, with long windows and hardwood floors. The first floor of the building is for administration, with offices and a visitor lounge (for patients past the second week). The second floor houses the common room with the little kitchen in the corner and windows looking out over the frozen pond where the thick willow trunks dangle their spindly branches down over the ice. Rooms for group therapy and study groups are on this floor, and the cafeteria is at the far end. The third floor is a long row of dormitory-style rooms, men on the west side, women on the east. A staircase runs up the middle of the building and this is what we have to use, even the fat people.

In the common room, people lounge about, reading, making notes, having quiet conversations. Even with all the AA and recovery stuff, the posters, the Steps and Traditions hanging everywhere, if I shut my eyes and listen to the sounds of paper, voices, and shuffling feet, it could almost be university, which would mean the book in my hand wouldn't be the *Twelve Steps and Twelve Traditions* but a text on pre-Socratic philosophers, maybe lyric poetry from the Archaic period, maybe the Persian invasions of 490 and 480, B.C.E.

"Okay people, rock and roll. It's almost time to meet your buddies. You have ten minutes left, not a minute more. We have a schedule here at the Weeping Willows and it does not change. Do you understand? It does not change for anyone. You are only here for twenty-eight days, so you learn the Willow rules as fast as you can. Carry them around on a piece of paper if you need to. Ignorance is not an excuse here."

That's how I know it isn't university — the loud voice of Charlie, one of the seven drug and alcohol counsellors, with searchlight eyes. He's the closest thing to Grammie I've ever encountered, that is if Grammie rode a motorcycle. The counsellors, and the hospital bracelets we have to wear for the entire twenty-eight days, remind us we are at the Willows, here at the Fundy Regional Hospital in Bigelow Bay.

I'm sitting with Hannah, and we are the youngest people in treatment, with this intake anyway. Hannah is twenty-two and though we are only two years apart in age, she's nothing like me — she is one of the few patients who is self-referred. The rest of us have been sent here by hospitals, doctors, judges, counsellors, spouses. Hannah sits in her overalls and Birkenstocks, reading, drinking decaf coffee, composed, dead serious about *recovery*. There is something very formal about her, like she is here on a course. Hannah is a recovery dictionary, with the lingo down perfectly: *sobriety*, and all the things that you do with it like getting it — getting sober, staying sober, maintaining sobriety, quality of sobriety. And then there is denial, relapse, dysfunction, co-dependence, all these AA slogans: One Day at a Time, But for the Grace of God, Think Think Think.

And she says she has a bad case of *perfectionism*; this is her main downfall, reaching for the unreachable. She's here from Ottawa, she tells me, because the Willows is supposed to be one of the best treatment programs in the country. She wants the best sobriety, though she's been sober for a year already. Not clean and sober because she wasn't into drugs, just beer. Not that there is anything wrong with drugs, she says. Not that she means that drugs are good. What she means is a drug is a drug is a drug, liquid, pills, powder, herb, whatever.

"Well, if you are a Nova Scotian, you must know how to cook a lobster," she says. We've both finished the questionnaire, so there is time for conversation.

"Yeah, sure," I say. "Don't you?"

She shakes her head. Hannah is a vegan and she doesn't eat any kind of meat or animal product, not even honey — cruelty to bees. She is against any kind of captivity. She doesn't wear leather. When she did eat lobster, Hannah says, she was a kid, it was in a restaurant, and they served it dead. She's curious how we get the lobster meat out of the shell. So I tell her that all you need is a hammer and then the same tools you use for cracking nuts, a metal cracker and nut pick. Some people use metal clippers, but we just use the hammer and give the lobster a smack that cracks the shell. You separate the tail from the body, take off the big front claws. "The antennae are my favourite part to suck on. And the little legs on the side. You can suck out the meat," I tell her, summer memories coming back.

Hannah's face distorts with each detail I give her. "I feel like I'm at the Nuremberg trials,"she says. "Where did you learn how to do this?"

"Well, we boil them first, of course." I can't resist.

Hannah rolls her eyes and makes a yuck sound. I think she's off her rocker with that comparison and I shrug as Grammie speaks to me: *This is the problem with bloody extremists, they see their cause everywhere.* It's hard to remember learning how to cook up a lobster because I've always known how to, we always helped my parents, my Grammie. Hannah can't imagine having to boil it alive.

Hannah shudders. "I hear they scream when you drop them in the pot."

"No," I laugh. "Maybe that's steam in their shells . . . maybe. I've never heard of that one before." I smile and shake my head.

"It's not a stupid thing to ask," she says. "You're boiling them alive, you know. You boil them from life to death." She shakes her head and smooths her questionnaire.

"Well, it's not like we put them on the barbecue and slow cook 'em," I reply.

"It's cruel," she says. "And you should at least know that, be aware of it."

I've never looked at it that way before. A lobster doesn't seem alive, not how I think of life anyway. I nod and busy myself looking over my checks in all the little boxes on the self-assessment questionnaire as there is no use continuing this conversation and making enemies less than one hour after my arrival. "We end as we begin," Grammie always says, and I want this to end well.

Percy had gone back to Toronto, grim and quiet, his slight body hunched over as he waved to me from the driveway when Cyril drove him in to the airport. Elizabeth was gone after Boxing Day, to Antigonish to meet Reggie's family and then back to the city to work at the bar. And poor Dearie was stuck in Florida until after New Year's, but it wouldn't matter if they were all still in the Valley because I can't make any phone calls anyway, and no visitors for the first two weeks. Sunday was always intake day at the rehab. There were a maximum of sixty people in treatment, fifteen new people arriving every Sunday, fifteen completing the program, with the intake number going up if there were kick-outs and drop-outs and there were almost always drop-outs and kick-outs, because treatment is no soak in the hot tub, as Charlie would inform us, right from that first night, as he supervised the paperwork aspect. In the intake room he had handed out questionnaires and little red pencils, pointing out the decaf coffee urn in the corner. No milk or cream, just powdered stuff, a bowl of sugar and fake sugar packs in a glass jar.

The treatment program incorporates some of the AA philosophies, though it isn't formally based on AA. The questionnaire was adapted from a pamphlet from Alcoholics Anonymous to help with self-diagnosis, because we have to figure out if we are in fact, alcoholics, *we* have to believe or we'll never stay clean and sober. SO ARE YOU AN ALCOHOLIC?" it asks at the top. Yup, I nod. At the bottom, printed right under the last question, "If you've answered yes to three or more, then you are definitely an alcoholic." I've answered yes to all the questions — that must make me a heavy-duty drunk. There's nothing like seeing it in print, my mark in every "yes" box. Yes: tried to quit on my own, never going to drink again, then hammered in the Lobster Trap. Yes: drinking has caused trouble in my home life. Yes: I've done stuff drunk that I've wished I never had, like London, and all those drugs, not that I even know what drugs I've taken. Just call me the Blackout Queen, 'cause, yes, I black out when drink. I'll drink whatever booze I can find at a party; yes, I'll steal booze. Oh yes: I've had trouble related to drinking in the last six months, the last year. And of course: I keep thinking I can stop whenever I'd like to, but then I end up loaded. Definitely: I've missed time from work, school in my case, from drinking. Yes: I've woken up feeling remorseful after drinking. And, certainly: my life would be way frigging better if I didn't drink. I can't imagine what it will be like, not drinking, but anything will be an improvement, even just being sober and sitting quietly in Meetings until I grow old and die. It's hard to imagine anything more at this point.

Charlie calls for us to go up to the second floor to the common room where we will be introduced to our program buddy, the person who will help orient us for the first two days. After that we will be on our own, sort of — we are still supposed to help each other, look out for each other.

"Long way since Bible camp, Serrie," Fancy says in Lupin Cove twang, as though she has been expecting me, which I realize she has. Charlie says he sees he doesn't need to make any introductions and leaves us alone. This Fancy looks like an older cousin of the girl I remember, long hair permed so curly it floats half a foot out from her back, tattooed eyeliner black under her bottom lashes, huge alien eyes. She's smoking with long nails, bits of red where the nail polish remover didn't penetrate. Her collar bones stick out of her blue angora turtleneck — she's as skinny as I am. Fancy offers me a smoke and points to the chair beside her and I feel the relief only familiarity brings. And panic, because seeing Fancy makes the overdose real, my alcoholism not just a problem but a disease, and the Weeping Willows exactly what it is, a twenty-eight day treatment and rehabilitation program to deal with the disease. Panic, relief, panic, relief, I'm in a rocking boat feeling sick and shaky, squeezing the cigarette almost in two, so Fancy takes it, lights it, and gives it back to me, rubbing my shoulder. "It's okay," she says, "it's okay, Serrie. Everyone feels like this at first. Don't you worry, now." My mouth is watering and I don't want to fall apart, so I clamp my lips on the filter and suck in really hard, nodding. Only one tear slips down and disappears in the filter. Fancy says nothing about my shaved head, my nose ring. She just pats my hand, like she's been through this many times before. She tells me she has a little girl now, Melissa, in a foster home in Toronto. She's hoping they will give her visits if she can stay straight this time.

It's weird to think of Fancy as a mother. I still think of us as kids sitting around a table under the pines, making a Jesus mosaic, giggling into hot summer days. The last time I saw her was after finishing grade eight at the Foster School, and then getting on the bus with Percy to Fundy Central that September, wearing my new high school outfit that Grammie had bought for me. Fancy would be in the back of the bus for that month, sitting with the kids from Lupin Cove, all the Ryan brothers. She wore aqua-blue eyeshadow and tight jeans

and T-shirts, the kind some buy to look sexy, the kind that people like
Fancy wore because they had outgrown them but didn't have anything else. She was in grade eleven with my brother, in Percy's home
room. One day Ms. Brown came in to do home room attendance and
she slammed her attendance clipboard on her desk. Ms. Brown was
a marathon runner and she lived in Bigelow Bay, where all the Valley
culture was, the Valley intellectuals, what with the university. Percy
said she was so mad her face turned splotchy red. Ms. Brown just
wanted the class to know that Fancy Mosher had come into the office
that morning to drop out and get her things from her locker. It didn't
matter that her grades were high, it didn't matter that she wrote the
most interesting papers in the class. She was sixteen years old that day
and she was dropping out. Her boyfriend was there with her, some
guy who lived over on the Mountain. He was thirty years old and had
been away in Toronto but was back now. "Another life wasted," Ms.
Brown yelled. "All that potential lost, just like that," she said as she
clapped her hands together, then yelled out each name as though
they were individually and collectively responsible for the fact that
Bright Light Fancy Mosher was now a high school drop-out. She
apologized to the class at the end of the day.

I'm wondering what happened to her old-guy boyfriend, when
Fancy says the point of the group therapy here is to get you working
on the Twelve Steps of Alcoholics Anonymous, you just work on the
first three in treatment and then they want you to join a group when
you finish, an AA group, where you will do the remaining nine
steps. She rattles them off, taking a drag of her smoke between each.
She says Step One is about admitting that we have no power at all
over booze, or anything else for that matter — our lives have gone
crazy. "Sounds some simple, right? If only." She laughs. "The second step is about findin' a Higher Power, you know, believin' that
God, or whatever you want to call it, can help us get back on track."
Fancy says softly, "I like that one there, makes me feel hopeful. And
the third one, that's about decidin' to let the Higher Power take

over, you know, askin' for help. That's the hard one. You have to trust, Serrie. I'm bad at that, real bad. It's like climbing a mountain with your eyes glued shut."

That night Fancy takes me down to supper but I'm not hungry and just pick at my food while Fancy does all the talking. After supper she brings me to an AA meeting on the second floor of the facility, where all the meeting and group therapy rooms are. The meeting at the Willows is put on by one of the Valley AA groups. Members of that meeting come in to the hospital and host it. She says there is a meeting in Foster I can attend when I get out. The people are nice there and I shouldn't be embarrassed because they are all drunks too, that's the best part of AA, being in a room full of people where there are no explanations needed. The meetings at the Willows are closed-discussion meetings, like the ones in the Nova Scotia hospital, and only people with *a desire to stop drinking* can attend, no family, no friends, no doctors or counsellors. Only if they too have a desire to stop drinking. They call it *carrying the message.* You are a *newcomer.* Some people are just *coming back*, like Fancy Mosher — that means they've relapsed. Fancy whispers that I'll get used to the jargon, the program-speak, she calls it. I see Hannah over in the corner having an earnest conversation with her buddy, this lady wearing a blonde curly wig. The meetings aren't a formal part of treatment, but you have to go. Not going is one of the things they will kick you out for.

It's the first night and I've got insomnia coming out my pores, lying in the bed trembling. In the dark I count the deep and full sleeps of the last year and only need nine fingers. Maybe all my problems are from sleep deprivation. Exhaustion is supposed to make people do crazy things. It's a tiny bed and the wool blankets are thin. There are extra ones in the closet, but I'm too cold to get up so I just shiver as much as I did on the ski slopes yesterday. Yesterday is years ago. I already feel like I've been at the Weeping Willows forever and skiing was only a dream.

Boxing Day skiing. They picked me up at 4:00 and we were on the slopes by 5:00. It was already dark and the lights were bright on the snow. Reggie and Elizabeth waited while I went and got rentals. Reggie was helping her put her skis on, new skis he had given her for Christmas. My old ski pants from high school, they were so baggy I had to belt them on. Elizabeth didn't last long on the slopes, going back to the lodge. The best thing about skiing is the solitude. The hill is covered in people and so you are in it together in that way, but you are by yourself, making sure you get down the hill, you surrender to every turn, every pull of gravity, and your body and mind just merge and there are no more thoughts or worries, just soaring. There's not time to think about anything except what you are doing. Reggie didn't like to stop and he also didn't want to leave me alone. He was keeping his vow to my family to look after me, make sure nothing happened. It was a good thing it wasn't cross-country skiing, what with my case of smoker's lung. You think when you grow up you'll grow up healthy, wealthy, and wise, but it's just a crock.

Growing up makes every single simple thing complicated, like having fun, you know, like being healthy. Fortunately, you don't need good health to go down hill, just balance and technique. Even a zombie like me could go down a hill. The one time I fell, I was looking at the stars, thinking that I loved night skiing more than anything, when the end of the ski caught as I turned, cartwheeling me over two times. But I was so relaxed it was like falling in water, great splashes of snow going up and then gently covering me. I hopped up and waved to Reggie.

On the lift, Reggie said I was a good little skier, surprise sticking all over his voice. He thinks I'm a little poor girl and poor girls don't do things like ski and travel — they stay in the Valley and work as cashiers, wearing uniforms: *Thank you, sir. Over there, sir. Come again, sir. Have a nice day, sir. Fuck you, sir.* Even if Reggie doesn't think this, obviously I do, and then, in the ski lift, it made me want to just scream and then whimper, like everything did since the hospital. Reggie patted me on the arm and that made it worse, because these days every bit of kindness hurts, my achy feelings plastered over my flesh in bruises. Shrinking away, I began to fall out of the chair lift. "Steady, Serrie, steady," Reggie said as he pulled me back in.

Steady, steady, I hear in my head, all through the night, dozing on and off, every time I shut my eyes feeling cold ski wind on my cheeks until it is 6:00 a.m. and the wake-up bang hits the door. It's one of the jobs for the patients, wake-up duty. You only get one wake-up call. Late for breakfast two times and it's kick-out.

When you think about it, treatment isn't that different from Bible camp. You do things in groups, and you have to sit with people to eat, and before you can eat you have to pray. We are supposed to be opening up to the idea of a Higher Power, praying and meditating scheduled in, though don't let that stop you from asking your HP for help at any other time of the day or night, Charlie likes to point out. The counsellors always take turns doing everything and they all seem the same to me, except for Charlie, who's always watching. I study the weekly schedule at breakfast, and see that Fancy is right, every single minute is accounted for, every second. Breakfast. Group. Lunch. Quiet time. Study time. Exercise time, splashing in the pool and doing yoga. Then workshops on rotating topics: nutrition and physical exercise, feelings, anger management, building a healthy sobriety, prayer and meditation, signs of relapse. Supper. AA meeting Monday, Wednesday, Friday, and Sunday nights. No television, no radio, no newspapers, no outside world.

When we do have a few moments, we are meant to be reading, reflecting, meditating.

Group therapy lasts for two hours, without a break. There is a topic, and we all have to talk about it, how we feel. There is a counsellor, a different one every day, and every Sunday, new patients join. It keeps us in a state of disorientation. At least it is in the same room. There is homework, answering questions about Steps One, Two, and Three. We don't hand in homework, but share in group, and give feedback to each other. The patients who have been here longer say alcoholism is a disease about feelings, alcoholics are people who can't deal with feelings, they stuff them, squash them, mush them, pack them, drown them, anything to not feel bad. Is it a spiritual, mental, and physical disease? Is it genetic? They say there is no cure, only abstinence, a daily reprieve. And there is AA, where you can help each other get sober, you get it by giving it away.

The main point they hammer into us is that we have to start *getting honest*. That's how they put it, getting down to honesty and truth. Lies and deceit are part of what makes alcoholics sick. We drink because we are full of self-loathing and this horrible compulsion, and then we get into trouble and lie to cover up and then lie to cover up the lie and it is just a maddening cycle of lying and cheating and stealing, on every plane, until we don't know truth from fantasy.

"If you can't face the truth, ladies and gentlemen, we will put your face in it," Charlie says.

After the first two days, I only see Fancy in the lounge in the evening. It's her fourth week, but they want her to stay for an extra session.

"Twenty-eight more friggin'days," she tells me that Friday night after the AA meeting. It will be my first week on Sunday and I can't imagine having to do the program twice. Fancy says they think she is making progress but it's her third time in treatment, the other two times in Ontario, and she hasn't managed to stay clean and sober. "I always seem to get right scared, you know, when things are comin' together, and what that means, you know, when life starts openin' up right in front of me. And then I relapse on stupid stuff like mouthwash toddies and cookin' sherry soup. Next thing you know, I'm back on the cocaine and the whisky."

She's always wearing that blue angora turtleneck and as she lifts her teacup, the sleeve falls back and I see pale pink vertical scars on her wrists. She tugs the sleeves down without looking and lights a smoke. "Fuck, eh, Serrie, who'd'a'thought?"

I just nod and shrug.

This young guy, in a black T-shirt that says "Who's home at your house?" comes over. He's in the same week as Fancy, and blushes when she looks at him.

"This here is Serrie," she says and he nods. "Ronnie, he's from over in New Brunswick. He's kinda stupid but he's a good feller, aren't you, Ronnie?"

He laughs and nods again, then offers me a smoke. I'm holding a lit cigarette and show it to him, but no engine seems to be starting up in his head.

"She's got a smoke, Ronnie," Fancy tells him. He nods and I stand up because if he nods one more frigging time I'm going to scream.

"See you later, Serrie." Fancy says. "Let's sit together at breakfast. How 'bout it?"

I start to nod and stop myself. "Okay, Fancy," I whisper.

Fancy smiles and bounces her foot. She's wearing sneakers. They won't let her wear high heels, she told me, or nail polish. An ash falls off the end of her smoke — her hand is shaking.

Over by the window, I curl up in a chair and look out over the town, the lights bright in the night, beacons of the world we have temporarily stepped away from. And I'm thinking about a Higher Power, you know, the idea of this Divine Light, when Charlie comes barging into the common room. He snaps off the huge whirring fan that sucks up our smoke and a still nicotine silence fills the lounge. He points at this middle-aged woman in the corner, someone I don't know. She's a week ahead, not in any of my groups. She looks to each side, thinking perhaps Charlie is pointing at the person beside her, but there is no one on either side of her so she looks back at Charlie and waves.

"Cynthia, please stand up," Charlie says.

Cynthia puts down her notepad and stands up, smiling and chewing her bright red bottom lip at the same time.

"Cynthia, you have sleeping pills in your room."

"No, no, Charlie," she says with a weak laugh. "That's not true."

"People, when you sign your admission forms you sign a section that gives us permission to search your room. We point that out to you."

They do, it's true. They went through the admission form line by line, before we were allowed to sign it.

"Cynthia is being removed from treatment because she broke our rules, the rules she agreed to."

Cynthia is crying. "But I couldn't sleep. It's not fair."

"If you can't sleep, then you come and talk to us. You know that. There is no second chance for using any mood-altering substance. Go pack your things."

And that's it. Charlie isn't kidding about not breaking the rules. Cynthia leaves the lounge crying, her face the same colour as her lips.

Charlie isn't through. "Benjamin, would you please stand up."

Benjamin is way in the back by the kitchenette and he stands by the fridge. I don't know him either. "Benjamin, how many times have you been late for group?"

"Well, once last week."

"And yesterday?"

"Well, I got there in the afternoon just when it was starting."

"Your counsellor said it had already started and you walked in when someone was sharing. Are you saying she is lying?"

"No, no, I'm not saying that. I was just a minute late."

"So you were late. And then what about today?"

Benjamin gets pissed off. "Well, I had to take a leak." He looks around to see if anyone is laughing, but no one will meet his eye. "Why didn't anyone say anything to me when I was late?"

"Because you had a warning the first time. Because we aren't here to babysit you, Benjamin. We are here to help you get sober. If you can't be on time for group therapy, if we can't trust you to be on time after we've asked you to take responsibility for this, then how can we believe you are willing to be responsible for your own recovery? And when you are late you affect every single person in your group. Step One, people: *We* admitted *we* were powerless over alcohol, not *I* admitted. We recover by helping each other. Benjamin, go to your room and pack your things."

Benjamin is a big man and I'm scared he's going to pound Charlie, but he just saunters out pretending he doesn't care, but you can tell he does, his hands are in fists. I'm shaking now and my stomach is in a knot as I flip through the last week, wondering if I deviated from the rules in any way. This is nothing like the sedated haze that draped the entire ward in the NS.

"That, people, is an attitude, and an attitude like that is deadly. Why?" He snaps his fingers and the sound cracks out and bounces off the wall. "An attitude will have you relapse faster than you can blink. This program is about honesty, and it's about being able to count on yourself, being able to trust yourself. It's about wanting something enough to do the work, one day at a time. Now you are here because you need help. Most of you are referred here by agencies, but you still don't have to come. No one puts a gun to your head, unless you've put it there yourself. Oh, it may get you some leniency with the judge, Robert, I know why you are here. And Beth, you think it will help at the custody hearing you have in two months."

Robert takes a drag of his smoke and Beth, Hannah's buddy, tugs at her wig and pulls it lopsided.

"Well, that may be enough to get you here but it's not enough to keep you here. You get with it, you start getting honest, or you are out. This is your only warning. Now, if anyone here thinks they know how to stay sober, then I would ask you to stand up and tell me how you happened to end up in a rehabilitation program."

No one moves. No one looks at Charlie. We are waiting for the next kick-out. He sweeps his eyes around and then walks to the door. He flicks the fan back on and we sit there in the hum and whir.

It takes me a long time to get to sleep, and I only have three hours of rest when the wake-up bang hits my door. I fall back asleep, just for a few minutes, and then lurch out of bed. There isn't time to shower and I rush down for breakfast, hoping Fancy saved me a seat. Two stairs at a time, so fast I'm past the second floor and almost on the ground floor when I bang into Fancy and Ronnie. They are smiling, with red eyes. I smell pot. And then I turn around and run back up the stairwell. I hear them come behind me, muffled laughter.

We get to the cafeteria with a few minutes before grace time, and other people are just filing in so we get in the line with our trays. I take my food to the far table and sit down beside Hannah. Fancy joins us, and spends the entire breakfast buttering her toast and covering it with jam but she doesn't even take a bite. Hannah eats granola, explaining that factory eggs are about the worst thing you can possibly eat. The chickens live in metal cages with their beaks cut off, with artificial lighting to make them lay, denied their pecking order, literally being driven into chicken madness. Fancy keeps putting more and more jam on her toast, Hannah watching her as she talks about soy and protein alternatives, Fancy not once looking up at us, fixated on her toast.

I spend the whole day quiet, with my stomach in a knot. There is no way Fancy won't get caught — they know everything here. In the evening Fancy comes and sits with me, but neither of us say anything about her dope smoking. Some buddy, is all I can think. And I'm scared for Fancy Mosher because I don't know what the hell she is doing or what it's going to take for her. That night, in the lounge, everyone is uneasy, waiting for Charlie or some other counsellor to come barging in. But no one does for the next two nights and then it is Monday night, and I'm into my second week. Those quiet reflective evenings would almost be serene if I wasn't so fucking scared all the time.

I'm still silent in group. My group members comment on the fact that I don't say anything and I shrug and whisper that I don't have anything to say yet. We have Charlie that day as our counsellor, and he asks me what I'm feeling. I whisper I don't know what I feel, that I'm confused. He asks what I'm confused about.

"About how long recovery takes."

"Well, Serrie, that's like asking how long a string is."

And I nod. It makes perfect sense, echoes of Grammie. And then I share how Dearie, Elizabeth, and I started drinking down in the graveyard on Saturday nights. Why? Because I felt like I could fly when I took a sip, with a glow on, my stupid family blurring into some sepia dream. But it didn't last and I kept hoping to get that warm feeling back with every sip, gulp, guzzle and chug-a-lug. But it was just one big blackout after another. I tell them about Trevor, that he told me once you start getting high you'll be chasing that first high for the rest of your life, like a gambler chases that first win. But it's always elusive after that, for the addict. I was found drunk and stoned with Trevor on the front steps of the school one Friday morning, after a big party the night before. I never knew how we got to the school. The principal found us there when he came in early to hoist the flag up, his morning ritual. My parents thought I was at Elizabeth's house, and I thought I was, too, until I saw the flag pole looming overhead, the principal staring down at us, flag in hand. I was only suspended for a week, because I had high marks. Trevor was suspended for a month. His mother didn't even think about where he was that night, because she didn't make it home either.

Charlie says, "So you fell between the cracks in the system."

I think of Fancy Mosher. "I *live* between the cracks, I was born there. And now I'm stuck here in the crack of life," I whisper.

"Well, here's to crawling out," says Robert, sitting across from me, and everyone nods.

I spend the rest of the week trying to be mindful. I am on time for meals and eat everything on my plate. I empty my ashtray, go to all the AA meetings, splash in the pool, focus on my breath in yoga, read quietly in the lounge until it is time to go to my room, and then fall into dull sleeps. I walk down the hall beside the wall as not to take up too much space. I feel like I am a part of the hall — a long empty space full of echoes.

I go to the ecumenical church service on Sunday morning in the hospital chapel and that afternoon my family come out for a visit. They all drive in together, my mother, Galronia, and Grammie, everyone but my father, who has to do some work on his solar project, but I know he just doesn't want to be in a rehab place, too many bad memories. The ladies sit in the lounge, where all the other patients are with their visitors. Some of the visitors have flown in just for that one hour and I can tell by their accents that they aren't from Nova Scotia, or any of the Maritime provinces.

"Americans," Grammie says. "God love the Americans." The friendliest people on earth, she thinks, and nods at every one who says hello to her, which is almost everyone in the centre. Gallie thinks they must have lots of air-mile points to come all that way just for a bloody hour in the middle of nowhere. I talk about the weather, the godawful unending unmerciful snow, and Galronia slowly sinks deeper and deeper into her chair, lest a Meissner be seen at the Willows. She points out Fancy Mosher on the other side of the room. Fancy's mother is there. She's brought Fancy a big box of chocolates.

"Now Fancy's been in up Toronto for a long time and this is her grand homecoming. I guess this is what comes of being raised on the Mountain," Gallie says.

Grammie swats her. "Oh, Gallie, you be quiet. Serrie's been here two whole weeks. She's doing fine. Put on a bit of weight too. Now how about a cup of tea for us?"

I bring them steaming Styrofoam cups on a little tray and my mother stirs with the little plastic stick. "Gallie went on a date, Serrie." She takes a sip and starts stirring again.

Gallie sits up and her tea slops on the napkin in her lap. "Martha, good Lord, that's nobody's business."

My mother takes another delicate sip. "She went to the fire hall dance with David Starr."

Grammie waves her cane. "Serrie, she looked lovely, what with the lipstick and perfume. It was like she was a girl again. Going to go out again, Gallie?"

Gallie rolls her eyes. "Now David Starr is a fine man, but they're all the same, aren't they? It's just like being in a garden, one vegetable after another. Speaking of vegetables, that Clarence

Burgess has just up and moved to Bermuda to manage a condo-
minium complex. Whole family went with him. Sold the place to
someone from the city who's going to make it a country inn. Tax
man's after him, so they say."

Martha slurps her tea and stirs it so fast it sloshes out a bit. I pick
at my nails.

"Well, you'd have to have been slow in the head not to have
seen that coming. I'm half senile and it's no surprise to me."
Grammie pats my knee and says I'm looking a bit better, but she'd
like to see some hair on my head and meat on my bones, that it isn't
right for someone as young as me to have so much strain in their
face. I know she means I'm going to look just like my mother.

As they are leaving, Dearie arrives in the lounge. Elizabeth
can't get time off work, so she has sent out a present from Palm
Springs. She went to Las Vegas, too, and flew over the Hoover Dam
in a helicopter, Dearie tells me, like she's a reporter. Elizabeth's
working at the Dome all the time and when she's not working she's
partying. Dropped out of all her classes. She's still with Reggie, she's
still living with Clare, she's never got any time to see Dearie, so why
would she have time to come out to the Valley to see me?

She has sent presents out for me, though, lots of little things
wrapped in purple cellophane. There are tacky postcards, a sou-
venir ashtray, and a red lace push-up bra from a sex shop in Los
Vegas, but as Elizabeth says in the card, it's a classy sex shop and the
bra is real silk. Dearie checks the label to make sure and then shakes
her head when I hold the red bra up in the visitor's lounge.

"Oh, my sweet fuck, where does she think you'll wear that?"

I feel this surge of anger, sliding up from my belly. I look at
Dearie. "What do you mean?"

"Well, you don't even wear bras."

"Maybe I'll start."

"Maybe you should let your hair grow in and your nose, too,
while we're on the topic."

I fold up the bra and the wrapping paper and then light a smoke and stare out the window. "Fine, then, take it back to the city."

"Now, that would be thoughtful. Someone gives you a present and you send it back. Oh, Serrie, you're too sensitive. Don't go get in a huff just because you don't need lingerie. You need practical stuff."

I must be learning in these groups, because I know she is busy *projecting* all her dissatisfaction and disappointment in the world right onto me. "It's not my fault you aren't making any new friends and that Elizabeth is neglecting you," I tell her.

Dearie opens her mouth and then shuts it and sits quiet. She grabs my cigarette and takes a puff. And then Dearie goes off: she hates university so much she's praying the whole place burns down, her father keeps threatening to cut her funding if she drops even one course, which she already has, three courses, but she only tells him things on a need-to-know basis.

That night Charlie comes in with another counsellor, but they are talking and laughing as they get a cup of tea. They sit down and talk to a few of the new patients. After awhile we forget they are in the room and that's when they snap the fan off.

"On Saturday morning someone was smoking dope at the bottom of the stairwell on the east side."

Everyone is still and my stomach shrinks as my hands start shaking.

"Now does anyone want to admit to this? Remember, people. It's about honesty on every level. Not just here with me, in front of friends, but inside, being honest with yourself."

Silence. All this recovery lingo is so trite, I think. My eyes are shut.

"Serrie? Anything you want to say?"

I squeeze my hands together. He must have seen me coming up the stairwell, coming in with Fancy. Who knows what they know. I think about this stupid total honesty thing. And then I nod, "I think it was Fancy Mosher, Ronnie." My eyes are still shut and I can hear the willow branches out there on the icy surface of the pond, scraping away the last bit of my childhood code.

"Serrie, next time you come to me right away. This is your only warning. Fancy? Is this true?"

She stands up with her smoke in her hand, long fingernails red again. "Yeah, it was me. Serrie's tellin' the truth."

"Ronnie?"

"She's lyin', man, she's lyin'. She was smokin' the dope, man. Honest."

"Oh, shut up, Ronnie. You know she's not lyin', you arsehole."

Ronnie stares at Fancy like she's crazy.

"You see, people, Fancy Mosher doesn't care about herself. It's your third time in treatment, Fancy. I want everyone to know this. Every time she gets close, she starts breaking rules. Because she's scared, isn't that right, Fancy? Because you are so full of self-loathing you think you don't deserve a chance and so you never really give yourself one, you never let us in enough that we can really help. It's all about walls with you. And it's a shame, ladies and gentlemen, it's a shame, because this young woman is going to die if she keeps this up. And that is a waste, it is a waste, because every one of you is precious, every one of you counts in this world and the only people who can't see that is *you*, so you just go on killing yourselves."

I open my eyes and look at Fancy. She doesn't say anything, doesn't look at me, just puts her hand on her hip. She's not even in the room anymore, you can tell by the way her head is on the side, letting Charlie's words slide off her and fall down on the floor.

"Fancy, Ronnie, go pack up your rooms." Charlie's voice is quiet. He's disappointed.

They leave the room and Charlie starts going on about how Serrie may feel bad for turning in her friends and others may judge her for being a snitch but we've just go to understand that covering up would have been the real betrayal.

"Covering up, ladies and gentlemen, is killing them. Yes, you may as well just take a slow-firing gun and point it at their heads. Looking the other way is pulling the trigger. Do you see, covering for your buddies just adds another strand of lies to a web we are trying to take apart here at the Willows. And if someone is smoking pot in treatment, then they obviously don't want to be here, they are not ready, and they are showing us this by their actions. They may as well be back out there, using, because you can't get straight when you don't want to. That's how simple it is. Without the desire, you have nothing. And with the desire, you are going to walk into freedom, one day at a time. It takes courage, ladies and gentlemen, it takes courage to start taking honest steps." He runs his fingers through his hair and his voice breaks. Charlie takes a deep breath as though he is going to say something, but then he just leaves the room.

We just sit there in sandpaper silence. I wonder about this marriage of fear and courage, I see the Reverend Rafuse stand among the pines at Bible camp: *knock knock, who's there?* Hannah is looking at me from across the room and she gives me a little smile and nod, some kind of recovery support. I look down at my chewed nails. At least I'll always know what I'm doing now, when I put a lobster in the pot.

SEVEN

I'M CHOPPING RHUBARB AT MIDNIGHT.

Stewie, the night supervisor, whistles, "Serrie, you chop rhubarb like nobody's business, some good, yessir." I tilt my head and shrug, chopping all the while, going at it like I'm some whirly-snip-late-night-mail-order-chopping-sensation, the rhubarb-o-matic slicer dicer. I better not let the chopping compliment go to my head. Last thing I need to hear on a break is that Serrie's too good to talk because *Serrie can chop rhubarb like nobody's business.* But I really am glad Stewie likes my rhubarb chopping. My life has never been so easy — if I can chop rhubarb, I can do anything. I chop alone until my hand just keeps going, so numb that it belongs to the knife now. I can't stop, even when the rhubarb is gone, my right hand slicing through the air, the left groping for more stalks in the bin by my side, but it's empty. In the fluorescent light, the knife is silver-blue and red juice drops fly as I chop chop through Stewie's laugh as he brings in a new bin of rhubarb. I stick a piece out and the knife cuts through at high speed. He laughs again, "You look just like a robot, you do." I smile, but not taking my eyes from the stalks, not missing a beat or a slice. My technique is perfected — I am becoming a robot, soon to be friends with the buoybot, still waiting in the workshed for its day in the sun, ha ha, while the alternate energy project moves on.

"Break's in ten minutes, Serrie. Don't forget. Got to take a rest sometimes, you know."

And off Stewie goes to check on the good ol' boys. I stare at the clock. It's almost the end of June. Summer was sudden this year. It had been a cold winter. It had been a cold spring. The land was chilled, greening hesitantly, until summer clunked down last week in a heat wave. All the fruit crops are late this year, strawberries, raspberries, only reliable rhubarb had been growing from May. It's a remarkable and underrated fruit, in my opinion. Now summer has arrived, it's unbearable working in the factory in the heat. There has been no time to adjust, to adapt, no time for acclimatization, and we are reined in by the hot close air.

Break time at last and I sit outside on the bench. Cow moos hang on the pungent dark and frogs groan in the meadow pond. How could it have been freezing winter at the Weeping Willows and now boiling summer at Zimmer's Pies? My life is being spent in large buildings, punching time cards, accounting for every minute. There's nothing like shift work to disrupt clocks, calendars, and the nine-to-five work week. On the night shift I must learn to be a vampire, loving the night hours, so tired in the day that I shrivel from the sun. I passed the probationary three-month period at the end of April — I am being well rehabilitated. I got a fifty-cent raise, too. There will be another job review at the end of July, which will make half a year of my life spent at Zimmer's Pies. Hans Zimmer interviewed me himself and then Timmie Ogilvie, the general manager, a local guy from Foster. I had gone to 4-H with his youngest brother. It was the end of January when I had the interview, just out of rehab, back at the Spinster's house in my old room in the tower, going nuts with nothing to do and I had really wanted any job at that point. It was through the Employment Centre in Bigelow Bay. The job counsellor had told me about a program where the government paid half the wages, the employer the other half, and then after six months, if the worker was satisfactory, the employer would take over the full hourly wage. Each business in the Valley could have one employee through this program and Zimmer's Pies just happened to need a new employee. Hans Zimmer didn't ask me much, just stood there leaning against the wall with his arms crossed, all handsome in that fresh-out-of-the-box way. Hans Zimmer looked so new, so perfect, just as he had in the mall at Christmas.

"Yes, you know, you are ideal for the job," he said, "church caretaker, working on Baxter's Strawberry Farm." My former employers all said I was a hard worker. Hans liked a good work ethic, it made all the difference. His voice was soft, velvety, with almost no accent.

"Serrie," he had said, looking at me, perfect blue eyes. He spoke my name as though he were tasting it, sampling and appraising it. Hans wanted to know why I dropped out of university.

"Wasn't ready for university, didn't know what I wanted to do," I had whispered.

He had nodded, it was important to know why you were doing something or there was no point in doing it. Timmie Ogilvie would speak with me next, Hans had said, and he hoped he would see me around.

Timmie didn't bother with the resume crap — he knew all he needed to know about my manual labour skills from Smokey Baxter, who said I could run a strawberry field and drive a tractor like nobody's business. Smokey's word was good enough for him. Timmie said the only thing they could give me was the night shift, I'd be working for Stewie the night manager. I nodded. He was sorry, he said, sorry to hear I'd had so many problems but I was a Meissner, hardy as my grandmother, and I'd get through it. I didn't bother telling him I was a Sullivan. And then he said all the other workers knew about the rehab work program and they might be a bit funny but not to pay any attention, to let him know if there were any problems. After I'd been around awhile, maybe a spot would come up on the rotating pie table where all the other ladies worked. It's the place to be, the pie table, and it only runs in the day. The women, or the ladies, as everyone calls them, always arrive as I leave to go home to bed and they say hello, but nothing more. I'm a pariah now, drop-out, drunk, freak. Grammie says if I want to fit in more, then I should at least consider letting my hair grow.

"It's so much easier to be a bald factory worker in the hot weather," I reply.

Of course, she shakes her head. "You'll have to get to the point where you are willing to make compromises to fit in. Not sacrifices, but compromises." She says, "There is a difference between sacrifice and compromise, and you'd best learn it."

It makes me think of Fancy Mosher, her whole life some kind of sacrificial ritual, trying to escape her past and then being gobbled up by it. Grammie was the only one who asked me about Fancy, and all I knew is that she had left that night. She did tell Charlie to tell me that she thought I did the right thing, being honest, that I shouldn't feel bad. Charlie said she had set the whole thing up, she knew I would have to be honest, because she knew I had the desire, that's what she had told him. And while I know it was the right thing, it makes me mad that Fancy would do that, just give up like that, knowing she would get caught, that she would make me, you know, make that choice. Some choice, is all I can say. I like to think Fancy went away and then had this spiritual awakening, but somehow I doubt it. There wasn't even word around town of where she was, Gallie said. But that was back in the winter, just before I started at the pie factory. Maybe if I let my hair grow in, the pie ladies will tell me if they know anything of Fancy, because they know everything about everything. None of them more than nod at me, even though I know most of them from school, from Foster, the surrounding area. This is the hard part now, being back in the Valley, with everybody knowing everything, every mistake I've ever made.

And so I slide into the comfort and safety of my shift work, the routine, working here six days a week, Saturdays off, and then back on Sunday night. It's a twelve-hour shift, from six to six. I sleep right through until mid-afternoon and then help out in the gardens, or read in Outhouse Number Nine with a glass of icy lemonade. Grammie says there is nothing better than good honest work, and I should be proud I'm holding down a job, it will help me get back on my feet. They all agree on this, Martha, Cyril, Gallie, Grammie, and Percy, who is in Ottawa working as a summer researcher for the Public Archives. He starts his Ph.D. in the autumn. Grammie says my day will come to do something else, but right now it is one foot in front of the other. They all think I've turned around and I have — just like a ballerina in a jewellery box, going round and round.

The factory is in the country, down in the Valley, about six miles west on the Back Street, the road that runs along the base of the Mountain, what the government calls Route 991. When I was first out of treatment, Martha and Cyril would let me take the truck over, and when spring came, I took one of the old bikes out of the Spinster's barn and drove down, watching the trees bud, the leaves unfold, the flowers start to bloom in the fields, the late apple blossoms on the trees. The hardest part, of course, was riding up the Mountain at six a.m. It was clear the smoking was going to have to go, but I was willing to keep those contradictory elements up and running right through the summer, maybe something to consider in the autumn. One day at a time, one step at a time, they say in the Foster AA meetings — the meetings that I never get to now because of my factory work.

I have no social life, no time to make new friends, not that there would be anyone around to make friends with. Maybe there would be, but it's impossible to know that. For three months I went to after-care meetings at the Willows, every Saturday night, my only night off, and specifically Saturday night off so I could go to after-care. Everyone in the factory knew. After-care meant sitting around talking about how the week was, how we were making out. By the end of April it was over, but I didn't miss it — I was too tired to miss anything, or to know anything was missing.

Break will be over soon. It's always over soon. It's cool outside at four in the morning, sitting on the bench. The knife has been temporarily exchanged for a smoke and the good old right hand putting it to my lips with the same cutting speed. The June breeze swishes in the poplar trees and it's nice to have a few minutes to myself. The guys are all out behind the factory, by the loading bay where there is a big orange outdoor light. They don't like standing around in the dark talking — maybe it's a man thing. I know they are back there chatting about their barbecues, these big black propane numbers everybody's got for sizzling up steaks and burgers — a meat extravaganza all summer long. I'd give my right arm for a big cool glass of water. Grammie says there used to be a refreshing drink from Maine. Moxie, as it was called, claimed to be a cure for imbecility and helplessness. I'd give both my arms for a glass of that.

"Serrie."

It's like he's taken a juicy bite out of the pungent night air. Hans is following the red glow of my cigarette, a beacon if there ever was one.

"Serrie, you sure smoke a lot." His sandals crunch on the gravel and stop as he moves onto the grass.

A cigarette is a girl's best friend. Where would I be without smoking? It's the most social thing I know how to do. I'm aware it's deadly, but if it's really that dangerous, then why can you buy them? The government looks out for you, right? Percy says it's all about commerce, not health, and so far, that seems to be the case about a lot of things.

I just laugh when Hans asks if he can sit down because who says no to the boss? Certainly not me. His cedar-and-spice smell floats through the smoke into my nostrils. It's more than that, there's a warm flesh smell that makes me lick my lips.

"So, Serrie, are you enjoying working here?"

The heat of my cigarette burns my tongue as I suck on my smoke. "Yes," I whisper. "It's a nice change of pace."

"Yes, you were travelling before."

"Well, if you want to call it that."

"Maybe someday you will travel in a more productive way. For instance, there are many exchange programs, did you know?"

It's clear Hans doesn't really understand the world I live in. I'm a pie girl now and pie girls don't travel, don't go to university, they just chop until they drop. He had just stopped by on his way back from a late-night trip to the airport where he had taken his parents to catch a flight to Frankfurt after their summer visit. Hans Zimmer is a controversial man. He's created many jobs in the Valley with the pie factory, and before that he had started a bakery on the South Shore with a man from Switzerland. That bakery was sold to a large American company and then he had come to the Valley. He drives back and forth from Lupin Cove, going right by my parents' place. Sometimes when I'm sitting outside, trying to wake up in the after-noon heat, I'll wave. He always beeps and waves. Friendly feller, that Zimmer is, my mother says.

"Do you want a ride home, Serrie?"

"Oh, my bike is fine. Anyway, I've got to finish my shift."

"Of course, but I will be here until then. And I will put your bike in the back."

"It's really no problem to ride."

"I insist," he smiles.

I capitulate.

Driving up to my place Hans tells me about his old home in Lupin Cove.

"I know the one, the old Cruickshank place."

"Ah, yes, you would know. You are a local."

"Yeah, that's me, a local," I giggle, letting the window down with the push button. Hans's automobile is brand new and has that wonderful just-off-the-line smell. It's this sports utility kind of vehicle with all the features.

"Do you drive a standard, Serrie?" He shifts as he speaks.

I nod, "Yeah, I learned to drive in my dad's truck, and then I drove a tractor on the Baxter's farm."

Hans nods, looking pleased. "I don't understand you North Americans and your automatic transmissions. Scared to shift gears, scared of a clutch. It's so silly, you know, bad on fuel, less control of the car. Automatic everything here."

I press the window button on his car and a breeze comes in. He laughs. "That is actually a convenience, this master panel." He puts my window up and I wipe my hands on my shirt, I'm grimy from the factory, sitting on the genuine calfskin leather, folding my hands delicately on my lap.

"How are you enjoying the pie factory?" He glances over with this little smile.

"Just fine, glad to have a job."

The sun is rising in the east as we come around the oxbow bend and up to the brow of the Mountain. Hans puts on his sunglasses as I play with the push-button windows and we turn in the driveway.

"You know, Serrie, your father's outhouse collection is very valuable. Some people, they enjoy collecting these kinds of buildings and they will pay to have them shipped all over the world."

I nod, just look straight ahead, hoping he isn't a Burgess clone. He doesn't say anything else about it as he stops the car and gets my bike out. I say goodnight and we laugh because it's morning, and then I wave as Hans backs up. Inside, on the kitchen table, a phone message in my father's scrawl — Dearie wants me to call. We haven't spoken in almost a month and I wonder what she wants. A truce maybe, though I doubt it. Dearie seems to savour other people's confusion, maybe because she has so much in her, she doesn't want to be alone — it's hard to tell about Dearie. She had constantly driven all the way out from Halifax for Saturday night, my one night off, just stopping in for a cup of tea, and complaining. And the first nice Saturday night in May she had pulled up as I was on my way out the door to Lupin Cove for a walk. I had only been up for four hours and was hardly awake, but she had a whole picnic itinerary. And there I was, climbing in the white van. I should have just said no, followed my plans, but it's hard to break a lifetime of habits. It's weird to think that at twenty I could even have a lifetime of habits. As we had driven into Lupin Cove, Hans Zimmer had passed us in his fancy Mercedes. I had waved.

"Oh, so are you and old Hans big buddies now?" Dearie asked as she parked the van by the wharf.

"Well, he's my employer, Dearie."

She put on the emergency brake, a huge pedal that her short legs could barely reach. "Well, at least it's a job. You should be grateful. You better keep it so when we get a place you can pay your rent."

"Dearie, you know, you sound just like Galronia. God. I don't want to stay at the pie factory forever. Is that what you think my life's goal is, to work at Zimmer's Pies? And I didn't know we were planning to rent a place together. You haven't even asked me. God."

"Stop saying 'God'. You're not much fun this evening."

I carried the picnic basket down Echo Beach, and made a driftwood fire to roast weenies, direct from Stronach Meat Packers to her father's freezer to our fire, Dearie talking the whole time.

"And I don't see why I have to study Business. I mean, I didn't even pick it. He did."

I never talk about the Weeping Willows or the hospital, none of it, and Dearie never asks. Just talks and talks like she thinks talking is going to change things. How she can't stand university and how Elizabeth works so much she never comes home, spending all her time off with Reggie.

I was tending to the fire, because she never did. Sometimes she'd throw a big stick on it, smothering the flames, scattering the coals, laughing when I raised my eyebrow at her. She was going on and on about how maybe she would move back to the Valley, we could share a house. Her father might buy one for her, if she worked at the drugstore, if she finished up her Business degree part time, summer courses, night courses, driving down to the city one night a week in the winter. She had dropped two courses this year and one last year but her father didn't need to know, she would just take an extra course in the summer or something, correspondence. I nodded, placing a piece of driftwood on the fire and turning my roasting stick, watching the skin on the wiener puff up and turn golden brown.

"It'll be great. Maybe we can get a house over here on the Mountain, have a garden, you know, renovate the house."

"I can't see your father buying an old house, Dearie."

"Well, maybe one of those modern cottages, you know, an A-frame."

My hot dog was bubbling through its skin, the bubbles charring blacker and blacker until it resembled a finger found in the aftermath of tragic fire — all that remained was a crooked charcoal finger, the newspaper report said. I dropped it on a grey stone pounded smooth from the water. Anthropology, I thought, looking at the blackened hot dog.

"What a waste of a wiener, Serrie. What the hell are you doing?"

I knocked the weenie into the fire and ate a cold white bun, fresh-freezer-burned from the Melanson freezer.

"Well, I'm trying to figure out what I want to do, too, and I thought it would make sense for me to come out to the Valley, so at least my father would leave me alone."

"Then maybe you should just do what you want and stop worrying about your father."

"But he's got the money."

"Well, you've got lots of money saved."

"That's for New Orleans —"

"Then go to New Orleans —"

"It's not that easy, Serrie . . . you think everything is so easy."

"No, I don't think anything is easy. Does my life look goddamn easy? I can't believe you'd say that."

She yelled, "Well, you didn't have to go be an alcoholic. I mean, I'm not an alcoholic."

They don't call it Echo Beach for nothing.

alcoholic . . . alcoholic . . . alcoholic

bouncing back at me and up to Lupin Cove. It was too much. I yelled, "I didn't grow up planning to be an alcoholic. This isn't what I thought my life would come to, you know. How do you think *I* feel about it? Not too fucking good, I'll have you know." Screams were coming out of my mouth and I just put down my hot dog bun and took off around the harbour, leaving Dearie there, hot dog in hand, mouth open. By the top of Moonrise Hill, by the graveyard, I was so out of breath I stopped and bent over, as self-pity wrapped around me in endless strips, stiffening my joints, my entire body rigid.

I walked along that old country road like a tin man in the chilly May dusk, arms twisted in front, pretending not to see the locals who drove by — gawking, of course. *Saw that Serrie Sullivan on top of Moonrise Hill and she didn't even so much as wave.* But I didn't care about their gossip because, as Grammie says, "other folks will think what they think and there's not a damn thing you can do about it. What you think, now, that's what matters." Just like what they say in AA. I was so alone then, there on the Lupin Cove Road. Sometimes dusk just makes everything worse, the world becomes one big shadowy indecipherable maze and you are supposed to just trust that it is out there. When I was little, twilight seemed to make everything better, softer, and I liked the mystery then. At the ripe old age of twenty, I was wishing my life was bigger than the pie factory. My plan was to hitchhike to the highway and then get a ride some-where, just away. Of course, not one car came by, except Dearie. She pulled up and rolled the window down, but I kept walking, so she drove slowly alongside of me. "Serrie, are you okay?"

I shook my head, because I wasn't okay, but it was dark and she didn't see me, I guess.

"Serrie, look, I'm sorry. I don't know what it's like. I didn't mean what I said. Why don't you get in the van? It's getting dark."

"It's okay, Dearie," I said but my voice came out in scratches that were lost in the engine rumble. I couldn't look at her then or I'd cry and I wasn't ready for that.

"Look, give me a call, okay? I'm really sorry, Serrie." Her voice broke and she drove off. The air was so still I could hear the van all the way over the North Mountain, the gears shifting as she went down to the Valley. Grammie always says we have to try to love the ones who are hardest to love, because they need it the most. Right then, it was impossible for both of us.

I walked another few miles until the Spinster's place loomed out of the twilight.

At the end of June, I have my six-month job review a bit early and I get promoted, but not to the rotating pie table, or even to the day shift. My promotion is to the warehouse section, still at night. They need someone who can do a whole variety of tasks, Timmie says. I'll be doing everything from packing boxes and driving the forklift to filling the pecan pie shells, wearing rubber hip-waders. I'll get to "manage" a big, hot sticky hose that oozes pecan pie filling into dainty little shells in aluminum pans. That's what they call it, *managing the hose*. I have to wear a hard hat, too; it's a rule in the warehouse.

And so, night after night, I pack-lift, pack-lift, manage-the-hose. The shift dotted with those precious few breaks outside, where I can smell pecan rising off my skin, sweet and sugary, coming right out my pores. I tidy up the pies after I fill them, after they have cooled. Fill them, take a break, and then come in and tidy them up with a knife, scraping and pulling away the spilled filling from the aluminum pie edge. After eating a pile of the delicious chewy filling bits I lose my taste for pecan pie forever. It's not that it doesn't taste good, it does — it's just too much of a good thing. We are allowed to take a damaged pie home every shift and my mother and father eat them as fast as I leave them on the kitchen counter at dawn.

One night at the beginning of July, I catch a glimpse of myself in the long window in the little room at the back of the warehouse where the pecan pies are filled. It's Serrie, in the green hip-waders and rubber boots, stained white tank top, yellow hard hat and pierced nose, dripping sweat. "A sight to behold, you are," I hear Grammie say. My life will never be built, I think, too tired to manage the hose that thrashes in my grip, a snake held by its tail, spewing sweet goo all over the room. When I finally get my slippery hand on the off valve, I trip and land in the filling on the cement floor. It's cooled down on the cement or I'd've been scalded. And I sit there, all sticky, scratching at my head, trying to get the energy to stand up and find a mop. I have to clean up, get the boxes ready for loading. It must be three in the morning. I turn to check the clock. Hans Zimmer is leaning against the wall watching me. He is wearing safari shorts and a polo shirt, and sandals. He is everything I will never be, perfect and finished, confidence in every movement, a master of all realms.

Sweet warm goo drips down from my head and lands on my left breast, right smack on my nipple. We both look down and then up, right at each other. I don't giggle, just keep looking at him. He reaches down to take his sandals off. Oh my God, he's going to strip down right here, I think. I can hear the forklift in the hall. My tank top is bunched up around my ribs and my belly button ring is shining in the fluorescent light. There is a pecan stuck to it. Hans puts on the rubber boots in the corner and walks over to me. He takes the pecan off my belly, holds it to my mouth. He stares at the pecan and then into my eyes. My heart is pounding as I take it. Our fingers stick together. He stares at me with his blue eyes, but in this light they look black. More filling drips down from my head and lands on my nose ring as Stewie drives in on the forklift.

It takes us a long time to clean up. The boys are moving the wooden flats with the loader and it's too loud to talk. I don't make eye contact with Hans. My co-workers keep glancing over, wondering what the hell the big boss is doing cleaning up. I'm sure they can figure it out. After work, Hans puts my bike in the back of his Mercedes and drives me home, telling me that he is going hiking in the Rocky Mountains for the rest of July, that maybe when he comes back we can go down to Lunenburg for a day, I can show him where my German ancestors lived. Dating the boss, I think to myself, will wreck everything at the factory. No one will talk to me. I'll never make the day shift. I just need time for myself this summer, if that's okay with him, I explain. He looks surprised, and then nods in this matter-of-fact way. "Yes, yes, certainly, you are very busy with the pies."

Two days later, on Friday afternoon, we are called in for a full staff meeting. Hans has sold the business to an American frozen dessert company. He comes in to tell us and says the new management will arrive on Monday, that we shouldn't worry about our jobs. And no one does, except me, with the least seniority, on a work program and so on and so forth, so it's easier to let me go. Stewie, red in the face, tells me at the end of the meeting, after Hans has left. They are giving me two weeks' severance pay, he says, walking me out to Cyril's truck. It's the first of a lot of layoffs, he tells me. The new owners are going to build a big factory in the industrial park near the highway by Bigelow Bay, so if I can hang on until Christmas, then they can hire me back when they need more employees. I just stare at my feet and then give him a kiss on the cheek and drive off.

To his credit, as my father says, Hans Zimmer calls me at home that night, at suppertime, to apologize. Hans wanted out of the food industry, he has other business interests, and is so, so sorry, they had said they would keep all the employees on. It was a sudden sale, they came to him, and he felt terrible that I wasn't given more notice. And then he asked me out for dinner so we could talk about it. But I said no, no, I wasn't feeling well. And I wasn't. Who would be? What would I talk to Hans Zimmer about? Being a screw-up? Unemployment? My great plan to do . . . nothing? Alcoholics Anonymous? It was enough humiliation without savouring it through a fine dining experience. He said he would call me again, when he came back from his hiking trip, he had bought an old hotel and maybe he would have a job for me.

I won't hold my breath, I think.

Later, I force myself to go to bed at ten o'clock, a normal-person bedtime. Thoughts rattle through my head: unemployed, an alcoholic university drop-out without a job. "It's always best to face the bright side," Grammie always says, so I try again: I am a recovering alcoholic, who is an unemployed university drop-out living with her parents with big student loans. Crying would help, but my insides are stone. All night I try to make an action plan, thinking of what they told us in treatment, to look after ourselves when we are feeling vulnerable, which is what I decide the this horrible raw feeling is. I think of HALT, one of those recovery acronyms: hungry — angry — lonely — tired. We are always to watch for these when we are feeling bad. Well, I'm angry, socially isolated, and exhausted, so maybe that has something to do with me wanting to just run down the stairs, out the door, and down the road to any place but here. So much for the bright side, I think, just breathing thin shallow gasps until it is morning and my mother is at the door with a cup of coffee that steams in through the keyhole.

"Serrie, Serrie, do you want to go picking strawberries with me and Gallie? This is the last weekend there will be berries. Elizabeth came home last night and she's here for the day. She called this morning but I didn't want to disturb you."

"It sounds great," I whisper to the ceiling, head still on the pillow.

"I can't hear you," she says. "Can I come in?"

"Sure," I say in my loudest voice, as she opens the door and hands me the coffee.

"Maybe a better thing to do is to cart you up to the funeral parlour or prop you up in an outhouse with some ice. See if they can revive you in fifty years. Just look at you."

"Ha-ha," I say.

"Well, lord, look at you."

My arms are folded on my chest. I've slept that way. We both start laughing and she says I've got a morbid streak that must come from the Sullivans. I sit up and rub my head — the hair is growing in and it's itching, but I'm too tired to shave it.

"You look nice with a bit of hair, Serrie. Like a French cap. Soon I'll be able to put a ribbon in it like when you were little or we could just glue a little one there now. I know you're discouraged and it would do you good to get out."

At Baxter's we pick in the south field and I go like a machine. Gallie meets us there, telling us that Grammie is not feeling well, very congested.

"We should expect that, what with her being eighty-nine years old," my mother says as she kneels on the straw between the rows.

Gallie compliments me on my technique. "You sure learned a lot at Zimmer's Pies. Too bad they fired you."

"Gallie, please, not in this heat. She learned to do farm work right here at Baxter's with Elizabeth, working here every summer since she was twelve years old. You know that. And she wasn't fired, she was laid off. At least she can collect the unemployment insurance."

"They call it the employment insurance now. Isn't that just like the government to go meddling with the language to try to fool us . . ."

Thankfully Gallie goes off on the government and I just keep picking, *picking the row clean*, as we say in the business. The berries are enormous and red under that scorching white sun up there. I pick two flats of berries in thirty minutes, more than enough for jam and for freezing. The Meissner girls are crisp against the blue sky in their shorts, white blouses and big straw hats. I walk up the row to Elizabeth's house and turn back. They could be twenty years old, those two.

The row leads right to Elizabeth's back yard, where she is lying on a blanket on the lawn.

"You should be using your lawn-chair bed," I call out to her.

Elizabeth sits up and shouts back that she's had enough of lawn chairs for her entire life and then she comes running to the edge of the field in a yellow daffodil bikini. She hugs me, all covered in coconut sun oil. "Serrie, you look just great," she says. "A bit tired, but really great. Kind of pale and skinny, but really great. Dearie's right, you really are getting it together." She laughs. Sometimes it's hard to know whether Elizabeth is making a joke or being dead serious.

"Dearie's never ever told me that. The last time she was out I could hardly get a word in edgewise."

Elizabeth snorts, "Oh, you know Dearie. She can't say anything nice to anyone's face. It's like it would kill her or something. But she did say it. I think Dearie's jealous of you."

Just then Ardyth brings us out lemonade and strawberry short-cake. While I sip and eat, Elizabeth rubs my head with suntan lotion, telling me I should let my hair grow in more.

"Why would Dearie be jealous of me? I'm a loser," I say.

Elizabeth slaps my head. "You really shouldn't say that kind of stuff."

I smile. "So how's Reggie?"

She answers really fast. "Oh, he's working a lot and travelling, doesn't have a lot of time." She lies back on the chair and puts on a pair of sunglasses. I change the topic and tell her about Zimmer's, losing my job, about Hans asking me out on a date.

"He's awful good-looking, but isn't he something of a ladies' man, as your Grammie would say? Anyway, you should move to the city. God, I don't know what you do down here for a social life. After one day I want to blow my brains out."

I lie down on the blanket beside her and we hold hands and look at the sky.

"Serrie, I always knew you were, you know, not exactly thrilled about life, you know, not in the way Dearie is, not all sour. You get sad, like when flowers die and I think that must be hard because, like, flowers die, you know."

I squeeze her hand and she cries a little, telling me that Clare saw Reggie with some other woman down at Historic Properties at sunset. He had his arm around her, sitting on a bench, as the *Bluenose* was coming in to dock. I could imagine it: a herd of tourists with expensive cameras, the ferry going over to Dartmouth, the mental hospital on the other side, brackish smell of harbour heavy on the evening air, Reggie being an infidel.

"I called him up and he told me it wasn't true and then I asked him, 'Why would Clare lie? I don't think *she* is doing the lying here. Do you think I'm, like, retarded?' He said maybe she's jealous. What does he think, I'm an idiot? I just wasn't having it, Serrie, so I hung up." She says that two days later he came crawling back with wine and roses. And so they are trying again.

"People can change," Elizabeth says. Her eyes are closed.

After tanning at Elizabeth's, Gallie and my mother come pick me up and we go up to Grammie's place with our strawberries, to make jam. I'm sweaty and covered in suntan oil so, before I start hulling the berries, I rinse my head in the kitchen sink while my mother has a look and a listen to Grammie's chest.

"Well, it could be a summer cold," Gallie says, "you know how old people get the summer colds, and there is just nothing worse than a summer cold.

My mother rolls her eyes. "She needs a chest X-ray. It's no summer cold."

There is nothing worse than double pneumonia in an frail old lady and Grammie goes into the hospital the next day, not even making it to church.

On Tuesday morning I'm having a cigarette and coffee out in Number Nine, waiting to go into Foster to see Grammie. Martha has started her vacation. She has four weeks off now because she's been working for the government for so long now, and she says it's the only good thing about working for the government. A haze hangs over the Valley and it's going to be a burner of a day. Elizabeth has gone back to the city. I take a drag of my smoke, a sip of my coffee, and then dump it out. The air is too sticky for a hot drink, even for smoking. Cyril comes out and sits on the bench by the marble birdfeeder.

"Some hot. Could the farmers ever use some rain."

"Then there'd be even more mosquitoes," I say.

"Yup, well, this kinda warm weather breeds them, really. The mosquito goes back before the dinosaur. Never gonna get rid of 'em. All they need is a little bit of standin' water. Just a puddle." A hummingbird goes by. "Did you know, Serrie, a mosquito's wings beat ten times faster than a hummingbird's? 'Bout three to five hundred times a second, if you can believe that. That's what makes the whinin' noise. And the different species beat their wings at different frequencies, that's how they can tell who to hook up with, you know what I mean, tunin' into the same frequency. It's only the female ones, too, that feed on blood, for the eggs. So every time you swat one off, it's a lady. The males, they just eat up the nectar."

I nod. It's classic Cyril, detailed knowledge about the strangest and the most common things, and not a word about the things going on, like people in hospitals and families falling apart, that kind of thing. My mother is over standing by the car, so I stand up and step onto the lawn from the outhouse. Cyril waves to us from the shade as we head over to collect Gallie.

Martha stays in the car while I go inside to get Aunt Galronia. She is in a bad mood as she adjusts the fridge magnets. "So, Serrie, when are you going to get a new job? Your parents can't go supporting you. Percy's in university, with his doctorate, and the last thing they need is having you mope about the house." She shuts up when we get to the car, but as soon as we start down the hospital road, which is called Hospital Road, she starts again. "This must feel like your second home, Serrie."

My mother slams on the brakes, right in the middle of the road, and speaks in a whisper. "Just don't start now, Gallie, or you can get out right here. You should have enough decency to not take this out on Serrie. We are all worried."

And Gallie shuts up, just like that.

The geriatric ward is on the fourth and top floor. We wait for the elevator and when it opens Mrs. McIver walks out. She makes a little squeak when she sees me and Gallie says good day to her. She puts her hand out to the elevator door and starts saying something, but Gallie pushes her hand away as my mother hits the button. She keeps trying to talk and Gallie keeps saying, "Isn't it just a beautiful day, sun and blue sky, oh my my . . . " as they close ranks around me. And then the big sterile-smelling elevator that is enough to make you gag goes up and it occurs to me that this family will always be there for me in one way or another. The cigarette smoke reeks as the door opens and we walk into this sea of oldies hobbling along on canes and in wheelchairs, people going by on stretchers. I never realized there were so many seniors in Foster. Gallie and my mother stop at the nurses' desk and my mother tells me to go down to see Grammie in the last room on the right.

I walk down the hall, holding onto the handrail like I'm an oldie myself, and peek in the last room on the right. There is a big window looking out at the North Mountain. You can see our place, right at the top there. I just stare and then I hear this horrible gasping sound and take a step into the room. The sound is coming from Grammie's mouth. She's got this oxygen thing under her nose, and she's all curled up in a tiny ball like Le Mont. But she's not marmalade orange, no, she's a nice shade of blue, robin's eggshell blue, with needles sticking in all those big bulgy veins. So right, my Grammie looks like an Easter egg. I bite my lip and step closer. Holding my stinky smoke breath, another step closer. Grammie opens one eye and I think of television documentaries, crocodiles in the bayou.

"That you, Martha girl?"

I shake my head. "No, Grammie, it's Seraphina."

"Martha, I want to go home. I am almost ninety years old, I am." Her eye shuts as my mother comes in the room.

"Grammie thinks I'm you. She's gone back in time," I whisper.

"It's the medication, Serrie. Give your Grammie a kiss and go out in the hall," she breathes in my ear.

Grammie's cheek feels dry and thin. My nose brushes her hair, white and fine, a head of gossamer, and beneath the acrid hospital smells there is Grammie, lavender, jasmine, and rose, those deep scents that so slowly fade away.

I go out and lean on the car outside and cry into a cigarette. It takes my mother half an hour before she comes out. Gallie is going to be a few more minutes — she's telling Mrs. McIver off. We both start laughing like we're on drugs, and the tension fizzles away for a bit. I offer my mother a cigarette.

"We should both quit, Serrie."

I nod and light up her smoke. "Maybe we should make a quitting deal," I say.

She takes a drag and looks off at the big maple tree. We are parked just beside it, missing the shade by a foot. "Serrie, I've been talking with Yvonne, Yvonne out in Vancouver."

She must think I have no brain cells left. "I know who Yvonne is, Mother. I mean, she's only your best friend, she was your maid-of-honour, you grew up together," I snap.

"My god, Serrie, why do you have to talk like that?"

"Well, I didn't know you'd been talking to Yvonne." I can't stop being nasty, I'm just like Gallie.

"I don't tell you everything I do. And you certainly don't tell me everything you do. Look, I don't want to fight. Why is everything so hard all the time? It's just one thing after another." Martha takes a drag of her smoke.

She's right, everything *is* hard all the time, it's always been that way. "Life is hard," Grammie would say. "Not always, but often. That's how it is, the good with the bad." Sometimes I wish Grammie would shut up but not right now. I'd give anything for her to sit up in that bed and hold forth, even all blue like that.

My mother is still talking so I tune back in. " . . . it's her sister Lenore who, two years ago, bought the one-of-a-kind house over in Lupin Cove, you know, right where the road turns by the harbour, and you don't know Lenore so don't say you do. And I know you'd rather be in the city, but how you'll manage that is beyond me, so you'd best consider this because you can't be without work, it's not healthy."

She points her cigarette at me and I stay quiet. She looks at the red brick wall of the hospital and we listen to a plane drone over-head, a military one heading to the base down further east in the Valley, near the Bible College. I feel sad, because of Grammie, but this sadness has more to it, not that I know what else is involved, or even want to right now. My eyes water and I rub them. Crying only makes me feel worse.

She pats my shoulder and starts talking like words will make it better. "Now Lenore is a retired teacher. She's almost seventy, though you'd never know it and she's going to Vietnam, to do the curriculum development with teachers over there. I was telling

Yvonne about you losing your job, and she said Lenore was looking for a house-sitter. It would be for almost a year, from this September right through until the end of July, I do believe. There's the cat as well, Earl Grey. Isn't that cute? The Earl's old, so not much to do there. You can stay with us, of course, but it would do you good to have your own space. And you'd be close, still on the Mountain, just over in the Cove. You'll need to give Lenore a call soon. And you'll have to get a job, because there's bills to pay, and you'll need to keep busy. Lord, autumn will be here before you know it." My mother takes a drag. "Oh, Serrie, what will ever become of you?" she exhales.

And I just shrug. She puts her arm around me and we stand there, the helpless and the imbecilic, squinting off towards the bright side.

EIGHT

THE FRONT DOOR OF THE ONE-OF-A-KIND HOUSE IS PERIWINKLE BLUE.
From the porch swing on the verandah I see every car that drives
by, which is hardly any now in September, the smattering of
tourists gone, the summer residents all away for the year, just the
fishermen, the year-rounders, and of course, the Germans. I keep
waiting for Hans Zimmer to pass by, but he never does. He must be
away, too, and surprisingly, it's a disappointment to me, not seeing
him. Hardly anyone ever walks, just me and the odd kid, waving
and calling hello. Most people are at work in the day, except for us
unemployed, but it's not just that. Saying Lupin Cove is off the
beaten track is an understatement — you have to know of it, you
have to have a reason, like visiting, to go there, or let's say, house-
sitting, unless you take a wrong turn at the bottom of the
Mountain, or maybe you are looking for an investment in shore-
front property. It's not listed in the provincial tourism guide, there
aren't any fancy road signs, and with the huge tides and rocky
beaches, it's not like you're going to go tacking about the bay in a
ferro-cement sailboat with a big keel or anything, because once the
water is out, the keel would snap like a cracker. There used to be a
community centre, once the Lupin Cove School, and while the
clapboard building with its peeling paint still stands, there are no
more community dinners and the church is only used every other

Sunday during the summer months. I don't know about high summer, but now, in the autumn, everyone seems to spend most of their time watching television; the blue glow of the TVs is all I can see when I go out walking in the dark. No one closes their curtains at night. It's sort of odd, living in a place so small and having so much privacy, but it's perfect for me, and I can even feel my stomach calming down, relaxing into the quiet pace here. I even make porridge in the morning, with raisins, and try to cook meals, not that I am much of a cook, but I'm trying, buying fish right off the boat. And then I rock the early evenings away in the porch swing. Sea Breeze Cottage, it says on this little antique brass plaque, not that the cottage is in direct line of a sea breeze, tucked away into the knoll right at the bottom of Moonrise Hill, where the road turns by the harbour, just before the bridge. You still have a view, but it is protected from the winds off the Bay. I can hear the water at night, the waves on the rocks, even when it's calm, and it calms me from head to toe.

"Finely built peasantry, some people call it," Lenore said in August at our tea party to set up the house-sit. "However, that's misleading, as enormous thought went into the decorative style. The arts and crafts movement was not just architectural, it was a whole philosophical movement."

"Sounds like my life," I said, taking a bite of a ginger cookie served on a blue Depression glass plate.

"You're just like your grandmother, Serrie," Lenore laughed, refilling my cup with tea, and pointing to framed blueprints on the wall — the house had been designed by a Halifax architect, which was rare in those days, and meant the folks who built it had money. Most homes were designed and put up by local builders, from experience and pattern books. Sea Breeze Cottage was constructed as a year-round home, a modest dwelling, one-and-a-half storeys, with a bedroom and study in the top, sloped ceilings, and one gabled window looking out over the verandah roof. It was early-twentieth-century, 1915 to be exact, and the original American owners had hoped to move there permanently, but they never did, and the house was passed down through the generations as a summer place until this generation had sold it to Lenore. Her grandmother had owned the farmhouse back up the road before the church, she said, so there was a special connection for her here, here where she had played on the wharf with my mother and Yvonne, walking barefoot, like Percy and I had, over the harbour bottom at low tide, playing on the outer wharves, something we had never done, those wharves having crumbled by the time we were toddlers.

"Seraphina, now how did you find that Hans Zimmer? You worked for him. People here are curious about what he's got planned for Lupin Cove. Hans is away now, but some obnoxious German is up there supervising the renovations on the Cliffside Hotel."

"He's very good looking," I whispered into my tea. "He's organized. Nice footwear."

Lenore let out this big whoop, and slapped the kitchen table, an old harvest table with a pretty lace runner on it. "Yes, he is a handsome man, I'll give you that. And quiet, composed, you know. He doesn't seem to say anything unless it needs to be said."

"Maybe his brain's full of his plans, his blueprints," I said, Lenore laughing again. "He was okay to work for, he helped me clean up one night." No mention of the pecan pie encounter. Locals girls don't take up with the Germans. "He liked my father's outhouses," I whispered.

"I like your father's outhouses too, Seraphina. He's onto something there. He's an innovator, your father. Just born in the wrong time, in my opinion. Would have done well in a university. Speaking of, will you be heading back to school?"

Another cookie. "Don't know, I guess we'll have to see how the year goes."

Two years ago, Lenore had bought Sea Breeze Cottage, moving back to Nova Scotia from Toronto after being away for almost fifty years. She is like no oldie I know, with her hair in a long braid, hiking boots and cat-eye glasses. She's spent most of her time renovating the house, not piling it up with stuff, no clutter, just lovely restored features, and a deluxe bathroom with a whirlpool tub and ferns. A fully modern kitchen with a kick-ass gas range. She's kept the old wainscoting in the house, all the quirky shelves, ledges, and cupboards, so the character of the house is intact; it's things like skylights that make it contemporary, bright and hopeful. The house was old and new at the same time, with such extensive renovations. No dust, no drafts, no creaks and groans, no must and mildew. There are select pieces of furniture, not that the place is empty, but it's spare, each piece you know is special to her, from the ultra-comfy Morris chairs in the front room with the airtight woodstove to the dining room with the round table and the fine china. The kitchen is white and the morning sun makes it glow, though in September I sit right out on the back step drinking coffee, looking at the garden that has begun to go to seed. Throughout the house are pictures of her grown kids, and her grandchildren, and of her husband, who passed on ten years ago. They travelled the world, teaching in Africa and India, the kids going along. In all the pictures they look happy, you know, a real family. It's like Lenore has gathered up everything good and precious in her life and brought it here to Lupin Cove.

There are funny columns on either side of the house, with a whole assortment of windows looking out on the harbour. Most of the houses in Lupin Cove are traditional saltboxes. There are some dressed-up saltboxes, with classical revival features and rigorous symmetry, with pillars and cornices, you know, balance and order. But not the one-of-a-kind house. The arts and crafts style was always asymmetrical, very much the romantic ideal, Lenore had said as she toured me through, looking for Earl Grey, who was asleep on top of the fridge. She didn't want her house empty during the winter. And the Earl was too old to be relocated for ten months. He was retired, she said, and deserved to stay put in his retirement home. Lenore was supposed to be too, but she said she wasn't ready to surrender to summer days of lemon iced tea and gardening, winter days of crackling fires and reading books, another kind of romantic ideal.

"Well, after this last year, I'm ready to retire," I had whispered, and Lenore laughed and gave me a set of keys. And then she was off to hot and humid Vietnam, and it was just me and Earl Grey at the one-of-a-kind house.

There's no smoking at Lenore's place, so as soon as I moved in the last pack of smokes went into the woodstove. In treatment they said to replace a bad habit with a good one, so running filled in the giant hole left without smokes. At first it felt like self-imposed punishment, because I'd never trained for anything in my life, I'd never had any kind of physical regimen at all. When you start running, it is a killer. And when you don't know what you are doing, well, you end up puking in a ditch. My legs don't hurt too much because I've been biking, but my lungs are on fire and by the time I get to the top of Moonrise Hill, I'm ready to roll down into the harbour and drown. And the next day my thighs feel as though I've been beating them with a club. It's madness and it is like this for all of September, me running with a screwed-up face, in complete agony, pain in my side, gasping. But it gets easier, especially with the method of running and walking, stretching afterwards. And running every other day, not every day, so my muscles can repair. It doesn't take long until I'm running all over the Mountain. My mind just stretches out, becomes as long and as peaceful as the road, the world falls into perspective, and time, as I know it, falls away.

By late September I have a final cord of wood delivered, just to be ready for winter. When it's summer in Nova Scotia, you can forget winter even exists; it stops even being a memory, and becomes a story people tell, like a fairy tale, the white days of bitter ice. Lenore has a woodshed, and so I set to chopping and stacking. And that's how Hans Zimmer finds me in Lupin Cove: outside chopping wood, exercising my work ethic, wondering why I'm always chopping at something, swinging the axe just like Cyril has taught me, when I get this feeling I'm being watched. I have that feeling all the time so at first I ignore it. When I turn around, Hans is there, leaning on the back porch.

"Serrie, you are always working."

I stand up and wipe my forehead. We both smile.

He holds out his hand, and I wipe mine on my jeans and we shake. His hand is warm and his skin is soft as his firm grip holds my hand for just a moment too long. "So, you are house- sitting." He asks about my Grammie right away.

"She's home from the hospital," I say, "but not the same." Her mind is wandering off, back in time to simple days, riding a horse at night when roads were dirt and she could drive down them at any speed she wanted. The house is never warm enough for her and Gallie frets constantly that they will both dehydrate to husks, so there are humidifiers everywhere, which Grammie says make her feel like she's living in an arboretum. I keep hoping Grammie will rally, and go to visit her every Friday night.

"How were the Rocky Mountains?" I ask.

"You know, Serrie, they are very big. Different than the North Mountain." We both laugh, because it doesn't take much to be bigger than this beloved hill.

"And the Rockies are different than the mountains in Bavaria. You should go some time."

"To Bavaria?"

He laughs. "Yes, yes, of course, to Bavaria some time. You know, everyone should go to Bavaria. But you should see the Rockies. They are magnificent. The people are very nice in Banff. They are more open than Nova Scotians. The Bavarians, they are snobs too, you know. They even think their German is special, Bayerisch."

Hans is from Frankfurt, he tells me. He has a brother and sister over there, older than he is, settled with kids and stuff. They send pictures. He came to Canada on a holiday, to visit his Swiss friend on the South Shore. I don't ask him about his dead wife.

He fell in love with Nova Scotia, with its potential, he says. "Except the people, they are hard to get to know, all this mistrust of outsiders, people from away, my God, even people from Ontario, you know, you think they are from away, calling them Upper Canadians. You still hate us for the war and them for the country's confederation. Always thinking outsiders are going to do something very bad. Like this house, you know. Some people won't sell to Germans."

I chop the axe into a piece of wood and lean against the house.

"I wanted to buy this house but it was a private sale."

"Well, you have to understand folks around here, the culture. Change is slow, people just don't like it," I say, and kick the axe with my foot. "People have to know what you're about, know you appreciate who they are. It takes patience, living here."

He nods and contemplates the woodpile. "I just want to make things better here. Lupin Cove is a gem, an unpolished gem. A shabby little place but with some polish, so attractive. But people here, they don't want that. They would sit on the verandahs of their lovely old homes and have the roofs fall in. You have forgotten your history." He picks up a piece of wood. "Would you like to have some help, Serrie?"

I wipe my forehead again. I know all about verandahs, and how much it costs to replace them. "Sure, a bit. My father is coming over later. He likes to help me with this," I whisper.

Hans nods, as though he understands all about father-daughter bonding. I start splitting and he stacks. "You know, it takes money to do what you are talking about and people here don't have any. Times are hard, with the economy and all, the fishing industry collapsing," I say.

"Yes, yes, ja, sure, I know this, Serrie. But that's from overfishing. You Canadians just think it won't end, these natural resources, you know. We Germans, we know, we have learned. But you don't want to learn from us, from Europeans, because we are *from away*. This is not a good reason, you know. And here the fishermen catch lobster and scallops. They make money. Why don't they spend it on their wharf? They just want the government to do everything. In Germany, we know what can happen when you let the government do everything."

I nod, but not everything is always logical and rational. How do you explain that to a German? "How about getting people here involved, you know, community effort?"

He stretches his shoulder. "They are lazy."

I start laughing. Gotta like a man who gets to the point, I think.

"My cousin in Cape Breton, he has a fishing lodge and his workers are always quitting, coming late, coming to work drunk. Believe me, it's very hard being an employer with people who don't like to work. You like to work, Serrie."

"Yes," I laugh. "So do the lobster fishermen. They aren't lazy. It's no easy job, especially in winter. You'd never catch me out there, and I like to work." I laugh again, because I never thought about whether or not I like to work, I just do it, you know, habit, instinct, some combination of the two.

Hans nods. "Yes, yes, it is a hard job. But you know, why are their boats so shabby?"

"Jeez, Hans, I don't know, I don't think of them as shabby. Because they're busy fishing. I mean, they keep the boats working great. There's only so much you can do in a day, my Grammie says. Lupin Cove was a real place, you know, it had a post office, and stores, it had ships in and out all the time, it had a school. But trains came, you know, industrial innovation, it sucked the life out of here, and places in the Valley took off. It's still a real place, you know, with its own kind of reality."

I wished I remembered more of what Percy had always gone on about. "There were two hotels here at one point. A big celebration on Canada Day. It was called Dominion Day back then."

"It is hard to imagine that. Maybe it can come back to life, you know." And he walks into the shed with a wheelbarrow of split wood. Hans is kind of odd, but then so am I. One of the things I like about Hans is that he doesn't take the axe away from me. He lets me do all the splitting and I know most guys from around here would let me do most of the stacking. But he doesn't care about that kind of thing, he cares about the work being done, he tells me, as we take a break on the back porch, drinking ice water. "Serrie, can I ask you something?"

I nod.

"Why do you have a hole in your nose?"

"Oh, Hans, it's a long story." It's the first time I've called him by his name.

"Youth rebellion, yes?"

And I just laugh and drink my water.

When Cyril comes over in the afternoon, I've got most of the wood split and he helps me make neat piles in the shed, bark-side up. I tell him Hans Zimmer plans to operate the Cliffside like a bed-and-breakfast, that he is aiming to have people in by Thanksgiving, maybe even before.

Cyril nods and adjusts his hat. "Maybe you can get a job, Serrie. For the year."

I tell him I already have one, starting mid-October, working at the front desk, as a chambermaid, all-around handy girl.

Cyril nods again. "Hope you'll get back to the university though, sometime, Seraphina."

That autumn is the best of my entire life, like a holiday, enjoying Lenore's house, looking at her paintings, the stained-glass windows, and how the light comes in. Reading her books. Running helps me sleep more than sherry ever did. Imagine, me, Serrie, thinking I have a great life. Hopeful, I guess, is what it is. If I had my way, I'd never come down from running across the Mountain, never go near the Valley, but the AA meeting is in Foster every Friday night, and so I come down for that. Someone drives over to Lupin Cove, picks me up, and then drives me home. It's a whole network. I'm the youngest person there, and it's not like I make a whole new gang of friends. I mean, I don't just start opening up and going on and on about all my insights, because of course I don't have any. But it's good to walk in and have people know my name, to know the names of everyone sitting around the table. It's the routine I like, that's my main discovery, that I'm a sucker for a good routine. Knowing I have a job is a huge relief, and I can feel the tension drain out of my body at night, rising out and floating out the window, pulled away by the fog.

I'm always up early for the sunrise — unless, of course, it is foggy, white everywhere, the end of the driveway just disappearing into the mist. I love the way sound comes through the fog, the sound of waves, voices across on the other side of the harbour, the fishermen on their boats. They go out in the fog, sun, rain, wind, any weather; they go with the tides, starting up at all hours. At first I hear the boats out there, but after awhile, even if they wake me, I just fall back to sleep with the Earl curled up at my side. The boats coming and going soothe me as much as the water sounds, this security, fishing, as old as the ages, and here in Lupin Cove for almost two centuries. Of course it's a deluded feeling of security, given the state of the fisheries, but I feel it nonetheless.

Gallie said everyone was skeptical that Hans thought he could make a go of a B&B open year round. Working at the Cliffside at the beginning of October, I could see how Hans would be successful. He has marketing plans for the whole village, a future vision; he can see what it was and what it can be. When I tell this to Grammie on a Friday night before my AA meeting, she says that's well and fine, but it's important to have present vision, to understand the time and moment that you are in. Everyone is glad I have a job, even though it is with *the German* again. I ask Hans about the present and he says the problem is people are stuck in the present. That doesn't make much sense to me, and so he tries to explain as we paint an upstairs rooms that looks out over the Bay.

"What I mean, Serrie, is that you work today to make what you want tomorrow. You know, you keep your eye on the prize, that's what they say, don't they? Always think about tomorrow."

I skip my Friday AA meeting (which I'm not supposed to do) the first Friday in October when Dearie and Elizabeth drive out from the city to spend a night. Dearie and I are friends again, ever since she sent me a card. There were two seagulls on the front, soaring over the waves. Inside the card, the printed message "You are a good buddy to go the distance with" above her signature, and where she had written she was sorry. And it was enough. Good old Dearie, she's had a hard life, and she carries that hardness around with her. If only the rest of her floated like her curly Acadian hair.

They arrive just as the sun is setting, and come in by the fire. It's the first time they've spent a Friday night not drinking since elementary school, but they don't even bring it up, just sit by the stove, telling me this and that, about working at the bar. They don't want to talk about university because neither of them are making it to class, and who wants to think about problems, Elizabeth says. Dearie keeps going out on the verandah for a smoke and she's there when Hans drops by. We hear their voices through the glass window, and Elizabeth and I go out. The air is cold and damp, summer already seems like some piece of exotica shoved away in the Spinster's attic.

"Ah, Serrie, so you do have friends. We call her the little *Einsiedler*, the little hermit." The three of us laugh. We all know, without saying, that it's hilarious to be in Lupin Cove with a handsome German. Hans just looks at us with a little smile, his teeth white and straight. He doesn't understand twenty-one-year-old girls, not that I'm twenty-one yet, three more weeks until Hallowe'en.

"Do they work as hard as you? Maybe they can work for us next summer," he says.

That night the three of us pile into the bed in the attic room and they tease me about Hans. "He likes you," Dearie says. "It's as plain, as, like, warm rice pudding."

"No, he doesn't," I whisper.

Dearie snorts. "Oh, you lie like a sidewalk, Seraphina Sullivan. You like him, too."

I blush and Elizabeth yawns. "Serrie doesn't need a man, Dearie. They are more trouble than they are worth. That's my two cents. Now I have to get to sleep if we are getting up to be back in Halifax for work," Elizabeth says. And she falls asleep, just like that, no late-night worries or pains interfere with Elizabeth's sleep time.

Dearie and I go sit in the two rocking chairs by the window, wrapped in quilts. A foghorn blows out on the Bay.

"Serrie, I'm thinking I'm going to go to New Orleans next year. Take some time off and travel. That's what I'm planning," she whispers.

I rock back in surprise. Like Grammie says, if you can't be surprised in life, then you aren't alive. "That's great," I reply, balancing the rocker again, pulling my feet in under the quilt.

"Maybe you can come with me. You know, work and save some money. We can take off and just see some of the world, like you were always on about in high school."

"I can't afford it," I whisper.

"All you have to do is just keep working, and saving some money, like I've been doing. It just takes planning, that's all. I've been planning this for years. Sometimes I think I should just pack up and head off."

"Maybe you should do that, Dearie. If you aren't even making it to class."

There is a long silence and a wind comes up. We can hear the waves on Echo Beach, out beyond the harbour. I creep down the stairs and put another log on the fire and tiptoe back up the stairs. Dearie hasn't moved, and I'm amazed she's gone this long without a smoke.

"Serrie, I just think I should plan the trip out more. You know, do it when I'm ready. I know you just up and do things but, no offence, what does that lead to? I like to plan it out, step by step. No offence, right?"

"None taken," I whisper as we crawl in bed, on either side of the snoring Elizabeth.

"What do you want the trip to New Orleans to lead to, Dearie?" But she is asleep already, snoring away with Elizabeth, as the foghorn sounds again out on the Bay.

By Thanksgiving, there are people staying at the Cliffside, and I'm back to working like a maniac, doing shift work, too. The Cliffside has ten rooms, seven looking out on the road, and two over the cliff on the Bay side. Those rooms are the most expensive. At first I don't know where he gets all the guests. None of them are locals, everyone is German or American. He advertises in upscale tourism magazines in Europe and the United States, and with travel agents, he tells me. Hans still wants to try to stay open year round, though I think he's deluded. Maybe through Christmas, I tell him. He nods, he'll see.

The season is busy, through the changing of the leaves, Thanksgiving, my birthday, each day blending into the next, answering phones, doing double washes, making up rooms, serving in the dining room, looking after Lenore's place, feeding Earl Grey. I use one of Hans's cars, doing my errands when I grocery shop for the Cliffside. We mostly serve German-style food, so I'm driving all over the Valley to various farms run by Germans to get *wurst*, all this Ocktoberfest kind of sausage. Not that I know how to cook any of it; there is an older German woman who does that, her hair in a thick grey bun, always wearing dresses and practical shoes, never talking to me. She looks like someone should stick her right up there in the widow's walk in the Cruickshank House. And there is Joachim, childhood friend of Hans. Hans says Joachim's parents are both disgusting drunks, that Joachim has had a very hard life, he just needs to take it easy on the bottle. Hans wishes Joachim would take control, like I have, he says. Joachim supervises the renovations and does lots of them himself. It's hard to figure out what he did in Germany, something with beer and wine, Hans told me, selling it, not drinking it.

"You are the only local here," Joachim announces one day at the end of November, as I'm heading home on a Friday night. "*Local*," he says again, and laughs like it's the funniest word he has ever heard of in any language dead or alive in the entire known universe. This is Joachim's outstanding feature, not his sense of humour but his own personal enjoyment of his sense of humour. It's a two-man play, but there is only Joachim, saying something and then answering back. "Ah, ja, Joachim, that's a very good one." And then he bends over and slaps his knee. Joachim is the same age as Hans, but not aging in the same way. Big pot-belly hanging over his belt, head bald on the top with a grey-and-red fringe. Hard to believe he is thirty-five. I guess it must be all the beer and sausage. He's from Frankfurt, too, as is the German woman, but she doesn't speak English and so I don't know anything about her, just what Hans says, which is that she is his aunt, his *Tante*. Whether they are here on work visas or what, I have no idea, and don't bother asking.

Hans and I become lovers in November, when the leaves have fallen off the trees and everything is stark and bare. It's cold and damp living on the Bay, and every night after work, I go back to his house at the top of the hill and have hot chocolate with him. Another thing I like about Hans is that he couldn't care less that I don't drink. He knows my whole story and seems to just put it off to character building. Grammie says what doesn't kill you makes you stronger, I tell him, and he nods and says that's fine as long as it doesn't cripple you. That night we become lovers; it is after my shift, when Joachim passes out on the kitchen sofa and the aunt who never talks to me goes up to the little apartment Hans has put in for her above the kitchen. I help Hans take a truckload of summer furniture up to his place and we unload quickly as the first snow of the year is dusting down. We stack all the lawn furniture in the basement and as we go up the stairs, I slip and fall back. He catches me and kisses my neck and carries me up through the kitchen, up the next flight of stairs, then the next, to his third-floor bedroom that looks out over the harbour and the Bay. There is one bright yellow light down by the wharf, a light that disappears as his warm skin covers me, and my body unfurls in a huge sail that twists and rises and falls.

After, we are in bed, and the wind bats against the glass.

"It will be a hard winter," Hans says quietly, one hand in my little bit of hair. His toes are peeking out of the flannel sheets, and the duvet is twisted through his legs. He is lean and strong, muscular but with soft skin, his body warm and hard and clean. He is perfect, I think, looking at a terrible painting of the Alps at the end of the bed, by the window, in a huge frame.

"Is that the German Alps?" I say, putting my head on his stomach where I can hear soft noises.

He sighs. "Ja, that is German Alps, yes, painted by my former wife, Ute. She just wanted to paint. That's all she wanted to do, paint pictures. But she only talked about it most the time, doing it, you know, plans, plans, plans. That was Ute, always talking, always the talk. She was always so angry, *zornig*, we call it. And she always said it was me, that if I understood her she would be happier. But I never understood her, I never understood how she didn't want to do anything . . . nothing. She was supposed to come over here to Canada with me, but it was too much packing, she said. 'I hope you get it,' she said in her note, 'that packing is not something I am willing to do.' I got the point, you know."

And then he is quiet, and I don't say anything, just lie there until I fall asleep, as he strokes my hair and whispers that it took him by surprise, how much I wanted him. I nod and think that it's not just him, it's this whole warm and renovated world I want, where things function, and hard work pays off; I want order. But I don't tell him this, I fall asleep, just like a man, he says the next morning, serving me breakfast in bed. He went downstairs to call Joachim at the hotel.

The napkin on the tray has writing on it: *I love you*, letter perfect.

I don't tell my family that Hans and I are seeing each other. Gallie tells them at Sunday dinner in early December. She's heard it from Mrs. Tweedie, a year-rounder who was alive back in the Lupin Cove glory days, who says that Hans has been coming in and out of my place at all hours, me out of his place. Not the Cliffside, but the old Cruickshank House.

"I thought Mrs. Tweedie was dead," I say. Grammie's at the table, quiet, looking at her food, and she perks up.

"So did I, Serrie. So did I. Well, if you've got a boyfriend, you better bring him round for us to meet." You never know when Grammie's going to be lucid.

That Sunday, Hans and I drive over from Lupin Cove and stop to pick up my parents. My father wants to take a picture of us, outside, even though it's freezing. We stand by the Mercedes as my father holds the camera up. "You look like Mia Farrow in *Rosemary's Baby*," he says.

My mother elbows him, "Lord, Cyril, what kind of thing to say is that, even if it is a seventies movie."

"Well, direct from Bombay with that nose ring. How about that?" He must be focussing on my nose.

My mother is standing behind him and she rolls her eyes and winks at us. She asks if I'm letting my hair grow.

Hans answers for me. "Yes, yes, the shaved head, you know, it is not very pretty."

"It's time I had some hair again," I say. "Winter is coming, it was too cold last year." Hans doesn't like my "military hairdo," he's getting skin burn because it's like making love to an electric sander.

We drive into Foster together, where Gallie and Grammie are dressed up and waiting, Grammie telling Hans stories of Grampie Meissner's family in Lunenburg. We eat roast beef and potatoes, and Gallie serves sauerkraut she made in the summer. There isn't one argument, everyone on their best behaviour for me. Grammie asks me about the house-sit and says it's good to see me in one place, not blowing around like the wind. Martha and Cyril nod and I know it's because they are relieved I'm seeing Hans, finally settling a bit, not alone all the time.

On Friday night I come in to see Grammie before the AA meeting, wearing a new sweater and skirt. Gallie says it's the first nice outfit she's seen me in since I used to go to church and Grammie asks me whose clothes I have on.

"Mine, Grammie. A gift from Hans."

"I see," she says, as she takes a wobbly sip of tea. "He's dressing you now, like a baby? Hope you aren't planning to stay over there. You're only twenty-one years old, you know. Whole world out there. More to life than being a chambermaid, my girl. Does he need a passport or something like that?"

"Oh, Grammie, he's a landed immigrant. Why does everyone hate the Germans? It's racist," I say. I still don't know about the rest of the Germans over there in Lupin Cove, but I keep that to myself.

"We are not racist, Serrie. Mind your mouth." Gallie says to me and then turns to Grammie. "Well, it's a job, Mum." Gallie pours more tea. "She's lucky to have a job. And it's amazing that Hans Zimmer has people coming from all over at this time of year. Who would have thought Lupin Cove would have been a tourist destination again, and in December, of all months. Just imagine. Whatever do they do over there at this time of year, Serrie?"

"You know, sit by the fire, read, eat meals in the dining room. Most of them seem to bring their work with them, they just want to hide out. They go for walks and stuff, all bundled up. A retreat kind of thing."

Grammie puts her teacup down and stands up. "That's well and fine for the tourists but you're no tourist, Seraphina. You're my one and only granddaughter."

I don't know why Grammie is in such a bad mood and so I try changing the subject, but she's not having it. "You should be in university. Now, I don't want to tell you what to do, but maybe I should have. Last thing I want is to see you go and marry some foreigner who is almost old enough to be your father. Serrie, you are always looking for the easy way out and you never see it's the hardest path of any. Lord God almighty."

I just sit there staring into my teacup, in my nice little pale pink cashmere twin set.

Gallie stands up. "Never heard you go at her like this before. First time for everything, I suppose. Maybe it's time for bed, Mum."

Grammie says she doesn't need any babysitting and she heads up the stairs, her cane thumping on each one. She doesn't say goodnight.

Gallie and I just sit in the kitchen and listen to the clock go tick-tick, almost meeting time. She says Grammie's just tired these days, but she's proud of me, working so hard, that they all are. "I know I don't tell you that enough, Serrie, but it's the truth, you've really pulled things together, and I'm sorry I'm not a better aunt to you. Sometimes it seems that there isn't time to be kind, you know. So much to do. It's easier just to try to fix what needs fixing than to appreciate everything that's already working. Hans is an industrious man and that's good enough for me. You go up and say goodnight to your Grammie now. She'll have forgotten all about it."

Aunt Gallie says it like it's a good thing that Grammie's memory is going, but I can't imagine anything worse. I go up the stairs and see her light spilling out of her door onto the floor.

"You're going to be late for your meeting, Serrie," Grammie says as I reach the top of the stairs.

"Grammie, how do you know it's me and not Gallie?" I walk to her door.

She coughs. "Gallie walks up the stairs like the major general. You come up them like a ghost." Grammie is tucked in her bed, with her book, in a pink flannel nightgown and a hair net.

"I'm sorry for my sharp tongue, my dear. I'm not myself these days. Don't want to see that happen to you. Your twin set looks very nice."

She turns a page. "Goodnight, Martha," she says.

I don't bother going to the meeting that night, just drive back to Lupin Cove with my hands digging into the steering wheel. And I don't go up to the Cruickshank House, just crawl in Lenore's bed with the cat. I've hardly been sleeping there, and the old thing is so happy to see me he purrs right through the night. Hans calls early, wondering where I was, annoyed that I didn't call. "Well, the roads are very slippery now with snow, and you should think of how I feel when you don't call."

It isn't an unreasonable request, but it feels that way, intrusive. I tell him I'll try to do better next time.

"Are you planning on not coming over tonight as well?"

"That isn't what I mean, Hans. I'll try to remember to call." I tell him about Grammie.

"Oh, Serrie, she is old. This is nature, you know."

I look at Earl Grey, curled up in the bed with me, and my stomach hurts. His fur is soft and thick in my fingers, and I want him to live forever. "I need to spend more time here, to do a good house-sit. I promised Lenore to do a good job and I'm not."

And Hans doesn't say anything, because to him doing a good job is everything. That's how he is, you start and you finish — you see things through.

Mail comes to my parents' house for me. It is from my Classical Studies professor at the university. Martha and Cyril don't say anything, but I can tell they are waiting for me to open it. I've stopped in on my last run for the winter. It's too cold for me now and Hans worries I'll fall and break my leg. I tuck the envelope in my jacket, pretending I don't notice their eyes. Back to Sea Breeze Cottage and I read it in front of the fire, after I have a shower and put on warm clothes. It is a Christmas card from my professor. He'd heard I'd had a difficult time, and he was sorry, hoped I would think about resuming my studies, he would always be available if I wanted to call and talk. The department would be happy to re-admit me, and as we had discussed a year ago, he still felt I should consider graduate work, there were funding possibilities we could discuss.

I hide the card in my underwear drawer.

A week before Christmas Grammie gets sick again and they call me down off the Mountain. Galronia and my mother are in the kitchen arguing when I arrive. The phone is ringing and there is so much noise they must be overreacting. How can anything be wrong with that much commotion? Serious matters are always quiet, sombre, sober, subdued — that kind of stuff. My mother points to the living room. Grammie is sitting in her chair, in just her nightie because the heat is up so high, and because she has a fever. She is so thin now she may as well be a skeleton decoration bought at the drugstore and then forgotten, not put away after Halloween. She's rasping these outboard-motor sounds as she tries to breathe.

"Get me a drink of water," she croaks.

When I give her the glass, it wobbles and the water splashes. I reach to steady her hand and she swats me away, the swat taking most of her energy, the glass falling down on the carpet.

"I do not need any goddamn help," she wheezes.

Gallie rushes in with another glass of water and puts her hand on my shoulder. "Now, Mum, you let me hold the glass," Gallie orders in a schoolmarm voice. And Grammie, she drinks the water like a baby.

I back out of the room and bang into the door, but they don't notice. I don't know if I am crying from the pain in my elbow or from seeing Grammie, but I sniffle past my mother to the porch. It's bleak, dead and withered. My mother comes out and we stare over at Dearie's house, where Dearie's father is staring back at us from the kitchen window. I put my arm around her and we stand there until Gallie comes out saying she could use some help inside.

Grammie goes to bed that night and stays there until Christmas Eve. Hans is looking after Lenore's cat and checking on the cottage. It's not good for him to come over, I explain, I'll keep him posted. He says he understands. I call Percy. It's the first Christmas he hasn't come home. He's busy with his thesis and wanted time to write and he's waiting now to see what happens before he flies home. I tell him I'll keep him posted and then call Dearie, leaving a message, Grammie is very sick. I know she'll come out right away. I leave a message for Elizabeth and she calls back on her break from work. The bar noises are so loud in the background I can barely hear her, noises I immediately recognize. Bars are something I don't miss at all. She's telling me Dearie's already called her and told her what was happening. And then Ardyth called, too, so she's heard it from the whole circle, she says. I ask her how Reggie is and she says things aren't going so good but her break is over and she has to go.

I cook the meals for Gallie and my mother, answer the phone, do the laundry, all the chores, the same as at the Cliffside, I just transfer the skills. I want to be one step ahead of Gallie and my mother, to let them just be with Grammie. We keep changing Grammie's sheets and her nightie, so she will be fresh and cozy. I carry neatly folded piles back to the linen closet in the upstairs hall. Beside it stands an old bookshelf with glass doors on each shelf, glass doors that slide up and inside. These are Grammie's books, going back to her school days, the nursing days, books with hard covers and illustrations, little pieces of tissue paper over the pictures, Grammie's name and date in the front of every single one: in the old, old ones, Islay Mary McKay, and then Islay McKay Meissner, written in spidery writing with faded blue fountain pen ink — she collected books like my father collects outhouses. When I am sitting with her, watching her little chest heave up and down, I look at all the pictures on her walls, so many black-and-whites in fancy wooden frames, ladies in long dresses, kids in big fancy getups with giant hair ribbons, old houses and cars, pictures of Grammie and Grampie, Gallie and my mother in Lupin Cove, at some long-ago beach party, class pictures in front of old schoolhouses.

I sleep in the same room Percy and I had when we lived with Grammie and Gallie that summer I was eight. The bunk beds are still there, and my mother sleeps on the bottom, me on the top, thinking how short the climb up is now that I'm an adult. None of us get any real sleep, with Grammie's breathing louder and louder. We take turns sitting with her. When Gallie or Martha are there, and I still can't sleep, I sit in Grammie's chair in the parlour, looking out at the quiet little town, thinking about her stealing her brother's car, pulling out my tampon, Grammie woven through my life, threads now at an end. And I go outside in my nightie and peek up at the stars. The days may be bleak but those winter nights are painfully bright.

Inside it's as though time is passing around me, as though it were the air itself, and when I walk carefully up the stairs without making a creak, I can feel all the days attach themselves to me. I peek in Grammie's room and both my mother and Gallie are asleep, my mother in the pressback chair by Grammie's head and Gallie across the foot of the bed. I put blankets on them. Grammie's wheezing away. I can hear her even as I brush my teeth, peering in the mirror for lines. I know they are there, in fact, waiting just under the skin, for it must be this way for all humans, moving through the day which is really time and not knowing until it moves around and through us and settles on our bones and skin. Like Grammie. And me too some day.

Dr. O'Leary comes by in the morning and I walk him out to his car. As he opens the door he tells me my Grammie was a nurse, she knows what not going to the hospital means and it's what she wants. I nod.

"She's ninety years old, Serrie. We should be so lucky. She's lived her whole life with her mind sharp and clear like a bell," he says.

My mother is in the kitchen making a fresh pot of coffee when I come back in, bringing a rush of cold air in the door with me. She runs her hand over my back, saying, "God bless the small-town doctors."

At midnight on Christmas Eve, I sit down in Grammie's living-room chair and shut my burning eyes for a minute. There are no Christmas decorations out except for a single candle in the window. And with my eyes shut, it seems as though I can still see it, this single candle, and then soon it is a silky grey dawn. I am still in the chair. My mother's hand is on my forehead. I am still sitting upright, hands folded in my lap. My neck is stiff and sore as I look up at her in the silence.

Upstairs, Gallie keeps saying Grammie went just how she wanted, in her own bed, in her own home. She just took a deep breath, one final sample of the earthly world, and then died without even waking up, just as the stars faded out.

And the three of us nod, and then at the same time take a deep breath in. We sit with her body, waiting for Dr. O'Leary to come and pronounce her, Gallie in the pressback, Martha at the foot of the bed, and me on the window ledge. And then the ambulance attendants come and take the wisp of Grammie from her old spool bed, covered in a white sheet, out the doorway and by her bookshelf, down the creaky stairs by all the family photos, and out of the house she owned free and clear, to an ambulance, with us following behind. Dearie's father is standing at his door, Dearie at his side, and the neighbours across the street. Who didn't think Islay McKay Meissner would live forever? My mother and Gallie are on the porch in nighties and slippers, and me, I've been in the same clothes for two days. Our white breath floats on the air, arms around each other as the ambulance backs out. It's Christmas morning. Gallie starts crying and my mother hugs her.

There is hoar frost and the sun shimmering off those naked tree branches, trees like Grammie now, the terrible and delicate beauty of the dead.

Upstairs in the bathroom, I can feel the whole house vibrating with all the people down there talking and crying, pounding back hot rum toddies, gin-and-tonics, sherry, all Grammie's favourite drinks. Percy flew in from Toronto. Gordie and his five-year-old son Bobby flew in from wherever it is they live on the Prairies, and the whole family, all the first, second, third cousins, once-twice-three times removed, showed up from all over the Maritimes. Even old hobbly Irvine McKay from California with the McKay blue eyes — he's ninety-five and it was the first time I'd ever met him outside of a photo. He didn't seem resentful with regards to the car theft, in fact, didn't seem to know what I was talking about when I asked him, not even when I began to explain, stopping abruptly when Gallie rammed her elbow into my ribs. He just kept patting the top of my head, saying I looked just like Islay did as a girl, his voice breaking, as his heart trailed back over all those years that had passed.

The family had stood outside by the front of the church waiting for the usher to give us the cue so we could march down the aisle in front of the congregation and then sit in the front pew for the service. When the usher opened the door, we all marched up the stairs and down the aisle, everyone standing and looking at us. I was on Percy's arm at the end of the procession, Gallie at the front of the line. I saw Hans sitting there, with Dearie and Elizabeth. I smiled at him, you know, a sad little smile, which he returned as Gallie's knees buckled. Gordie grabbed her, all of us stopping. Gordie steadied her and we all took our seats, me with Percy on one side and Bobby on the other, Gordie sitting by him. Bobby grabbed my hand for the whole service. Grammie was in an urn so it wasn't a funeral, but a memorial service, "as per her request," Gallie told Gordie when he first arrived in Foster, demanding to know why we burned the body up like a bunch of pagans. My mother had hissed, "Gordon Benjamin Arsenault." She had taken over like I'd never seen her do before, hustling him out on the porch while I got Gallie a good stiff drink and gave Bobby a gingersnap.

Gordie stayed shut up until the service and then even he cried for the memory of his Grammie. All these people Grammie knew got up and talked about her, how the police took her license away when she was eighty-five because she went speed crazy and wouldn't pull over when they'd try to stop her. They gave her three chances and she blew every one. The whole church was laughing, and I looked around at the oak walls and stained-glass windows in a building I'd spent so much time in I could never count the hours of cleaning, praying, dope smoking, reading, crying, you know, all the stuff living people do. And thinking there couldn't be a better ritual for putting my past away, making the church a fresh place for me, you know, letting the dead bury the dead and all that AA stuff, rite of passage and blah blah. I looked at Gordie's cowboy boots on the floor, polished, and then his face, eyes scrunched up, praying like he had gone all religious.

Then, back at Grammie's, handing out good stiff drinks, helping my mother with Aunt Gallie, going out on the porch for a cigarette with Dearie and Elizabeth. Dearie whispered that Hans looked like he had just jumped out of a men's fashion magazine. Hans was busy talking to Dearie and Elizabeth, and putting his arm around me. He was saying his ears hurt from the pipe music that was at the service, when we had to parade back out of the church following behind this bagpiper who came from Pictou, some old guy named Sean Sutherland that Grammie grew up with. My mother had thought it was too much, but Gallie had insisted, Grammie was Scots, she was a good McKay, and she'd have a piper at her funeral if Gallie had to pipe herself. Martha had conceded immediately.

Sean had appeared from one of the choir entrance doors back by the altar, looking so wobbly it seemed we might be turning around and having another memorial. Then he started blowing away on the pipes, maybe thinking he could blast some life back into Grammie, but she was in an urn by then so it was too late. The music bounced off the oak beams, the Reverend Rafuse up there at the altar waving at us to stand and march out. Halfway down the aisle Gallie fell apart again, laughing and crying, not stopping until we were at home plying her with liquor. Gallie was a wreck, Percy said, because Grammie was her roommate for most of her life. And she'd get more of a wreck as time went on. That's the thing about all the death ritual, it just keeps the pain away, you know, at arm's length, and after it's all over, it swoops in and knocks you down, and when you are sitting on your butt, then you know it happened.

I walked Hans out to his car after he had said hello to everyone. I could tell he liked being there with my family. It was his first time at a local event, if you could call Grammie's funeral reception an event. Outside, by his car, he took my face between his hands and said he thought we should get married, that my Grammie would have wanted that. It's the last thing she would have wanted, I thought, me getting married at twenty-one. But I didn't tell Hans that, just kissed him and nodded. He hugged me and headed over to Lupin Cove, beeping the horn as I stood there in the Valley snowflakes, waving. When I turned back to the house, the whole family was watching me from the window, though you would never have known it from how they were all back in their chairs and talking to the guests by the time I came in the kitchen door. Dearie and Elizabeth were in the kitchen with Gordie, who was on his fourth beer. "So, taking up with the Germans, are we?" He put his empty on the counter. I just ignored him and took a tray of crackers and cheese into the living room and went up to the bathroom.

There is a lot of cleaning up to do. Most people have gone now and my cousin Gordie has gone too, gone religious, in that fundamental way with a religion called Church of the Prairie Grass. When I come in the kitchen, Gordie's holding forth to Elizabeth and Percy on the Primary Sins, the first sin, *the sin of the homosexuality* (which is why he doesn't go to the United Heathen Church of Canada anymore, since they ordain fruitcakes and lizzies as ministers, though he made an exception for his Grammie's memorial, seeing as she didn't mind being around a bunch of queers); the second sin, *the sin of abortion*, practised by the whorish feminists as nothing more than tax-paid birth control; and, of course, *the sin of being a screw-up and shaming the family*, he tells me when I say the Church of the Prairie Grass sounds like a pagan thing if I've ever heard of anything pagan. Percy starts laughing into his coconut squares. Bobby comes in and asks what a pagan is.

Gordie points at me. "Your first cousin once removed, that's what a pagan is. What's this nose-hook business?"

I do my best to ignore Gordie, it's the easiest thing. Dearie hands me a glass of mulled apple cider.

"Your grandmother was quite a character," Elizabeth says to Gordie.

Gordie looks at her. "What's bright young girls like you and Dearie doing spending time with a crazy drunken slut like that right over there? A slut like her who is going about with a Nazi white supremacist." He makes a continuous jabbing point as though he urgently needs an elevator.

"Arselicker," I whisper, as Elizabeth downs her drink and Percy grabs my arm. Gordie is opening and shutting his big mouth but no words are coming out. Dearie walks in from the living room and tells Gordie to shut the fuck up and she announces that Percy, Elizabeth, and Serrie are going for a drive, to get our coats and be snappy about it. Gordie's jaw just hangs off his big alien head and my mother comes in and gives him another shot of rum and shakes her finger at him. Bobby wants to come for the drive, but Gordie finally yells, "No fucking way will you go out and be corrupted." Bobby runs crying into the den.

We zip along through the countryside, over to Canning, and up the mountain to the Look Off where I put Percy's quarters in the telescope and stare out over the Valley at the Minas Basin. You can see for miles. Elizabeth is standing at the edge of the platform the hanggliders use for launching. "So how you been?" I say, like we are acquaintances. We are still looking out at the Valley, at the farms.

"Okay, you know, working a lot. Not doing so well in the courses. I'm so sorry about your grandmother." And then she just falls apart, crying in this blowfish way. "Reginald and I broke up. He kept seeing other people and lying about it and I couldn't take it. You know the only time he told me he loved me was when he was drunk once and he didn't even really tell me he loved me. He said, 'Lizzie, I know you love me and that's a valuable feature.'" And then Elizabeth starts laughing with her head on her shoulder. "Can you believe it? A valuable feature. Like, what does that mean anyway? My love is valuable? Loving him is a valuable feature for me? Like power steering or heated car seats?" And she goes off laughing again, in between snorts.

I start laughing too. And then she starts crying again. "Serrie, do you remember that summer we cut the blossoms off the first-year strawberries, so they wouldn't grow fruit? And we had those stupid little scissors that left marks on our fingers, remember the middle finger? I can't stop thinking about that, how we were, like, so stupid. I thought those strawberry days would just last forever, but it's not that way. I feel like one of those dumb little plants out there in the big field, Serrie. Nothing has been the same since you went in the hospital. Dearie's right, you know. Growing up means you just lose all the people who ever meant anything to you in the first place."

I nod and bite my lip. "Sorry," I whisper, as though this is my fault.

Elizabeth stares at the Basin, her lips moving, she is counting the tiny waves. "It's okay. Forgiveness is a valuable feature," she whispers back, as though she too thinks this is my fault.

It's getting dark, so we take the highway back, and the cars are gone now. Hans is there in the Mercedes, waiting to pick me up. In the driveway we hear Gallie and Gordie screaming at each other. Bobby is outside standing alone in the dark. I pat him on the head and he starts crying, he wants to go back to Alberta. Dearie takes Elizabeth over to her place to use the bathroom and Percy and I go inside with Bobby. My mother is standing in the kitchen with her arms crossed, crying, and my father is putting on his boots. He just shakes his head at me. Gallie and Gordie are in the living room, Gallie screaming that it is no time to be discussing Grammie's will, she's an executor and when it's time she'll goddamn well let Gordie know who gets what, but not until she's good and ready to deal with it.

It's funny how you can walk into all that pain, like a fly to a sticky strip, stuck there, unable to get off. We will never make it without Grammie, I think, my poor crippled family. My gut twists into every knot imaginable as my mother comes over to the door, hugging me and Percy. She's all maudlin from death and wine. It's at times like this I miss blackouts, not drinking, just the efficiency of blackouts.

"Oh, I wish they would just have some respect for Islay and stop this," she weeps. "Serrie, when Percy goes back it'll just be you left, my little girl."

Gallie's voice shrieks out from the living room. "There is no way in hell I am going to sell this house just so you can have a chunk of money. I'll disown you, Gordie Arsenault, if you ever suggest anything like that again."

I leave my mother with Percy and nod at Cyril, who nods back, holding his hat.

On the way up the Mountain, big fat fluffy snowflakes fall on the windshield, and I loathe each and every one of them. And back at the Cruickshank House, right up there on the top of the hill looking out over the Bay of Fundy, I fold into Hans, into his warmth, his solid, steady, and tidy presence. He doesn't care that I'm a drunk or a drop-out, he cares about what I do, and right then and there, that's enough for me. I'll be glad to be his wife, I whisper.

The same dream comes to me over and over the winter months, and into spring, as I make beds, sweep floors, buy supplies, talk to hotel guests, and plan the wedding. I am modelling for life-drawing classes, the kind at the art college in the city. I am in the poses of every photo I have seen myself in, and then in the poses of Grammie, in all her photos, standing by the stolen car. No colour, just contrasts, black-and-white, shadows, expanses of skin interrupted by eyes, dark and deep and as glossy as buckets of water. My body takes each position as though it has been in it hundreds of times before, as though I was born in those postures. From one move to another and then back again, always in black-and-white, always in the same order, caught in a pattern of moments that will be repeated over and over, each detail exact and meticulous. There is a breeze blowing and I look up for a fan and then, the only colour: watery blue, pale yellow, white faded — Grammie's eyeball, as she flips the page of the photo album, and I'm pressed in between.

In late March I tell Hans about my dream and he says it is some kind of Freudian pre-wedding anxiety. We are busy renovating a new house he has bought, further down the Bay Road, a house to rent out in the summer, but wedding guests from Germany will stay there first. His parents will be staying with us, up at the Cruikshank House, arriving at the beginning of May, six weeks before our marriage. I'm doing all the wedding plans. My family is excited; it will keep me in the area, and with Grammie gone now, no one wants me to go, Percy away is enough, and no one wants Gordie back. "Oh, I love a June wedding," Gallie and my mother keep saying, as I make arrangements. I write it all out on charts and show Hans twice a week. He likes to hear about the details, the caterer, the flowers, the dresses for me and Dearie and Elizabeth — they will both be standing for me. Hans has his hands full with the hotel, and with two other properties he's purchased over in Mahone Bay. There is much work to be done to have the hotel ready, where more guests will be staying. Hans leaves me lists of chores in my mail slot at the front desk. We all have a slot, the guests, the staff. Sometimes he leaves me love notes on napkins, stapled to an errand and chore list. Hans says work is the best cure for grief, and that I will forget all about Grammie eventually, I just need to stay busy. I tell him about university in Halifax, not about the card from my professor, just that I'm thinking about whether I should finish my degree. Hans says education is a good thing but something practical is better than Classical Studies. Maybe I should think about studying tourism, or marketing, or public relations, something that will help us with the business. And if he is going to be paying for it, he wants it to be something worthwhile.

I don't talk about university any more. I must stay busy, busy like Hans, who has his hands full with Joachim. Now that some good weather is starting and the snow is beginning to melt, Joachim has started complaining about everything the melt reveals. And not just the dog shit and the garbage, Joachim says there is too much driftwood on the beach, all that wood dirtying up the rocks. He tells Hans he wants to take a can of gasoline and burn the beach clean. The beach is covered in wood of all sizes: logs, trunks, branches, all washed up to the high-water mark, wood that has silvered with the sun and salt. Some people come from miles to collect it, Hans tells him, and if he so much as lights a match he'll be on a plane to

Deutschland. Joachim just spits in his handkerchief and shoves it in his pocket. It's like his cocoon is opening and a cantankerous old man is crawling out. Hans says Joachim is always grouchy in the spring, but this is the worst so far. Joachim wants the potholes and frost heaves in the roads fixed, he says the wharf is an eyesore, the shabby boats are an eyesore, the shabby locals are eyesores (he says this like I'm not in the room), the village houses are so very painful for him to have to look at, soon the harbour will stink of fish, and the lobstermen will start the diesel engines of their shabby boats in the middle of the shabby Nova Scotia night, waking up all the guests to whom Hans is promising Bay of Fundy peace and serenity. He doesn't even listen when Hans who explains he should have a bit more appreciation for the local colour, that the big draw of Lupin Cove is that it is an actual working fishing village.

"Vorking?" Joachim snorts. He slaps his knee, "vorking, ha-ha-ha," and he goes off on one of his five-minute laughs.

Hans says Joachim is drinking too much, and I should consider taking him to an AA meeting. Joachim yells at Hans that he is no drunk like his stupid Nova Scotian hillbilly girlfriend. It's no skin off my back because, hey, I've been called worse.

And it's a good thing Joachim doesn't want to go to AA, because I'm not going to AA in Foster on Friday nights anymore, haven't been since Grammie died. No one knows, except of course for the AA members. A few people call me, but they just let me do my thing, that's how it is at meetings. They think I'll be back when I'm ready, that's what they always say about other people who stop coming. I have no idea if I'll go back, I just know there isn't enough alone time right now, not even being at the one-of-a-kind house with Earl Grey. There are no private moments and I'm just sick of everyone telling me what to do. I'm not clock-punching anymore, but I'm still checking in all the time, accountable for every minute, except my Friday nights. My stomach is in a knot all the time, and it hurts to explain, so I just start disappearing on Friday nights.

I usually drive into Bigelow Bay and have a coffee and a dough-nut at Tim Horton's. I don't know anyone who lives there, so it's a safe place to be, thirty minutes out of Foster. On the way back I fill the car up with gas so Hans won't know how far I've driven. He doesn't check the odometer, as there is always someone hopping in to go over to the Valley, but he does keep his eye on the gas tank. And I sit in the back, where no one would see me anyway, wearing a ball cap. My hair is growing in now, so I don't have to hide my shaved head, but the brim of the cap covers my nose ring, and my face. I sit there and think about the Classical Studies department, and sometimes I read books. There is never time for reading at the Cliffside. But after my doughnut, I can just sip away at the coffee and read by the fluorescent lights, step back from all the noise and confusion that makes my head and stomach hurt.

And this is where Dearie finds me at the start of May, just before Hans's guests start arriving. I can feel someone looking at me, and at first I think I'm being paranoid, because who would see me here? I'm reading *Agamemnon* and am just near the end, where everyone is going to be done in by Clytemnestra. Cassandra is wail-ing away, and I peek up. There is Dearie, holding an apple fritter. We just look at each other, and then she comes over.

"Well. Well, what are you doing here?"

I hold my book up and smile this stupid smile.

"I see. Well, I thought you were at an AA meeting. I called up Hans to say I was coming over tonight, instead of tomorrow. Got the night off. Can I sit down?"

"Sure," I whisper.

She offers me a piece of her fritter and I shake my head.

"So, Serrie, what are you doing here?" she asks again.

"Just hanging out, you know."

Her mouth is full and she nods her head. She does know. Dearie is different since the blow-up on Echo Beach. She keeps chewing. "What's going on, Serrie? I know you. Can't fool us locals. That's what that Jock-em, or whatever the hell his dumb name is, called me when I telephoned. He put the phone down and yelled, 'Hans, it iz zee local on zee phone.' What a freak, Serrie. Glad you're not marrying him. My father said I should hook up with him and then we can run the place. Well, my father can just go fuck himself."

I start laughing, tear off a piece of her apple fritter, and tell her I am thinking about going back to university, that my professor wrote to me.

"What does Hans think?"

"Not much. I mean, he wants me to study Commerce."

Dearie starts laughing and shakes her head. "Lord love a duck," she says.

Later that night, when we get back to the Sea Breeze, Dearie's sitting by the fire with Hans, showing him the patterns for the bridesmaid dresses, and you'd never have known we had hacked a fritter apart together a few hours earlier. Hans goes back to his house, and Dearie and I crawl into the big bed upstairs, Earl Grey at our feet, purring away. She's asleep in no time, just like Elizabeth, but not me, so I head outside to Echo Beach. There is a full moon and I can see the Isle Haute out there — it reminds me of the drawing in *The Little Prince*, the one the grown-ups see as a hat, though it is really a boa constrictor digesting an elephant. Where is Fancy Mosher, I wonder? Did the pirate come and chop her head off, and throw her down a hole? The sound of the waves doesn't calm me anymore. So much for the halcyon days.

The future in-laws arrive — I think of them as the Zimmer-in-laws — at the beginning of May. I have a bad feeling about meeting them, but at least it's just a feeling, and feelings can change. Things are already bad for Hans. Now the boats are back in the water and the lobster season has opened, Joachim has started harassing the fishermen. He gets loaded and goes down to the wharf, complaining about the engines at night, the noise is too loud. And it's not like he's even asleep — he just sits inside his apartment in the hotel on the third floor, right above the Aunt's set of rooms, drinking and looking out with his binoculars. And then as soon as the engines start, he's stomping down the hill. The next complaint is how the fish they use for bait smells like fish. He doesn't get it when the next day bait boxes appear at the side of the wharf, bait boxes that were never left there before. Joachim starts in on them about where they are parking their trucks, saying it is his property and he has enough money to buy them all. And then he calls the RCMP, to complain about the engines. They come over and start explaining: in order to get the boats on the Bay the boys have to start the engines, which involves noise, unless they paddle out, but who wants to paddle a Cape Islander, unless of course, Joachim would like to offer his services, that is, if the fishermen would even be interested in having an oarsmen. Joachim doesn't think it is funny, not like the fishermen, who are all hanging about the wharf, laughing into the harbour. He starts yelling at the Mounties, that he won't be patronized, and that's when Hans, completely humiliated, orders him up to the hotel and apologizes to the Mounties, sending me over to apologize to all the guys at their boats. They just nod and scuff their boots. I can tell they think I've lost my mind.

Back at the hotel, Hans has a big fight with Joachim, shouting that he is single-handedly ruining good relations with the locals who just happen to be our neighbours. And if he keeps it up he must go back to Germany, he is only here as a tourist, and this kind of thing is going to get him reported to Immigration.

The next day the Zimmers arrive from Frankfurt for the wedding, which isn't until the middle of June. They are going to be here for almost two months before the wedding, during the wedding, after the wedding. Hans says they love Canada and want to have some time here, that I should be more understanding, they are old people. I'd be more understanding if I understood them — they barely speak any English and we just wave and nod at each other. His father just mutters away at me in German all the time, pointing at my nose. I'm trying to support Hans, since the stress level is almost enough to blow out the attic when Herr Zimmer walks around the house like an inspector, just like Aunt Gallie. He tells Hans he's been thinking, since his visit last summer. And what he has been thinking is that Hans paid too much for this cottage and should sell it. Joachim is sitting in the corner with a beer and translates everything for me. Hans says it was a good price. And then they start this arguing, the kind that you can tell they must have been doing since Hans was a kid. Herr Zimmer shakes his head and says the house was overpriced considering the work he had to put into it. "It was not," Hans says. "Ja, ja," his father replies and then they start screaming at each other while Frau Zimmer tries to intervene.

When Frau Zimmer starts crying I take her outside. We can hear them yelling from the road and we walk around the harbour. She speaks almost no English and keeps apologizing, "Es tut mir Leid, Es tut mir Leid," she says over and over and I pat her hand and link it through my arm. It strikes me that Hans has told me nothing of his family, not that I've asked much. His father has some big soap factory, and a jam factory, in Germany and in Poland. His mother goes back inside and I creep up the front steeps and to the bathroom. The Zimmers are downstairs fighting and I'm waiting for it to end. I try to think of what Grammie would say, but nothing comes, she's not there. Hans and Herr Zimmer are still shouting and I've got enough sense to make out that Herr Zimmer thinks I'm after the Zimmer fortune. The battle is closer now, at the bottom of the stairs. I put my hands over my ears and move them up and down, trying to rub the noise away. It works until Hans starts pounding on the door. I just sit there and look at my dumb face and wonder how I can look like such a baby when I feel so old. Hans bangs on the door again.

"Go away, go away," I yell.

And at long last, a gulp of silence. Heavy breathing and I realize it is my own. I can see my chest heaving.

"First my father and now you. *Scheisse.*" And then he pops the door open, the old latch flying across the room and hitting the window.

I wonder how his shirts can stay so pressed and clean with all the commotion. "I'm not Lupin Cove, you can't renovate me, you can't improve me, I'm no frigging fixer-upper. I don't need any fixing," I scream at him. He slaps me across the face. *What goes around, comes around*, I hear Grammie whisper. There is a trickle of blood on my lip and it has us both quiet. Hans tries to wipe it up but I push him away. He apologizes as I splash water on my face and then, when I don't reply, he goes downstairs. I sit down on the floor and Frau Zimmer comes in.

After Frau Zimmer has done her pantomime best to mother me, I sneak down the back stairs and out the front door, in my running shoes. By the time I get to my parent's house, the knot in my stomach is spreading to my chest and into my shoulders, and I have no perspective. My parents have been doing some gardening, the soil by the front and side outhouses is freshly turned. I wipe off my running shoes in the back porch and go into the kitchen, where my mother is sitting at the table, glueing the Limoges teapot together, the one we sold to Mr. Burgess that spring I finished high school.

She tries to put the pieces in the box, and then puts her arms over them, like I'm not going to notice. "Serrie, I thought you were with the Zimmers."

My thousand-year-old voice startles us both. "Yes, yes, I was with the Zimmers." I point. "Now where did you get that?"

My mother's voice is quiet, she tries to make it sound casual. "At a garage sale. The people who bought the Burgess place had a garage sale. I guess he broke it. Seeing as he paid us so much money for it, I imagine he couldn't bear to toss it in the garbage."

And then that knot stretches right up to my head and bounces out this horrible rage: "So are you planning to glue the fucking thing together and put it back in the dining room? Do you really think these mysterious American relatives aren't going to notice, whenever the hell they arrive to claim their inheritance? It's like waiting around for a bunch of ghosts. A bunch of ghosts who are going to get broken china, which is at least a fuck of a lot more than I'm inheriting. What do you and Cyril think you are passing on to me and Percy? This fucking house that's just going to keep falling apart? These stupid genes? This great life in the Valley?"

"Percy doesn't live in the Valley anymore." She starts to cry. "Oh, Serrie."

I scream, "Yes, and did you ever wonder why Percy doesn't live here? But do I leave? No, I just can't get the fuck out of this place. I'm trapped here, because all we've got is family, and we are all supposed to get along, and act like nothing bad has ever happened. Do you want to hear a story about the teapot?"

She's just looking at me from the table, the tube of glue oozing over on her fist, she's squeezing so hard. "No, I don't want to hear a story about the teapot, Serrie. I know I've not done right by you, I never understood enough how things might affect you . . . this isn't how I imagined life would turn out when you were little and running around in bare feet. I think maybe you should go to an AA meeting, Serrie. Did something happen today?"

I scream, "I don't want to go to a stupid meeting and I don't want you to start telling me how hard your life has been. What about mine? Look at what I'm having to do just to crawl out of this stupid trap I'm in. And what would ever make you think something happened to me today?"

She looks up, and then down at the porcelain. "You have a

bruise on your face," she cries softly, tears falling on her ragged fin-
gertips, on the broken pieces of china.

When I get back to Lupin Cove, three of the Zimmers friends have
arrived from Cape Breton. They are all going up to Cape Breton the
next day. I'm back just in time to help with the big meal in the hotel,
and try to act like nothing has happened, serving food and cleaning
up, avoiding my fiancé's eyes. His mother keeps patting me on the
back, and I keep patting her hand. Herr Zimmer laughs and eats as
if nothing happened, ignoring me, just like the weird old aunt who's
never so much as looked at me the entire time I've been around.
Hans is quiet and I don't say anything to him when we are in the
kitchen together. The only thing he says is that he wants me to stay
all night, and he looks so sad that I do. We don't talk, though, not
even walking up the hill to the house, not until we are in bed, both
of us looking up at the ceiling. I can feel that his eyes are open and
all I can think about is how good a big smoke would taste, how much
I would like to get rip-roaring drunk. I put my fingers to my lips and
bite them as he tells me how horrible it was growing up with his
father, how nothing was ever good enough and nothing has changed,
that it doesn't matter how far away he goes or what he does, it is the
same thing. And he is worried about Joachim. He knows he should
send him back to Germany, but Hans is the only friend he has, he
doesn't even have any money, and can't hold a job. And then he cries
like a child, saying I can't leave him, he needs me more than ever.

Dawn, at long last, and I'm up just before the sun rises, a bit of red
twisting in the sky. Hans is snoring and his parents are sleeping
soundly. The guests are at the hotel. I creep down the stairs, pulling
on my boots, and then walk down the hill to the harbour, where the
tide is almost halfway in. I stop at the Cliffside, where all is quiet,

and grab a bottle of cooking sherry from the kitchen, shoving it in my knapsack. First I head over to the Sea Breeze and feed the Earl, who meows and rubs at my ankles, like he knows what I'm up to, trying to get me to just have a bath and go back to bed, call someone in AA. Do I know what I'm doing? Oh, yes, I sure do, no justification of how it's just going to be one drink. I don't give a sweet blessed shit anymore. Feeling this way has just got to stop and I cannot wait to get wasted. The old grandfather Ryan is out there already, doing work on the lobster traps as the sun rises up in the east. I walk over to him.

"Morning, my name is Serrie Sullivan," I say.

And I'm an alcoholic, I think.

He nods and looks at my bruise and then in my eyes. He knows who I am, he says, Islay Meissner's granddaughter. Thinking about Grammie now hurts almost as much as my face, so I change the subject and ask if I can borrow their dory for some morning exercise, and he supposes so, the boys won't be going out on the Bay until later.

I row hard, eyes shut, full of shame for my bruise, for having let things get so bad. But I didn't even know they were getting bad. Denial, the outstanding characteristic of the alcoholic, I remember. When I'm out far enough, I open my eyes and look back at Lupin Cove. It looks so strange from out here on the Bay of Fundy, not even like a village, just a smattering of buildings. Not even Dearie is going to show up out here, just me, the Bay and my bottle. It's been years since I've been out here and I bob up and down in the swell, barely perceptible at first, but after I've been sitting there for awhile, I feel the constant rhythm of the ocean, moving, just like the Arctic ice, alive, always shifting, not that I know a thing about the Arctic ice, but that's what they say. Frozen life. Fluid life. I think about that. What do you want, Serrie? Frozen life or fluid life? Grammie wouldn't put it like that, but I do, taking a big swig of the sherry. It's been a year and almost five months since I've had a drink.

The sun is up now, promising a gorgeous day, but I'm praying for a blackout. I take another swig. My head spins and I've never been so happy to be getting drunk. But it doesn't last for long. We drink to forget, they say, and that's what I'm doing now, but it's not working — the drunker I get, the more I remember.

"Oh, Grammie." A whisper breathed across the water at high tide.

The silence blows back her voice:

> *Break, break, break,*
> *On thy cold grey stones, O Sea!*
> *And I would that my tongue could utter*
> *The thoughts that arise in me.*

Sunday afternoon in April at Mr. Burgess' Antique Shop. Seventeen years old. He had tried to take the box from me at the door, but I had insisted, didn't need his help, it wasn't that heavy. I should have had a better grip, but I was hurrying, to be in and out fast, not taking care, not being mindful, tripping and clunking the box down on the counter, something going crack. Mr. Burgess standing close, his aftershave chemical sweet. It was late in the day and he had locked the door behind me, his wife and daughters in the city, I'd heard on the phone when I'd listened in. He said they weren't due back until late that night so not to worry. The light was dim, one antique floor lamp on at the front, the shop stretching back endlessly. All the antique furniture set up in display rooms, living rooms, dining rooms, kitchens, a pantry, bedrooms.

"Yes, it's about time your mother sold me this china," he said. "Old Miss Sullivan, now she wouldn't sell it, no matter how much I offered her. Let's take a look-see." He smiled at me with his mouth half open, gold fillings glinting.

I whispered, "I think I broke something."

"I know you did, Serrie," he said, taking out the Limoges teapot, now in seven pieces. "But that's okay, we are going to work it out. Don't you go worrying. We can take care of this."

He carefully unwrapped each teacup and saucer as I stood there, one hand in my long hair, the other across my hard stomach, one foot on top of the other, twisted like a candy stick. It was the most valuable, the teapot, *intact* that was, a complete intact set. Couldn't get anything for it glued together. He knew we needed the money. And he'd touched my hair where my hand was, my hand that dropped down and he rubbed the soft skin on the inside of my wrist. We could make an arrangement, Martha didn't have to know. And then the smell of lemon oil, like the church, as I lay on the divan, from France, Mr. Burgess said, direct from France, the antique springs underneath the original upholstery digging into my body, leaving marks I would never get rid of.

A wind has picked up with the still rising tide and the dory is held in a current, but the current is not going in, it heads down the Bay, dipping into eddies, the boat beginning to whirl as I sit there sipping sherry, hearing Grammie telling the eight-year-old me, "Don't open the curtains, don't open the door, just let him knock until he goes away," but my mother opening the door, me letting him right in the door. Oh, my poor Martha, she would have wanted me to bring the cracked teapot right back home.

Grammie's voice swirls up from the water:

> O, *well for the fisherman's boy,*
> *That he shouts with his sister at play!*
> O, *well for the sailor lad,*
> *That he sings in his boat on the bay!*

I keep seeing my mother at the table, crying, looking at my bruise, knowing she only wanted those big sky dreams for us, for all of us, for her girl and boy playing in the waves by the beach. The waves on the bay are rolling now, and the dory crashes up and over them. I try to row but it makes no difference.

I cleaned up in the bathroom at the back of the shop and when I came out there was an envelope full of cash in his hand, for everything, including the teapot. The next time he would give my mother a fine price with the same arrangement. Six more times on the divan. The final time the end of summer before third-year university started, before I ran to London. The antique mah-jong set with real ivory pieces, the Italian end-of-day glass vase, the art deco perfume bottle, they were all gone now, just small pieces, no one would notice them missing, Martha had said, chewing her nails. The last time a rare Clichy paperweight Mr. Burgess had been after for years, he told me as he held it up to the light, little yellow and white roses surrounding a large pink rose, blue underneath, like flowers floating on water. On top of me, Mr. Burgess whispering the classical period for glass paperweights was from 1845 to 1865. Next he wanted those Cheyenne saddlebags, he'd give us the best deal ever, the Spinster Sullivan must have met a wealthy gentleman in her travels, giving her gifts, us getting such a fine price, for the Clichy, fifteen hundred dollars. And there was the Spinster, summoned by her name, by our betrayal. Only I could see her, only me looking up, him groaning in my ear that the millefiori technique was used to make this unique Clichy paperweight. I knew that much Italian, a thousand flowers. A thousand sorrows in the Spinster's eyes. And I would not do it again, not for all the tea in China, not for all the verandahs in the world, not for the finest price ever.

But there had been no fine price. That October, back at school, in the kind professor's office, talking about graduate school and scholarships, I'd seen the Clichy on his desk. I hadn't heard what he was saying, wanting to know about the paperweight.

"Seraphina, it was a gift, from my sister, Penelope. A reproduction, of course." He had smiled and waved his hand. "The real one would need to be kept in a safety deposit box, worth anywhere from ten to fifteen thousand dollars, I would think. Penelope, in London, she collects."

And he had carried on about me doing a master's degree while I sat there, Grammie's voice in my ear, "Always know what you are worth," as a host of angels tossed down a thousand rotten bouquets, burying me in thorns.

I open my eyes and Grammie is there in the bow, skinny, wrinkled, holding a cup of tea. I wonder just how drunk I am. Her look is so soft, her heart breaking for all of us. "Some things are never to be spoken of," she had said to me that long-ago summer in Foster. And even tipsy in a dory, I know there is no peace to be gained by coiling the past around our necks.

The wind is strong now, the sky clouding over as cold salty waves splash into the dory. I yell for help, and look back to the distant shore, and then to the bow, the space filled with Grammie's voice:

> *Break, break, break*
> *At the foot of thy crags, O Sea!*
> *But the tender grace of a day that is dead*
> *Will never come back to me.*

And the blackness finally comes.

E BB T IDE

THERE IS NO BREEZE COMING IN THE OUTHOUSE DOOR NOW, AND SO I have taken the old calendar off the wall to fan myself. Sweat trickles down between my breasts, running under the already soaked red bra and into my navel, the ring shining in the bit of sun that reaches inside. Standing on the cushion, I stretch, and then take down the tobacco and matches from the old ledge, and roll a smoke. I'm on the wagon again, but I want a smoke, even a stale one. I take a pinch of tobacco. It would have been nice to have it all end neatly, you know, to have just walked away then, just like it would be nice to be able to do a rollie as fast and perfect as Kenny Mosher always did. Sometimes you really want to do the right thing, but the right thing is what would appear to be the wrong thing, so you do the right thing which is truly the wrong thing. But then you live and learn and do what you knew you should have all along.

There had been an entire month until the wedding, and Dearie wouldn't have wanted me to postpone or cancel, that's what everyone said. Even if she wasn't there, she would be in spirit, and she would have wanted me to go ahead with it. I knew this, but it wasn't until I was at the altar, and that pure voice began to sing, "Hail, O star of the sea," that I understood what going ahead really meant.

I had come out of the blackout on the deck of the *Ruby R* as she came into the harbour, old grandfather Ryan feeding me instant coffee he had made below. They were standing on the wharf: Hans, Joachim, his parents, and their friends, as well as the rest of Lupin Cove. Hans's father and his friends were holding these expensive bird scopes and binoculars. So much for a private moment.

Hans had been quiet as I stood there on the boat with the fishermen, bruise on my cheek, the two eldest brothers on either side of me, the boys I had ridden the high school bus with, steadying me. I'd only had a few sips of sherry, so I didn't know if it was lack of practice or lack of sea legs, or just lack of heart, but I couldn't get out of the boat without them helping me up and on the ladder, climbing up to the dock, Hans there at the top, his hands gentle on my shoulders, carrying me over to the one-of-a-kind house. He had put me in a bath, saying he would forgive me, because it had been a very bad few days, I was upset, I didn't know what I was doing. And I didn't say anything, just listened. There were no words any more, for explaining, for making it better. I was like Fancy Mosher, hearing the words and watching them slide over my face and into the tub. As he dried me, he said Dearie and Elizabeth would be coming over soon, to stay for the night, to show me their bridesmaid dresses. He was going to go away with his parents, to give me some space, we needed a time-out, he knew that, he felt like he was driving me to drink. No one can do that, of course, but I didn't say anything. Hans was a good man, I had thought, sprawled in the tub, my body like jelly, as he sat on the toilet, his face in his well-manicured hands.

I put more tobacco on the paper and roll, picturing Dearie all crouched and small in the corner of the outhouse after her grandmother died. It's easy to remember her, silent and shaking, writing her name on the wall with a pencil stub, just like the one hanging there now. The match lights on the first strike, and the flat smoke makes me dizzy. Coughing, I lean back on the hard outhouse wall. That day I got drunk in the dory, after Hans and his family had left for Cape Breton, I had been walking around the harbour. It was mid-morning by then, high slack tide, and all the boats were out. The water was still, in those few moments before it would turn, and the air was cold. I'd gone over to the closed-up store, to lean against the wall for shelter, waiting for my friends to arrive.

And then Dearie's van had appeared at the top of Moonrise Hill, as little white caps rippled across the harbour, a bit of rain spitting down. The old buildings were worn after the winter, but beautiful in that languishing way. I had waved at Dearie and Elizabeth, Dearie beeping as they came down the hill. It happened in slow motion, the white van on Moonrise Hill, the van hitting a wet spot, Dearie braking, the brakes screeching, the screeching stopping as the brakes failed, too fast for the turn by Sea Breeze Cottage, the van flying over the water, bashing engine-first into the freezing harbour, water foaming up, the van beginning to sink with Dearie and Elizabeth seat-belted in like the good little girls they were. Me screaming and running around the harbour road, slipping in a pothole as some old Acadian folk song from the sinking van warbled across the water, accordion music pumping away, then shorting out, me screaming, *Dearie, Elizabeth, swim, fly,* white boils of water as the van went down. I had climbed on the wooden railing and jumped. The salt water burning in my eyes, diving down and seeing nothing but blurry foamy white bubbles, body numb, coming up gasping. Back down again, grabbing the door handle, but it wouldn't open. Elizabeth floating by, me pushing the door handle button in because if you pushed the button then it would open, but no opening, just swallowing stings of water, Dearie struggling, the seat belt jammed in the door, the sky again, coughing and choking and gasping, eyes burning. Earle Baltzer running in rubber boots on the road, Elizabeth floating, her blue lips pulled back like a dead cat's. Down again, the van on the harbour bottom now, Dearie slumped over the wheel. The window open, I had reached in and grabbed at her, feeling so much hair but she wasn't moving and I was weak and stiff, instinct pulling me to the top. Earle threw me a buoy, falling close. Not just your life passes by when you are freezing, when you are drowning, the whole world slides before your eyes, and every bit of pain and joy you have ever known lifts you up, and every moment you have lived comes together, and that is who you are, as you lie dying, a voice whispering, *And the stately ships go on, To their haven under the hill.*

A truck was parked on the side of the harbour, the licence plate, *Nova Scotia: Canada's Ocean Playground.* An old man in rubber boots with a pipe between his teeth hung over the harbour railing, one hand holding the end of a yellow rope, the rope stretched out in mid-air, suspended in the moment before it will fall to the water. An old fisherman in a dory, his face lined like a sand dune from years of sun and wind. Flags blowing on the rooftop of a house beside the harbour. There are only two of us being pulled into the little boat, Elizabeth's face ivory, purple lips, palm outstretched.

My voice whispering,

> *But O for the touch of a vanish'd hand,*
> *And the sound of a voice that is still!*

My palm open as Grandfather Ryan reached for me, my scratched palm, burning from the cold and the salt, a clutch of curly hair in my fingers.

Dearie was right, way back then: nothing would ever be the same again. But that's life, nothing ever stays the same, not the small children, or fishing villages, or boats and hearts that bounce on the Bay of Fundy waves. White vans will never fly, and little girls will never be mermaids. You never know when the timer's going to ring.

I cry, sitting in Number Nine from Tatamagouche, tears rolling down my cheeks, and onto my thighs, my weeping filling up this little house, then fading, until there is only the soft sound of my breath. With the rollie between my teeth, I take the little pencil and write on the wall beside the nine-year-old's careful printing:

Islay Mary McKay Meissner

Deirdre Margaret Melanson

And then I stand in the doorway. The sticky red bra pinches my back, so I take it off, and pull away the last shreds of the antique wedding dress, tossing everything behind me into the outhouse. I will always imagine Dearie in New Orleans, walking through the French Quarter, her hair floating, and I run behind her with my hand out, just long enough to touch her curls.

A final haul on the rollie and I throw it into the marble bird feeder, where it sizzles out in the bit of water at the bottom. The green grass is cool on the soles of my feet as I step from the outhouse and look out to the Lupin Cove Road, then down over the Mountain and into the Valley below, everything old and familiar, everything mine.

ACKNOWLEDGEMENTS

First, I wish to acknowledge the encouragement and support of Leanne Pawluk in Banff, Alberta. This book would not have been without her.

Gratitude to my mother, Mary Louise Conlin, for her ceaseless support, and sense of whimsy. Thanks to my brother, Dan Conlin, for his stories, and generous historical consultations. And thanks to my aunt, Margaret Ann Thornton, for letting me and my papers commandeer the kitchen table in Berwick, and for drinking my sludge-like coffee and pretending to like it. Thanks also to my father, Murdy Daniel Conlin, my brother, Peter Conlin, my sister-in-law, Patricia Acheson, and my aunt, Angela Conlin.

Special thanks to my editor and publisher, Maya Mavjee, my agent, Denise Bukowski and to Samantha Mitschka at Doubleday Canada. To Bernice Eisenstein, my editor on the final revision, heartfelt thanks for her sagacity and her commitment to this work.

I'm indebted to those who read this book as it grew from those first few story pages and so generously gave their comments and insights: Rick Maddocks, Sara O'Leary, Tim Carlson, Madeline Thien, Sandra Birdsell; and Linda Svendsen, Keith Maillard and Peggy Thompson at the University of British Columbia Department of Creative Writing.

Sparkly thanks over the water to Caroline Robeznieks-Drennan, Willie Drennan and Eleesha Drennan in Northern Ireland, for the stories, the music and so many tasty meals.

Special appreciation to Sheila M. Diakiw and Mrs. Murphy, Carolyn Arnold, Donald and Jennifer Paterson, Heather Brown, David and Betty Cameron, Millie and Maurice Laporte and the Wolfville Monthly Meeting (Quakers).

Gratitude also to Sandra Shields and David Campion, Jon Wood and his music, Kara Arnold, Robin and Olivia Apsara Purohit, Spider and Jeanne Robinson, Kim Goodliffe, Karen Connelly, Kevin Chong, Marika Morris, Laurie Pardoe, Morag York, Janet Martini, Verna Hammond, Dr. Margaret Brown, Dr. David MacKinnon, Susanna Steinitz, Thomas Schmitt and A Western Theatre Conspiracy.

Many, many thanks to Helen Lenton for having me as her last minute, off-season lodger. Thanks also to Fred and Mary Walsh, for their willingness to hide me in their spare room.

Thanks to Nell Den Heyer, for bringing the world to Maynard Street.

Appreciation to all at (and associated with) Arsekick Productions.

And finally, so much gratitude to Lynn Coady for her incomparable friendship and constant drollery.

CAC
Vancouver/Northern Ireland/Nova Scotia
1995–2001

ABOUT THE AUTHOR

Born in Nova Scotia, Christy Ann Conlin has worked as a seasonal fruit picker, a factory worker, an antiquities sales clerk, a teacher, a researcher and a science grant writer. She has travelled and lived in France, England, Germany, Switzerland, Korea and the United States and recently worked as a storytelling apprentice in Northern Ireland. The first short story she wrote was a prize winner in the 1996 *Blood & Aphorisms* fiction contest, and that story, in a somewhat different form, became the opening pages of *Heave*. A graduate of the MFA program in creative writing at the University of British Columbia, she was named one of B.C.'s best young writers by the *Vancouver Sun*. She lives in Halifax and in Turner's Brook, a community on the shore of the Bay of Fundy. This is her first novel.